HIDDEN ENEMY

WindStorm
PRESS

Praise for Hidden Enemy

Another passionate and fun romp on land and in the skies from J.P. McLean. Her adventure fantasy series, while full of tense and dangerous moments, is also playful and expansive.

—Bill Engleson, author of *Like a Child to Home*

The story holds you from start to finish, and the author's descriptive powers are immense. She is also the mistress of unpredictability. So many twists and turns, so many surprises. You will never regard this story as a comfort zone – just a truly exhilarating ride. This urban fantasy goes from strength to strength and takes the reader with it.

—Charlie Bray, author of *The Trouble with Celebrity*

Praise for The Gift Legacy

" J.P. McLean possesses her own unique gift: the ability to bewitch her readers with her boundless imagination.
—Elinor Florence, Globe and Mail bestselling author of
Bird's Eye View

" A profoundly intelligent story of a captivating young woman whose victories and struggles with a unique gift will grab your every emotion.
—Jennifer Manuel, award-winning author of
The Heaviness of Things That Float

" A deftly crafted, impressively original and inherently compelling read from first page to last.
—Midwest Book Review

" Danger, suspense, and mystery all bundled into one perfect read.
—Urban Lit Magazine

" A fast-paced, compelling read.
—Ev Bishop, award-winning author of
the River's Sigh B & B series

" Tense with an under element of potential sinister about it that throws the mind every which way.
—Pat McDonald, British crime author

" Exciting action and conflict of loyalties make this a fantastic page-turner.
—Kristina Stanley, author of
the Stone Mountain Mystery Series

" JP McLean has created a thrilling combination of mystery, paranormal, urban fantasy and a touch of romance. It is a compelling read.
—Karen Oberlaender, author of *In a Small Compass*

" Exposed secrets, hidden enemies, and a new, gut-wrenching reality for Emelynn create a gripping read you won't want to put down.
—Debra Purdy Kong, award-winning author of
The Casey Holland Mystery series

TITLES BY JP MCLEAN

THE THORNE WITCH NOVELS

The Never Witch

Hexborn

THE DARK DREAMS NOVELS

Blood Mark

Ghost Mark

Scorch Mark

THE GIFT LEGACY

Secret Sky

Hidden Enemy

Burning Lies

Lethal Waters

Deadly Deception

Wings of Prey

THE GIFT LEGACY COMPANION

Lover Betrayed (Secret Sky Redux)

NOVELLAS

Crimson Frost (A Supernatural Noel)

HIDDEN ENEMY

The Gift Legacy

Book 2

JP McLean

Hidden Enemy
The Gift Legacy ~ Book 2
First Canadian Edition

Copyright © 2018 by JP McLean
All rights reserved.

Previously published as *The Gift: Revelation*

ISBN
978-1-988125-31-2 (Paperback)
978-1-988125-32-9 (MOBI)
978-1-988125-33-6 (EPUB)
978-1-988125-34-3 (PDF)

Edited by Nina Munteanu
Copy Edit by Nancy Wills
Book cover designed by JD&J with stock imagery provided by
Konstantin Kamenetskiy & Progressman © 123RF.com
Author photograph by Crystal Clear Photography

This is a work of fiction. All of the names, characters, places, organizations, events and incidents, other than those clearly in the public domain, are either products of the author's imagination or are used fictitiously. Any resemblance to actual persons, living or dead, is entirely coincidental and not intended by the author.

Cataloguing in Publication information available
from Library and Archives Canada

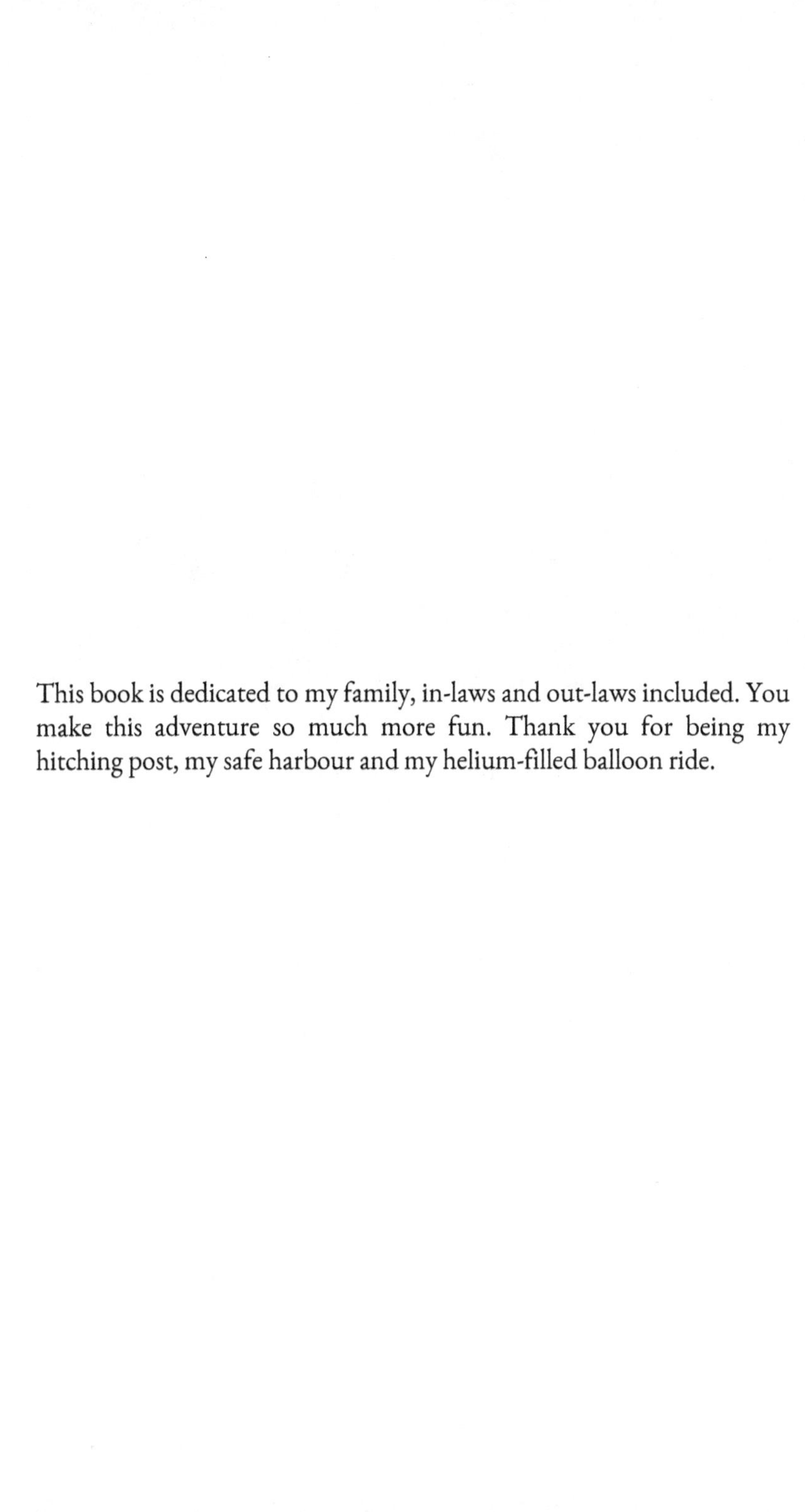

This book is dedicated to my family, in-laws and out-laws included. You make this adventure so much more fun. Thank you for being my hitching post, my safe harbour and my helium-filled balloon ride.

The shell must break before the bird can fly.

—Alfred, Lord Tennyson

CHAPTER ONE

Someone was in the house. My eyes shot open. I strained to hear the noise repeat, but I couldn't hear a thing over the pounding of my heart.

The bedside clock projected the time on the ceiling: 2:55 a.m. I kept absolutely still and concentrated on my breathing. Damn! I thought I'd gotten over this weeks ago. My nerves were now officially fried.

I pushed aside the covers. Living alone meant it was up to me to check the cottage for intruders. Sweat trickled down between my shoulder blades as I tiptoed the perimeter of the bedroom, then slid into the hall.

My search of the small cottage revealed nothing out of place. The doors and windows remained locked—just as I'd left them when I went to bed. Was I losing my mind?

The covers were still warm when I crawled back into bed and curled into a ball, holding my knees tight to stop the shakes. I squeezed my eyes closed and tried to push away the fear. I hated this feeling.

Tonight was just like the previous times. I could have sworn I'd heard footsteps out on the deck or shuffling up on the roof, yet not once had there been any evidence. Not a single footprint in the dew; not one finger smudge on a windowsill.

The lack of evidence suggested my imagination was playing tricks on me, but maybe a little paranoia was normal when you'd been shot. I just needed more time to adjust. Besides, this cottage had always been my sanctuary, and I'd be damned if I was going to let fear, imaginary or not, drive me from it. This cottage was my home.

Tomorrow I had an appointment with Avery. This time, even if I had to beg, I would convince him to prescribe sleeping pills. A couple weeks of undisturbed sleep would fix me up and then I'd be back to my usual upbeat, glass-half-full self.

The next day, at my eleven o'clock appointment, I learned Avery wasn't quite as convinced as I was about the whole sleeping pill solution.

"It's a bad idea, Emelynn." He frowned over the top of his ebony-framed glasses and released the blood pressure cuff with a rip of Velcro. "I'm not surprised you're feeling somewhat vulnerable and anxious, but sleeping pills aren't going to fix that."

He walked over to the small wooden desk and scribbled a note on a scratch pad. Avery was tall and fit. He kept his blond hair short and the only thing that gave away his fifty-plus age was the greying at his temples, which you had to look closely to notice. He turned from his note and leaned back against the desk.

Avery Coulter was my doctor, but he was much more than that. He was my friend and confidant, and he'd saved my life—twice. For that alone, I would always be grateful, but that wasn't what made him so special to me. It was because I'd come to think of him as my stand-in dad.

My father died in a plane crash when I was twelve years old, and though ten years had passed, I still missed him. Dad had also been a doctor. His name was Brian Edison Taylor. He was forty-two when he died, so he and Avery would have been about the same age. They also shared a similarity in their casual manner and confident styles. I could talk to Avery about absolutely anything, and I liked to think that if Dad were alive today, we would have the same kind of relationship.

"We'd be further ahead if we addressed the underlying cause of your anxiety instead of masking the symptoms with drugs." Avery, as usual, was maddeningly logical, but I'd already heard this speech.

"That's what you said last time, Avery. All I want is to sleep through the night. Is that really too much to ask?"

"The pills will help you sleep, Em, but as soon as you quit taking them—*if* you don't become dependent on them and *if* you can actually quit taking them—you'll be right back to hearing noises in the night." He crossed his arms over his chest. That was never a good sign.

I huffed in exasperation. "Well then, what would you suggest I do?"

"Last time we talked about this, your new fitness regimen was helping. What happened? You're still working with Malcolm aren't you?"

Malcolm Perreault was the personal trainer I'd hired after Avery cajoled me into it. Actually, that wasn't the entire truth. In the early days of my recovery, I started having these late-night wake-up calls. Avery, working from the theory that an exhausted body rested better, suggested a fitness regimen.

At the time, it was hard for me to disagree. I was physically weakened from the damage the bullet had inflicted, and still reeling from the naïveté that led to my involvement in a situation for which I was ill-prepared. What on earth possessed me to think I could come out on the winning side of a physical confrontation, let alone one that involved guns?

"Yes, Malcolm's great. We're up to 8K now. It gets easier every time out, but it's still a challenge." I remembered my first runs with Malcolm. Between my calf cramps and side stitches, he must have thought he'd taken on an albatross. "Poor Malcolm."

"Don't feel sorry for Malcolm—that's what you pay him for. Besides, trainers like Malcolm run that distance just to pick up the newspaper."

Malcolm Perreault was almost six feet of flawless, dark skin melted over smooth muscle. I'd met him at the local YMCA after paying drop-in fees at half a dozen gyms in my search for a trainer. He was a refreshing change from the others I'd met, most of whom were Lycra-clad, muscle-bound men and women full of themselves and self-congratulation. Malcolm was different. Within moments of our introduction, I knew I'd found my man. Well, not my man in that sense, though he could easily be a contender if I ever got into that frame of mind again.

Avery finally uncrossed his arms, but that put him back to staring at me over his glasses. "What's changed to set off your anxiety? Why the uptick in cold sweats in the night?"

"I have no idea. When it's happening, all I can think is that someone's trying to get into the house. It's terrifying, but by the time I'm able to think straight, the noises are gone and I never find any evidence that someone's been lurking. I can't keep doing this."

Avery walked behind the desk and pulled a phone book from the drawer. He flipped to the back and ripped out a page. "Home Alarms." He pointed to the column of ads he'd handed me. "Maybe it's time you invest in a security system. It'll take the guesswork out of these noises you hear in the night."

"This is your solution?" I said, underwhelmed, as I looked at the flimsy sheet of yellow paper. He was the only one I knew who still used a phone book.

I considered his idea for a nanosecond before I started ticking off counterpoints. "Sleeping pills are quicker . . . less complicated . . . smaller," I said, touching my third finger, though that last one was a stretch.

Avery shook his head and smirked. I knew that look well enough now to know he wasn't about to give in. "A sleeping pill won't scare away intruders or alert the police." He had a good chuckle at my stubborn stance. "Ah, come on—being a victim doesn't suit you. Take the reins and get back out in front. Let's give the non-chemical approach a shot first and if that doesn't work, then we'll talk about alternatives."

Avery bent to put the phone book back in the drawer, but changed his mind and set it aside. He twisted his mouth and flipped through the drawer's contents. "That's odd," he said, puzzled.

"What's odd?"

"I could have sworn I brought your chart down here this morning, but it seems to have grown legs and walked away." He replaced the phone book and came around in front of the desk again. "If only they made a pill that could cure absent-mindedness."

I stared at him and blinked—just once. "Surely you're not suggesting chemical intervention?" I barely hid my amusement. Avery arched an eyebrow. My bid for sleeping pills was lost.

Perhaps his suggestion of a home alarm had some merit. "I suppose I could look into a security system. Cheney might be able to recommend a company." I brightened at the thought.

Cheney Meyer was the twenty-five-year-old mechanic who'd resurrected my father's old red convertible. I'd discovered the abandoned MGB in the garage when I returned here to our family's cottage on the west coast a few months ago. Cheney and his dad, Jack, restored it so it spewed exhaust like the day it came out of the factory. Cheney had contacts. He'd know someone in the security business.

"I bet he could," Avery said. "Lie back."

This was our Tuesday routine. First, he took my temperature. Then he checked my eyes and reflexes. Next, he took my blood pressure. The last step was checking the bullet wounds. The paper crackled under me. I lay back on the red vinyl exam table and hiked my shirt. The bullet hole that caused such terrible pain just seven weeks ago was now a dime-sized shiny pink circle. The exit wound wasn't as pretty, but it was on my back, so I didn't have to look at it. He examined the wounds with gentle fingers, palpating around them. We did the, *does this hurt? how about that?* routine and then tugged my shirt back down, and I sat up.

"The night sweats, the sudden waking—they're typical symptoms of anxiety. You've been through a lot these past few weeks, physically and emotionally. You need to process it." Avery pushed his glasses up into his hair. "Let's give it more time. If your symptoms persist, we'll discuss it again, but my preference will still be to try behaviour modification therapy before chemical intervention."

I frowned. My preference was still the quick fix of pharmaceuticals.

"But we're getting ahead of ourselves. Your work with Malcolm has already helped heal your body. A home alarm will put your mind at ease and don't forget about Eden. She knows what you're dealing with and she wants to help. Besides, she's one of us—discreet is in her DNA."

Avery was right about Eden. She started off as one of my teachers, but the intensity of our time together had turned our bond into a close friendship.

Eden Effrome was four years my senior and five foot nothing to my five foot seven. Her spiky red hair looked nothing like my long, curly mop, and her eyes were bright blue, whereas mine were green. The physical differences made it impossible to mistake us for real sisters, but she's exactly who I'd pick for my sister if I could. I hopped down from the exam table and straightened my clothes.

"Do you think Jackson was telling the truth?" I asked. "You know— about the military or organized crime, knowing about us? Looking for us?" Jackson Delaney's integrity had been obliterated in the wake of a deception by him that left us questioning if anything he'd told us could be trusted.

"Honestly—I don't know. Everyone with contacts has put feelers out searching for more information. I just hope we're not stirring up a hornet's nest with all the speculation. Just a few days ago, one of my contacts had his computer hacked. His first thought was that someone was on to him. It's worrisome."

I agreed, gathering my things. We walked out of the small exam room into the empty waiting area. Avery's home office was in a converted garage attached to his Victorian-era home in an old-money neighbourhood. The stately old house dominated a large city lot with a small back garden. Avery and I had shared many mugs of coffee and pots of tea in the kitchen, and it was upstairs in one of the bedrooms where I'd recovered after the shooting.

Avery put his arm around my shoulder and walked me to the door. "Don't wait too long to look into an alarm. The sooner we address the anxiety, the faster you'll get over it." He opened the door for me. "And call Eden. Are we still on for Thursday?"

I sighed. "I'll be here." I stepped into the bright August sunshine. Tuesdays were physical checkup days, but Thursdays were when the real work happened. On Thursdays, we challenged my *gift*, the source of so much pain and angst. The *gift* was the secret we all kept, but only three people knew mine was different. That difference would cost me my life if my secret got out.

"Looks like you've got company," I said, seeing Victoria emerge from the sleek, navy blue BMW she'd parked behind my little red MGB. Victoria Lang belonged to the class of beautiful that turned all heads, male and female alike. She was as tall as Avery and graceful with long blonde hair that she'd tied back into a ponytail today. Victoria had the look of an heiress; I think it was her confidence.

A glance at Avery confirmed they were indeed still an item. He was all but drooling. "You know they call these 'lunch dates' nooners." I chuckled and he rolled his eyes. I headed for the MGB. "Hey, Victoria."

"Em." She walked between our cars. "You're looking good." She would know, having helped Avery nurse me after the shooting.

"Thanks." I opened my door. "See you Thursday," I called over to Avery as he pulled Victoria into an embrace.

As much as I wanted to go straight home, there was one more stop I had to make. I'd promised to have lunch with Molly. She worked at Rumbles, a quaint old bookstore that I'd discovered shortly after my return to Summerset. I'd known Molly Connolly since kindergarten. We were friends until my dad died, but lost touch when my mother fled the coast and moved us to Toronto. Our old friendship bobbed to the surface after our reacquaintance.

Finding Molly was both a blessing and a curse. When I left Toronto, I promised myself I'd make the effort to change my life. Gaining control of my gift was my biggest priority, but another one was reaching out and making friends. Molly's ready friendship filled that void. Of course, that was before I learned the full extent of the secrets I guarded.

It would be safer for both of us if I eased out of her life, but I'd only just found her. She lived a life that would have paralleled mine if I'd never accepted Jolene's gift. Molly was smart and funny and upbeat. Spending time with her never failed to remind me that there were things in this life that remained uncomplicated and normal. She grounded me in a good way.

I'd been avoiding her and she knew it; she just didn't know why. We'd talked since the shooting, but I hadn't been by to see her. It was easier to lie and hide my leaky emotions over the phone. I wasn't so adept in person, but I was stronger now. Today I would tell her the "why." Well, not all of it, I could never do that, but I could at least reassure her it had nothing to do with her.

I eased out of Avery's quiet neighbourhood and headed back to Deacon Street. In the three months since my return to Summerset, the scenery had changed from cherry blossoms and magnolia blooms to fluttery summer leaves in every shade of green imaginable. Now the leaves showed their age, leathery and thickened with the kiss of August's sun.

I never once regretted returning here. The coast's beauty was tied to nature, not architecture. Even the city of Vancouver, a short thirty-minute drive north of Summerset, dripped in all things green. The heady scent of blooms and mown grass permeated the air. Snow-capped mountains played hide-and-seek with skyscrapers and bungalows, providing an ever-changing view.

Molly worked on the stretch of Deacon Street that locals referred to as *the strip*. Each side of the strip had its own feel. The south side was home to impersonal chain stores. It was pleasant enough, with mature trees shading the sidewalk, but it lacked the personality of the north side.

The north-side stores were smaller and original to the neighbourhood. Despite the fact that almost all the shops had been renovated, they'd kept their small-town charm.

I found parking a few doors away from Rumbles, picked up a Reuben sandwich from the deli, two coffees from Starbucks, and pushed open the door to the bookstore.

A bell jingled to announce my arrival. The door didn't close automatically like modern stores. It needed to be pulled shut. Molly often grumbled about having to close it behind inattentive customers. The old store had character. Its tall ceilings accommodated book stacks that reached up so high Molly needed a ladder to get to the top shelves. The old oak floor was bare of finish in places and creaked underfoot. I breathed in the familiar aroma of crisp paper and fresh ink with an undertone of dust.

"Hi," Molly said, from my left. She'd already cleared the small table close to the front window and had settled into one of the worn wingback chairs. The store was empty of customers, as it seemed to be most of the time. Some days, I wondered if Rumbles ever turned a profit.

Molly had restrained her short dark curls behind a lime green hair band. She dressed like she often did—as if the fifties had never ended, not that she'd ever experienced that decade first-hand. Today she wore a sleeveless tailored shirt tucked into perfectly pressed capris.

We shared a love of books and similar taste in music and movies, so were never lost for chatter. I think we'd both been surprised at how easily we slid back into our old friendship. It felt comfortable. Not so close that keeping a few secrets threatened it, but close enough to share some genuine laughs.

I handed her a coffee. "A sprinkle of cinnamon and a dash of whole milk—did I get it right?"

"Perfect." She pried the lid off the coffee and blew across the top. She watched me, waiting. "You've lost weight," she said, and I knew that she'd debated whether to say that out loud.

"Maybe a bit." I'd always been on the light side of the scale and Molly had always been on the heavy side. We'd both fallen into the typical girl trap of being self-conscious about our body image. She suited her weight: it made her curvy and sexy. I assured her of that as often as she assured me I wasn't all knees and elbows.

"How are things with you and Cheney?" I asked, stalling as I searched for the words to explain my absence. Luckily, her new relationship absorbed much of her spare time.

"We're tight, still having fun," she said, blushing. I pictured Cheney's handsome face and the thick brown hair that Molly probably ran her fingers through. Initially, Cheney had been interested in me, but I'd steered him in Molly's direction more than two months ago. They'd hit it off and been dating steadily ever since. Some days I regretted pushing him away, but at the time it was the right thing to do.

"I'm glad." I unwrapped my sandwich while she slowly stirred her fork around in her salad. It looked like tabbouleh. Silence crept in between us.

I took a deep breath and steeled myself. Working from the Band-Aid theory, I decided to blurt it out and get it over with. "Jackson left."

If she was surprised, I couldn't tell. "I'm sorry. I figured it was man trouble that kept you away." She savoured a forkful of her salad and looked out the window. "Was his leaving your idea or his—or maybe you don't want to talk about it?"

"No, it's okay. He just wasn't the man I thought he was." I felt embarrassed to tell her the truth. Jackson had betrayed my trust with one of the oldest possible deceptions and I had been too caught up in him to catch what, in hindsight, were some strikingly obvious clues. "Turns out he was married."

"Oh, that sucks." Molly looked like she'd bit into a sour cherry.

"Yeah, but I'll get over it." That was said with more bravado than I felt. Jackson had been my first lover, so his betrayal was particularly painful. I'd been attracted to him almost from the moment I'd met him, but it took a near drowning to put me in his bed. I could picture his pale hazel eyes and feel the way his smile made my insides quake. I hated that I still thought of him as handsome; hated feeling used and discarded; hated feeling angry and hurt. Apparently, I was a long way from being over it.

"Sure you will," Molly said, much more upbeat than I was about it. "I'm glad you came for lunch. I got worried when you put off seeing me. Thought maybe you'd had another fight with the rocks on the beach." She smiled with a little chuckle. "Last time you went AWOL, you showed up with a horrible bruise on your face and told me the rocks had won. I thought maybe this time they'd finished the job."

I did remember my *fight with the rocks*, but that wasn't what caused the bruises. It was one more reminder of the secrets I kept. "I'm sorry. I just didn't feel like pretending everything was okay."

"At least you called—saved me having to plaster missing-person posters all over the neighbourhood." Molly set her lunch down. "You've got me wondering." She hurried over to the computer and retrieved a sheet of paper from the shallow drawer underneath.

"Was his wife's name Alexandra?" she asked, glancing at the paper as she walked back.

I frowned. "She uses Sandra, the short form, but how would you know her name?"

"You told me the name of Jackson's boat, remember? I looked it up on the Internet." She offered me the piece of paper. "The *Aerial Symphony* is registered in New Orleans to one Alexandra Delaney."

"Now I feel like an idiot. Do you know how many hours I spent on the computer researching the Delaney family and their development business? I even knew he had a *friend* named Sandra, but I never suspected she was his wife." In fact, the reason Jackson Delaney had come to Vancouver from New Orleans was to organize Sandra's rescue. "If only I'd thought to Google the *Aerial Symphony*. It would have saved me a whole lot of hurt."

"Hardly. I looked it up and it never occurred to me. I just figured the boat was owned by his mom or a sister. Didn't give it a second thought."

"I suppose." I'd managed to ignore or write off all the other things that should have been flapping red flags—why not this one too? "Let's not talk about it anymore, okay?" I'd hit my *you're unbelievably naive* limit for the day.

"Sure. I'm sorry it hurts, Em, but he's not worth it."

He absolutely wasn't worth it, but it still hurt.

Chapter Two

I felt relieved that I'd come clean with Molly. Not that I'd told her everything—I would never be able to do that—but I valued the parts we could share. And though I often felt guilty about keeping secrets from Molly, thanks to Eden's sage advice, I was coming to terms with it. The secrets protected her.

Back home, I expanded on Avery's list of home alarm companies. There were half a dozen possibilities, but which one to choose proved an impossible task, so I played my "Call a Friend" card and phoned Cheney.

It was good to hear his voice. "I'm got back from lunch with Molly."

"I'm glad to hear it. She's been worried about you. You okay?"

"Yeah, thanks, I'm fine." Cheney had always been kind to me and easy to talk to. When you added in his sky-blue eyes and great physique, you'd have a difficult time finding a better catch. It made me sorry to think I'd passed him up. I cringed knowing he'd soon learn I'd been dating a married man. It was humiliating. "I was hoping you could offer a recommendation. Do you know anyone in the home alarm business?"

"Why? Did you have a break-in?"

"Nothing like that. It's just a precaution. Living alone and all."

"You are fairly isolated out there. The company that looks after our garage is Prime Security. They're good. I can ask David to give you a call if you like?"

"Thanks. That would be great." Prime Security was one of the companies on the list.

I should have said goodbye right then, but I hesitated and Cheney jumped into the void. "Any news on the Wrights?"

The Wrights looked after the cottage during the ten years my mother and I'd lived in Toronto. Charles Wright was a good friend of Cheney's father, Jack. In fact, it was the Wrights who'd recommended Cheney for the MGB's restoration. Charles and Gabby had gone missing two months ago.

"No, not a word. You?" I asked.

"Nothing. Dad can't believe they took off like that without telling anyone."

The police, Charles and Gabby's friends, and their faithful clients were all keeping a vigil, hoping for their safe return. I knew better. They weren't coming back.

Charles's duplicity still stung. I'd called him a friend, but the surveillance pictures told a different story. They left no doubt he was the one who'd planted a high-tech spy camera on my property. It was a fatal mistake. The Tribunal Novem made certain Charles and his wife would never be able to spill the secrets Charles had uncovered. Cheney knew nothing of all that. It was just another one of my dark secrets.

"Maybe something will turn up," I said, with as much sincerity as I could rally.

Less than twenty minutes later, David Donelli from Prime Security called. We set up an appointment for the next morning when he would assess the cottage. I hung up feeling like I'd accomplished something and then checked in with my mother.

It was only six in the evening Toronto-time, and she wasn't answering at her lab. She picked up at the condo on the third ring. "Wow, you're home. Did the lab burn down?" My mother, a dedicated behavioural research Ph.D, worked at the University of Toronto's Behavioural Sciences Lab.

"Very funny. I get home for dinner on occasion."

We both knew that wasn't very often, and never before 8:00 p.m. I wandered into the breeze of the open patio door. "I had a visit with Molly today. She says to say hello."

My mother and I didn't have one of those all-consuming, touchy-feely, mother-daughter relationships. Ours was an arms-length one that worked well for both of us. A weekly phone call was all it took to maintain. Right now, the distance between us was a blessing because the things I had to work out were best done in private.

She updated me on her most recent article in the *Journal of Neuropharmacology.* "Do you remember Edgar Stein?" she asked.

"The doctor in pharmacology?"

"He invited me to lunch yesterday. He's intrigued with my research into chlordiazepoxide's effect on the optic nerve in rats. His interest is pediatrics, but his line of thought reminded me of some research of your father's. I'm considering giving him your dad's notes. Who knows? Maybe the work your father started will result in some new research. He'd like that, don't you think?"

The rarity of this moment stopped me cold. An awkward silence hung in the air. My mother didn't talk about my father. Ever. My father's death was nearly the end of her. It was certainly the end of her social life. To my knowledge, she'd never dated nor even shown any interest in men after him.

"I—I think that's a great idea. Yes, he'd like that."

Perhaps my mother was finally putting his death behind her. She was a workaholic before he died. Afterwards, she re-doubled her efforts and used her work like a shield to protect herself from her grief. Neither one of us handled his death very well, but I never could muster the anger that should have been mine when she shut me out and kept me distant. I just got used to it.

As I wandered back to the bookcase, I told her about getting an alarm installed. She liked the idea and even offered to pay half the cost.

I absently fingered the framed photo of her and my father. Dad looked content. His blue eyes squinted against the sun, his arms wrapped protectively around her, unaware that his short brown hair was sticking up with the wind that must have been at their backs. The photo was taken in Seattle on their honeymoon. They made an attractive couple. She'd worn her hair long then. It was a darker shade of brown than mine and without the auburn highlights that I'd inherited from Dad. Her hair was short now and greying, but I liked the way the grey set off her green eyes.

"I know it's still early days, but have you put any feelers out in the job market?"

I knew my mother. She was not pushing, just curious. My graduation gift from her was six months of all-expenses-paid living here in our old cottage. It was the perfect gift. I was halfway through my six-month freebie and hadn't done any serious looking yet. Of course, she didn't know about the reward money from Sandra's family that now cushioned my bank account.

"Not yet, but I will. Soon."

After hanging up, I made a cup of tea and took it out to the deck. In the mornings I was a slave to coffee, but in the afternoons, there was nothing better than a big mug of milk-infused orange pekoe. I had a few hours to fill until it was dark enough to fly.

I leaned on the railing and inhaled the pungent aroma of a low tide. The small Arts and Crafts cottage I now called home sat on two acres perched on the Pacific. Below me, pockets of grey sand had settled between the shale and sandstone rocks. The stone slabs were dressed in green and red seaweed left behind by the receding tide. All but one side of the property was surrounded by either ocean or Sunset Provincial Park. It felt like my private paradise.

My father had bought this gem before he met my mother and we'd lived here until he died. My mother moved us to Toronto after his accident. She couldn't handle the pain of Dad's memories that saturated every room. To my young mind, the move seemed abrupt and pre-mature. Grief and anger proved bitter company. I think that's when I first started calling her Laura.

This cottage was a large part of the reason for my move back to the coast. Though it was modest—just two bedrooms, a small study and one bathroom—it was everything to me. It was comfort and security. Unlike my mother, I loved the memories it held of my dad. Even the fact that we called this place a cottage was due to him. He'd adopted the quaint term of endearment from the original owners, to whom the small dwelling truly was a cottage.

But my return wasn't only about coming home. I also needed the privacy and the open space this setting provided to sort out the mystery that was Jolene's gift: a gift that had wreaked havoc on my life. My first attempts to figure it out lasted exactly five days. On the fifth day, I made a colossal blunder that caused me to fall from a very great height. It bought me a two-day stay in the hospital complete with a concussion, contusions and stitches.

It wasn't, however, a complete loss. I found Avery in the ordeal, and he held the key to the mystery. He was the ER doctor on duty the night I was brought in, unconscious. He knew what I was the moment he examined my eyes and the severity of my injury was proof enough that I was in trouble.

That trouble started with Jolene. I'd met her on our beach the summer my father was killed. She was a quiet woman my mother's age. She dressed like a hippy in long blousy sundresses and hid her wavy blonde hair under a wide-brimmed hat. On the last day I saw her, she offered me a gift I was too naive to turn down.

I expected pretty paper and a bow. Instead, she positioned our hands, careful to ensure that our fingertips touched, and recited some gibberish that didn't do much but put me to sleep. Soon after that visit, I discovered I could see as clearly in the middle of the night as I could at midday. The perfect night vision made me understand why Jolene had insisted I promise to keep her gift a secret.

The night vision wasn't difficult to conceal; I switched on lights even though I didn't need them. But as I grew older, the gift began to change, and I realized that what Jolene gave me wasn't just perfect night vision. No, that was just the tip of Jolene's iceberg. If it weren't for Avery and the covey, that iceberg may very well have sunk me.

I kicked off my sandals and descended the stairs that ran off the north end of the deck. Passing by my usual perch on the bleached driftwood logs, I continued to where the sun heated the sandstone. I stretched out on a large slab and let the rock's heat seep into me.

The beach was alive with all manner of creatures but not a single person. This wasn't a volleyball beach. Rocks the size of bowling balls laid shoulder to shoulder, presenting an ankle-twisting maze that didn't tempt many visitors. Being two kilometres from the nearest public access didn't hurt either.

When Avery brought me home after the shooting, I never thought I'd feel anything good again. Jackson's betrayal came on the heels of Charles's duplicity and the damage he'd done had seared my heart. I felt ruined, like the charred chimney left standing after the house has burned to the ground.

I spent the intervening weeks healing, walking the beaches and berating myself for my error in judgment. Avery had warned me to protect my heart, but I didn't know having it broken would hurt so much. I didn't think I'd ever be able to rebuild my life from the smouldering ashes, but time and self-discipline had worked their magic. The pain now only flared up in my weakest moments.

I'd also learned something about myself: I had an unhealthy need for control. I hadn't been conscious of it before, but now I could see that it had been a part of me for a long time. Dealing with Jolene's gift had been the impetus, but I applied the control to every aspect of my life. Unfortunately, right now my life was a sheaf of papers blowing in the wind and no amount of control could rein in all the loose sheets. It

wasn't just the gift and its implications—it was the myriad little anxie-
ties: the "why" behind Jolene's choice of me, and of Charles targeting
me; the "how" behind blending my worlds and moving past Jackson;
and the "what" behind the hidden threats and the unfathomable future.

It was arrogant and presumptuous of me to think I could control
any of those things, but that freakish part of me kept trying and kept
failing. It was exhausting. I needed to let it go. Think positive thoughts.
Send the impossible stuff out to the universe. Live in the moment.
Yadda, yadda, yadda.

A bumblebee the size of a grape landed without grace on the warm
rock near my head. I turned to watch it. "You really weren't built for
flight," I said. It stumbled like a newborn foal on hairy limbs, its tiny
wings buzzing ineffectually. Scientists had only recently discovered the
aerodynamics that made bumblebee flight possible. When would they
figure us out, I wondered?

I focused on the heat seeping up from the sandstone, the sun on my
toes and the warm breeze that wafted the briny smell of the ocean over
me. But mostly, I tried not to think—just to absorb the quiet calm of
the beach and wait for the cover of darkness to provide a release.

Chapter Three

Back in the cottage after dark, I donned the uniform: dark hoodie, dark yoga pants, black Rocket Dogs. I adjusted the sleek Ryder racing goggles and fastened on my newest addition—a wrist-mounted Garmin. I'd lost my old Ryders and my last GPS during Sandra's rescue. This GPS looked too big for my wrist, like a man's watch, but I was so adept at getting lost that I didn't go far without it.

I pulled my hair into a ponytail and stepped out onto the deck, locking the patio door behind me. It was a warm, cloudless August night, and the stars twinkled, beckoning me to join them. It felt decadent, like eating a pint of Haagen Das from the container. The night was my friend on these sojourns, cloaking my presence in the dark.

Using my mind's eye, I reached deep within myself and called forth the crystal that powered my gift. The crystal wasn't a physical thing, but I knew what it looked like, and I could sense it within me always. It had been revealed to me in a dream that was twisted up with memory fragments of my father. If I could hold the crystal in my hand, it would be the width of my palm. It would be clear and warm to the touch with six smooth sides and a six-sided prism capping each end.

I wrapped metaphysical fingers around it and concentrated on the steady hum of power that coursed through my limbs, fueling an all-consuming high. The crystal was my talisman, the key that awakened my gift and it begged to be released.

When the power peaked, I raised my arms, twisted to the left, and felt gravity break loose. I lifted free of the deck and rotated as I drifted silently into the night. When the deck was far below me, I lowered my arms, shifted into a horizontal position and then moved without a whisper over the trees of the adjacent park.

This is what I lived for. It was pure, unmitigated, self-indulgent me-time. Sweet beyond any measure I'd known before. I was omnipotent in the night sky and even if the rest of my life felt out of control, in this slice of heaven I was in charge. If it was just an illusion, I didn't care. This was my opiate of choice, and I was a happily devoted addict. This is what Jolene gave me: The gift of flight was her legacy.

I was almost as good a Flier as those in my covey who were born with the gift. A covey wasn't something you joined: it was more like a family. But it wasn't genes that bound you, it was your gift. I'd had good teachers and living adjacent to the park as I did, I had the opportunity to practice frequently. My endurance had diminished after the shooting, but I was rebuilding it.

Sunset Provincial Park was a treasure, but it was no Stanley Park. Both were roughly a thousand acres, and each bordered the Pacific, but that's where the similarities ended. Vancouver's Stanley Park had clean restrooms with running water, restaurants, well-tended and well-lit paths and heavy foot traffic day and night. By contrast, Sunset Park's trails weren't clearly identified on the park's signage and the three unisex outhouses weren't identified at all. It was perfect.

I liked to fly slow and steady. It allowed me to see more clearly and have better control over wind gusts and unexpected up- and down-drafts. My skills, though still new, were solid and improving all the time. I rarely poured on the speed that lurked within my gift. I'd learned that flying at those speeds came with a different set of rules. Once in a while I'd let it loose, but I kept it on a short leash; I didn't want to take the chance of losing control. Been there, done that, nearly drowned and not going back for seconds, thanks very much.

Tonight's plan was to find the old lighthouse that Molly and I had rediscovered during a hike weeks ago. It was one of the coastal lighthouses that had been automated as part of cost-cutting measures under a previous government. The lighthouse still beamed out its warning, but due to prohibitive costs, the grounds had been closed to the public: abandoned to all but minimal maintenance and locked against vandals.

I concentrated my efforts on flitting in and around the treetops, like a dog on an agility course. It was an excellent skill-building exercise that required considerable focus to avoid contact with the scented boughs.

The sweep of a flashlight beam crossed the path below. I stopped short. Damn! I'd become used to having the park to myself after dark. When had I become so complacent? The voices of the couple below drifted up to me. They were arm-in-arm, walking their dog. The trees in this area were spindly, leaving me feeling exposed.

I kept perfectly still, barely breathing, hoping my thumping heart didn't give me away. I watched their bowed heads follow the criss-crossing beam of their flashlight. Just a few more yards . . .

My cellphone trilled to life.

Oh, Jesus! I flew backwards, side-swiping a cottonwood with my shoulder. Crap, Crap, Crap! The dog barked once, twice.

"What was that?" I heard from below.

Don't look up, don't look up, I pleaded silently, fumbling with my phone. The blasted thing sang out again and lit up brightly in the palm of my hand. Where was the freaking mute button?

From below, a voice said, "It's not mine."

I found the mute button on the side and pressed it. A cold sweat bloomed.

"Not mine either." This was accompanied by now incessant barking.

Frantically, I looked around for cover and spotted an ancient cedar in the distance.

A male voice called out, "Who's there?"

I twisted, narrowly missing an erratic beam of light that flashed up to search the trees. I darted toward the cedar at a reckless speed and dropped behind it, stepping onto a sturdy branch. I held my breath.

My carelessness would be the death of me. The dog's barking faded as the couple beat a swift retreat.

I was safe again, but admonished myself. How could I have forgot-ten to put my phone on mute? It wasn't just my freedom at stake. If I was discovered, the whole covey would be in danger, and I didn't even want to think about what the Tribunal would do.

The night slowly settled again and so did I. The GPS gave me my bearings and I lifted off. Once airborne, I stretched the tension out of my limbs. Cautiously, I headed south flying above the trees that leaned out over the Pacific.

As soon as the coast curled around to the southeast, I saw the blink of the lighthouse. The white structure sat on a cliff that jutted from the southernmost tip of the park. I approached from the water. It stood like a solitary sentry, alone at the edge of the ocean, proudly carrying out its soldier's duty.

I circled it slowly. The forest had been cleared from behind it. A small entry door at ground level was painted red. Five stories up, another red door graced the top, giving access to the metal-grated catwalk that circled the structure just below the lantern housing.

I landed on the catwalk and tested the door. It was locked. I peeked in the window and saw a small lumpy cot on the far side of the room. Steep steps led up to the lantern room. Electronic gadgets lining the curved wall, closest to the ocean, showed no sign of life. The sparse contents looked lonely in their abandonment.

I breathed a heavy sigh of relief and leaned back against the wall sinking to my haunches. Jesus, that was close. The covey would not be impressed with me right now.

Who had called? I retrieved my phone. Eden. It was late for her to call. She was probably still working. I dialled her back.

"I hope I didn't wake you earlier," she said.

"No, I was up—just couldn't get to the phone." *Up in the treetops with near heart failure.*

"How are you?"

Reeling. It took me a moment to gather my terms of reference for this conversation. "I saw Avery today. Asked him to prescribe sleeping pills."

Eden laughed. "Don't hold your breath for drugs from Avery. You're lucky he gave you any when you were shot." Eden was a nurse and she and Avery had a professional respect for one another. "Are you not sleeping well?"

"I've been hearing noises in the night. Makes me think about Jackson's warnings about outsiders knowing about us, looking for us. Maybe he was telling the truth. Maybe the covey really is in danger."

"I think about that too. It scares me, but we can't let fear run our lives. We stay vigilant. If we learn Jackson's theories have substance, then we'll take precautions. But I can't live my life like an anvil's hanging over my head. I won't."

"Avery suggested I get a home alarm."

"That's a good idea."

"Cheney knows a guy. He's coming tomorrow to take a look."

"Good for you," Eden said. "Did Avery have any news about his contact down in Portland?"

"He mentioned that some guy's computer was hacked."

"It's the man who maintains the message board we call Infinity. We've been waiting for word on whether it's still secure."

"I can ask Avery on Thursday when I see him."

"Don't trouble yourself. Alex will call him tomorrow." Alex Klause was Eden's live-in love. "But that's not why I was calling you. I'm working my last night shift at the hospital tomorrow and thought I'd see if you wanted to get together?"

"I'd love to. What did you have in mind?"

"First, did you connect with Molly yet?"

"Yes, this afternoon, and you were right, she was great." I knew that would make Eden happy; she'd been encouraging me to reconnect with Molly. Eden knew I struggled with the two very different lives I lived. She'd been trying to help, showing me how she and the others managed that balance. After all, every one of us lived two lives, and we all interacted with the rest of the world in some capacity; we worked there, banked there and shopped there. It was only rocket science to those of us who had difficulty forming meaningful attachments to anything more significant than a Chia pet.

"I told her about Jackson, too," I said. "She barely blinked." Eden knew about my involvement with Jackson. I had filled her in after Sandra's rescue. It was just too big a hurt to hide from her and she had been unfailingly supportive. Neither she nor anyone else knew that he was married, let alone married to the woman who'd gone missing. Jackson had left out that tidbit when he asked our covey to help him find her and free her from her kidnappers. That omission had cost him his integrity, a valuable commodity in the small Flier community.

"I'm not surprised," Eden said. "Good friends are like that, and with that in mind, how do you feel about introducing us? We could have a girls' night out." Eden was nothing if not optimistic. I inhaled through my teeth. "Oh, don't be like that. We'll have fun. What do you say?"

It was hard to say no in the face of that much enthusiasm. "All right, but don't get too excited until I see if she's even interested."

"She will be. Text me when you know." An urgent overhead announcement blared in the background. "I've got to go, but I'm looking forward to meeting Molly. Don't forget to call her. Yaletown. You, me, Molly. This weekend."

I returned my gaze to the unobstructed view, spectacular under the stars. Above me, the lantern's motor hummed and clicked as it made its semicircular trek back and forth inside the tower. Water lapped gently at the shore, the moonlight reflecting off the surface in a mesmerizing display of sparkles.

After one last look around, I headed home.

When I landed back on my deck, I was spent. Not so much physically tired, but flying was a little like being on a roller-coaster ride and the duration of the adrenalin rush took a toll.

You might think the adrenalin withdrawal would help me sleep, but the opposite was true. I self-medicated with a much-too-large glass of red wine. Not because I was being self-destructive, I just wanted to sleep through the night.

CHAPTER FOUR

I didn't wake until nine the next morning. It was bright outside and the view from my bed was stunning—too beautiful to hide behind curtains. I'd had a scare a few weeks ago when I found footprints in the sand at the foot of the stairs, but I hadn't let it change my open-curtains policy. I headed to the kitchen to make my morning pot of coffee.

David from Prime Security was due at ten, which left enough time for a quick shower while the coffee dripped. I turned on the Bose and checked the CBC headline news while I topped up my caffeine level. I glanced at the shrink-wrapped GPS manual. Eventually I'd have to register the thing online.

I was dressed for summer and sitting on the deck when the doorbell rang.

"Ms. Taylor." David Donelli offered his hand.

"Call me Emelynn." He was a large man with a thick neck. He wore a white shirt with a blue-flecked brown tie. His grey slacks had shiny patches on the thighs. He looked more like a bodyguard than a salesman, but maybe that was the image Prime Security was going for. He made a point of showing me his ID before accepting my invitation to come inside.

"How many people live in the house?" he asked as we made our way to the kitchen. His demeanor was serious, strictly business.

"Just me. Would you like a coffee?"

He declined. His gaze darted around the room, pausing at windows and doors, but not venturing to the view.

"How long have you lived here?"

"Four months, but I grew up here. I've been away. Moved back in May." His questions felt like an interrogation. Had he even smiled yet?

"Do you mind if I look around?"

"No. Please, go ahead," I said, following him.

David started his tour at the front door, measuring and marking doors and windows on a template attached to his clipboard. The solid oak front door pleased him and the length of the plunger in the dead-bolt got a passing grade. I felt a warm blush of pride.

The cottage followed a basic centre-hall design with rooms running symmetrically off either side. He started up the north side. The first bedroom was the one I'd used as a child. He shook his head at the brass window lock. The room also had a leaded glass porthole window, like my father's study across the hall. Next was the bathroom, and he was equally unimpressed with its window lock.

At this rate, he was in for a lot of disappointment because the entire house had all its original hardware.

He moved on to my bedroom at the far end of the house and inspected the patio door. "You need to beef up security on this door." He then, much to my horror, drove his point home by removing the locked patio door in about two seconds. He just lifted it right out of its track.

He repeated the demonstration with the patio door in the living room. "It needs a deadbolt just like your front door and I'd like to see a security bar in the track and floor bolts."

We rounded my mother's blue sofa and started back through the house on the south side. He noted the narrow rectangular window on the wall behind the dining-room table. The kitchen window beyond the breakfast bar was next. I could tell by his dour expression that it, too, had earned a black mark. The last room on the south side was my father's study. It was slightly larger than the small bedroom across from it, but its window also failed inspection.

He started his sales pitch as we walked back to the dining room. "Prime Security offers a wide range of protection. We install locks (he pronounced *install* like it was two words) and motion detectors as well as window and door sensors."

I motioned him to take a seat at the table. His knees didn't quite fit. He sat sideways and continued his spiel, rhyming off round-the-clock monitoring, two-way radio communication, and direct access to the local police and fire departments. "We even install safes and panic rooms," he added.

I didn't need a safe or a panic room, but I also didn't need any more convincing. He had my money the moment he'd lifted the patio door out of its track. "There's nothing here to steal. I just want to feel safe, and I want to sleep. That's all."

"You're installing a house alarm because you're having trouble sleeping?" At that, I finally saw some facial expression. He raised an eyebrow.

"I'm sure it's nothing. I've been waking in the night—hearing noises."

"What kind of noises?" he asked, again, just a little too seriously.

"Scuffing, thumping noises—sometimes I hear rattles. Of course, I imagine the worst and think it's someone trying to get in."

"Do you have reason to think someone might try to get in?" Now it was my turn to look perplexed, so he went on. "Has anyone threatened you in any way?" he asked, and though I didn't think it was possible, his serious level went up another notch.

"God no, it's nothing like that," I said, embarrassed now that I'd caught his drift.

"You're sure? Because if there is someone—say, an ex-husband or former boyfriend—trying to scare you, then an alarm won't help. You need to call the police. Someone that determined will find a way in."

And now I felt foolish *and* embarrassed *and*, apparently, I could add potential divorcée to the list. "It's nothing like that. I've never been married and the only boyfriend I've ever had is very former and living in New Orleans, far away. It's probably just my imagination or maybe it's living alone. I lived with my mother in a high-rise condo before moving back here."

He settled back against the chair, relaxing a bit. "In that case, you should consider a panic button, just until you feel more comfortable here. It's a little gizmo—looks like a key fob. It'll even work outside if you're in range of the sensor."

After a detailed discussion about what I needed, David excused himself to check the perimeter.

He returned with a written estimate. "I've included new window and patio door locks as well as sensors and motion detectors in every room. I've also included a panic button." He checked his itemized notes. "Have I left anything out?"

"I'm not sure you noticed, but there are two small attic windows as well."

"Yes, I saw them, but they're inaccessible without the use of a ladder. Do you keep a ladder that size around?"

"I don't think so." But David didn't know that the people who might do me harm wouldn't need a ladder. "I know it's probably over-kill, but I'd feel better if you'd install a motion detector up there too."

"Certainly." David made a note on his clipboard. "Is there anything else?"

"The stairs to the beach?"

"How about a trip alarm? It's similar to those used in retail stores to alert proprietors when a customer crosses their threshold." I nodded my agreement, and he scratched another note. "Let me make some phone calls, get you a firm price and an installation schedule." He returned to his car to make the calls.

His estimate was pricey, but my peace of mind was worth it. I gave him the go-ahead and signed the papers.

"Because Cheney is such a good customer, I'm going to push this job to the front of the queue. If it's all right with you, a crew can be over here today to work on those locks. If we don't run into any snags, the whole system could be up and running by end of day tomorrow. Will that work with your schedule?"

"Thank you—yes." David insisted my presence wasn't required when I told him I had an appointment away from the house.

"We're bonded," he said. "Your house is in good hands." It occurred to me that if you couldn't trust the company installing your security system, then who could you trust?

I left him a key and headed out to meet Malcolm at the YMCA. Twice a week we met at the gym where we'd do weight training, the other three days he met me at my place, and we went for a run. Malcolm believed that the human body needed a variety of challenges to achieve optimum fitness and he was a prime example.

A waft of chlorine and stale sweat greeted me at the door. The Y reminded me of high school with its colourful poster boards and noisy bustle. I signed in at the front desk and glanced through the glass wall opposite into the weight room. The equipment, though plentiful, was well used. A bank of lockers lined the hall to my left. I claimed one before taking a seat to lace up my running shoes.

Malcolm was busy with another client, but he saw me and waved.

For the most part, the people using this gym weren't hard bodies wearing fashionable Lycra. They were all ages and shapes and most wore old T-shirts and shorts.

Malcolm's fitness plan for me included a foundation of cardio, ramped up with strength and agility training. He'd shown me how to use every piece of equipment, and which muscle groups each machine targeted. I'd done okay, for the most part, but I had to drop weight when I did anything that targeted the muscles around the wound on my left side.

Avery had insisted I tell Malcolm about my injury, but we fudged the details; doctors are legally required to report any gun-related injury and there was no way he could do that. So as far as Malcolm knew, I was recovering from a freak bike collision with a pointed piece of metal fencing.

I started my warm-up while Malcolm finished with his elderly client, using the mirror to watch him in action. Earnest is how I'd describe him. He wore a T-shirt that was too big for him over baggy shorts and his shoes were comic-book huge. His hands were the same—disproportionately large for his slight build.

After escorting his client to the ladies' change room, he walked back to me. "They've posted the times for the intermediate self-defence class. First one's Sunday, ten to four." His voice had a calm, quiet quality.

I'd taken the beginners level two weeks ago. "I'll sign up before I leave." The first self-defence class had covered personal safety: being aware of your surroundings; anticipating potential problems; parking lot safety—simple things that everyone knows but needs to be reminded of from time to time. The most fun that day was the screaming. It's not often you get a chance to practice that. The intermediate class promised more hands-on training.

"You warmed up?"

I nodded and we headed to the circuit. Malcolm varied the machines each time, so my routine was always different. Today's circuit took me through lat pull-downs, leg presses and arm curls, a round of stomach crunches and a set of push-ups. We repeated the circuit three times. The hour melted away.

Malcolm was already working with another client when I finished my stretch out. "See you tomorrow," I called, heading to collect my things from the locker. Unlike some patrons, I preferred to shower at home. I signed up for Sunday's self-defence class on my way out.

David and the Prime Security crew had come and gone by the time I returned, and all the windows had shiny new locks. The patio doors had bolts through the frame at the floor and metal bars in the tracks. He'd left a business card on the table with a note to say that he'd be back tomorrow morning to finish the work. He also said he'd signed for three large boxes that crowded the floor in front of the dining-room table. The delivery slip confirmed what I'd hoped when I first saw the boxes.

I phoned Alex right away. "The laser tag equipment arrived," I said, when he answered. He said he'd pick up Danny after work and come by to have a look.

We had Sandra's family to thank for the equipment. When I divided up the reward money amongst the four of us who'd taken part in her rescue, we decided to invest some of that money in the covey. Coveys were an important line of defence. We all belonged to one. Even a visiting Flier checked in with the area's local covey. Custom dictated it, not for territorial reasons, but for protection.

Sandra's rescue had taught us a valuable lesson. The covey had to be better prepared to protect one another. Danny had the initial idea of switching up our training to laser tag. He and Alex then researched it and found an equipment supplier. Ours was a custom order, so we'd had to wait for it, but it would be worth it. The paintball games we'd been using for training and team building had been fun, but the equipment was cumbersome. The big barn at the paintball park was great indoor space, but with the new laser tag equipment, we could train anywhere.

The growl of Alex's motorcycle announced his arrival shortly after six. Being the owner of a custom motorcycle paint shop, it was a given that he'd have an impressive bike, and Alex's Norton Commando was that. The black feathered wings on a pearl backdrop were a subtle nod to our gift. Danny was on the back. I had the door open before Alex had the kickstand down.

"I thought you'd never get here," I said, watching them set their helmets on the bike.

Alex had turned thirty in July. He was five foot ten and his thick brown hair looked as tousled coming out from under a helmet, as it did when he flew. He had the habit of running his hand over the top to tamp it down, though it took several passes to get the job done. Alex had a sturdy frame and was a strong Flier. His flight was powerful and controlled. He reminded me of an Olympic athlete in the tumbling events.

Danny Thornton was early twenties. He was shorter than Alex with dark skin and the dreads he wore sprang free from his helmet completely unaffected by their close quarters. Danny was always in motion and wound like a tight spring. He trained as a kick-boxer. I'd seen Danny in action during Sandra's rescue and knew how big a punch he packed with both his fists and his feet. There was sinew, speed and technique behind those shoulders.

It was the first time Danny had been here. He looked around nodding appreciatively. "Nice place," he said.

Soon the living room was covered in plastic bags and crumbly bits of static-laden Styrofoam as boxes were flung open and their contents unpacked.

We'd ordered fifteen units, one for each of the covey members, and some spares. Each unit came with a lightweight mesh vest, a headset and a laser. Danny and Alex had been like kids in a candy store when they'd selected the lasers. They'd picked a combination of rifle and handgun styles that looked frighteningly real. In fact, the only visible sign they weren't, was the flexible coil that connected each laser to its vest.

Units like these were typically covered in colourful flashing lights so players could easily identify who was on which team. Laser Sports only agreed to make ours with no lights after they'd received our down payment. They'd tried to talk us out of it; told us it was a mistake, but we'd persevered.

Each unit was fully programmable to operate singly or as part of a team. It came with a command centre for programming the equipment and keeping track of the players, their hits and reloads. Base units were also included that could be set up to represent team camps or other types of targets, like buildings or vehicles.

"It'll take a few days to charge everything," Alex lamented, counting the number of pieces that needed charging. The cottage was old, and the outlets weren't plentiful, so we figured three to four days at least.

"I'll look after the charging. You just organize the game," I said. We hadn't yet told anyone about the laser equipment. It was our gift to the covey, but I'd have to let Avery in on the secret soon. He was the only one who drove to the paintball park, so I was counting on him to deliver the equipment for our next game, where we'd spring the surprise.

The covey was about to have a whole lot more fun.

CHAPTER FIVE

I couldn't wait for dark. The wonder of flying never failed to put my worries on hold. When I was above the trees, broken hearts and disturbed sleep seemed insignificant. It hadn't always been like that. Getting to this point had been a difficult journey. I'd hidden Jolene's gift for ten years. It hadn't been easy given my ever increasing tendency to float away at inconvenient times. I now knew that those episodes were precursors to flight. I shuddered to think where I might have ended up if Avery hadn't found me. I could have done without meeting Jackson, but I'd be lost without Eden and Alex in my life. They'd taught me to fly and gave me the confidence to embrace Jolene's gift.

I thought of Avery on nights like this. He was an oddity in the Flier world—a Flier who couldn't fly. In a sombre moment of reflection, Avery had told me the story of him and his best friend playing a game of dare, as young boys do. Their curiosity had been piqued by their discovery of incantations in an old book. They had no idea they were playing with powerful words that would change their lives. Luckily, Avery escaped the incident with his night vision intact and he could still harness the energy associated with his eyes.

Avery's father blamed the young friend's family for carelessly giving the boys access to a lethal and ancient book. He sought vengeance through the Tribunal Novem. They ruled in his favour and arranged for the fatal accident that claimed Avery's friend and his friend's parents.

Stories like that were why the Tribunal was universally feared. The Tribunal Novem was centuries old and born of an alliance among nine of the oldest and most powerful coveys. Most Fliers abhorred their methods, but the Tribunal was the only group powerful enough to deal with rogue Fliers. No one was strong enough to oppose them. In the absence of any other judicial presence in the Flier world, the Tribunal remained judge, jury . . . and executioner.

The Tribunal chose a dead dove as its calling card to announce that vengeance had been served. How cold and heartless did you have to be to kill such a beautiful, fragile creature and present it like an offering?

The thought chilled me.

While I waited for darkness to fall, I called Molly and invited her to Eden's and my girls' night out. Though I still had mixed feelings about it, she seemed genuinely excited.

As the blue hue of my night vision slowly replaced the golden glow of daylight, I stepped out to the deck and locked the new deadbolt. The tingle in my limbs gathered strength as I reached in my mind's eye for the crystal and pulled its power into my core. Stretching my arms above my head, I broke free of gravity, and rose over the cottage roof. The relief of being free from my bonds to the earth was overwhelming. I hoped I never got used to it; taking this for granted just seemed wrong. On nights like this, I thanked Jolene for her gift, for this freedom.

Tonight's plan was to fly the stretch of the park that bordered on the homes north and west of my place. I kept close to the tree canopy and travelled silently and slowly. Light seeped from the houses that shared a backyard with the park, but I stayed well out of sight above the trees. I plotted points on my GPS as I made my way across the park. When I reached the far edge of it, I turned back but instead of going home, I detoured to the lighthouse.

I approached from the forest, flying a slow wide circuit around it. The white tower stood in stark contrast against the night sky. I alighted on the catwalk. The door was locked. A quick glimpse through the windows revealed nothing new. Who serviced the lighthouse? I pictured a bent old man smoking a droopy black pipe and wearing a Greek peaked sailor's cap squinting out to sea.

I sat down and leaned back against the curved wall. The lantern's mechanical drone was constant. Its light swept in a pendulous arc across the sky. The clicks were out of sync with the rhythm of the waves below.

It had been a good day. Of late, I'd had more good days than bad, and that was progress. There were times when I felt my life marched two steps back for each step forward, but in the aftermath of the shooting, that had changed. With Avery's nudge and Malcolm's guidance, I'd made it change. I didn't ever again want to be that vulnerable, naive young woman. I would not backslide.

Physical fitness was one critical component in making the change. Mastering my gift was the other. It had been a steep learning curve. I couldn't control all the chaos in my life, but I'd taken the reins of the things I could control. I'd accepted that I had a role to play in protecting the secret of the gift. The covey's freedom and safety depended on it, and I wanted to be an asset to them, not a liability. The small group of Fliers were my family now.

And if that wasn't enough to motivate change, Jackson's betrayal certainly was. I hadn't even realized I'd given him my heart until he stomped on it. It wasn't like I'd been the first woman to learn she'd been the unwitting mistress of a married man. Jackson may have been my first lover, but he would not be my only love. I was made of stronger stuff than that. Besides, I enjoyed the physical part of our relationship. I just had to work on being smarter about who I chose next time.

I stood up and cleared my thoughts, then reluctantly said goodbye to the lighthouse.

Back home, my thoughts returned to the noises that robbed me of sleep. Tonight was going to be different. I had new locks that I'd already checked and I felt more secure than ever before. I crawled into bed and drifted off to sleep thinking those reassuring thoughts.

A noise jerked me awake. The moment I realized it was my alarm clock, my heart rate calmed. I'd slept through the night! It had been the best non-wine-induced sleep I'd had in weeks. I stretched out under the sheets luxuriating in the warmth and comfort. What a coup.

David was due in an hour, which prompted the morning bathroom-coffee-dress routine. The first three laser tag units were charged, so I plugged in the next lot. Even with three units out of the way, the equipment still dominated the room. I closed my laptop when David arrived.

"We'll have the remaining install done by the end of the day."

In stall. I turned my head so he wouldn't see my smirk. "I'll be in and out this morning but I'll be back midafternoon," I said, estimating my schedule.

"Good. We'll need to test the system with your cellphone when we get it up and running."

"Laser tag," I said, in answer to his curious gaze at the scattered equipment. But he raised his hands as if to say "None of my business."

"All right then, I'll get out of your way." I filled my water bottle and went outside to wait for Malcolm just as a Prime Security van pulled in behind David's car. Two men got out and nodded to me before disappearing behind the van's rear doors.

Halfway through my warm-up routine, Malcolm pedalled up and propped his bike on its kickstand in front of the garage. Charles and Gabby used to leave their bikes in the same place.

"What's with the security?" he asked, joining me.

"I'm getting a home alarm installed."

"I thought this was a good neighbourhood."

"It is. It's just the whole living alone thing." I didn't like to admit to hearing noises. It made me feel like an idiot.

Malcolm never made me feel like an idiot, even when I was one. Like the day of our first run. He'd taken one look at my black Rocket Dogs and suggested I get shoes with more structure, more cushioning. Not judgmental, just instructive. "Your feet take a lot of punishment when you're running." He'd been right, and I'd been running in Pearl Izumi ever since.

"Are you okay leaving those guys in your house while we run?"

"I think so. They're bonded. Besides, it's not like I have anything in there to steal unless an old laptop and three-year-old Bose stereo interest them."

"Okay. Let's go."

The running had been Malcolm's idea to kick-start my fitness program. Efficient was the word he'd used, but I liked that we could do it outside.

We headed into Sunset Park. Cool, damp air enveloped us. Even on the warmest days the sunlight never reached down far enough to chase the damp away. Malcolm picked the path and set a fast walking pace.

Before I started the cardio training, I hadn't thought I was in bad shape. I knew I could have used a tune-up, but didn't think I was a three-toed sloth. But I was wrong—oh, was I wrong. Never before had I worked so hard on my cardio health. Running made my heart pound so hard it ached and my thighs and lungs burned. Four weeks in, and I still felt the burn.

We were gone a full hour and returned to find Prime Security still busy at work. While I huffed and puffed through my cool-down, Malcolm stretched out in total serenity.

"How do you do that?" I asked, mesmerized by his total lack of exhaustion.

His dark eyes sparkled with the slight upturn of his lips. "Practice. Lots of practice." A faint sheen of sweat made his flawless skin glow. "I love running. It gives me time to think."

When we finished our cool-down, he motioned toward the house. "You want me to wait until you make sure everything is okay in there?"

"No, but thanks. See you tomorrow."

"Don't forget I won't be here until noon," he said. Our weekly schedule had been shaken up with the annual maintenance of the Y's equipment. He mounted his bike and rode down the driveway.

David and his crew politely stayed out of sight while I gathered clothes and locked myself away in the bathroom. I rushed my shower and left the house with wet hair.

Avery was huddled behind his laptop when I arrived. I knocked on the door frame of the exam room and he looked up at me over his glasses.

"I was just thinking about you," he said, returning to his keyboard.

I hopped up on the exam table across from him. "Oh, why's that?"

"I was checking for a response from Greg," he said, focused on the computer. "He's using a new email address and should have answered by now. Thought it might have fallen into my junk-mail folder."

"Greg?" I asked.

"Greg Jeffries—the contact who found the information on Jolene."

I knew the name. "Why'd he change his email address?"

"He's the one I told you about—it was his computer that got hacked." Avery continued to work the keyboard, looking puzzled, while I connected the dots. Greg was the Portland contact Eden had mentioned, the one who maintained the secure Infinity message board.

Greg was good at finding things. He'd uncovered Jolene's identity with very little information to go on and learned she was, or maybe still is, a painter. She sold some of her work through the Sun Meadows Cooperative in San Francisco.

Inexplicably, one of her paintings hung in my father's study. It was a stunning seascape that showcased her talent and had been one of my dad's favourite possessions. He'd acquired it before he met my mother, and I had no idea how he came to have it. Whether he bought it here or in San Francisco or found it at a yard sale, I would never know.

Avery scratched a note on the pad beside his computer. He pressed his lips into a thin line and stared at the screen. The pen in his hand tapped out an impatient beat. He huffed in exasperation and turned his attention to me. "How did your research of home security systems go?"

I smiled, happy to supply some good news. "Prime Security is finishing the installation today."

"Finishing?" He leaned back into the swivel of his chair. "Well then, just as fast as sleeping pills after all."

It was hard not to laugh at his triumphant expression. "They started yesterday. It should be working by the time I get home."

"That's fast. I'm so proud of you, Em. This is exactly what I meant by 'taking the reins.'"

I laughed. "Yeah—not that you gave me much choice. You know sleeping pills would have been easier."

"Cheaper too—but not nearly as effective," he said, enjoying himself. "I don't suppose you've had any breakthroughs in the ghosting realm?"

Ah, ghosting. Yet another disturbing facet of Jolene's ever-evolving gift. Thankfully, I was with Avery the first time it happened, otherwise, I might have lost my mind. Turns out I'd inherited the rarest of Flier gifts—ghosting.

"No such luck I'm afraid."

Ghosting was aptly named. When it happened, my body disappeared into thin air—I could even take someone along for the fade if I touched them and held on. I hoped it was the last of the Jolene surprises.

Unfortunately, neither of us knew what triggered my ghost. We also didn't know how often or how long I could stay in that form. Those answers were critical because, unlike flying, which exhilarated me, ghosting drained me and left me weak.

We were operating in a vacuum and researching the topic was a tricky business. Ghosting was coveted, and like all Flier gifts, could be stolen, a process that would likely kill me.

When Avery had exhausted his own resources, learning no more than what he'd found in Flier lore and fairy tales, he turned to Greg. So far, Greg had not unearthed any new information. And now Greg's computer had been hacked.

Avery's computer beeped. He frowned. "Now I'm really baffled. Greg's email just bounced back—'Unknown Recipient.' That's strange."

"A cyberglitch?"

"Could be but I'm going to send out some feelers and see if anyone else has heard from him. Give me a minute, would you?" He bent back to the keyboard.

"There." He hit with flourish what must have been the send button. "Someone out there will know something." Avery closed his laptop.

"If Greg really has dropped off the radar, where else can we go looking for info?" I already knew ghosting resources were like water in the desert.

"We could ask James. He might know something." Avery watched my reaction, but I didn't flinch. James Moss was the only other person who knew I was a Ghost, and that was one person too many. It wasn't information I had volunteered. He'd witnessed me ghost when I was shot in the midst of rescuing his sister, Sandra.

"It's a risk," he said.

"I don't know why James makes me so nervous. He shouldn't. After all, he brought me safely back here to you after I was shot. That's more than I can say for Jackson."

"James thought you knew Jackson was married, Em. You can't blame him for trying to protect Sandra. She's his sister."

"No, you're right. I'm just having trouble ditching my first impression of the guy." I remembered how dismissively James treated me when he thought I was Jackson's eager mistress. He'd frightened me. He'd even taken a swing at Jackson. Of course, now I wished he'd taken more than one swing.

I couldn't shake the feeling that there was more to James than I knew. And it wasn't just the menace he threw off. It was the way he held himself, quiet and aloof: like he was one step ahead of everyone else. My intuition kept raising *he's dangerous* flags.

Avery said, "He was just as angry with Jackson as you were when he found out what Jackson had done to his sister *and* to you. Believe me. I heard plenty of his ranting while you were upstairs recovering."

"We don't know much about James Moss."

"No, but he's kept your secret safe so far—as he'd promised. Unfortunately, Jackson was our main source of information about James and I'm not about to ask Jackson anything. Him, I flat out don't trust."

"Now you tell me," I said, grinning.

"Look who's getting her sense of humour back," Avery said with a chuckle. "How about I give it another few days and if we don't hear anything back from Greg, I'll get in touch with James and see what he says?"

"I'm keeping my fingers crossed for Greg."

"Me too," Avery said.

"Just be careful, okay? I know I don't have any basis for it, but I have a funny feeling where James is concerned."

"I will. Now, let's get to work."

On Thursdays, Avery stretched the limits of my gift. He'd been a patient teacher and freely shared his knowledge of the Flier world. He'd explained that a Flier's eye has a second lens. It's what we used to project the energy of our gift. Thanks to Avery, I could now produce and recognize the eye *flash* Fliers used to identify and signal other Fliers. I could also produce a whole spectrum of effects that ranged from a mild tap-on-the-shoulder *spark* to a full-blown, consciousness-sapping *jolt*.

Not all Fliers could access the power at the lethal end of the range, but I could, and Avery had suffered more than once at my clumsy efforts while he taught me to control the full range of power. Equally important, Avery had taught me how to put up an energy *block* to shield me from those same effects. Jolts worked on Fliers and the non-gifted alike, and with the secrecy and strange goings-on in the Flier world of late, the skills were important to master.

There was, however, one other eye effect that Avery and I would never work on. It was referred to as the *rush* and though Avery explained it to me, it was Jackson who'd demonstrated it. At the peak of passion, he'd lock his eyes onto mine and set my libido on fire, sending me into a mind-blowing orgasm. I considered it his one redeeming feature, given what a bastard he turned out to be.

Avery and I strategically placed one-gallon plastic milk jugs filled with water at various distances and heights in his back garden. My job was to hit them with a jolt that would either topple or explode them, at Avery's discretion. The accuracy of my aim had markedly improved but my judgment on strength needed more work. We also needed more milk jugs. I'd already raided the recycle bins twice. Personally, I think Avery found toppling the jugs plain old boring, so he had me explode them far more often than not. Truth be known, it was more fun to explode them, but the fun was over when the last jug burst, and we had to call it quits.

While he walked me to the door, I filled him in on the laser tag equipment. Like me, he'd heard of laser tag even though he'd never seen a game. However, the concept was so like paintball that he grasped the advantage of it right away. He readily agreed to play mule and transport the gear to the park for our next game.

"You can be our game master," I said, enthusiastically. Because Avery didn't fly, his role in our games had been neutralizing paintball splatters to get players back into the game. Now he could take charge of the command centre and keep track of the hits and reloads. "Why don't I email you the instruction manual?" I left him with his curiosity piqued.

The Prime Security vehicles were still parked in my driveway when I got home. The front door was unlocked. But when I opened the door, an ear-piercing shriek shot through the house. Immediately, I yanked my hand back, and bolted a distance down the driveway, covering my ears to dampen the siren.

One of the crew raced down the front hallway and skidded to a stop just inside the door. He fiddled hurriedly with the controls and seconds later the sharp noise stopped. The quiet was deafening.

"Sorry about that," he said, looking sheepish. "The good news is—it works." His humour didn't quell the feeling that I'd been electrocuted.

"I've disarmed it now. You can come in," he said, extending his arm.

"It's so loud," I said, crossing the threshold.

"Your neighbours are quite far away. It's the highest decibel siren we install residentially. I'm Martin, by the way." Martin was a dishevelled twentysomething and his jeans were torn and faded. He wore a leather tool belt over a tattered T-shirt. "We're almost done, so we'll be out of your hair in a few minutes. David will stay to show you how to operate it."

I thanked him, and after Martin and the crew left, David walked me through the house pointing out all the new hardware. Back at the front door, he showed me how to turn the system on and off at the panel that was now mounted to the left of the door.

"If the alarm is triggered, it will send a text message to your cellphone with details on what's been compromised. If you don't disarm it within sixty seconds, the police will automatically be alerted." David assured me that the horrible shrieking alarm would only engage if I didn't disarm it. The panic button, however, bypassed my cellphone and went directly to the police.

David took me through several dry runs including setting the alarm off accidentally and testing the panic button. David suggested I program the house alarm's ringtone to emulate a fire truck's siren, so I'd know immediately that it was the alarm and not a phone call coming in. It was an impressive set-up, and one I hoped I'd never set off accidentally.

Chapter Six

I was ready for our workout when Malcolm arrived. He waited on the porch while I bit my lower lip and set the alarm. It was the first time I'd done it without David here to fix it if I accidentally set it off.

"I hope you know what you're doing," Malcolm said in that quiet voice of his. "If that alarm goes off, the last thing I need is your neighbour reporting a black man running from your house."

I darted a glance his way, and he quickly straightened his face. Funny man. "Don't worry. You'll have sixty seconds after I enter the code before it goes off. You're fast—you can get all the way into the park by then." He wasn't the only one with a sense of humour.

Thankfully, the alarm didn't go off. I set the GPS, and by the time we hit 6K my legs were on fire.

"No, we can't stop, Emelynn, just slow your pace. Work through the burn." If there was such a thing as an annoying inspiration, then Malcolm was certainly that. I was on the verge of coughing up a lung and he was merely breathing heavy. Sweat beaded his forehead, but was nothing compared to the creek that was running down my back.

"We're almost there. Come on, you can do it." He had to know my lungs were burning, and my legs felt like rubber stumps, but still, he urged me on. Some days I questioned if Malcolm was a good trainer or a closet sadist.

If he wasn't running along beside me, and it wasn't broad daylight, I'd be tempted to lift off and fly the rest of the way. Sorely tempted—sorely being the operative word.

We rounded the end of Sunset Park's boundary and slowed to a walk. This last leg of the route, around the cul-de-sac and up the driveway to the cottage, was our cool-down.

"How are you feeling?" Malcolm asked when he saw that I'd recovered enough to talk.

"Winded." And I wasn't exaggerating.

"Your stamina's improving. Eight K today. That beats 3K from our first run." We started our stretches. "How about on Monday we take a circuit from the beach? You can show me where the public access is north of here."

"Sure, but we won't be able to run the whole way because of the rocks."

"We'll make up for it on the road. Besides, I want you to get a feel for the differences between running on pavement and running on trails."

I liked the way Malcolm worked. He used my interests and goals to manage my fitness plan and keep me encouraged and on track. That's why we ran outside and not on a treadmill. It's why we used the park rather than a track. Malcolm was refreshingly open and honest, qualities that I was drawn to and truly appreciated.

What I didn't particularly appreciate, at least right now, was the way my legs were complaining. Hopefully, they'd wait until tomorrow to seize up because tonight was girls' night out. Malcolm hopped on his bike and left. I'd see him again on Monday and we'd start the torture all over again.

After a shower and lunch, I had a stare-down with my closet. This was really not the time to conclude that I had little in the way of *night-out* clothes other than one sundress, one pair of black slacks and a half-decent pair of capris that I couldn't find. Oh no, scratch the capris: they hadn't survived the blood stains after Sandra's rescue. And I'd already worn the black slacks both times before when Molly and I had been out to dinner.

That left the pale blue sundress, which had its own memories. It was the same one that I'd worn to lunch with Jackson on the *Aerial Symphony*. Just looking at it brought back memories of that day. Bittersweet best described them: tasty lunch, fantastic sex, married man. That was the only time I'd worn it.

I pulled the dress out of the closet, careful not to let the spaghetti straps slide off the hanger. Small white and yellow daisies decorated the pale blue cotton which was smoothly fitted throughout the heart-shaped bodice and bloomed into a lightly gathered short skirt. Perhaps after tonight, the dress would hold better memories.

Eden arrived just before five wearing her hospital scrubs and lugging an oversized handbag. Since we'd agreed to take transit tonight, it was quicker for her to come here directly from work rather than go all the way home first.

As soon as she arrived, I dragged her down the hall to show her the laser equipment. "Kate's going to love this," she said, laughing. Kate Dennison was the one Flier who always seemed to end up being pelted with the most paintballs by the end of the night and she didn't hold back telling us how much they hurt.

Eden looked around at the assorted gear and duffle bags. "I didn't think there'd be so much of it." What had arrived compactly packed into three boxes, had exploded and multiplied like guppies in my living room.

She turned for the bathroom. "I'll go shower and get ready. Give me half an hour," she called over her shoulder. I liked that Eden was comfortable and made herself at home here.

While she showered, I got dressed and put on my makeup. Eden came out of the bathroom transformed. She wore navy blue cropped slacks and a white high-collared halter top. She could have stepped out of a glossy A&F ad. Even though she was six inches shorter than me, I had no doubt she had shoes that would compensate. Her spiky red hair put me in mind of a pixie, but she was anything but. She was brave and strong and sassy. Eden and Alex had both become good friends, and it was a relief not to have to guard secrets around them.

"Great dress," she said, helping me with the zipper.

"Thanks, my mother bought it for me," I said.

"I like her taste," Eden said. "Are you ready to go?"

"Are you sure we can pull this off?" I still wondered how Eden and I could pretend to be normal for an entire night in Molly's company. Wasn't she worried about us slipping up? leaking something about flying or Sandra's rescue?

"We can do this Em, we all do this. There's not one of us who doesn't have friends outside the covey. Just remember, if you have to lie, keep it simple and stay as close to the truth as you can. It makes the lie easier to remember, like the cover story for how we met. It was at the hospital, remember—when you tripped on the rocks?" She gave my arm a reassuring squeeze.

"I just want to be careful with Molly. I don't want to hurt her." I especially didn't want to compromise our rekindled friendship.

"I know, but trust me. It's going to be okay—just follow my lead if we get into a dicey situation." Eden's confidence calmed my nerves.

We gathered our jackets and purses and stopped at the alarm's control panel at the front door. "I'm nervous of it. You'd know what I meant if you heard the alarm—it's loud enough to cause hearing damage." After I set it, we closed the door and waited a few anxious moments. When it didn't go off, we started toward Rumbles.

We arrived early. Molly was still working, but she was already dressed and ready to go. She looked her usual retro-fifties style in a floral, sleeveless, shirt dress. She even had the pearl necklace and a little clutch to go with it. Eden and Molly shook hands and exchanged kind smiles and mutual compliments and I took a deep breath: so far, so good.

They spent the entire bus trip talking fashion. It was a topic close to Molly's heart. She'd graduated with a Bachelor of Fine Arts from Emily Carr, and fashion was her passion. Apparently, Eden was passionate about it too. Who knew they would find so much in common? I didn't know the first thing about fashion or designers but Eden and Molly were flipping out names and styles like cards in a game of fifty-two pick-up. At one point they moved away from clothing and on to home décor. How could these two people, who spoke a completely different language from me, both end up being my friend?

I'd worried for nothing. They were getting on like old chums and the conversation was deep in safe territory.

We got off the Skytrain at the Yaletown-Roundhouse station and walked up Mainland Street looking for a place with outdoor seating. Yaletown was an old warehouse district that had been claimed by developers and rebuilt to accommodate high-density urban living. The odd hold-out establishment from its grittier days still existed, but they were the exception now. Art galleries and shiny retail stores were the new norm, interspersed with coffee shops and restaurants. Lots of exposed brick and concrete defined the building exteriors and former loading docks were now wide, raised sidewalks.

A fashionable Friday-night crowd was gathering steam. Perfectly tousled hair and French manicures let you know that the rumpled shirts and tattered jeans they wore were expensive designer duds and not from the bottom of the laundry hamper. Laughter and music spilled onto the streets from open patio doors.

Molly recounted her night here with Cheney. We paused at the Keg then headed in. The hostess led us upstairs to one of the last tables on the patio and handed us menus.

"Can I get you a drink to start?"

Molly ordered a beer but changed her mind after Eden and I each ordered a glass of wine. "Let's get a bottle. After all, we're not driving."

After devouring a tray of sliders and a plate of calamari, we dipped into uncomfortable conversational terrain.

"He's cute," Molly said, nodding at a dark-haired man seated close by. Even though she'd never met Jackson, she had managed to pick someone who resembled him: tall, lean, and thirtysomething.

Eden played co-conspirator to Molly's match-making game. "Yes, and well-dressed too. He probably has a good job."

I dismissed his handsome packaging without a second thought. "Cute, well dressed and likely married."

Molly scoffed and resumed a conversation that was plainly meant for me even though it was aimed at Eden. "What about the blond guy over there?" She gestured covertly toward a man standing in mixed company across the room.

Eden nodded. "He was looking our way just a few minutes ago."

"Better look for a wedding band in his pocket first," I quipped. They looked disappointed, like I'd kept their ball rather than throw it back over the fence. "Don't you two have some fashion drawer you haven't opened yet to talk about?"

"We're mixing it up a bit, keeping it interesting." Eden flashed me a silly wink.

Molly declared that we needed a fresh bar. "Let's settle up." She signalled our waiter.

The street was busy before; now it was jam-packed. The people who weren't walking were crowded around restaurant doorways. We strolled to the end of the street and around the corner where the crowd was thinner.

I pointed to a bar across the road with large, open windows. "How about there?" Eden and Molly nodded. We crossed and paused outside the front door. Joss Stone's smoky voice leaked outside.

Molly opened the door to a gust of saxophone and happy voices. There may not have been a lineup outside, but the bar was standing room only. We pushed inside and found an empty patch of floor space by a pillar. A narrow ledge encircled it, just wide enough to hold a few drinks. Molly volunteered to press through the crowd at the bar and get us drinks.

The room's honey-coloured wood flooring combined with subdued lighting produced a laid-back feel. Sporadic laughter burst from the surrounding groups. These were workmates or good friends celebrating the end of another work week.

Molly made her way back to us juggling three martinis. "Do you know how hard it was for me to show cleavage in this dress?" She laughed as she passed us our drinks. "Believe me—that was the only thing that got the bartender's attention. I hope you like them dirty."

"Thanks for the sacrifice," Eden said.

I'd never had a martini before, dirty or otherwise. I brought the drink to my lips. It was a test not to spill it over the rim. Wow—salty and strong enough to take my breath away.

Molly tapped me and Eden on the shoulder, motioning toward a woman making her way through the crowd. She wore a leather braid around her forehead that twisted into her waist-length blonde hair. To say she stood out was an understatement. She dressed like a seventies-era hippie wearing an ankle-length dress with a chain belt. We weren't the only ones who watched her navigating the crowd. If she noticed the attention, she didn't pay it any mind.

During the next lull in the music, Molly told us about her. "She's a psychic. Cheney pointed her out when we were at Brix a few months ago. She works the bar circuit. He says she's impressive. Told me a bunch of his friends had her read their palms. They swear she's the real deal. Want to give it a go?" She flashed a hopeful smile.

"I've always wanted to do that," Eden said, her eagerness shining through.

The skeptic in me made an appearance. "Really?" Eden and Molly looked so disappointed by my reaction that I immediately retracted it. "All right," I said, "I'll give it a go."

Molly motioned the woman over and she nodded in acknowledgement.

"If you want to see your future, it'll cost you twenty dollars," she said, as the music started up again. "Not here. Meet me outside." She turned around and headed toward the exit.

"Shall we?" Eden asked, keen to have her palm read.

Molly upended her drink. "Yeah, let's go. We'll never get another drink here anyway."

Fuelled by dirty martinis, we followed the psychic outside. I let myself get caught up in their excitement, tamping the skeptic down, determined to be entertained.

"My name's Cassandra," the blonde woman said, as we gathered around her outside the club. "Let's go over there." She pointed to a stone bench that sat on the edge of the sidewalk away from the lights and music that escaped from the bar.

We each ponied up twenty dollars and Cassandra tucked the cash into a fringed handbag she wore on a thin leather strap across her body. She sat down and beckoned Eden to sit beside her.

"I'm Eden," she said, angling her body toward Cassandra. Molly and I stood by eagerly watching the process.

Cassandra nodded then reached for Eden's hand. Cassandra didn't look at her hand, just held it like a fragile bird that might fly away. Cassandra closed her eyes and took forever to respond. When she did, it was with a heavily creased brow and a look of confusion. She lowered her gaze from Eden's eyes and concentrated on her palm, stretching it out and running her fingers over it, then cocking her head from the right to the left.

Cassandra shook her head. "I'm sorry, Eden. You're shrouded in a haze that I can't see through. I can't make sense of it." She dropped Eden's hand, rummaged in her handbag and returned Eden's twenty-dollar bill. "I won't take your money today. Seek me out next time you're here. Maybe the clouds will lift." Eden looked disappointed as she relinquished her seat.

Cassandra turned to Molly, inviting her to replace Eden on the small bench. Cassandra repeated her efforts, closing her eyes. This time she smiled even before she opened her eyes. She pressed Molly's hand flat and bent closer to get a better look at her palm. She trailed her fingers carefully over it.

"You have a new man in your life." As far as opening lines went, Cassandra had a winner, but I had to give Molly kudos for her poker face: she didn't even blink. I suppose it could have been a bold guess on Cassandra's part. A knowing smile lit Cassandra's face. She continued with confidence, like she was used to being challenged by those who didn't believe in her kind of magic.

"Your mother's from this soil. She's an ancient soul: but not your father. He's far from home."

Molly glanced up at me, giving away her surprise at Cassandra's remarks. I knew that her mother was First Nations and her father still spoke with a thick Scottish brogue. Maybe Cassandra really was the real deal. She certainly had my attention.

"Is there something you want to know, Molly, about your future?"

Molly shot Eden and me conspiratorial glances. "Will I be married?"

"Yes, but sooner than you expect. Is that all you wish to know?"

"Who?" Molly blurted out. "Who will I marry?" She was more curious than cautious now.

"You're a lucky woman, Molly. You'll marry the one you love." At that, Cassandra dropped Molly's hand. Her smile remained as she looked from Molly to me. I guess that was what twenty dollars bought.

I was surprised to find myself nervous as I took Molly's place on the small bench. I held out my palm, like Eden and Molly had done, but she didn't take it. Instead, she looked at me long and hard and adopted a furrowed brow similar to the one she offered Eden earlier.

"Are you two related?" she asked, looking from me to Eden—so much for her psychic talents.

"No," I answered, disappointed.

Cassandra looked at Eden as she took my hand. "You two are surrounded by the same haze, but it's different with you," she said, turning a leery gaze back to me.

She closed her eyes and adopted a look of concentration while Molly, Eden and I exchanged *don't ask me* shrugs.

Still with closed eyes, she asked, "What's your name?"

"Emelynn."

"Emelynn." She repeated my name slowly, as if testing it.

She opened her eyes and the depth of wariness within them made me uncomfortable, like she was afraid of me. "The haze is thick—like gauze, but there are thin patches. I can't see your ancestry, but I see blood—you've been injured."

"She's right, you have," Eden offered, much too quickly. "On the beach—you remember?" Her eagerness had transformed into caution. She was guiding me.

Molly added her confirmation. "What a coincidence. We were talking about that just a few days ago."

"We should get going," Eden said, clearly wanting to put an end to Cassandra's palm reading.

But Cassandra ignored Eden and kept hold of my hand. "What would you like to know, Emelynn, about your future?"

I did have something I wanted to know. It had been on my mind for weeks now. I glanced up at Molly; she was expectant. I saw worry in Eden's face and I knew she wanted us to get out of here. She'd asked me to follow her lead, but my curiosity was stronger than the pull of her lead right now.

I pressed on. "Am I in danger?" I asked, hoping Molly wouldn't think I was nuts. I felt Eden's hairy eyeball drilling into the side of my head. I was willing to risk her wrath if Cassandra could say whether nefarious agents were out to get me—and by extension, other Fliers.

"Can you be more specific?" she asked, keeping her eyes closed.

How else could I phrase it without sounding paranoid? "Is someone searching for me?" I finally asked, disregarding Molly's questioning gaze. Maybe that did sound paranoid.

"I get a sense of many arms reaching for you, but I can't tell if they're dangerous. It's like they're reaching right through you as if you were nothing more than smoke. I don't know what it means." She opened her eyes and released my hand. "You shouldn't wear amber. It doesn't agree with you."

I reached to my earrings. What an odd remark. My mother had brought me the amber earrings from a conference in Copenhagen.

Eden moved in and reached for me. "Okay, Emelynn. Molly," she said, motioning me up. "My apologies, Cassandra, but we've really got to go."

Cassandra looked up at Eden. "I've had visions my entire life—I trust them implicitly." Eden took a step back. Cassandra leaned in close to me and whispered, "I see weddings, funerals, children—I don't see arms reaching through spectres. Something is wrong and I think you know it. You and your friend need to be watchful." Eden had turned away, but she was listening.

"Thanks," I said, standing. Eden had already stepped away and held her hand out to me. "We've got to go." I left Cassandra on the bench and caught up with Eden and Molly. We hurried across the street and headed back to the thinning crowd on Mainland. Eden led us through the bustle and straight into an Irish pub.

"Can I buy you a beer?" Eden asked.

"Guinness for me," Molly said.

"I'll have wine." I'd never developed a taste for beer.

"You don't order wine in an Irish pub," Eden said. "How about a cider?"

"Sure."

Eden leaned into the bar. "Two Guinness and a Strongbow, please."

"What was with that question you asked the psychic?" Molly said, looking puzzled.

"I couldn't think of anything to ask on the spur of the moment."

"I think you threw her," Molly said.

Eden handed us our drinks. We took them to a small stand-up table against the far wall. Laughter cascaded around us, lightening the gloom that Cassandra had cast over us moments earlier.

"To Cassandra," Eden toasted. "What a whacko."

"I don't know. She was bang on with me. Maybe it's a hit and miss thing with psychics," Molly said, as if she needed to make an excuse for Cassandra. Her comments about Molly's parents had certainly been specific.

"Lucky guess I'd say, but I bet she makes a good living doing the hocus pocus thing," Eden said. Guess or not, she had connected Eden and me to one another, even if it was based on the haze she "saw" around each of us. Maybe Cassandra could see the blocks we used to protect ourselves?

I fingered one of the amber earrings that dangled from my earlobe. Try as I might to dismiss Cassandra, her words had shaken me. Had she glimpsed my ghost in that spectre she mentioned? Whose arms were reaching for me?

I shook my head, clearing the troublesome thoughts from my mind. I needed to get back in the moment, back into girls' night out and apparently back to more futile matchmaking efforts if Molly and Eden's analyzing glances around the bar were any indication.

It was after one in the morning when we poured ourselves into a cab and headed home. Our first stop was Molly's apartment. She got out after tipsy hugs, and then Eden and I were back in the cab on the way to my place.

Moments later, the shriek of a fire engine erupted from my purse.

CHAPTER SEVEN

I t's the house alarm!" I searched frantically for my phone, grabbed it and pressed talk. The small screen lit up. "It's the attic's motion sensor," I said, looking up into Eden's expectant face. Panic's familiar tendrils wrapped around my chest.

Eden had her cellphone in her hand and Alex on the line in a flash. "Emelynn's house alarm just went off." Eden paused. "The motion sensor in the attic," she said, answering a question I couldn't hear. "Emelynn,"—she touched my arm. "Can you disarm it remotely?"

"Yes." We were still within the sixty seconds allotted to do that before the audible alarm went off.

"Okay, we'll wait for you." Eden hung up and turned to me. "Go ahead. Disarm it."

I entered the disarm code and crossed my fingers that it worked.

"Alex is on his way." She turned her back to the cabbie. "He's flying," she whispered. "He doesn't want us to go inside until he gets there."

We travelled the last fifteen minutes in anxious silence.

The neighbourhood was reassuringly quiet when we got out of the cab a half block from the cottage. I prayed Alex was flying hard.

We crept forward passing the end of my driveway to stand deathly still under the overhanging willow branches behind the low brush that partially obscured our presence.

Eden leaned in and whispered in my ear, "I think I'm sober now."

I turned my head and saw her smiling face. Leave it to Eden to try to lighten the mood. "Was this a waste of a good night out?"

"Almost, though Cassandra was interesting, don't you think?" After a few moments, she breathed freely. "Alex is here."

I hadn't seen him. We stayed put.

Eden jumped and pulled out her phone. It had been set to vibrate.

"Damn it, Alex," she all but yelled into the phone. "You nearly gave me a stroke. No, we're at the end of the driveway," she said, pulling me along by the elbow toward the house. I saw Alex absently taming his hair on the front porch.

"What's going on?" I asked, when we got close.

"Squirrels."

I frowned. "Squirrels?"

"Yeah. You know the air vent on the north side of the attic?"

"Not really."

"Well, there's an old wooden air vent over there with a couple of broken louvres."

"Are you sure?" I asked.

"Yes, about the broken louvres, maybe, about the squirrels—but only because it could have been a large chipmunk or a small raccoon. But my money's on squirrels. I'm fairly sure that's what I saw disappearing into that vent."

"Squirrels," I repeated, shaking my head. I bet that's what it's been all along. "I can't believe it."

"Why don't you open up and I'll check it out from inside," he offered.

Eden and I stood beneath the attic hatch in my bedroom closet while Alex investigated.

"Definitely squirrels," he said, coming back down. He handed me three hazelnuts. "I don't know how many of the critters are up there, but they're using that vent for sure."

"I've been terrorized by squirrels?" I could have wept with relief. That alone was worth every penny the house alarm cost.

Eden started to laugh and soon Alex and I joined in. Our laughter sounded borderline manic. I hadn't realized how tense we'd all been until then, but the laughter drained the tension out of us.

"I should have let the security company deal with this. That is, after all, one of the advantages of having a security system. Squirrels are hardly worth Alex risking an emergency flight all the way over here."

"Except isn't it the police who would get called out?" Alex asked.

"Yes, but what if it had been an intruder instead of squirrels?" I said.

"Maybe," Alex said. "But if the intruder turned out to be a Flier, then the police would only complicate matters."

"Besides which," Eden said, "look around. This laser gear looks real enough to send the police into commando mode."

She had a point—the living room resembled a combat staging area. "As much as I'm relieved it's only squirrels, now I have to get rid of them," I said, turning the hazelnuts over in my hand. "Before the camera incident, I would have asked Charles." Eden reached out and squeezed my arm. We had both been traumatized by that incident with Charles Wright and his surveillance camera.

"You might want to move those boxes out of there until the squirrels are gone," Alex said, brushing off his jeans.

"What boxes?"

"Toward the front of the house. It looks like there are four maybe five of them about this size." He estimated two feet square with his hands. "Do you want me to bring one down?"

"Would you mind?" What on earth were boxes doing up there?

Alex scrambled back up through the hatch and I heard his footsteps above us. "They're heavy," he shouted back to us. "I think they've been here a while." He pushed the box to the edge of the hatch and backed out, pulling the box down after him. "I'd better take it outside."

I rushed ahead of him to open the deck door. He set the box on the railing and blew a small dust cloud off the top.

"What's in it?" Eden asked, her curiosity second only to mine.

Alex unfolded the flaps. "Looks like books," he said, pulling one out and handing it to me.

I read the cover. "1976. *Bioengineering Applications in Modern Medicine.*"

Eden took another one. "*Radiographic Diagnosis and Classification.* Looks like 1970."

"These must be Dad's." I thought my mother had gotten rid of all this stuff when we moved to Toronto.

"Looks like more of the same," Alex said, going through the rest of the box. "No squirrels though." He smirked. "Where do you want me to put it?"

"The spare-room closet if you could." At least tucked away in there I could take my time going through it.

Alex secured the hatch and I thanked him again before he and Eden headed home.

I lay in bed for the longest time, waiting to hear the squirrels in the attic, but I guess they had gone to sleep too.

Another good night's sleep put me in a fantastic mood the next morning. I hummed the "Happy" tune as I brewed my morning caffeine fix. It was the squirrels. The furry rodents hardly seemed heavy enough for the huge weight that had lifted from my shoulders.

I poured a to-go mug of coffee and stepped outside wearing just my nightshirt and housecoat. I pulled the collar up and tightened the belt. The dew on the deck was cool on my feet, but I hardly noticed. Cold feet were not going to stop me having my coffee on the beach. I loved this morning ritual and I'd missed it the past few days.

The sun rose early in August and it was already at work warming the rocks and patches of sand. Seagulls screeched overhead and smaller birds flitted in and out of the bush where the greenery tufted out at the shoreline. Sea fleas and tiny flies tickled my ankles as they jumped about my feet. I squinted, looking down the beach for other people, but as usual, I was alone. The neighbours were spaced widely apart, and I rarely saw them down here.

I sat in the sand with a bleached out log at my back and tucked my housecoat under me. The driftwood was warm against my back. I closed my eyes and inhaled a cleansing breath of briny sea air.

Last night was fun. Molly and Eden had gotten along like old friends. I thought about Cassandra. Was she the real deal, or were her predictions like newspaper horoscopes—so vague that any reader could apply the words to their own lives. And what was with her comment about amber? Maybe she didn't think the colour went with my skin tone. But I liked those earrings, and did I really want to take fashion advice from a woman who wore a headband?

I tried to remember the words she'd whispered to me, something about seeing *weddings, funerals and children, not arms reaching through spectres,* and that *something is wrong.* She'd warned me and Eden to be *watchful.* What did she mean? Maybe Cassandra was picking up on the anxiety I'd been feeling. It was a potent mix of late-night wake-up calls, Jackson's dire warnings, the computer hacking, and the covey's safety.

There were eleven of us in the covey. Not only did we all protect the Flier secret, but we also watched out for and protected one another. They were all born Fliers. Luckily for me, I'd been so naive when Avery and the covey discovered me that they didn't suspect me of stealing my gift. Otherwise, I might have been reported to the Tribunal.

The covey had been honing our skills at the Pinecrest Paintball Park and it was paying off. We were working well together as a coordinated unit. The laser tag would make us even better. I had visions of the whole covey hovering around my attic with their toy guns chasing squirrels and laughed out loud.

Squirrels. I shook my head and looked out across the water. Had I really been that easily frightened? My imagination had turned rodents into intruders. It made me angry to think how vulnerable I had allowed myself to feel. I hoped someone in the covey learned something soon. Waiting to discover if Jackson was being truthful about the military and organized crime looking for proof of our existence was putting a strain on everyone.

Jackson hadn't just betrayed me; he'd lied to the entire covey, and now we didn't know where his lies ended and the truth began. Jackson's integrity had taken a backseat to his agenda. He was obviously a firm believer in the end justifying the means. He'd known all along that it was his half-brother who was responsible for Sandra's kidnapping. I wished he hadn't lied to us. Hell, I wished I'd never met him. I shook a dime-sized crab off my foot before it could climb higher.

We had all been so naive, not only in trusting Jackson, but about our physical safety. Guns had been on both sides of that rescue operation and we'd acted like a bunch of cowboys. It was only dumb luck that someone hadn't gotten themselves or Sandra killed. Stupid mistakes could have cost lives. If it wasn't for James, mine might have been one of them.

James, of all people, should have had my trust. Unfortunately, that trust had been shaken, and I didn't feel comfortable with the fact that he knew I was a Ghost. Where exactly did James's loyalties lie? After all, he must have suspected that Jackson had misled the covey. He'd certainly never let on that he was Sandra's brother, or that Jackson was his brother-in-law, though it did explain why neither of them wanted the Tribunal involved.

There was a lesson to learn here. Maybe Cassandra had a point: I had to be more watchful. I needed to be strong and so did the covey. It was more important than ever.

On a more immediate level, I had to find someone to deal with the uninvited guests in my attic. Maybe David from Prime Security could help. I dumped the now cold dregs of my coffee into the sand and plodded back to the cottage to shower and dress.

David didn't work Saturdays, but Banjeet, the on-call tech from Prime Security, who spoke with a sweet, sing-song voice, gave me the name of an exterminator. "It's something we come across a lot," he said.

It only took me a few minutes to line up Andy from A-1 Pest Control. Happily, he did work on Saturday.

"Yes, you've got squirrels living in there," Andy concluded after inspecting the attic and dragging another box down behind him. Andy was spry and energetic. He'd been very accommodating and agreed to move the remaining boxes out of the attic for me. This was number five. I took the box from him and dusted it off on the deck before piling it with the others in the spare-room closet. "That's the last of the boxes," he said, pushing his glasses back into place. Andy was in his sixties with a bald patch and unruly thinning hair that needed a trim.

A short time later, and after a few trips to his van, Andy secured a temporary one-way rodent exit to the broken air vent and cleaned up the debris the squirrels had left inside. He told me I was fortunate they hadn't damaged the wiring.

"You're lucky you caught it when you did," he said. "They'd found a warm, dry home up there and were making a nest. You would have had kittens in here in no time—they breed in the spring and again right about now. They've made a mess of the insulation in the far corner, but I can fix that up for you."

Andy packed up his things. "I'll leave that one-way exit in place for a few days, just in case there's a straggler. When I come back, I'll fix the vent so they won't get back in."

"Thanks," I said, walking him to the front door.

"My pleasure. I'll call before I come to finish up."

I waved goodbye to the back of his van. It wasn't even noon and I already had a major item ticked off my to-do list.

CHAPTER EIGHT

Next was shopping. I set the house alarm and drove to the Richmond Mall.

The Y insisted on clean indoor shoes and my Pearl Izumi runners were no longer fooling anyone. I picked out a pair of Pumas in the second shoe store I went into. The ease with which I found the runners set my shopping luck for the day. My next find was a sleek pair of Stella McCartney ankle boots and that sent me wandering through stores looking at fashion with fresh eyes. I hadn't shopped for clothes since Toronto and back then my focus had been on finding reinforced pockets strong enough to hold the divers' weights that kept me on the ground.

The smell of fried food drew me to the food court. I bought a falafel pita pocket and chose a table close enough to see the nearby shop windows while I ate. Was that a Flier's flash reflected in the glass divider in front of me? I turned around to search, but couldn't find the source. I reminded myself that there was a fine line between vigilance and paranoia.

I dropped my empty lunch tray by the recycling bins then went to get a closer look at a beautiful pencil skirt I'd spotted in the window at The Gap. They were having a big sale. Soon, I had another shopping bag to add to my armful and a big smile on my face.

I walked toward the mall exit and checked over my shoulder one more time. Maybe it was the flash I thought I'd seen earlier. I was almost at the parking lot when my phone rang. It was Avery.

"Hi Em, where are you?" he asked.

"Just leaving the Richmond Mall. What's up?"

"Do you think you could drop by on your way home?"

"Sure, but if I'm late, it's because I had to stop and buy a bigger car. I hit the shopping jackpot today." I got the chuckle I expected out of him. "What's going on?" I asked.

"I want to show you something," he said. "I'll go unlock the door. See you soon."

I looked around as I got into my car, unable to dismiss that funny feeling of being watched. I shook it off and reminded myself: vigilant not paranoid.

Avery called me back to his kitchen when I got to his office. He and Victoria sat at the round table with his Brown Betty and a plate of maple leaf sandwich cookies. I took a seat and Victoria poured me a cup of tea.

I helped myself to a cookie and nibbled the points off. "The shopping gods were very good to me today. My credit card was smoking."

Avery didn't even try to conceal an eyeball roll.

"But the best news of all, thanks to my new house alarm, I now know what's been waking me in the night."

"Oh?" Avery said, leaning forward attentively.

"Squirrels," I said, and then explained.

"What a relief." Avery sat back again. "I'm so glad that's cleared up."

"The pest-control guy has already been up there and taken care of it. He's not done yet, but he thinks the squirrels are out of there now."

"I've got to go," Victoria said, standing. "But I'll be back for dinner. Don't get up." Victoria kissed Avery goodbye. "Nice to see you, Em." She headed down the hall, and the front door clicked closed behind her.

"You two look good together," I said.

Avery was still watching the doorway. "I feel like I've known her forever." He turned back to me. "How's your tea?"

"I'm tea-ed out."

Avery stood and cleared the table. When he returned, he had an envelope in his hand. "This came this morning." He handed me the enclosed sheet of paper. "It's from Greg."

"He sent you a letter? Why not an email or a phone call?" I asked, unfolding the letter.

Soon enough the letter explained everything. Greg's computer had been hacked a second time, and he worried that Avery's might have fallen prey as well.

"He's given me his new Hotmail account, but I can't use this computer—it may have been compromised.

I continued to read. Greg confirmed that Infinity, the secure message board Greg maintained, had been compromised. Greg was lying low while he figured out who had hacked him and why.

"Greg's hacker has his contacts?"

"And possibly mine," Avery said.

I kept reading. Until I got to the part in the letter where Greg mentioned Jolene. I felt the blood leave my face.

"Jolene's name triggered this?"

"Someone knows I've been asking questions about her. They wouldn't know why, but they might suspect, especially if they knew Jolene and what she was capable of."

"But Greg's computer was hacked two weeks ago. The hacker might already know who we are and where we live. They might already be here!" Panic squeezed my lungs.

"Nothing is certain. Greg had a lot of contacts, and we weren't the only ones looking for information on Jolene. Besides, I never mentioned you. Greg doesn't have your name, your email, your address, or know anything else about you, so take a breath. I need to touch base with him and see what he's learned since he wrote that letter."

"When will you do that?" I asked.

"Right now. I'm going to the hospital to use the computer there. This hacker might just be an old friend of Jolene's. She's still missing after all. Maybe they're looking for her too."

"If that were the case, don't you think they'd email rather than hack?"

"I don't know. But let's not think the worst. Not yet. I'll see what I learn from Greg. If there's cause for concern, we'll call the covey together."

"Call me when you hear from him."

"I will. In the meantime, go home, hang up your new clothes and try not to worry."

When I got home, I did what I always did when I felt at loose ends— I cleaned the house. I dusted, vacuumed, cleaned windows and scrubbed the bathroom. I mopped the kitchen floor and did the laundry. When I ran out of things to clean, I turned on the flat screen and flipped channels. Nothing caught my interest, and I had a hard time keeping my thoughts from going places they shouldn't.

Finally, Avery called.

"I've had an email back from Greg. He found what he calls a Trojan Horse embedded in the Flier network. It triggered when Jolene's name appeared on the subject line of an email. The hacker's IP address is masked, but Greg's sure he can find the source."

"How long will it take?"

"He couldn't say, but he's sent me a program he wrote to clean the virus from my laptop. I'm forwarding the program to everyone else to run, too. And then you'll need to change your passwords. Greg thinks he'll know something by tomorrow. We'll have some answers soon."

"Avery, if the hacker got into your computer, he'll know you've been asking questions about ghosting. He'll have your contacts."

"Unfortunately, that's a possibility. I need to call the covey together. Warn them. It's just a precaution until we know this hacker's motives are."

"I'm sure it's not to invite us to join the Jolene fan club," I said.

"No, but someone might simply want to know what happened to her," Avery said, ever the voice of reason.

"Or they might want to take back what she gave to me."

"You don't know that and spinning out the worst-case possibilities won't help, Em."

"I'm sorry." I should have been thinking about the covey, not myself. "When are you setting the meet?"

"Tomorrow night at eleven at the paintball park. I thought your new laser equipment would soften the blow of the hacking and its implications. We're due for another practice. How about I come by your place just after ten to pick up the gear?"

"Sure. Alex was going to set up a game anyway. Are you taking Victoria?"

"Only if you're okay to fly on your own."

"Yeah, I'm good."

My racing thoughts refused to settle. I needed a distraction. Perhaps my dad's boxes?

I wandered down to the spare room and went back through the first one. There were both textbooks and medical journals. Some of the journals had check marks next to articles, others didn't. I absently flipped through the pages, unable to decide what to do with them. Finally, I sat down at the computer and sent my mother an email. Perhaps she'd know if they were of any value.

That evening, when the blue hue of darkness finally took over my vision, I dressed in my dark flying clothes, crept down the stairs to the beach and walked south. As long as there was a threat out there, I would be cautious and not take the chance of lifting off from my deck. I picked my way over the rocks, watching and listening for anything out of place. There was no wind to hamper my hearing and the rhythmic lap of waves was distant at the edge of a low tide. When I got to the sandy stretch of beach where I had first attempted flight, I made like a tree and stood silent on the rim of the park's forest.

Gradually I let go of the paranoia and walked free of the tree line and out onto the sand. Without further hesitation, I let the crystal break me free from gravity's grip and lifted off over the trees and into the park. I set my GPS to take me to the lighthouse and followed the shoreline, travelling south. The guttural call of a long-legged great blue heron pierced the night. They obviously had good night vision too.

I approached the white tower from the water and circled around behind, out of the reach of its bright light. As I drifted upward, I checked the lighthouse for signs of occupation. Like before, it was dark inside. I landed softly on the catwalk and reached out to turn the door handle. It was locked. I peeked in the window and glanced around the now familiar interior with its rickety cot and quiet instruments.

It was quiet here, peaceful. I stood at the rail and looked out across the vast expanse of water. Is this what Kate Winslet's character saw when she stood on the prow of James Cameron's *Titanic*? The night sky twinkled above with its carpet of stars stretching out to infinity. If you had no fear of heights, this vantage point was the best one in the entire park.

I let my mind wander. It was easy to suspend the nagging voice of worry up here.

My thoughts were miles away when the door clicked open.

A man's voice whispered, "Beth?"

A cold chill crept up my spine. I couldn't ghost and I couldn't risk flying. I kept my back to the voice. Damn! How could I let myself get so distracted?

"Beth?" he repeated cautiously, and I slowly turned around to face him. This wasn't the ancient, bent-over, pipe-smoking lighthouse keeper I'd imagined. This man couldn't have been more than thirty. He had blond windblown hair, longer on the top than on the sides, and wore a loose hand-knit sweater and blue jeans. His bare feet sported a pair of

Keens. His expression morphed from hopeful to crestfallen when he saw my unfamiliar face.

He took but a moment more to adjust his expression to match his darkening mood. "You shouldn't be here," he said, his voice hardening as his anger edged out his curiosity. He looked around. "How did you get in?"

"What do you mean?" I asked, beaming innocence.

"The lighthouse is closed. And locked. It's off limits to the public." His voice was utterly void of emotion.

"The door was open," I said.

"Sure it was. And I suppose you didn't see the posted signs." He looked around the catwalk and jiggled the door's handle. "You're damn lucky I turned up tonight. I might not have come again for days and this door is locked. When you let it close behind you, you locked yourself out here."

"I guess it's my lucky night then," I said, making an effort to look contrite.

He hadn't shaved, and though I knew that was the fashion these days, I got the feeling with him it wasn't intentional. The delicate skin around his eyes had the blue tinge of sleep-deprivation. He would have been handsome were it not for that haunted look on his face. Terrible pain had taken up residence there and if I weren't so anxious to protect my butt and make my exit, I would have lingered to uncover the story.

"I'll show you out," he said, completely unaffected.

He ushered me through the small red door and into the lighthouse tower. But I'd never been inside before and hadn't a clue how to get to the staircase that led down to the ground level.

"After you," he said, herding me ahead of him.

I looked about for a door, but there wasn't one. "I'm sorry. It was dark when I made my way up here." If they gave out awards for lying, I'd be getting a trophy.

"That way," he said, his voice impatient. He pointed to an open trap door on the floor at the foot of the cot.

I stepped down and made my around a winding spiral staircase that I'd only imagined prior to tonight. A dim light reflected up from the lowest level.

As I descended, I saw other levels inside the structure. Perhaps there was more living space beyond the closed doors. The lowest level of the structure was an open area that looked like it was used for storage. He reached around me to open the ground-level door, which I'd only previously seen from the outside.

"What's your name?" he asked.

"Emelynn. What's yours?"

"Case," he said. "If I find you in here again, Emelynn, I'll report you to the police and have you charged with trespassing." He closed the door in my face as if he needed to emphasize his point. He didn't. But I did wonder how a man got to be that cold, that disconnected.

He'd asked me if my name was Beth. Who was she, I wondered?

I escaped into the shadows at the edge of the clearing and found Case's vehicle. It was an old Jeep and the hood was warm. He must have just arrived. In future, I'd be more careful. I didn't dare risk another encounter like this.

Returning to the forest, I found a concealed place to lift off from. Flying took my mind off things for a time, like it always did, but back home again I picked my worries up right where I'd left them.

Chapter Nine

In the morning, I donned my runners and did a quick warm-up before taking off into the park at a slow jog. I missed Malcolm's company on my weekend runs. Avoiding all paths that lead to the lighthouse, I opted instead for a short loop that would have me back home in thirty minutes.

The workout revitalized me. I booted up my laptop and clicked on an email from my mother, anxious to learn what she knew about the boxes in the attic. It surprised me that she hadn't known about them. Given the dates on the journals were late seventies and early eighties, when Dad was in medical school or doing his residency, her guess was they were Dad's from before her time at the cottage. She was excited that I might find some of his original research and asked me to check through them carefully. She'd already agreed to give my father's notes to Dr. Stein, and anything new could be important. I wrote her back promising to keep aside anything that looked like research.

I picked up my phone and headed to the deck. Someone had called when I was in the shower. I settled into a deck chair and checked the message. My skin bristled and the hairs on the back of my neck stood up when I heard Jackson's voice.

> *"I know I'm the last person you want to hear from, Emelynn, but something's come up and I need to talk to you. It's important. Please call me as soon as you get this."*

He was so much further down the list than *last*. What an arrogant ass. I erased his call with more furor than necessary and checked twice to make sure it was gone from my phone. Like noise pollution, his voice rang in my ears long after the source had quieted. I pictured his pale hazel eyes and the dark curls that were always too long and felt the familiar pain flare in my chest.

Why would he phone me? Didn't he realize how much he'd hurt me? I may have been an idiot about him the first time but there was no way I was giving him an opportunity for a second shot. He wouldn't be getting a thing from me: not a phone call; not an email; not even a "screw you."

It was bad enough that his call made me think about him again, but I resented the hell out of the fact that it still hurt so much to remember him at all; to remember us. It's not like I thought Jackson was "the one," or expected the "happily ever after." I'd let him take my virginity without any false illusions. I'd nearly drowned and he'd rescued me. We both needed more affirmation of life that night than a drink could provide. I didn't regret the sex, but I never expected him to hurt me. And then, to learn that he'd done it on purpose, with forethought— that cut deeper than anything else.

Maybe Eden and Molly were right—I needed to put myself back out there, find a guy to have some fun with. Someone who could help me push Jackson out of my head.

Molly was off today. I phoned her at home and told her about Jackson's call.

"What a prick," she said, and it warmed my heart. This is what friends were for—support, encouragement and name calling with just the right amount of indignation.

We hung up with promises to get together soon, and then I headed to the Y for my self-defence class.

I was one of twelve women. The only man in the room was the instructor, Ken Gillespie. He was in his mid-forties with mousy brown hair. His qualifications included a first-degree black belt in tae kwon do and a third-degree black belt in ju-jitsu. It sounded impressive, but I knew nothing about the martial arts and he looked absolutely ordinary in jeans and a T-shirt. If anything, he looked on the small side though his arms were well defined.

He introduced himself and asked us to take the seats surrounding the black mats he'd placed in the centre of the room. His bare feet smacked the mats as he paced and explained his approach to self-defence.

"Most women," he said, looking at each of us. "Women like you, are smaller and weaker than anyone who would pose a threat. That's what predators count on. I'm going to show you that you're capable of fighting effectively against bigger, stronger opponents by turning their strengths against them. I'll show you how to use your attacker's own weight and momentum to your advantage to give you the opening you need to get away."

Wow. Ken Gillespie had raised the bar fairly high and the smaller, weaker women in the group—all of us, apparently—looked hopefully at one another.

The door behind us opened and a hulking man entered. Ken had set up a demonstration and at first glance, it looked like he'd over-stepped. The would-be attacker was larger in size and poundage, but of course, that was the point. Ken introduced his opponent, Jake Oliver, also a black belt in one of the martial arts. Jake was intimidation personified with his shaved head and thick, tattooed neck.

They had obviously done this before, but it was no less impressive with the repetition. Jake Oliver took a run at Ken Gillespie with the intent of knocking him down while his back was turned. Ken twisted on impact, bending at the hips, and Jake spilled to the mats in a tumble. Ken ignored him and continued talking to us. Jake got to his feet and when Ken turned to face him, Jake lunged as if he had a knife in his hand. Even without the weapon, it looked like a frightening move. Ken waited until the last moment before grabbing Jake's wrist and flipping him onto his back with what looked like an effortless twist of his hand. Ken didn't miss a beat in his presentation.

"Your goal is to get away. Every move your opponent makes gives you another opportunity to do that." Jake moved in close behind Ken and reached around as if he were going to grab the smaller man by the throat. Ken bent at the waist, forcing Jake forward. Ken kicked back at the same time as he sunk his elbow into Jake's abdomen. Once again, Ken ended up standing while Jake lay flat out on his stomach on the mat. It was a convincing demonstration.

During the class, the men took turns showing each of us how to think about the moves our opponents might make. They made us think in terms of momentum and how to use that momentum to our best advantage. They also taught us about painful pressure-points and how to use our elbows, heels and hips to best advantage. It was enlightening, and even if I never had another opportunity to use the new skills, it was encouraging to know that size and gender didn't necessarily turn us into victims or render us weak. I left the Y pumped with confidence.

Back home I repacked the last of the laser units and lined up the equipment in the front hall. I stood back and viewed the mountain of assembled gear. Would it even fit into Avery's tiny Porsche?

By 9:45 that evening, I was dressed for flying and entered the Pine-crest Paintball Park's address into my GPS. On pavement, it was a thirty-minute drive east, but I'd be flying, travelling over dark tracts of land and forest to avoid lights and high-rises. It would be the longest flight I'd taken since my recovery and it was good practice with the new GPS.

Avery surprised me by driving up in an SUV, not his sleek black Porsche. Victoria got out of the passenger seat, her long blonde hair trussed in a black net. "You need some help?" she asked.

Avery came around the back of the vehicle. "Is everything ready?"

"Yes and yes," I said.

Avery opened the hatch. "I read through that material you sent me."

I handed him the first duffle bag. "What did you think?"

He nodded, smiling. "These lasers are really going to spice up the game." He took another bag from Victoria.

"I'm looking forward to trying something different," Victoria said with enthusiasm.

After several more trips, Avery closed the hatch on what turned out to be a Land Rover.

"There's room to spare. Sure you don't want a lift?" Avery said.

"No, but thanks. I've been looking forward to flying."

"Okay, then. We'll see you there."

After they left, I took off, dodging condos and checking my GPS to see that I was on course. The big old barn of the paintball park was hard to miss from the air. It was an enormous structure with a rusting steel roof that was the only brown patch in a sea of green fields.

It was Jackson who'd initially found the paintball park and culti-vated the relationship with its owner, Jerry. When Jackson left, Avery took over. Jerry rented out most of the surrounding farmland. It was his son who'd started the paintball business, renovating the barn and buying the equipment, but he'd abandoned it when he couldn't turn a profit. Now Jerry let charities and not-for-profit organizations use the space in return for a donation toward the insurance costs.

Deidra and Kate had arrived ahead of me. I hadn't seen either of them in over a month. Deidra Lewis had strawberry blonde hair just long enough to pull into a blunt-ended ponytail. She and Eden were neck and neck in the contest for shortest member of the covey. She reminded me of a lollipop, top heavy with slender legs and tiny feet. Kate Dennison was more of a pear-shaped woman. She's the one who often ended the paintball game with more splatters than anyone else. Kate had shiny chestnut-coloured hair cut into a bob, which suited her heart-shaped face. Both women were teachers, in their early thirties.

We exchanged polite hellos and pleasantries and turned to greet Sydney, who arrived next. Sydney Davenport was taller than me with dark eyes and jet black hair, razor cut so it flowed like silk around her face and shoulders. She was of mixed heritage, and though I couldn't identify the exact combination, Asian was certainly represented there somewhere. She would have been beautiful even without the exotic undertone. Sydney was reserved. Not aloof, just quiet, like her privacy was important.

Alex and Eden arrived soon after and though Eden was in her flying gear, Alex had improvised. It looked like he'd come straight from his shop and had pulled on a pair of dark coveralls over his paint-spattered work clothes. As usual, his brown hair was sticking up all over the place. Alex seemed to tower over Eden, but everyone towered over Eden. She might look like a sprite on the ground, but in the air, Eden was special. She was the first Flier I'd ever seen in full flight and I still remembered her arching swan-dive off the side of the *Aerial Symphony* and the ballet performance that followed. She was a prima ballerina in the sky.

Danny was the next to arrive and he rarely stayed still. If he wasn't shifting his weight from one foot to the other, he was fiddling with his fingers. "Hey," he said, as he approached, and I returned his smile. I liked Danny. He was game for anything.

"Avery's got the gear," I said. "He should be here any minute."

Gabe and Steve arrived together. Gabe Aucoin was a fit man in his early fifties with an olive complexion. He had a bandana tied around his head in the style of a do-rag that made him look more like a badass biker than the lawyer I knew him to be. Gabe's dry sense of humour and quick wit kept Avery on his toes. When Avery first introduced me to Gabe, he'd mocked that Gabe was embarrassed about being a lawyer. He wasn't, he was just discreet. He represented some extremely wealthy families, who guarded their privacy as well as their money.

I thought of Steve Elliott as the universally average man who could disappear into any crowd if he chose to. Nothing about him stood out. He was of medium height and build with short brown hair and brown eyes. He rarely spoke and his movements were so unobtrusive that he drew little attention. Steve remained a mystery. He'd flown in with Gabe though, so perhaps I'd quiz Gabe about him later.

The last to arrive was Avery. Instead of leaving his car at the edge of the parking lot like he did when he came in the Porsche, he drove up close to the barn, spitting loose gravel and bouncing over the dry pot holes. He and Victoria emerged from the Land Rover laughing and took their time saying hello to everyone.

Avery finally broke up the lively chatter and called for attention. "Thanks for coming out. Jerry's given us use of the park until 3:00 a.m., but first I have some news to share, and then Alex has a surprise for us." Expectant eyes shot to Alex, who gleefully rubbed his hands together.

Avery handed each of us one of his business cards. "As most of you already know, Greg Jeffries's computer was hacked and our Infinity message board has been compromised. The intruder pilfered Greg's contacts and through him, got to me and my contacts. Unfortunately, we can't be sure who else has been compromised, so before any of you access the new message board or my new email address, you need to run Greg's virus program. I emailed you all a copy of it earlier today. Run it on any computer you've used in the last four months and then change your passwords."

A collective groan went up. "Yeah, I know. I'm sorry about this, but it's necessary. My new email is on the back of that card, as well as the new URL for the secure message board."

"Do we know what happened?" Danny asked, fingering Avery's card.

"It was an embedded Trojan Horse virus triggered by the keyword *Jolene*."

"Who's Jolene?" Danny asked.

"A woman we've been trying to locate. Unfortunately, using her name set the thing off. Someone out there has been monitoring the network, but we don't know who or why."

"Why the interest in this 'Jolene'?" Kate asked.

Avery's gaze sought me out and he smiled in reassurance. We had discussed this already and knew it would come up. We wouldn't lie to the covey about Jolene. It wasn't necessary as long as we kept the ghosting out of it.

"Jolene is the woman who gifted Emelynn and then disappeared. We'd like to find her."

Kate turned to me. "You were gifted?" Her expression was part curiosity, part accusation.

"Yes," I said quietly. I didn't want to elaborate. Only a few of the covey knew I'd been gifted. The rest had made whatever assumptions they needed, to explain my inexperience.

"Do you think Jolene survived the gifting?" Deidra asked, looking apologetic. She needn't have. I'd already learned that the gifting process would have stripped Jolene of all traces of the gift, and I also knew it may have fatally weakened her. Death was an outcome in over half of the cases of gifting.

"I hope so, but I understand it's unlikely," I said. I'd had no contact with her since the day she gifted me.

"But not impossible," Avery interjected. "We're not giving up."

"I know we've all heard it before, but this is a new threat so don't let your guard down. Until we know who's behind the breach and what their motivation is, be extra careful, especially of strangers."

"Does the Tribunal know about the breach?" The question came from Steve.

"I don't know."

"Will you bring them in on it?"

"It's not my preference, but I think it should be a covey decision if we do. Any one of you has the right to pull that trigger, but if you do, I think the rest of us would appreciate a heads-up."

A tense quiet surrounded us as we sought out each other's face looking for solidarity perhaps, or reassurance.

"Is there anything else?" Gabe asked, breaking the silence. He'd already tucked Avery's card into his pocket.

"No, we're done with the bad news. Alex, you want to take it from here?"

All heads turned to Alex, who stood close to Avery's SUV. Alex looked as antsy as Danny, who now stood beside him. "You all know that these games are more than just a fun night out. It's training and I think you'll all agree it's been effective. I've seen a big improvement in our aerial agility and I know the teamwork is improving our cohesion as a group. I can speak first-hand about how useful the training has been; we used it when we helped rescue Sandra.

"That experience left us questioning if we could do better and, thanks to Sandra's reward money, we've found a way. Our covey is now the proud new owner of its own custom-made laser tag equipment." Avery had already opened the rear of his Land Rover and called Danny to help him pass out duffle bags.

Murmurs of curiosity rose up all around and eager expressions replaced furrowed brows. "Let's take the gear inside," Danny said. "We'll set it up and explain as we go." Everyone grabbed what they could and made their way through the small door that opened into a staging area just inside the cavernous barn.

Alex raised his voice. "Each player needs a vest, a headset and a laser gun. There are two styles of lasers. They're interchangeable, so don't worry about getting stuck with one you don't like."

Danny and Alex checked the equipment and helped everyone suit up. Avery busied himself with unpacking the command centre like he knew what he was doing.

Victoria held a vest to her chest. "These are so much better than the jumpsuits!" The quilted jumpsuits we wore for paintball protected our clothing from neck to ankle, but the extra padding hindered flight and did little to lessen the sting of paintballs taken at close range.

"Kate, look at this," Deidra said, showing off a vest.

"Is there no helmet? No face mask?" Kate asked.

"You don't need them," Danny said. "There's no impact with lasers."

Deidra giggled. "It's going to feel like skinny-dipping."

Excitement flitted through the air. Laser beams flashed in short red bursts and long lines, like bright thread all over the barn, as we got a feel for the trigger and the balance of the lasers. I chose a handgun because I liked its compact size, but noticed that, except for Steve, the men had all selected rifles. It might have been a mistake, but I was willing to trade off the advantage of the rifle's scope for the convenience of a smaller weapon.

Danny explained the concept of the new game including the fact that our lasers would automatically be incapacitated, and we'd be out of the game, if we were hit with a kill shot, or hit three times within a three-minute window. "Aim for your opponent's vest or headset," he said. "Each time a hit is registered, your laser will shut down for ten seconds, so you'd better find cover if you want to stay in the game. The lasers are modified to be silent, but you'll hear the hits over your headsets. You'll also be able to communicate with your teammates through the headsets unless you're taken out. Avery's gear keeps track of each player's hits."

Danny showed Gabe the kill shot area of the vest. It was a large swath across the chest but with my aim, it wasn't likely I'd hit it unless by fluke.

"The maximum number of shots in each magazine is eighteen. If your laser's on semi-automatic, it'll pump out three shots each time you pull the trigger." Alex upended his laser to show us how to switch to semi-automatic. "It's effective, but you'll run out of ammo quickly. You'll have two additional magazines that you load yourself by pushing this lever." He turned the laser to demonstrate. "If you reload before your magazine is empty, you'll lose the shots you didn't use."

You could feel the energy crackle in the air as voices got louder and the boasts bolder. Sydney was the only woman who'd taken a rifle and she was adjusting her scope, testing its accuracy. Steve was pretending he had a holster on his hip, playing like a cowboy in the Wild West. Alex and Danny made a final round of each of us, checking the laser settings and testing our headsets. Almost everyone had a question or two and those who weren't off playing around with their lasers stuck around to listen. Anticipation ramped up with every passing minute.

"Are you ready to pick teams?" Avery shouted over the din.

There was a murmur in the affirmative and Danny stepped forward. "I'll lead the green team."

"What is it with you and green?" Alex said, teasing Danny as he stepped forward ready to claim leadership of the red team.

"Wait a minute," Eden said. "How about the women challenge the men this time? What do you say?" We looked at one another and shrugged.

Danny thought for a moment before he said, "Just a sec," in a voice that said he smelled a rat. "That would give you a six-four advantage."

"Darn, thought I could pull one over on you," Eden said.

"I'll bow out and help Avery with the command centre," Victoria said. I hid a smile. She'd bow out all right—right into Avery's arms.

"Do you boys think you can handle us having a one-woman advantage?" Eden baited them in an embarrassing display of coy.

The men were already gathering together as if for warmth. "You are going to be so humiliated when the four of us whip all five of your butts," Alex said in a show of bravado that sealed our fates.

"And if we win at these odds, you ladies will be buying us each two beers," Danny added. Gabe and Steve were happy to nod their heads in agreement with that one.

The women were the red team, so we wore red armbands. The men wore green. After we'd got a feel for the lasers, we each paid a visit to Avery. He set up our radios while Danny and Alex loaded the lasers. "After I program your laser, don't pull the trigger until Avery starts the game. If you do, you'll lose those shots and suffer a time-delay penalty when the clock starts."

"Are you sure we can trust you?" Eden said, teasing Alex, who took her laser to program it.

"I should have negotiated less ammo for you ladies, to make up for your advantage," he said, handing it back to her.

"But you're all so big and strong." Eden fluttered her eyelashes, teasing, and then she checked the readout for all eighteen shots. "We need all the advantage we can get."

When the last laser was programmed and the radios tested, Avery shouted to get our attention. "I'll radio a three-minute warning. Okay?" With no objections, he and Victoria took their gear and headed toward the tent with the big red cross, which was set up in the centre of the lower floor of the barn.

The modifications that Jerry's son had made to the interior of the structure were minimal but effective for the game. Large sheets of canvas were strategically hung between stacked hay bales, which could either provide cover or, if you weren't careful, trap you.

Eden whistled. "Ladies, you're with me." She motioned for us to follow her to the second floor. Obediently, we floated up behind her. From there you could see the canvas walls that made the game more challenging.

The main floor was open up to the rafters. A wide, horseshoe-shaped balcony made up the second floor, which was accessed by loft doors that opened at this end. On the second floor, the hay bales were arranged haphazardly. When it was a functioning barn, the loft doors would have been used to load bales into the upper floor for winter storage. The livestock would have been housed in the lower reaches and the bales tossed down to feed them. Now the bales provided cover for players who sought protection on the second floor. Eden pushed the loft doors open and we followed her outside. She flew twenty feet straight up and we joined her in a cautious huddle, watchful for spies.

From this height, we could appreciate the massive length and breadth of the structure. All along the north side of the building, a covered lean-to protected rusty remnants of farm equipment, and though you couldn't see it from here, the area underneath that roof was also littered with hay bales to provide extra cover for players.

"I've got an idea for a strategy no one's used before," Eden said. "Instead of splitting up, like every team has always done, let's stick together. We'll form a loose circle with our backs together and take out all comers."

"They'll just gang up and get us all at once," Kate said.

"Maybe," Eden said, "but they've never done that before. They'll come out in ones or twos and won't be expecting all of us, so the surprise and our numbers should give us an advantage."

"If we position ourselves another twenty or thirty feet up, and centre ourselves above the barn, we'll also be in a formation no one has ever tried. Like a death star," Sydney added, wide-eyed. I liked Sydney's imagery.

"I'm not that good a shot," I said apologetically, knowing how often I missed my mark. "I don't think I'll be able to hit anyone unless I can get close to them."

"Yeah, me too," Deidra said.

"Okay, we'll break out of formation and attack en masse, then retreat and re-form after we hit them."

We looked at one another for reassurance. "Why not," I said, and Eden seemed to take that as a collective yes. She shot up and stopped about fifty feet above the centre of the barn. We gathered in a circle, backs together and then lowered ourselves to horizontal. From below we'd look like five spokes on a wheel.

Sydney whispered, "Keep your feet touching, and if you spot someone, kick to get our attention."

Our headsets crackled to life with Avery's voice. "We're ready to go. The game is going live . . . now!" We hovered in silence, wound up like springs waiting to pounce. Then we waited some more . . . and some more.

When the silence became uncomfortable, Eden whispered, "They're waiting us out, be patient." So, we waited some more.

Our patience was rewarded. Kate kicked. We looked in her direction and spotted the end of a gun poking out from the loft doors. The player ascended and soon his whole body was visible as he cautiously looked out toward the fields, all around. He ascended higher to look over the top of the barn, but he hadn't yet looked up high enough to spot us. Eden whispered, "In three—two—one—go!" We all shot forward and five lasers criss-crossed the guy's vest. I think it was Gabe. He was out of play and we were already re-forming our death star.

"What if he tells the others what we're doing?" Deidra speculated.

"His radio will be disabled," Eden said, and then reconsidered. "But just in case you're right, let's shift down to the loft end of the barn."

We moved into our new position and played the waiting game again. It didn't take long. This time the player came from the far end by the big doors on the ground floor and Sydney's kick got our attention. Eden counted it down, "Three—two—one—go!"

We shot down and went on the attack and that was the end of us. The two remaining green players came up behind us—from where, I don't know, but their lasers were on semi-automatic. They pulsed out a torrent of red flashes and one by one our lasers jammed up, putting us out of the game.

It should have been a humbling defeat, but I couldn't stop laughing. Kate cursed like a trucker in city traffic, not exactly elementary-school-teacher language, and Eden taunted the green team with inappropriate and unflattering names. If I didn't know better, I'd have thought we'd won. We flew into the barn in a boisterous whirlwind.

"That's two beers each to the green team," Avery shouted, handing out water and colas. The inevitable post-game analysis began. It happened after every game, but this time it was more animated and it was the new equipment that got most of the air time. There were a lot of pros and only one con. Fliers missed hearing the confirmation of a "hit" that you got with the sound of a paintball.

"I thought I fixed that," Alex said. "It's just a setting I need to change to send a signal through to your radio when you get a hit. Give me a minute to find it." While he looked for instructions, new conversations broke out discussing strategy—what worked, what didn't, who got hit, when and how. It was all part of the game.

Everyone was eager for a second match. Danny and Alex reset our lasers. This time, Alex assured us, we'd hear our hits.

The women abandoned the failed death star configuration and split up. We went back to a strategy that had worked well before. Deidra and Kate stayed outside and up high to pick off players coming in or going out the big barn doors. I would do the same at the loft doors, and Eden and Sydney took offensive positions. They would enter the barn through the loft and make their way through the interior, picking off as many green players as they could.

The moment Avery radioed the start of the game, two green players shot out of the barn doors heading straight for Deidra and Kate. Immediately, I abandoned my post and raced to help them. The women didn't fold when they were attacked. They stood their ground, knocking one of the attackers out of play and emptying their lasers, but it wasn't enough. Their lasers locked up with one of the green players still in action. Luckily, I was on him and he hadn't seen my swift approach. I locked him out of the game with an automatic burst of laser light and kept on flying. I think it was Steve. He'd spun around to find me, but I'd flown out in a wide arc and was already speeding back to my position.

Within seconds the two remaining green players pulled the same strategy with me. I was still in motion, not yet back in position. Miraculously, I hit one of them mid-flight and blew past my post, giving free rein to my speed to outrun the one who was left. His parting shot registered as a hit but it wasn't a kill shot so I was still in the game. I kept going to fly off my ten-second penalty then turned around.

I had to find him; he was the last man left. I flew a wide, cautious circle, making my way back to my position by the loft door. An impressive display of red light glowed from inside the barn and moments later my radio squawked to life to end the game. "Yes!" The ladies had won. I joined the raucous Fliers inside and my team slapped high-fives all around.

The post-game analysis flared up again and Gabe sidled up beside me. "I thought the rumours about you were just that—until I saw you in action tonight. I want you and that speed of yours on my team next game." He winked and bumped my shoulder then rejoined the others. I suppose it was inevitable that word would get out when I kept using my speed in these games. At least it wasn't embarrassing when it was acknowledged in passing like that.

We played one final game, which the men won and our beer debt grew.

Avery organized us to meet on Thursday night at Clam Diggers, an old pub in Seaside. A definitive date was the only thing that was going to shut the men up about the beers we owed them. We each took our vests and headsets home and Avery agreed to transport the rest of the gear. The Fliers flitted in and out of the small groups saying their goodbyes, and then they broke up and drifted off home.

While Victoria, Avery and Alex still had their heads together, I talked to Eden. "Jackson left a message on my phone today."

"What did he want?" she asked, and I told her his message. I expected the same reaction that I'd gotten from Molly, but Eden wasn't flinging insults Jackson's way. She frowned. "Have you told Avery?"

"Not yet. Why? What are you thinking?"

"I'm thinking about what Avery told us tonight about being hacked. Jackson had been looking for Jolene too. Maybe he has some information about it."

"I never thought of that." I should have. When it came to Jackson, my brains fell out. I was so busy being angry with him that I didn't see the obvious. We both looked over to Avery.

He sensed the dual stare and turned away from Alex. "What?"

"Jackson called Em, today."

Avery and Alex closed the gap in two strides. "What did he want?"

"I didn't speak to him. He left a message asking me to call him— said it was important."

"You didn't call him back." It wasn't a question. Avery knew how I felt about Jackson.

Eden addressed Avery. "It might have something to do with the security breach."

"I'll call him," Avery said, rubbing my shoulder.

"Would you please tell him to erase my phone number? I don't ever want to hear his voice again."

Avery smiled indulgently. "Of course. I'll make sure he calls me in future, okay?"

"Thank you."

We flew off our separate ways, and I hovered long enough to watch Avery's Land Rover clear the driveway and turn toward the highway.

Chapter Ten

The wheels of Malcolm's bike crunched on the gravel of the driveway distracting me from my thoughts. I knew Avery would be talking to Jackson this morning, and as much as I told myself I didn't want anything more to do with him, my curiosity was eating away at me.

Malcolm set the kickstand and removed his helmet. He squinted into the warm sunshine. "How was your weekend?"

"Good. I took the self-defence class yesterday. Do you know the instructor, Ken Gillespie?"

"I've met him. He stages martial arts demonstrations at the Y for the after-school kids."

"He's impressive. Showed me how to crush someone's windpipe." I probably shouldn't have smiled quite so brightly when I said that.

"I hope he emphasized that the whole point is to get away from your attacker, not join in."

"He mentioned that," I said with a chuckle. "Do you want to warm-up down there?" I pointed to the beach. We were doing the beach run today and the only way down there, other than scrambling over the bank, was through the house and down the deck stairs.

"Sure, lead the way."

I set the alarm at the front door and then we raced to the deck to beat the timer before the motion sensors kicked in. At the base of the stairs, we were caught between laughter and holding our breath. When the blast didn't come, we moved into our warm-up routine during which I entertained him with the tale of my resident squirrel-terrorists.

We set off northward. The rocks eliminated any chance of running, but Malcolm negotiated the hazard with exceptional agility. When the beach allowed, Malcolm picked up our pace, and we were running by the time we got to the public access. We hit the trail to the street without breaking our stride and jogged in place while Malcolm got his bearings. I looked around, watching for suspicious-looking characters. Had I seen that man before? The one with the navy shorts?

"This way," Malcolm said, a welcome interruption to my paranoia that seemed to be working overtime.

I set my mind back on the run, and we wound through streets I hadn't been on in years. Malcolm pushed our pace just enough to keep me breathing hard and didn't give in to my whining when I was sure I was going to die from the effort.

We made the turn onto Cliffside, slowing to a fast walk. Almost as soon as the cottage came into view, my phone went off. It was the siren again. "Sorry, Malcolm. It's the alarm." I dug the phone out of my fanny pack. Sure enough, it was the attic sensor again. Damn. I disarmed it and we picked up the pace.

"Are you sure it's just squirrels?" Malcolm asked.

"I can't be positive, but it's too much of a coincidence not to be."

Inside, I checked the alarm panel. Malcolm followed me in, his gaze darting around the space expectantly. He put on a brave face and neither of us said a word as we checked room by room for intruders. We finished in my bedroom and gazed up at the hatch in the closet ceiling.

"Let me," he said, as I snapped open the wooden stepladder. He nudged the hatch open and poked his head through the hole. "There's nothing up here," he said, shining a flashlight around.

"What a relief," I said.

"That alarm was almost as good as a run for getting my blood pumping." He climbed down and pulled the hatch into place, chuckling to himself. "Let's not do this again, okay?"

"I think I'll leave the attic sensor off until that trap is removed."

Malcolm stayed for a glass of juice, which we drank on the deck.

"I've got to go," he said, standing. "I've got another client. Weights tomorrow?"

"I'll be there," I said.

I had my head in the fridge when the phone rang. It was Molly. "Cheney and I are going to meet a bunch of his friends for drinks tonight. Do you want to come with us?"

"Is it all couples?" I asked, cringing.

"No, don't worry. You won't feel like a fifth wheel."

That might be fun. "Why not? What time?"

"Eight. We're going to Fast Eddies. It's on the water, down behind Cheney's shop. We'll pick you up."

We disconnected, but I didn't put the phone down. If I put off calling Avery, I'd be thinking about his chat with Jackson all night. I dialled him.

"I thought you might call," he said.

"My curiosity got the best of me. What did you learn?"

"Jackson's computer was hacked. Jolene's name set it off, same thing that happened to Greg."

"Why did he call *me*?"

"He didn't know how much you'd told me about Jolene. He was trying to do the right thing—protect your privacy."

"Yeah, right." Jackson—protect me? Not likely.

"I told him you didn't want him calling you. But he's not completely out of the picture either."

"What do you mean?"

"He's been working a different angle to find the hacker. I figured we might as well put our resources together and his are considerable."

"That's just great," I said with a heavy sigh. Sometimes I wondered if I would ever get to the point where hearing his name didn't make my chest ache.

"I'm sorry," he said. "But we'll get to the bottom of this faster with his help. He's got his entire IT department working on it."

"I'm sure."

"I know you're still hurting so I'll keep mention of his name to a bare minimum. Okay?"

I chuckled at his sincerity. "You know me so well."

"I wish you saw in yourself what I see. If you did, you would know that Jackson was just a blip on your radar. You're the one with the potential to break hearts—not him. You can already fly circles around most of us, who knows where the rest of your gift will take you."

"Thanks, Avery. You always make me feel better."

"Well, I *am* a doctor," he said, and I pictured his silly grin. "But Greg's news will make you feel even better. He and the-one-who-shall-remain-nameless are already making headway on the hacker. It's frustrating the hell out of them. I don't understand how it all works, but apparently, this hacker's led a chase around the cyberglobe and back again. The guy is doing something they call, believe it or not, *ghosting*."

"Are you joking?"

"No. He's using other people's computers without them even knowing it. The first trail led to Delhi where they lost him. Greg back-tracked and found him again in London. They thought they lost him there again, but the IT crew found threads that led them to Frankfurt and that sent them to Jakarta. Now it looks like they've zeroed in on him in the southern States. If we ever find this guy, I think Greg's going to want a piece of him."

We hung up with his assurances that he'd let me know when they learned anything more.

I sent Avery a note to let him know I'd run Greg's virus scrubbing program, and was back in the land of emails, and then I turned my attention to my night out.

Now, what to wear? After my recent shopping trip, that chore was fun for a change. I chose a gap-holed knit sweater with a deep V-neck to wear over a silky, white camisole. The beige stretch jeans fit like they were custom made, hugging me from hip to ankle. Finally, I stepped into my new Stella McCartney boots. The finishing touch was a small leather purse that was just big enough for my phone, some cash and my lip gloss. I left my hair loose and applied a smudge of eyeliner and some lipstick.

Molly stood waiting on the porch when I answered the doorbell. She was dressed in her typical fifties style with a pale pink sweater set over baby blue mid-calf-length slacks. Her bobby socks and hair band were, of course, pink. We had a quick hug hello and then I set the alarm and locked the door.

Cheney sat behind the wheel of an eye-catching turquoise convertible in the driveway. He hadn't dressed up, but I didn't expect that of Cheney. He was into comfort. He wore a plain white T-shirt and blue jeans. Molly held the front passenger seat forward for me and I caught the scent of Cheney's aftershave as I climbed into the back. I slid easily across the pristine white leather seat.

"Nice wheels, Cheney. A Mustang?" I'd recognized the emblem on the grill.

"Sure is. It's a '64 and a half, first year they made them. Dad and I restored it two years ago." Cheney spoke like a proud father as he stroked the oversized steering wheel.

He revved the engine and it let out a deep throaty rumble that promised serious power under the hood. Molly tied on a head scarf and it completed a picture; Molly with her fifties obsession and Cheney with his muscle car. A better match would be hard to find. She put her arm across the back of the seat and smoothed his hair.

Cheney drove out to Deacon Street and soon we passed the darkened stores on the strip. We turned down Fourth Street and drove past Stafford and Meyers Motors, straight to the waterfront. I soon spied the sign for Fast Eddies. Smooth cedar siding softened the building's modern industrial look. Cheney pulled into a parking space beside a Harley-Davidson motorcycle.

"Dean's here," he said, nodding toward the bike.

If there was a graceful way to extricate oneself from the backseat of a car like this, I didn't find it. I took Molly's hand and she hauled me out. I straightened my sweater and tugged my jeans back down to my ankles where they belonged.

"You look great," Molly said, hooking her arm in mine as we headed to the big double front doors. Cheney opened them for us and we stepped inside. I was nervous about meeting Cheney's friends but didn't feel the weight of trepidation I used to when meeting more than one person at a time. I took it as a sign that my social skills were improving.

The hostess' pedestal beckoned us forward. It sat squarely between two arches. The arch to the left revealed a room dedicated to sit-down, white-tablecloth dining. Beyond the other arch was a more casual setting. The hostess looked up. "Hi, Cheney. They're in the bar."

"Thanks, Dawn," he said, leading us to the right.

"They know your name?" I said.

"They should. Been coming here since it opened," Cheney said.

Music took a back seat to voices in the large open space, which was surrounded by an outdoor deck. Pool balls clacked on one of two green-felted tables at one end of the room, and a fireplace dominated the other. Leather sofas and chairs were arranged around low tables in intimate groupings, clustered near the fireplace. Elsewhere, bar stools sat beneath tall tables.

We headed toward a circle of people who had claimed one of the leather sofa and chair groupings. Cheney was all smiles, lit up like a Christmas tree, as he approached his friends.

He put his arm around Molly's waist. "Molly, you remember Jerry and Beverley." Jerry and Beverley sat together on a sofa, close enough to suggest they were a couple. Jerry's red hair and freckles gave him a child-like appearance. His girlfriend, Beverley, had shoulder-length brown hair and beautifully manicured nails.

"Good to see you again," Molly said. "This is my friend, Emelynn."

Similar introductions went all around the small group as I met Dennis and Dale and Annette. I made an effort to remember all their names. Dennis was the one with the light brown hair and a thin face. Dennis eagerly offered his hand. Dale had the dark, wavy hair and a mole on his face. He was shy and opted for a nod in lieu of a handshake. Annette had short, fine, blonde hair and a triangle-shaped face. She looked very much at ease, as if she were among family.

When Cheney got to the final introduction, he started with an apology. "Sorry about the bike, Dean," he said, shaking his friend's hand. "I just tapped it with my bumper, and it folded like a banana bike."

Dean was the one with the scar on his face.

Like Cheney, Dean wore a T-shirt and jeans. He laughed and tapped his fist to Cheney's shoulder. "Nice try, Meyer."

"Dean Mitchell—Emelynn Taylor, Emelynn—Dean. Now, can I get you ladies a drink?" Cheney asked.

"Thanks. A glass of Merlot for me," Molly replied.

"I'll have the same," I said.

Dean pulled two tall chairs away from the bar and arranged them around the group, offering them to Molly and me.

I was consumed with morbid curiosity about Dean's scar. It ran from his temple to his jaw in a corded line. I'd already assumed it was a motorcycle accident, but assumptions were about as reliable as rumours.

Cheney's group of friends were all about the same age, mid- to late-twenties. He returned from the bar and handed Molly and me our wine then went to sit beside Jerry.

"How do you know Molly?" Annette asked. When I'd finished explaining, she filled me in on the group's connections. She and Jerry were high school classmates of Cheney's. Dennis used to drive the NAPA truck that supplied Meyers Motors with car parts. Dean and Cheney met at trade school and Dale was a friend of Dennis's.

"You're the first of Molly's friends who we've met," she said, smiling, and it made me feel special.

We played musical chairs for the next hour while two or three conversations carried on at once. The friends drifted easily in and out of the huddles, adding laughter here or an anecdote there. I floated around the periphery and once in a while someone would ask me something to include me in their conversation.

At one point, Dean ended up beside me. I was telling him about finding my dad's MGB when I caught Molly eavesdropping. She quickly looked away.

I went to the bar to buy a round and Dean helped me carry the drinks back to the table. Molly watched our every move and my intuition flared. Being a mechanic, I thought the story of my car would interest Dean. Now I realized it wasn't the car that interested him. Suddenly I needed to join a different conversation. I turned in my seat and feigned interest in a Cheney school-story that Annette and Jerry were in the middle of telling. Dean wandered off to join Cheney.

I found myself looking at Dean with fresh eyes. He stood three inches taller than Cheney, maybe more, and was handsome despite the scar. Dean projected a no-muss, no-fuss kind of image. He smelled like soap, not aftershave. His hair fell forward without the influence of hair-care products and his Wranglers were loose fitting, nothing expensive or trendy.

There was nothing pretentious or intimidating about the man, but I could already feel myself running away. I didn't trust my judgment where men were concerned. Well, except for Cheney—I trusted Cheney. And Avery. Yeah, I trusted Avery too. And Alex—I trusted him. Oh, who was I kidding? The only judgment I didn't trust was my own about potential boyfriend material. It was a slice of Jackson's fallout and I hated it: hated that I still let his crap impact me.

I stood up and walked toward the windows overlooking the water. This part of the building rested on piers, and the ocean ebbed in underneath us. A stainless-steel shelf seemed to hang in mid-air around the windows in the corner. I rested my foot on the matching foot rail. My inner dialogue went from admonishment to pep talk before Molly joined me.

"You all right?"

"Yeah. They're a great group."

"They are. Welcomed me from the first time I met them." She turned her back to the window and looked over at her new friends. "Dean's watching you."

"He seems real nice."

"Then what are you doing over here?"

　　　　　　　　　　　　　　　　　　　　　　　

I twisted my wine glass in circles. "I guess I'm still wrestling with some unpleasant memories."

"Jackson?"

"How'd you know?"

"It wasn't hard." She leaned back with her elbows against the stainless counter. "If it's any reassurance, I can personally vouch for the fact that Dean isn't married, and doesn't have a girlfriend."

"Does he have an extra appendage I can't see?" I asked and Molly burst out laughing. Months ago, when I had first described Cheney to her, she accused me of hiding a similar fact about him. The laughter popped the negative bubble that had a hold on me.

Something tickled my arm. An errant lock of hair I thought as I smoothed my curls and swept them to the other side. I rubbed my arm to chase away the tickle, but then the sensation crept up my other arm and I jerked.

Molly looked over. "What is it?"

"Felt like a spider," I said, swiping at my arm.

Molly came closer to look then shrugged. "You must have got it."

But I hadn't. The creepy crawly sensation crossed my shoulders. I jumped again. Molly turned me around and swept her hands all over my shoulders. I waited a moment and the sensation passed.

"Thanks. I think it's gone now." I shivered and brushed my hands down around my waist and hips to make sure the spider wasn't clinging on somewhere waiting to crawl back up. Yuck. I massaged the back of my neck and my hand brushed against the dangling pale amber earrings. I think I wore them more often now, just to spite Cassandra.

"Let's go back to the group," I said, picking up my wine glass. We settled in beside a tall table. I set my drink down and rubbed my arms again as if that would erase the memory of hairy spider legs.

"What was that all about?" Dean asked, coming up behind my chair. He rested his boot on the side rung.

"Spider attack," Molly said, laughing. Dean rested his arm along the back of my chair. His thumb grazed my shoulder blade. I shot forward bowing away from the shock of his touch.

"I'm sorry." He held up his hands as if I'd slapped him.

My automatic reaction had caught me off guard too. His touch had thrown me and I recognized it for what it was: more Jackson fallout. "I thought the spider was back," I said, covering my overreaction, and then to prove the point, I settled back into the chair. Dean returned his arm to rest there, but he was careful not to touch me again. I felt like damaged goods and I couldn't stand it.

Cheney's friends were having a great time all around me, and I was suffocating. I headed off to the restroom and called a cab. When I got back to the table, I said my goodbyes. Molly grabbed her purse and stood.

"The cab's already here," I said, a small white lie to dissuade her and Cheney from driving me home. "And I don't want to spoil your fun. Thanks for the offer though, and the ride over. I'll see you sometime this week," I said to Molly, as I turned to go.

Dean followed me and I knew without a doubt what was coming. When we got outside he sprung the dreaded question. "Would you like to go out sometime?"

I turned to look into his handsome, hopeful face and thought, what's wrong with me? Thankfully, the cab pulled up with perfect timing. "Let me think about it, okay?"

"Sure," he said, but I felt like I'd kicked a puppy.

I knew it took courage to ask someone out and I couldn't let it go without trying to soften the blow. "Thanks for the company tonight." He smiled at that and I turned and climbed into the cab and didn't look back.

Back home, I disarmed the alarm and leaned back against the door. This was crazy. I was crazy. I was letting a worthless former boyfriend impact my life, and I hated it. It had to stop.

I changed into flying clothes, left the house and headed south, carefully watching for prying eyes. It was perfect conditions for flying: warm, clear and windless. I pulled the image of the crystal into my mind and ran phantom fingers over its smooth, warm facets. The hum of power surged, and I closed my eyes, enjoying the sensation. I felt no tension, no conflict, no stress: I was at peace, untouchable. Heaven, I thought as I concentrated the power and broke free of gravity.

The lighthouse called my name and I sought it out as if it could soothe my soul. It was the perfect place to stargaze and gather my thoughts—as long as Case wasn't around. Making sure he wasn't was my first priority. I scouted the grounds and then the tower itself. I landed on the catwalk and peered inside before I relaxed completely. I sat down, stretched out on my back and looked up into the night sky.

I could think more clearly up here, as if the clouds that muddled my thinking had less effect, and I came to a decision. I was going to make a date with Dean. I wasn't going to sleep with him, and I certainly wasn't putting my heart on offer, but I needed to make an effort to break the hold Jackson's memory seemed to have on me. It wasn't healthy, and dating Dean was a step in the right direction. With reluctance, I left the peaceful tower and flew home.

Chapter Eleven

Heavy rain woke me in the middle of the night. The patter of rain on the deck had stopped by morning, but it left a claustrophobic fog in its place and a heavy damp smell in the air.

For the first time in weeks, I pulled on my jean jacket and wasn't able to put down the top on the MGB.

After my workout with Malcolm, I headed home for a shower and got ready to see Avery. By the time I got in the car again, the sky looked like it might clear.

I filled Avery in on my night out at Fast Eddies while he ran through my checkup routine.

"Lie back," he said, getting ready for the final step: poking my scars. I lifted my shirt and felt the familiar taps. "Does your friend, Molly, know Dean?"

"He's Cheney's friend, but Molly vouched for him."

"What does Dean do for a living?"

"He's a mechanic. He went to trade school with Cheney."

I rolled on my side. When Avery finished examining the wound on my back, I sat up and tugged my shirt down. He made a few notes on a pad of paper, which reminded me. "You haven't found my chart yet?"

"No. I'm sure it's around here somewhere though. Where does Dean work?"

"A BMW dealership somewhere in Vancouver." I couldn't suppress a smile and Avery noticed. It wasn't just that he was acting like a father with the questions, but my own unemployment highlighted a glaring double standard.

"What? Too many questions?"

"No, it's sweet." And it was. It made me feel cared for.

"Just watching out for my favourite patient," he said, and offered me his crooked smile. "I think it's good for you to get out with your friends and have fun."

"Yes, it's time. I need to move on."

"Speaking of moving on, I think we're ready to drop these weekly checkups. It's been two months and you've been stable for a long time now."

"But whatever will you do with your Tuesday mornings?" I said, teasing. "You're going to miss me."

"How can I? I see you every Thursday."

I hopped down from the table and gathered my things. "Is there any word on the hacker yet?"

"No name yet, but Greg assures me that Jackson—sorry, he-who-won't-be-named—is close to getting the hacker's ID."

"That's great, but what then?"

"One step at a time, Em."

"I suppose," I said, turning for the door. Avery followed.

"Greg says he wants to get out of Portland for a while. He's going to lie low until this hacker is put out of business. I suggested he visit Vancouver. I'd like to meet him, thank him for all the help he's been over the years."

"Meet him? I had the impression you already knew him."

"Only online. We've been contacts for years, but we've never met in person."

"That should be interesting."

"Interesting?"

"Yeah, you know—see if his face matches the one you picture in your head." I opened the door. "See you Thursday."

I stopped by Rumbles on the way home. Molly was just finishing her lunch. "What time did everyone else go home last night?"

"Maybe an hour after you left. Did you have fun?"

"I did, and I liked Fast Eddies too." I looked to my shoes. If I wanted Dean's phone number, I'd have to ask for it and let Molly's teasing chips fall where they may. I sucked in a breath. "Dean asked me out."

"I'm not surprised. He was following you around like a puppy."

The visual of that made me snicker.

"Are you going to go out with him?"

"I think so. You wouldn't happen to have his number, would you?"

"No, but Cheney will." Molly whipped out her phone and called him. Then I suffered through her telling him that I was going to say yes to Dean. I don't know what Cheney said on the other end of that call, but Molly looked over to me and nodded like a bobble head.

She hung up and held out a piece of paper with the number. "He asked Cheney about you."

"He did?" I felt a flush of excitement. I reached for the paper, but she pulled her hand back.

"When are you going to call him?"

"Today, I guess." I raised an eyebrow and reached for the number again.

"Will I get a full report?" she asked, holding the paper hostage.

I snatched it triumphantly from her hand. "Maybe." I smiled as I tucked the paper in my pocket.

It was still overcast when I got home. Eden was working afternoons. I sent her a quick text teaser about Dean hoping it would prompt her to pick up the phone.

Thinking of Dean, I decided to call him before I chickened out. I hoped he didn't mind me calling him at work. It was the first thing I said when he came to the phone.

"Not at all. It's a pleasant surprise," he said.

An awkward silence followed, and we both ended up speaking at once.

"I wanted to—" I said.

"Did you change your—" Dean said. "You called me—you go first."

"Do you still want to go out sometime?"

He didn't hesitate with his reply and just like that, I had a date for Friday night. I agreed to meet him for dinner at Fast Eddies at eight.

When I hung up, I let out a breath and released the tension that had crept into my shoulders. I turned up the Bose and danced a happy dance with P!nk. Yeah—I had a date—my step in the right direction!

Despite the sunshine of my mood, the deck was still wet and a grey afternoon stretched out before me. With nothing better to do, I decided to go through Dad's boxes.

I brought my tea into the spare room and dragged the first box out of the closet. Sitting cross-legged on the floor, I flipped through each of the journals and textbooks. My father's hands had touched these pages. I needed to make sure I hadn't missed a piece of him: a doodle perhaps that I could keep, or a scribbled margin note that might be a critical piece of his research.

By the time I got to the second box, my knees insisted I move up off the floor. I continued my chore sitting on the edge of the bed. The third box held irregular shaped books and pamphlets which, at one time, were neatly bound with elastic bands. The elastics had disintegrated long ago leaving crumbage where they hadn't melded into the paper fibres. The pamphlets' topics ranged from teenage pregnancy to HIV/AIDS. They were the types of pamphlets you could pick up at any doctor's office or hospital. UCSF was stamped on the back.

Other than a tick mark or an underline, I had yet to find a personal note of my father's, and this job was growing old. I removed the last of the scattered pamphlets and uncovered an old Laura Secord chocolate box. My heart jumped a beat—finally, something interesting. I pulled my legs up on the bed and scooted back to sit against the pillows. Lifting off the cream-coloured lid, I gazed down at an odd collection of treasures.

Inside were half a dozen small sea shells that could have come from our beach, but it was hard to tell. Their colouring was more orange and peach than the white and purple that was typical of shells here. I turned each one around in my fingers and tried to think what made them so special that Dad would save them. I put them aside and picked up a miniature cable-car lapel pin. Under that was a small San Francisco Giants pennant mounted on a stick. I sensed a theme to this box of treasures. When I removed the pennant, I found two ticket stubs for a 1984 production of *La Traviata* at the San Francisco Opera.

I retrieved one of the pamphlets and turned it over then opened it up full. UCSF was the acronym for the University of California, San Francisco. Apparently, my father had spent some time in San Francisco in the eighties. How could I not have known that?

The Laura Secord box had a few more items. I picked up a plastic-wrapped cigar with "It's a Boy," embossed on the side in pale blue and a pair of tiny, crocheted booties with blue satin ribbon ties. My father was a pediatrician and often received gifts like these from grateful parents. These must have been very special to him. The last thing in the box was an envelope addressed simply "Brian." It wasn't my mother's writing.

I turned it over in my hand and saw no other marking. The flap was open. I pulled out a single sheet of paper that was folded in three. The texture felt more like linen than paper, as if it had been read and reread many times. Gently, so as not to tear the worn paper, I unfolded the letter and read it.

> *April, 1989*
>
> *I'm writing to let you know that I'm well. It's taken more years than I ever imagined, but I think, at long last, I'm able to start living again.*
>
> *Dr. Scott finally convinced me that you were right, and so it's with a clear heart that I say I'm glad you were able to put our son's death behind you and move on. I regret that I wasn't able to do that with you. The emptiness won't ever go away, nor the pain, but I suspect you already know that.*
>
> *I'm not sure what I expected to find when I came looking for you, but it wasn't a married man with a pregnant wife. Though you always were full of surprises, that one really threw me. You'd reached out to me so often after I left, that a part of me hoped you'd still be waiting. I'm so sorry I waited three years to find you.*
>
> *Mom and Dad still speak of you fondly and Mason misses you. I know they wish you well. As do I. I wish you and Laura all the happiness your hearts can hold and I pray for your little one's safe delivery.*
>
> *Be happy, be well. I love you.*
>
> *Jolene*

I read it twice more before my mind grasped the written words. My heart pumped a steady rhythm and air flowed in and out of my lungs, but time stood still.

Why is it there's never any warning? Out of nowhere an earth-shattering blow strikes, changing your life forever, and no one had the courtesy to warn you. I felt disoriented and clammy.

Jolene knew my father. Minutes ticked by before there was room for another thought in my head.

My father and Jolene had a child together: a child who died. For a brief moment, I felt the weight of a grief that wasn't mine.

My father had lost a son. I'd lost a brother. The urge to cry was stuck behind emotions I couldn't name.

Did my mother know? Maybe his anguish was too personal, too intimate to share with a new spouse. A new and different kind of grief for my father finally brought the tears. How he must have suffered. I hoped he hadn't had to bear the loss all alone—I knew the pain of that burden and the thought broke my heart.

I ran my fingers over the worn paper, no longer able to see the writing through my tears, and clutched it to my chest. Rolling onto my side, I gave in to the overwhelming emotions that rose from the depths of my soul.

When I came to my senses, I sat up in a rush and smoothed the letter, fearful that I'd ruined it. I felt a wash of relief as I examined the paper and found it intact.

Ten long years after Jolene approached me on the beach and I finally knew her connection to me. I wasn't some random stranger after all—it was my father who drew her to me. I still didn't know why she gave me her gift, and maybe I never would, but at least I had this much and that knowledge staggered me.

Now I had a much better understanding of my father's attachment to the seascape painting that hung in his study. He must have thought of Jolene and their son, each time he gazed at it. I felt a similar connection holding Jolene's letter. It was all I had of her. I wanted to hold it close, absorb it through my pores and breathe it deep into my lungs.

Carefully, I placed everything back into the Laura Secord box and carried it to my bedroom where I laid it reverently in the drawer of the bedside table. It seemed fitting to place it there, under the very spot where I kept my favourite photo of my father. I picked up the frame and looked into my dad's face. They were fishing the day my mother took this picture of him. She was expecting me at the time. Did my mother know that I would be his second child? Dad wore a floppy hat covered in fishing lures and a grin that told me he'd been having fun that day. Did his grief intrude on those happy moments?

Conflicting emotions tugged at me as I repacked the journals for recycling. Grief was the easiest one to identify, but there was also an unexpected joy in having found my connection to Jolene. Regret was mixed in there, along with a touch of anger.

It was getting dark. I packed the three boxes into the back seat of the MGB for recycling and pushed the remaining two into the back of the closet. I couldn't handle any more surprises today. What I needed to do was fly. Nothing else would clear my head as thoroughly and help me sort through these swirling emotions.

When it was fully dark, I set the alarm and left the house. I lifted off when I was well south of the cottage and absolutely sure no one was nearby. The lighthouse was again my destination of choice, and I kept my fingers crossed that my luck would hold and Case wouldn't be there.

It looked promising. I couldn't find his vehicle and I didn't see any signs of life around the grounds or through the windows as I drifted up the exterior of the tower. I touched down on the catwalk and looked in the window. How often did Case show up here? I couldn't exactly ask for his schedule, but I wasn't anxious to run into him again either. The coldness he projected would give a polar bear the chills.

With a breath of relief, I turned to face the ocean. The stars were hidden behind clouds tonight. Who would ever have imagined that this is where I'd end up feeling most at ease? Just a few months ago I struggled with the gift and now I was most comfortable when I was high above the madding crowd, alone and basking in the hum of power that shimmered just under my skin.

I sat down and settled against the tower. The tide was in tonight and the constant slap of the waves soothed me. The only thing on my mind was Jolene's letter. It was enough. I thought about me having told David from the security company that I had nothing to steal, but I did now. The letter was the only tangible thing of Jolene's that I had and I wanted to lock it safely away.

How did she meet my father? Had he seen her paintings first and sought her out or had the painting come later? Did he meet her at the university, the hospital, or around town? Had friends had set them up?

Another thought suddenly occurred to me: Did my father know about Fliers? Did Jolene reveal the secret when she became pregnant? Surely it would be within the rules to tell the father of your child, and yet, I didn't know. I didn't even know if the gift would be inherited when only one parent was a Flier. Avery would answer my questions, but not yet. I needed to hold this close to my heart a little bit longer before I shared it with anyone.

Sunk in my thoughts, time slipped by like the wind. When I resurfaced, I stood up and stretched out the kinks. Even without the stars, the night sky was incredible. Up here, I felt invincible.

But the moment I heard the click of a door opening, I realized I'd let that feeling lull me into complacency. Damn!

"Beth?" he said, in a quiet voice.

This would not turn out well. Turning slowly, I saw Case filling the door frame. He stepped toward me, reaching out, with a pained expression on his face.

When he saw my face, he pulled his hand back, but couldn't retract the tear that ran down his cheek. The depth of his emotion was palpable and I couldn't resist the urge to reach out to him. He closed his eyes and leaned his head into my palm. As I pulled away, he caught my wrist.

My heart broke a little bit at the anguish he couldn't hide. Case wasn't cold, he was hurt.

"It's you," he whispered, and then I watched his thought process play across his face as he considered the facts. He looked down to the locked door handle. I knew he'd also be thinking about the other locked door down below and maybe the last time he'd found me out here.

I saw him struggle to make sense of my presence. He was having some difficulty believing the impossible. He narrowed his eyes and stepped closer. "What are you doing here?"

I looked into his face, wondering why he was so despondent, so damaged. "I can't seem to stay away," I said, unable to retreat from his beautiful, sad eyes. "It's so peaceful here."

"How did you get in?" he questioned, holding my wrist firmly.

"The door was unlocked" I said, but this time he wasn't buying my lie.

"No, it wasn't." He was eerily calm. He rattled the door handle. "And this door is still locked, so I'll ask you again, how did you get up here?" He tilted his head to the side and looked at me strangely. "Did Beth send you?"

What? "No, Beth didn't send me," I said, not breaking his gaze.

"You look an awful lot like her."

"I'm sorry about that."

But he wasn't sorry. He pulled me closer with a tug on the wrist he still held. When he felt no resistance, he pulled me into an embrace the likes of which I hadn't felt since Jackson. That thought sent me reeling. I pulled away.

He let me go, but before I was free of him, he reached his hands to my face, leaned in and kissed me. Just a barely there brush of his lips. It was a kiss meant for Beth.

"I've got to go," I said, and bolted for the open floor hatch at the end of the cot. I ran down the staircase sprinting and burst out the main door then into the cover of the trees. He didn't follow.

That tiny little kiss had blown my heart to pieces all over again. I thought I was over the worst of Jackson's mess, but the ache in my heart proved otherwise.

I lifted off as soon as I was out of sight of the lighthouse and shot for home. This was a night for ghosts—first Jolene, then Beth, and now Jackson.

But the surprises weren't over. Flashing lights in the distance were the first sign that something was wrong. I slowed to a hover and saw two cars in my driveway. The police car was the source of the flashing lights. What the hell? It couldn't be the security alarm because I'd hear it shrieking from here, and besides, my phone hadn't gone off. I pulled it from my pocket. I'd put it on vibrate, but a quick glimpse told me it was dead.

Then another thought hit me: What if Case had followed through on his threat and reported me to the police? Crap. I didn't need any more trouble tonight. But there was no way to avoid whatever awaited me down there.

I landed in the park and pulled myself together, then jogged out as if I'd been on my usual evening run. The unmarked car was unoccupied, and it wasn't until I was abreast of the car with the flashing lights, that anyone noticed me. I was close enough to hear crackling voices over the police radio before the constable opened the driver's door.

"Do you live here?" he asked, getting out. He was my age, but baby-faced, so it wasn't anything physical that gave him his air of authority. It was his uniform and the way he held himself: no-nonsense. The gun on his belt helped too.

"Yes. What's going on?"

"May I see some ID?" He was firm but polite. Even so, I couldn't help him. All I had was my phone and my house key.

"I don't have any on me. It's in the house."

"May I?" he asked, reaching for the phone. I handed it to him. "Dead?"

"Unfortunately. Was it the security alarm?" Two men came around the side of the house just as a Prime Security car pulled in behind the unmarked police car. So it *was* the alarm, and now that I thought about it, I'd been distracted when I left the house and hadn't remembered to turn off the attic sensor.

I recognized Constable Tao Wong as one of the two men who approached us from the house. He had a broad face, short dark hair and dark eyes. Constable Wong was one of the police constables who drove me home from the hospital when I gave myself a concussion in an inept attempt to control my floating. That was a while ago—before I knew what the gift was. I didn't know his partner or the man from Prime Security. We all met in the red and white flash of the cruiser's lights.

"Ms. Taylor," Constable Wong said, greeting me as he offered his hand. "Your security alarm was tripped."

"Stanley Dobrowski," said Prime Security man, introducing himself. Stanley was a compact man, small but sturdy with thinning brown hair. He brimmed with nervous energy, as if the flashing lights and uniforms were the highlight of his night.

"There's no sign of forced entry," Constable Wong reported. "Can you identify which sensor was tripped?"

"The attic," Stanley replied and looked to me. "We have a report on file that you've had a rodent problem in that area?"

"I did, but the exterminators were here on Saturday." What I didn't say was that I'd forgotten to turn off the attic sensor when I set the alarm. All this fuss was the result of my mistake. It was embarrassing.

"I can check it," Stanley offered. "Is the house still locked?"

"I think so," I said, looking to Constable Wong who just nodded. I offered Stanley the key. He took it and started toward the house.

"You'll need to disarm it once we open the door," he said, over his shoulder.

Stanley opened the door and Constable Wong stepped inside ahead of us. I followed and entered the code to disarm the alarm. Stanley followed, but the other two men, whom I'd not been introduced to, stayed on the porch.

"Where's the attic access?" Constable Wong said, barring my way.

"There's a hatch in the bedroom closet," I said, pointing toward the front of the house. "The room to the right."

"Please wait outside," Constable Wong said and I didn't argue. I joined the two men outside and felt the awkwardness that a lack of introductions fostered.

"I'm Emelynn," I said, holding out my hand to the constable I had met first.

"Constable Nicholas Craft," he said, shaking my hand. Constable Craft looked like the kind of male hired to make up for all the large, tough-looking men on the police force. His pale skin and rounded face looked innocent, uninitiated.

"Detective Samuel Jordan," said the other man. This man represented the initiated. His handshake made no allowances for my slender fingers and his deep voice cut through any suggestion of casualness. He stood six two, but his military brush-cut gave him that second inch. I pegged him at mid- to late-thirties, but his hair was speckled with grey, which made me think that maybe he was older than he looked.

Neither man was inclined to make small talk, so we stood in silence, awaiting the results of the attic search. It didn't take long. Stanley and Constable Wong walked down the hall, unrushed and talking quietly. Evidently, this wasn't an emergency.

"All clear," Constable Wong reported.

Stanley approached me. "I would recommend you leave the attic sensor off until the exterminators are done. I know it's reasonable to think that after four days all the squirrels would be gone, but my guess is they have a stash of food up there somewhere and it's delaying their departure."

"Thanks for checking it out." I shook Stanley's hand. "Why didn't I hear the alarm tonight?" I asked, curious.

"Head office silenced it."

"I didn't know they could do that."

"The police are contacted automatically whenever an alarm isn't disarmed by the homeowner, but as soon as the police give us the okay, we silence it remotely—don't want to disturb the neighbours any more than necessary."

I nodded and thanked Stanley again.

"Glad I could help," he said, then turned and headed to his car.

"I'll start the paperwork," Constable Craft said, making his exit.

Constable Wong introduced me to Detective Samuel Jordan.

"We met when you were inside," I said. "Nice to meet you, Detective."

"Detective Jordan is investigating the disappearance of Charles and Gabby Wright."

I felt a flare of panic and knew my surprise had registered on my face. Normally, I was good at covering. It was a necessity when lying, and I had a lot of experience with lying, but it took me a second to get my game face on.

"I understand your family had a lengthy relationship with the Wrights." Detective Jordan made the statement sound like a question.

"Yes, my mother hired them ten years ago, when we moved to Toronto. They've been taking care of the place ever since."

"Did your family socialize with the Wrights?"

"No. I only met them after I returned here in May. Are there any new leads in the case?"

"It's ongoing." The detective reached into his inside jacket pocket for a pad, and I caught a glimpse of the butt end of a gun in a shoulder holster under his left arm. "Did I see you coming out of the park tonight, Ms. Taylor?"

I hadn't thought he'd seen me until I was beside the cruiser, so he'd surprised me again. "Yes."

"Do you mind me asking what you were doing in the park?"

I looked down at my yoga pants and hoodie thinking the outfit was self-explanatory. The shoes weren't right, but I had been going for black, not functional. "I went for a run."

"At this hour?"

I shrugged.

The detective frowned. "How do you manage in the dark?"

I didn't like the undertone to the detective's questions, but he had a point. "I know the park really well."

"Yes, you must," he said, raising one eyebrow to let me know he wasn't convinced.

"You're the young woman who had a serious accident in that park about six weeks ago?" He touched a thick finger to the tip of his tongue and flipped back through his notes. "May 17?"

"Yes, that was me."

"Do you like tempting fate, Ms. Taylor?"

Now he was pissing me off. "You think I should be afraid?"

"No. I think you could be more careful."

"Pardon me?"

"Light-coloured clothing for a start. A headlamp wouldn't be a stretch and a functioning cellphone is a no-brainer."

Did he just call me an idiot? If he wasn't so intimidating—and so right—I would have jumped all over that, but how could I? I'd probably think the same thing if I were in his boots. I wouldn't have phrased it quite that way, but I'd be thinking it. I stood there looking as close to contrite as I could.

"I'll be making the rounds and re-interviewing each of the Wrights' contacts. Will you be available to answer some questions?"

"Of course." As if I'd say no.

"Good. I'll be in touch." The detective nodded to me and turned to go.

Constable Wong tipped his hat. "Good night, Ms. Taylor," he said, and started down the steps.

Constable Wong joined Constable Craft, who had turned off the flashers. The detective pulled his unmarked car around the other one and made the loop back to Cliffside. I watched until both cars were out of sight then closed and locked the door.

Detective Jordan came off like a dog with a bone. Unfortunately, the Wrights' disappearance was his bone de jour and that made me very uncomfortable.

Chapter Twelve

Disturbing dreams haunted my sleep, and I woke tired. I rolled over and looked outside. It was overcast again but at least I didn't hear the patter of rain. My father's happy face looked out at me from under his silly fishing hat, his grin forever stuck inside the confines of a photo frame. I opened the bedside drawer and pulled out the Laura Secord box. Scooting up so my back rested against the pillows, I opened the lid and lifted out Jolene's letter. I read it again, touching the ink as if that would substitute for touching her. Her letter didn't provoke tears today, which was a blessing.

Malcolm would be here soon. The box went back in the drawer with Jolene's letter on top. I made coffee and ate a bowl of Cheerios while reading my emails. Eden sent me fair warning that she was going to call after she slept off her night shift and Molly sent a screen full of question marks. Funny girl.

Malcolm and I had both dressed with an extra layer for the run today. He caught me looking at him halfway through our warm-up.

"What?" he asked.

"You're always the same, Malcolm: quiet, content, serene. How do you do it?"

He gave me that smile that lit up his whole face. "I make a choice each day. This is what I choose."

"You make it sound so easy."

"It wasn't always, but I've worked at it."

His answer begged so many questions that I didn't know him well enough to ask.

Malcolm set the pace at a slow jog as we headed into the park. We interspersed our hour-long run with sprints and jogging. As we finished our cool-down on the lawn of the cottage, Detective Jordan pulled into the driveway and drove up to the top of the loop at the house.

"Do you know him?" Malcolm asked softly, wary of the big man who got out of his car and approached us.

"Sadly, yes." Detective Jordan was wearing the same jacket he wore last night and now that I knew it was there, the bulge under his left arm told me his gun was in its holster.

"Detective Jordan," I said, offering my hand. "This is Malcolm Perreault."

Detective Jordan's dark eyes looked too small under the heavy brows in his broad face. The detective nodded and shook my hand, then Malcolm's. "You were running again?"

"Yes." I hoped he didn't make a big deal out of it in front of Malcolm.

"You training for something?"

"Not particularly," I said, and then, thankfully, Malcolm made his exit.

"I'll see you tomorrow, Emelynn. Detective." He nodded warily then turned toward his bike.

As Malcolm pedaled down the driveway, I turned to the detective. "Would you like to come inside?"

"Yes."

Not "Yes, thank you," or "Yes, that would be nice," just "Yes,"—like the invitation was an expectation. I supposed that neither gruff nor direct would be out of character from what I saw of him last night.

He followed me inside and down the hall to the kitchen. After he declined my offer of orange juice, I poured myself a glass then joined him at the dining-room table.

He pulled the small notepad out of his jacket pocket and flipped through his notes. "When did you last see the Wrights?" he asked, diving right in. Something told me it was not good to be stumped on his very first question.

"I didn't make note of it and I'm afraid I've thrown out their schedule. I'm sure it's in the record. Constable Wong took a lot of notes when he was here investigating their disappearance two months ago."

He frowned at that, but I couldn't help him. "Do you remember the first date that they missed?"

I shrugged and shook my head. "No. It would have been on their schedule, but like I said, I threw it out."

"This schedule you had—what length of time did it cover?"

"A year, I think. Maybe six months. I don't remember."

He flipped another page and glanced at his notes. "They worked for your family for, what, ten years?"

"Yes," I said, relieved to finally have an answer. The relief was short-lived.

"Then how could you not know the period of time their schedules covered?"

His tone held an edge of accusation. "I've only seen the one schedule. They may have sent others to my mother in Toronto, but I never saw them." Did I sound as defensive to him as I did to myself?

"It seems strange to me that you've thrown it out already, like you don't expect them to come back."

This conversation was not going well. "I guess I like to keep the place tidy. When they come back, they'll make up a new schedule."

He sat back, narrowing his eyes as if contemplating another line of questioning. He made me nervous, but at least that kept me on my toes. "Have you made many friends since you returned?"

"A few. Why?"

"Have any of your new friends had contact with the Wrights?"

"Cheney Meyer is the only one who might have. He's the son of a friend of theirs, Jack Meyer. I'm sure it's in the file."

The name didn't surprise him. He didn't even check his notes. "Yes, I've already met with the Meyers."

"That's the only connection I can think of," I said, in my most helpful tone.

He flipped his notepad closed and put it away. It looked like the detective had run out of angles—for today, anyway. "I'll be in touch if something else comes up."

I followed him to the door. His broad shoulders filled the hallway, and I had no doubt that the bulk beneath his jacket was a solid mass of muscle. I felt very small and fragile in his wake. Maybe if I ignored him he'd go away, but somehow I doubted that. His questions had had an accusatory quality to them. I'd have loved to have known what he was thinking, but I wanted him out of the house more than I wanted to know his thoughts.

When he was safely out of the driveway, I showered and dressed. I wanted to see a friendly face. The MGB started in a cloud of exhaust, which it did with embarrassing regularity, and I pointed it toward Rumbles. It was nearly noon and the lunch crowd lineup hadn't yet hit Dimitri's. I ordered two Reubens to go, picked up two coffees and then headed over to see Molly. The store was empty, as usual.

"Oh, goody," she said, and I could tell by her tone that it wasn't because I had two coffees in my hands. "Give me the scoop. How'd it go with Dean?"

"Don't you want lunch first?" I asked, holding up the paper bag emblazoned with the Dimitri's Deli logo.

"No," she said, annoyed.

"Coffee then?"

"Come on . . . I'm dying over here. What did he say?"

"We're going out Friday. Happy?"

"Delirious. Now I'll have my coffee."

We sipped the heavenly brew in our usual spot, lounging in the wing-backed chairs closest to the front of the store. She unwrapped her sandwich like it was a Christmas gift while I filled her in on the detail: there was only one.

"I've never been in the dining room at Fast Eddies, but I've looked at their menu. They do the whole white-tablecloth and cutlery thing, but the food's only one step up from a pub."

"Not two?" I said, teasing, knowing how much she loved trying out different restaurants.

"No. Two steps is the Seafood House. Three steps take you into fine dining territory and Fast Eddies is definitely not that."

"Good to know." I agreed to give her a detailed meal description, if nothing else, after my date. She didn't like the *if nothing else* part.

The house seemed quiet when I returned. I put some laundry in and flicked the flat screen to life.

Eden called, as promised, and blew right past *how are you* niceties. She didn't even pretend to be interested in anything other than Dean. In fact, she was worse than Avery with the questions. "What's he like? How'd you meet him? Where are you going on your date?" She was relentless. It would have been annoying if she weren't so funny about it. "Granny underwear and a utility bra." This was her idea of the next best thing to a chastity belt.

We hung up, and I turned to BBC World News. I let it flash across the screen like background music to my thoughts.

Avery needed to know what was happening with Detective Jordan. I'd tell him tomorrow, but I hadn't yet made a decision about Jolene's letter. I went to the bedroom and read it again before tucking it safely away. It's not like I expected the words to change, but I felt this need to touch it. Something about that letter made me want to hold it close. I knew it was irrational, but I wasn't ready to share it yet. I would though. I'd share it with Avery because he deserved to know. He'd be hurt if I kept something this significant from him.

Thursday dawned bright and warmed up quickly. It looked like August was back on track. The tide was high. I walked my coffee down to the water's edge and let the cool water wash over my flip-flops.

I savoured these moments. September encroached, and it would be the first time since kindergarten that I wasn't headed back to school. My mother's graduation gift wouldn't last forever, and I felt the first real pull to get serious about finding work.

Later that morning, while Malcolm put me through my paces at the Y, he talked to me about the benefits of boxing training. Given his gentle temperament, the boxing component threw me.

"You're already doing most of it anyway. We'd have to change up your cardio to include rope work and ramp up your core and upper body training, but it wouldn't take much."

"I don't know, Malcolm. Punching people seems so barbaric."

Malcolm laughed. "It might look that way from the outside, but it's really more about reading body language and outsmarting your opponent. Tony's our boxing coach. He's good—got a way about him. He'll teach you the proper stance and show you how to throw a punch. How to take one."

"I don't have what it takes to throw a punch."

"It's really no different than the self-defence class you took. Ideally, you want to avoid getting hit, but if you can't, you need to be able to defend yourself." A smirk tugged at his mouth. The similarities were scant, at best. "You'll like the strength and speed you'll gain with the training, even if you never step into the ring."

I promised to think about it.

"That's all I ask."

We organized our run time for tomorrow and I headed home to shower and get ready for my appointment with Avery.

Avery had been in my thoughts all morning. I felt the weight of Jolene's letter in my purse as I opened the door to his waiting room. We usually worked in his back garden on Thursdays. I carried on through the waiting room, calling out his name.

"In here," he replied.

"Here" was the kitchen. A short hallway stacked high with cupboards lined either side of the entryway. The round table that sat in front of French doors was old polished oak; a table that had seen many meals. I found Avery standing behind the island to my right. The business side of the kitchen spread out behind him and from where he stood, he could look out over the kitchen table and beyond to the small back garden.

"Hi. I'll just be a minute," he said. He shifted his shoulders from the sink to the space on his right and hunched down behind the island where I knew the dishwasher resided.

"Take your time." I took a seat and made myself at home as had become my habit in Avery's kitchen. I pulled Jolene's letter from my purse and kept it safe between my hands and the table.

"Greg's making arrangements to come up this weekend," Avery said. "He doesn't know how long he's going to stay so I don't know if he'll get an opportunity to meet the covey, but I hope so." Avery turned off the faucet and disappeared behind the island. He resurfaced snapping the lid on a jug of dishwasher detergent. "He was going to book a hotel, but I offered my guest room. I feel like I know the guy even though I've never met him. Sure hope that's not a mistake." He closed the dishwasher door and turned it on.

My attention drifted back to the envelope under my hand.

"You're awfully quiet," he said, startling me. He stood next to me drying his hands on the corner of a hand towel he had draped over his shoulder.

"Oh, sorry—I'm a bit distracted."

"I can see that," he said, taking a seat beside me.

I felt like my time had run out. I had to serve up Jolene's letter, and I didn't want to.

"What's that?" he asked, spotting the envelope. The white paper stood out against the dark wood like a harvest moon on a dark night.

He caught my eye and I couldn't hide my apprehension.

"What is it? You look like you're hiding bad news."

I smoothed the envelope with my hand and ran my fingers over my father's hand-written name. "I found something."

"Oh?"

"It's a letter to my father." I felt Avery's eyes search my face for clues. "It was in one of the boxes Alex found in my attic."

I looked up. "I think I know why Jolene chose me." I took a breath and slid the envelope over to him.

He took it then reached out to squeeze my empty hand. I watched him read my father's name.

"Are you sure you want me to read this?"

"Am I that obvious?"

"You look like you're giving away your first born."

I forced a smile. "I don't mean to. Please," I said, motioning to the envelope.

He turned his attention to it, flipped it over and slid the letter out from under the flap.

My phone rang and I jumped. Later, Molly, I thought, seeing her name on the display. I let it go to voice mail.

Avery sought my gaze. I nodded, giving him permission to continue.

I watched his expression as he read and recognized the emotions that swam across his face as he hit each of the highlights: surprise, shock, and finally bewilderment. He set it down, staring at the worn paper.

"You didn't know?"

"No."

"That's a hell of a lot to digest," he said, finally looking at me.

"Yeah."

He stood and walked to the door that led to the garden and pushed it open. "Let's get some air," he said, stepping through and leaving it open for me to follow.

I walked to the far edge of the deck and sat beside him with my feet on the step. The scent of freshly mown grass sweetened the air.

"Do you think my father knew about our kind?"

"Yes."

"No hesitation?"

"None." He stretched his legs and moved his feet from the step to the paver below. "Could you hide your gift from someone you loved?"

"To protect them I could," I said.

"She *was* protecting them. Jolene was a Ghost. Her child would have been one as well. She would have needed your father's support to keep the child safe."

My dad knowing about us was one more thing I'd never imagined. The letter was its own little Advent calendar—a new surprise every day.

"Do you know for certain their son would have inherited the gift?"

"Yes. The Flier gene has complete dominance. It manifests in off-spring even if only one parent carries the gene. If both parents carry the gene, the skill set of the offspring can be any combination of the two."

"He would have been my big brother and I don't even know what his name was."

Avery wrapped his arm around me and drew me into his shoulder. "I'm sorry, Em."

"Me, too. I can't even bring myself to call him my *half*-brother. Somehow the *half* diminishes him."

"Did you find anything else?"

"Some mementos from San Francisco. There are still two boxes I haven't gone through."

"Maybe you'll find some answers in them."

"I'm not sure I can take any more *answers*."

He squeezed my arm.

"Oh, I almost forgot. I had a visit from a new detective working Charles and Gabby Wright's disappearance."

"Oh?"

"His name's Samuel Jordan and he asks a lot of questions."

"Wouldn't that be his job?"

"I think he likes his job a little too much. He hasn't accused me of anything outright, but he seems suspicious."

"You didn't do anything wrong, Em."

"No, but I didn't exactly help the investigation."

"And you can't. The detective can be as suspicious as he wants, but you don't know anything so you can't help him—right?"

"Yes, I know. It's just a bit unnerving."

"Nothing you can't handle. And the Tribunal won't have left any loose ends for you to trip over. You don't have anything to fret about."

I did though. Alex involved the Tribunal when Eden recognized the man caught retrieving the images from his surveillance camera. Days earlier, the same man had been to her ER with a less-than-compelling injury. Alex made no apologies for protecting her, and so he shouldn't.

Before the Tribunal arrived on the scene, we learned that Charles had been studying Fliers as if we were some genus of exotic bird. He had photos of Eden as well as other Fliers, some going back ten years, and he'd cross-referenced the photos to a map. They also found a research paper of his that would have exposed us and made him a fortune.

Charles thought he was on the verge of a discovery not unlike finding a lost Amazonian tribe.

Unfortunately, when the Tribunal arrived, they shut us out. We never did learn if anyone else had been involved. The Tribunal shares neither how it takes care of the problem nor the intel it gathers during the cleanup. Avery reasoned that the Tribunal's behaviour provided us with plausible deniability. That it kept their mystique alive and fed our fear of them was just a happy bonus.

Avery and I never did get around to working on my gift, and if he hadn't reminded me about owing the men's team a beer, I'd have forgotten about the covey's plan to meet at Clam Diggers tonight.

On my way home from Avery's, I picked up some comfort food at the Safeway. A few chewy chocolate chip cookies with a big cup of tea would help me bury my worries.

At least that was the plan, but no one told Detective Jordan. He awaited me like a bad omen, leaning against his brown unmarked cruiser as if he had all day and not a care in the world.

I got out of the car and then reached back to grab the Safeway bag and my purse. "Detective Jordan," I said, as I approached. "I didn't think I'd see you again so soon."

"A few questions came to mind. Thought I'd clear them up. Do you have a few minutes?"

"Sure." What was I supposed to say? No? Nothing says guilty like not answering the good detective's questions. "Come in."

We headed to the kitchen and I put the kettle on. I offered him tea because it was the polite thing to do.

"You have a few questions?" I prompted. The sooner we had this conversation, the sooner he'd be gone. He had taken a seat at the table and had his notepad out, pen poised.

"Where do you work, Ms. Taylor?"

"I'm not working right now."

"Lucky girl."

Sarcasm . . . really? "I just finished school, Detective. I haven't found work yet."

"Then you've been looking?"

"I will."

"But not yet."

I raised an eyebrow, taken aback. Even my mother, who was footing my bills, hadn't been this pushy.

"I don't mean to be uncooperative, Detective, but how does my work situation concern this case?"

"Did you know, of all the Wrights' friends and associates, your family had the longest connection to them?"

"No, but again, why the interest in my employment status?"

"I'm just being thorough. Money has a tendency to be a motivator. Where does your money come from, Ms. Taylor?"

Oh crap. Did he know about the reward? Did it matter if he did? I stalled while I thought that through. "My mother's graduation gift was six months of living expenses. That's where my money comes from." It wasn't a lie. I hadn't yet spent the reward money, unless you counted the fact that I'd distributed a share of it to Eden, Alex and Danny.

"As I said—lucky girl."

"Is there anything else?" I asked, peeved by his sarcasm.

"Just one other thing: What's your connection to Jackson Delaney?"

I flinched. There was no way to be prepared for that one and I couldn't hide my reaction. I turned my head to the whistle of the kettle, thankful for the distraction. "I don't have a relationship with Jackson Delaney." I excused myself, walked to the kitchen and poured boiling water in my tea cup, keeping my back to the detective.

"But you did."

I pulled the cutlery drawer open and reached for a teaspoon. "I knew him. It was a while ago." I felt myself withdraw, like I always did when that little ache started up around my heart.

"Molly Connolly thought you were seeing him around the time that the Wrights disappeared."

"Molly?" Oh, no. My heart sank.

"Yes, the girl you ate lunch with yesterday."

"You followed me?" The words didn't have the indignant bite they should have. The ache eclipsed my anger.

"As I said earlier—I'm thorough."

I went on autopilot: stirring the tea, removing the tea bag, getting the milk from the fridge, pouring it into the tea. I lifted the cup to my mouth, inhaled the aroma and took that first too-hot sip.

"Mr. Delaney has money, Ms. Taylor, and as I've already mentioned, money's a motivator. Did Mr. Delaney know the Wrights?"

Bloody hell! I put my game face on and turned to look at him. "Not to my knowledge, but perhaps you should ask him." I barely kept my ire under wraps. "I believe you'll find him in New Orleans."

"Yes. As a matter of fact, I believe he lives there—with his *wife*."

There's nothing quite as effective as someone trying to make you feel like a piece of shit to shake your anger free. A dead smile crept across my face. "Well, that is where they live, Detective. Is there anything else?" I wanted this Neanderthal out of my house.

"Did his wife know about your relationship?"

Relationship? Damn it! Molly must have told him. How else would he know? But why was it important? I couldn't connect the dots. "Again, Detective, I don't read minds. You'll have to ask her."

"Did the Wrights know?"

How the hell would Charles and Gabby have known? And even if they had, how did it figure in to their disappearance? I studied the detective's smug face as I rolled his question around in my mind.

Abruptly, the dots aligned. Samuel Jordan had played his trump card. He thought Jackson got rid of the Wrights because they knew about our affair. If only he knew how fucking far off track he was. Yet if the clever detective had a winning hand, why had he tipped it to me? Did he think I'd fold and fess up to murder?

"I'll be sure to ask them next time I see them," I said calmly. I refused to let him see that he'd rattled me.

He studied me with frightening intensity and then snapped his notepad closed. He took his time putting it and his pen away, flashing his gun in the process.

"I'll show you out." It was the edge of rude, but he'd used up all my politeness. He stood and I ushered him down the hall and out the front door.

"Thank you for your time, Ms. Taylor."

I couldn't muster words, just nodded my head and shut the door as soon as he was clear of the door frame.

Then I got as far away from him as I could, taking my tea to the deck at the other end of the house. The change of scenery helped me think.

How difficult would it be to prove the detective's assumption? Would he be watching me, hoping my actions would confirm his theory? Maybe that's why he'd tipped his hand. If I were guilty, I'd probably send Jackson a warning. Had the detective tapped my phone? Maybe he could trace my emails? He'd followed me to Rumbles—how long had he been tailing me?

God, I hated this guessing game. If the detective so willingly tipped this hand, how many other trump cards did he hold close to his chest? Just what did he know and how?

And then a more frightening thought crossed my mind: Was the detective an agent of those powerful forces Jackson had alluded to? Did he know about Fliers? Had he caught a whiff of something that he thought might lead to our discovery?

I felt powerless. Or was I being paranoid? Either way, the only thing I could do was carry on as if his comments did nothing more than offend me. I just hoped the Tribunal was as good as Avery said. This was not the time for a loose end.

And poor Molly—what must she think? I pulled out my phone and listened to her message. She'd been frantic. "It's me. Call me the minute you get this message. The police were just here asking all kinds of questions. It sounded serious. Call me."

I dialled and she picked right up. "Emelynn, where have you been? I left you a message two hours ago."

"I know. I'm sorry. I just picked it up now."

"What's going on?"

"Detective Jordan was here. He's investigating the Wrights' disappearance."

"I know, but why were they asking *me* about it?"

"I don't know, but he knew we'd had lunch together yesterday. He followed me. When did he talk to you?"

"This morning. He came into Rumbles and asked about your friends. I had to tell him about Jackson, Em. I'm sorry."

"You don't need to apologize. You just told the truth." I sighed, wishing she hadn't been quite so honest. "It's embarrassing, but it's not a motive for anything more than making me feel like trash."

"He made it sound like I was covering something up for you and Jackson. What the hell is that all about?"

"I don't know. He tried to make me feel guilty too—as if Jackson or I had something to do with the Wrights' disappearance."

"He did the same thing with Cheney's dad—tried to turn Jack's friendship with Charles into some kind of rivalry. Jack was furious."

Suddenly it all made sense. "I think you've figured it out, Molly."

"I have?"

"The detective—he's shaking the tree." It was so obvious now. I wanted to feel relieved, but with so many unanswered questions, I didn't dare, not yet.

"You're right," Molly said after a moment's silence. "That's exactly what he's doing. He's probably watching to see if any of us do something incriminating."

"You can't do anything incriminating if you haven't done anything wrong. I'm sorry you've gotten pulled into this mess."

"It's not your fault. If anyone's to blame it's the Wrights. Oh god, unless they really are dead. I don't even want to think about that."

And then we were right back to the lie. "Me neither," I said. "I hope they come back soon." And that was for Detective Jordan if he was listening in.

Chapter Thirteen

Clam Diggers called itself an old neighbourhood pub and its facade fit the description, or at least the *old* part did. It was a large, rambling, two-storey house—probably the area's original homestead. Homes like this were built in an age when acres rather than metres separated properties. I'd bet it had been converted to a business decades ago when the surrounding land was parcelled off and sold for building lots.

The front door opened into a wide vestibule. A console table sat against the right side. On the wall above the table hung a large chalkboard that proclaimed Clam Diggers had been serving the best chowder on the west coast for twenty-five years. Maybe, but that would have been long before tourists found the neighbourhood.

One step through the inside door and I could see that the owners had never bowed to pressure, tourist or otherwise, to re-model along more trendy lines. The bar was hopping, so I guessed the worn décor didn't hinder their business. Fish netting hung from the ceiling in billows to give a seaside ambience to the place, but both the net and the effect was old and dusty. The original net floats and dehydrated starfish that were strategically set in the netting were now joined by baseball caps and beer coasters. Would Molly rate the place at or below the pub step? In either case, I was glad I'd dressed casually in basic jeans and a T-shirt.

I spotted Gabe's grey hair like a beacon outside on the deck. No wonder he covered it when he flew. The covey had pushed two tables together in the corner and Deidra was speaking as I approached, "—he just kept repeating it. I thought I would die of embarrassment." She turned to me. "My youngest son. He's discovered the power of cussing, I'm afraid." Deidra's strawberry blonde hair curled neatly under where it brushed the top of her shoulders.

I took a seat beside her at the end of the table and said hello to everyone. Two jugs of draft were on the table, one at either end, and half a dozen glasses stood upside down on a tray in the centre. Avery and Victoria sat side-by-side close to Gabe at the far end of the table. Victoria had a glass of wine.

"I didn't know you had children," I said to Deidra.

She nodded. "Two sons, Nathan's six and Charlie is four. Charlie's the cusser." She took a sip of beer.

It struck me then that I hadn't considered children before in relation to the covey. And thinking of it now, I realized the covey didn't have elderly Fliers either. I asked Deidra, "At what point are children included in the covey?"

At first, Deidra looked perplexed by my question but her confusion faded quickly. "Of course—how would you know? Children can join the covey when they're eighteen, or at sixteen with their parents' consent."

"What about your husband?"

"When Nathan was born, Joe and I decided that one of us would opt out of the covey to stay with the kids. It's a little insurance in case the covey is ever compromised."

"What about elderly Fliers?" I asked and nodded hello to Steve who took a seat beside Gabe and poured himself a draft.

"Well, as you know, one of the covey's main functions is protection. So if a Flier, elderly or otherwise, decides they can no longer physically contribute, they can step aside. They're still covey and we'll protect them, but they don't attend covey meetings. It's safer for them. Thankfully, this covey hasn't seen much action. It's one of the reasons we live here."

"There's still so much I don't know."

Deidra reached over and patted my hand reassuringly. "I'm sure, but we're all here to help."

I smiled my appreciation and looked over the table. Most of the beer glasses were nearly full, so I hadn't missed much. Eden and Alex weren't here yet. I knew Eden would be anxious to hear about my plans with Dean when she arrived.

Danny touched my shoulder and took the seat to my left. "Beer?" he asked, reaching for a jug of draft.

"No, but thanks. I'll get a cider," I said, as he poured himself a glass. "You cut your hair." Danny's dreads used to touch his shoulders and now they were half that length and sticking out all over.

He shook his head of springy spikes and they danced. "You like?"

"I like." I smiled back at him. "I'll be just a minute." It looked like it would be faster to go to the bar than wait for table service.

Kate sat opposite Danny and reached for my hand as I turned to get up. Her shiny bobbed hair swung away from her face. "The guys decided that each of the women should buy a jug of draft to pay off our bet, so if you're going to the bar, get another jug would you?"

"Sure," I said, and headed inside. I ordered the drinks before I noticed Sydney talking to a woman at the end of the bar. She must have bumped into a friend. Sydney was engrossed in their conversation and didn't notice me. Nor did she seem to notice the admiring glances of the men close by.

Sydney spotted me just as my drinks arrived and nodded. I paid up and headed out to the deck holding the bottle of cider in one hand and the heavy jug of beer in the other. I held the jug away from me, afraid that I'd trip and spill it on myself.

But it wasn't a misstep that made me spill it. The sensation of a spider crawling across my shoulders caused me to shiver. It was exactly the sensation I'd felt at Fast Eddies. I rushed to our table to deliver the jug before I spilled more, then brushed off my shoulders. But my shoulders weren't bare. It couldn't have been a spider. What the hell was giving me the creepy crawlies?

I sat down and took a long drink of cider. Eden and Alex approached from behind and greeted the others. Deidra and Kate moved down closer to Victoria to make room for them to scoot in to my right.

As Eden settled herself, she bent down to my ear. "So? Do you have a date?"

"Friday," I said, grinning like a fool. Eden squeezed my shoulders then took a seat beside Kate.

"Hey, Em," Alex said, reaching down the table to snag two glasses. Kate picked up the closest jug and filled them, explaining the women's jug-debt to Eden as she did. Just then a waitress dropped two huge plates of nachos and a stack of napkins on the table. We descended on the mess like vultures, stretching cheese and dropping olives.

It was impossible to be dainty. I wiped a napkin across my chin and felt that strange crawling sensation across my shoulders again. This time

I scrunched my shoulders and tilted my head back, puckering the skin at the top of my spine and between my shoulder blades, but the sensation didn't dissipate, it changed. The creeping spider crawl morphed into what felt more like fingertips tracing a warm line from my right shoulder to my left. I twisted around in my seat fully expecting to find someone behind me.

"What is it?" Eden asked.

"I don't know." I rolled my head in a wide arc to loosen the sensation and after a moment it drained away. I half-smiled, feeling a little shaken. Was my anxiety finding a new outlet? Maybe I was on my way to developing a tic like the Chief Inspector in the old *Pink Panther* movies.

Sydney came to the table and pulled a chair between Danny and Steve. Danny stood and offered a toast. "Losers," he started. "Oh, sorry, I meant to say, ladies, thanks for losing . . . err . . . I mean, thanks for the beer."

Deidra threw an olive at his head, making him duck and slosh his beer. The table burst into laughter and Danny sat down but held out his hands to keep our attention.

"Next time we play, how about we change venue? The paintball park is a great space, but we're all too familiar with it now. We need a new space—somewhere that will challenge us."

Kate spoke up. "It might be fun to use the Allandale Fairgrounds."

"Don't they have after-hours security?" asked Alex.

"How about the park out by Emelynn's place? There's no security there," Danny said.

"What do you think?" Avery asked, looking at me from the far end of the table.

"It could work," I said. "I've flown there at night and hardly anyone uses it after eleven or so."

Avery nodded his agreement as another jug of draft was delivered. "I'll set up something for next week then. We'll give it a try."

The nachos got picked away to a scattering of bare chips that no longer looked appetizing. The last two jugs of beer were half full when the larger group conversation broke up into smaller ones around the table and I took the opportunity to pull Eden and Alex aside to tell them about Detective Jordan.

"He seems to know a lot of personal stuff about you, Em. Are you sure he's legit?" Eden asked, wide-eyed.

"He must be; it was a police constable who introduced us. But I should warn everyone. He's already followed me once. The covey needs to be prepared in case he follows and questions anyone else." I paused, putting my apprehension into words. "But I don't want everyone to know about me and Jackson. It's humiliating."

Eden looked to Alex and then back to me, nodding her head with a sympathetic expression. "I think we can do that. I'll tell Kate and Deidra." They were sitting to Eden's right.

Alex pushed his chair back. "I was going to say hello to Gabe anyway. I'll spread the word up there. You said the guy's name was Samuel Jordan?"

"Yes. I'll tell the others," I said. Eden filled her beer glass and turned her back to me, calling Kate's name.

Danny, Sydney and Steve took the news well. "We can handle it," Steve said, comfortably speaking for the three of them.

"If he's shaking the tree, he won't find anything falling from us," Danny said.

"We stick together, Emelynn," Sydney said, sounding as confident as she looked, putting her arm around Danny's shoulder.

They really were just like family. I knew it wasn't my fault that Charles used my property to set up his camera, but I still felt like I was responsible for this whole mess. Eden carried some of that guilt too. She was the only other one who Charles had singled out for a personal visit. How long would it be before the police declared them dead or did whatever else they had to do in order to close the case?

Alex and Victoria came back to our end of the table and Alex leaned down close to my ear. "Gabe wants to talk to you." He settled in beside Eden and I gave Victoria my seat. I brought the cider that I'd been nursing and shuffled in behind Gabe and Avery, taking the chair Victoria had vacated.

Gabe leaned across Avery. "This detective sounds like he could become a problem, Emelynn."

"I really don't think he has anything. He's fishing—I'm almost sure of it."

"Could be. I'll see what I can find out about him," Gabe offered.

"You can do that?"

"I have some connections in law enforcement."

"Do you think there's more to him than he lets on?" I didn't want to put voice to what were surely paranoid thoughts.

"No, but more info won't hurt. Just don't forget what he is. He's a trained observer. He'll see things in your reactions that you don't mean to give away and he can use all of that against you. He doesn't need much more than suspicion to charge you—take you in for questioning."

"What good would that do?"

"He might think he could scare something out of you."

"Well, if it's the truth he scares out of me, I'll be headed to the funny farm, not jail."

Gabe smirked and shook his head. "Just be careful. He's under a lot of pressure to solve this case and make an arrest. If you don't like the direction his questions are going, stall him and call me." Gabe handed me a business card. "I can help."

"Thanks, Gabe." I looked over to Avery. He wore the strain of his emotions on his face, and I felt the weight of his worry. Most of the time I thought of him as a father, but sometimes I saw the person behind that persona and that's when I felt like I took advantage of his kindness.

"I'm sorry, Avery. I know I'm always bringing crap to the table and imposing on the covey. I wanted to be a help, not a burden."

"Emelynn, that's not what I'm thinking at all. You *are* a help. You went out on a limb to help Sandra. Everyone in this covey knows that and we have no doubt you'd do it again for any one of us. I'm just sorry you've been put in the position of dealing with the *crap* as you so eloquently put it."

I gave him a weak smile. Words wouldn't make this better. The *crap* I brought was so much more than Gabe or the rest of the covey knew. It was Jackson, Jolene, ghosting and all the other complications that I dragged along behind me like the plague. Avery was being kind, as was Gabe, and I was grateful, but it didn't make me feel any less responsible.

"We'll get through this," Gabe said, taking my attention from Avery.

"I'll call if I get in over my head," I said.

Kate called down the table, "Deidra and I've got an early start tomorrow and twenty-five third graders gearing up for the weekend. We've got to go. We need all the sleep we can get."

"Next time we do this, you boys will be buying, and it won't be beer." Deidra laughed and winked and the two of them headed out.

Their departure was the stitch that unravelled our cohesive group and one by one we said goodbye and went our separate ways.

Friday dawned warm and sunny. That it was Friday used to be enough to ramp me up for the weekend, but ever since I finished school, Fridays didn't pack quite the same wallop. It was just another day. When I started working, Fridays would dawn with their old magic again.

I held in check my compulsion to reread Jolene's letter and made coffee instead.

Malcolm arrived, on time, calm and happy, as always. I didn't feel like myself today, but if Malcolm noticed, he didn't press.

Gabe's comments from last night worried me. Had the detective read more in my body language than I intended to give away? I wasn't sure I wanted to know the answer.

We passed the 8K mark on our run. After Malcolm rode away, Andy from the pest-control company came by to remove his one-way rodent exit.

"The squirrels have left the building," he said, making light of his work as he backed down the hatch for the last time. "You won't have any more coming in that vent. I repaired the louvres and stapled some wire mesh over it."

"Thanks." I was a relief not to have to worry about the attic sensor setting off the alarm again.

It had taken him less than an hour to finish up. With the whole afternoon in front of me, I made my first forays into the job market. I researched the leads I found online and tailored cover letters to which I attached my CV.

After I closed the laptop, I switched gears. My date with Dean was only a few hours away. Excitement and nerves fluttered in my stomach.

I walked to the bedroom and opened the closet doors. The perfect outfit was hiding in there somewhere—I just had to ferret it out. Dean was a T-shirt and jeans guy and Fast Eddies wasn't fancy, so I needed something on the nice side of blue jeans but not quite into skirt territory. I laid a pair of ivory capris on the bed beside a pair of dark grey skinny jeans and then held half a dozen shirts against both to see what looked best. Either Molly or Eden would have been better at this than me. Finally, I chose the jeans and a light grey sleeveless jersey that covered my butt. I wore red, open-toed pumps and left my hair down. A dash of lipstick and eyeliner, and I was ready to go.

Dean was waiting for me in the parking lot when I pulled in, leaning against his Harley with a black helmet tucked under his arm. The leather jacket looked too warm for the weather, but I imagine it was more function than fashion. He wore Wranglers. Black not blue, and new by the looks of them, but still jeans. They weren't tight, but I liked that. He didn't need to show off his thighs or his butt for me. I'd given him a passing grade in that department the first time I'd met him.

His reaction to my dad's car was heartwarming. He was either genuinely impressed with the car or good at faking it. I picked impressed.

The hostess greeted him by name and led us to our table. The MGB was still our topic of conversation as I took my seat by the window. He had the habit of jerking his head to the side to dislodge the lock of hair that fell in his face each time he tipped his head. Again, I wondered how he got the scar.

He removed his jacket and draped it over the back of his chair. Underneath he wore a printed T-shirt. The delicate jersey fabric clung to every muscle on his chest: a nice effect. Dean had put some thought into his date clothes despite their simplicity.

"A first date's probably not the time to confess to a minor—and I want to emphasize *minor*—deception," he said, finally taking his seat. "But I'm afraid if I don't come clean now, it's going to come up again later, and I'd rather get it off my chest."

It couldn't have been too serious an infraction because Dean's expression barely concealed a grin. "Deception?"

"Minor," he repeated.

"Uh-huh."

"I knew all about your father's car."

My face flushed. I remembered telling him about it on Monday night. "Am I repeating myself already?"

"No. I knew about it months ago. It was at Cheney's shop one time when I dropped by and he showed it to me, told me the whole story."

"And you let me drone on about it. Twice." I'd picked *genuinely impressed* when I'd first seen his reaction. I should have picked *faking it*.

"I liked hearing you tell me about it."

My judgment may be screwed, but that was pretty sweet. I shook my head and smiled at him. I am such a sucker for sweet.

We switched topics when our drinks arrived—his beer, mine wine, and started in on our respective schools. The music and favourite bands subject came up during the salad course—his Caesar, mine spinach. We were well into places we'd like to travel to by the time the main course came—his steak, mine blackened chicken. It was all very tasty, but I was too full for dessert so while he savoured an embarrassingly large slice of chocolate cake, I sipped the last of my wine. He thought it was funny that I was going to report our food selections to Molly.

"Remind me again how you know Molly."

"We met in kindergarten and were friends until eighth grade when I moved away."

"When your dad died?"

"Yeah." Most people didn't like to say it like that. They'd say *passed away or had his accident*. Dean's directness was refreshing.

"After I moved back here, I went into Rumbles to check out the store and didn't even recognize her. If she hadn't recognized me, I would have carried on right out of there. It's funny, we just seemed to pick up where we left off ten years ago."

"You know, I can see that happening with her. I don't know her very well, but she doesn't seem to have a lot of hang-ups. She sure has turned Cheney's head. He's crazy about her."

I liked that he thought well of her. "I think it's mutual."

Dean insisted on paying for dinner. I took Avery's advice and let him, offering to pay for after-dinner drinks at the bar instead. Dean tucked some bills into the little padded portfolio and stood, waiting for me to move ahead of him. I caught myself making a comparison in my mind that I didn't intend to, but watching him handle himself with the bill reminded me of Jackson. Dean was younger and not as polished on the outside, but he was just as practiced and confident in his motions. I pushed the comparison away. This whole night was about flushing Jackson out of my system, not using him as a measuring stick.

Dean escorted me to the bar with his hand on the small of my back. I felt the warmth of his palm and knew he could feel the play in my muscles beneath his fingers. He couldn't know how much that little gesture affected me. It was sensuous, but I wasn't ready for sensuous, and I felt myself stiffen under his touch.

I didn't want to be relieved when he removed his hand, but I was. We settled into club chairs set side-by-side.

"Tell me about how you and Cheney came to be friends."

"I caught him admiring my bike in the parking lot at school, though he'd never admit to it. He likes to rag me, but he appreciates the two-wheeled rides as much as his muscle cars. We've been friends ever since."

"What about family?" I asked. "Sisters or brothers?"

His hand shot to the scar on his face. It wasn't a conscious thing for him, more like covering your mouth when you sneeze.

"No, I'm an only child," he said, but his expression didn't match his words. He'd hidden something from me. "My parents retired to Chilliwack. Said they wanted to live the rural lifestyle."

Shades of Jackson, I thought, remembering the secrets he had kept, secrets that hurt me.

The waiter brought our drinks. It was the perfect opportunity to take a breath and refocus.

Dean wasn't Jackson. I didn't need to question his every response and the possible motives behind his words. Tonight was just a getting-to-know-each-other first date with a man who was single and kind and had a decent job.

"Tell me about your family," Dean said, settling back into his chair.

I told Dean about my mother and her research. It was difficult to explain the distance between my mother and me because people who saw the distance assumed we didn't get along, and that wasn't the case. It was just that neither of us had dealt with Dad's death well. We'd each built a wall to protect what was left of our hearts and that wall still stood between us.

The sky darkened just beyond the bar's floor-to-ceiling windows, and I felt the flutter I always did at this time of night when my night vision took over and my thoughts turned to flying. Sometimes when I thought about it too much, like tonight, the hum of power beneath my skin flared to life, threatening to spill over onto anyone who got too close.

It took an increasing level of concentration to keep myself in the room with Dean, so I suggested calling it a night. It was after ten and he didn't seem upset at the suggestion. He pulled on his jacket and offered me his hand. Though I tried not to, I felt myself stiffen again with the physical contact. Could I trust Dean? Had he been telling me the truth about his family? He was a handsome man, so why didn't he have a girlfriend? Could he have another reason for wanting to date me?

All these doubts flitted through my mind as we walked to my car. I knew it was my naïveté with Jackson that caused me to be wary, and regardless how baseless they might be, there they were.

"You've gone quiet, Emelynn. Is something wrong?"

I looked up at him, surprised to realize that it was true. "No." I didn't know what to add to that.

"I had a great time tonight," he said, taking my hand as we stood beside the driver's side door of the MGB.

What the hell was wrong with me? What more could I expect from a man on our first date? "Me, too," I said, and I meant it. He didn't deserve my suspicions or my Jackson comparisons, but I didn't know how to get rid of either.

I dropped his hand to find the car keys and leaned down to unlock the door. He stood a few feet behind, but too close for me to open the door. He took a step closer. I turned and saw in his face that he meant to kiss me, and I froze. I can't believe I thought that a date with Dean would magically erase my trust issues. How many dates would it take? Two? Five? Twenty-five? Would I ever be able to look at another man's face and not see Jackson? Would I ever not wonder what lies they'd whispered and what clues I'd missed that would have protected me?

He draped his forearms on my shoulders and tilted his head. If he had thought to kiss me, that thought had fled. "Something's been off with you and me tonight. What is it?"

I wanted to say "It's nothing," but that was such a girl answer. Would he minimize my concerns if I told him? Try to fix me? There was only one way to find out. "I have trust issues," I said.

He frowned. "Trust issues?"

"I think you're hiding something. My radar went off when you told me about your family."

His features fell and he lifted his arms from my shoulders. He took a step back and looked down to his boots.

"There's nothing wrong with your radar," he said, shaking his head. "I wasn't lying about my family; I just don't normally tell people I'm adopted on the first date. It leads to other questions I'm not always comfortable answering, that's all."

"I'm sorry, Dean. I won't pry, but I've been lied to before and it's made me cautious." My grand scheme to use another man to eradicate Jackson was not going well.

He looked up and met my gaze. "It's more than that. Every time I touch you, you freeze. You did it Monday and again tonight. You were scared. I saw it just now, when you thought I was going to kiss you." He took another step back. "I meant it when I said I had a good time tonight, but I don't know how to deal with whatever mess the last guy left. I'm sorry, Emelynn, but I don't want to be the focus of someone's fear."

Wow. That hurt. This was not a man who minimized concerns or tried to fix things. "You're right. I didn't mean to do that to you."

He nodded. "Let's just say good night. Maybe some other time I'll be able to tell you about my family. And maybe by then you'll be able to trust me enough not to frighten you."

Without waiting for a response, he turned and pulled on his helmet. I stood there, feeling a hurt worse than the ache that Jackson had inflicted on me. He kicked his bike to life and raced out of the parking lot, the straps on his helmet flapping in the wind.

I couldn't remember driving home—I just found myself there, keys in hand, standing on my porch. I shut the door behind me, disarmed the alarm and headed to the bedroom, stripping clothes as I went. I had only one aim now: I needed to fly. I wanted that power to overwhelm me and wash away the hurt, but the tears came and delayed my exodus.

How was I ever going to move past this? I couldn't inflict my baggage on someone else. It wasn't fair. I needed to get rid of it, but how did I do that? How did I get far enough past Jackson's betrayal to let someone else in? What did I have to do to break his hold on me?

These thoughts rolled around in my head as I found my flying clothes and donned the dark uniform. An idea formed; probably a bad one. Would it work? More importantly, did I have what it would take? I thought through the repercussions and came to realize that I had little to lose. I couldn't feel worse than I did right now.

I locked up, set the alarm and slipped down the deck stairs. My need to be free of gravity pushed me and the power within called out for release. I had barely envisioned the warm, clear crystal before my feet left the beach and I flew skyward, focused on one purpose, one destination. Jackson's time in my head and my heart was up, and tonight I was willing to pay the price with my pride, if that's what it took, to get free of him.

The lighthouse rushed at me as I broke out from the forest. My approach was too fast. Rather than land hard, I overshot my mark and circled back to land on the catwalk outside the red door. The purr of the light's motor thundered in my head as the bright orb swung in its half arc above me.

I took a deep breath. Please, I thought, let Case be here tonight. If he wasn't, I'd never be able to gather the nerve to do this again. With my left hand on the door handle, I peered through the window to the right.

With relief, I saw Case's blond hair. He was lying on the cot with his back to me. The cot looked small with him stretched out on it and the thin blanket only covered his nakedness from the hips down. He lay on his side with his head cradled on the shoulder of his outstretched arm. He looked peaceful, but I'd seen his eyes and knew the truth. If I was wrong about him though, losing my pride would be the least of my worries tonight.

I curled my palm around the doorknob and rattled it. Case's shoulders tensed. He rolled over and looked out at me with sleepy eyes. I didn't move from the window.

Case was exactly the kind of anonymous encounter I needed to erase Jackson from my memory banks. I could be Beth for him if that's what he needed. And maybe in return, he'd push Jackson out of my heart and put an end to the horrible ache that never seemed to go away. I didn't know him, and he didn't know me. It seemed a fair exchange all around as long as he didn't call the police first.

Chapter Fourteen

He shoved the blanket off his legs and swung his feet over the side of the cot. He wore boxers and a bewildered expression. As he stared out at me, I knew he was trying to work out how I'd gotten there.

He stood. I watched him approach with careful strides, not once breaking eye contact. He opened the door and backed away. "How do you do that?" I stepped inside and the door banged closed behind me.

I ignored the question, hoping I'd read him right. My intuition told me there was a lonely man underneath all that pain, but if I was wrong, this was going to be really embarrassing.

I kicked off my shoes and pulled my hoodie over my head, tossing it aside. He stood between me and the cot. I put the heel of my hand on his chest, intending to walk him backwards to the cot, but he didn't budge. Instead, he knocked my hand away and the shock of it registered on my face. He took advantage of my surprise and pushed me hard with both hands. I smacked into the back of the door and he rushed me, pinning my shoulders with his forearm across my chest. His expression was a mix of anger and confusion. I felt his breath on my face.

"What the hell do you think you're doing?" he hissed.

Okay, I was going to have to go with anger. Now what? I searched his face for any trace of the man beneath that heat. He narrowed his eyes and tilted his head one way then the other, making it look like his confusion was taking top billing. That was good. Confusion was so much better than anger. He loosened his arm, releasing my shoulders and straightened his head.

"How . . .?" he asked, but his eyes travelled from my eyes to my mouth. That was a look I understood, even if he didn't. I pushed up on tiptoes and kissed him. Neither of us closed our eyes. He jerked his head back away from me then furrowed his brow.

I didn't say a word. Cautiously, I put my hand against his chest and tried again to move him backwards. This time he let me and I walked him toward the cot until the back of his legs made contact. I moved my hands to his shoulders and gently pushed him down. There was no give under my hand, just muscle. He didn't protest so I moved in to kiss him again, lightly at first and then with more purpose. He opened his mouth and let me in. The skin on his shoulders was soft and warm.

I could tell the moment he decided to get with the program. His floodgates opened wide and his hesitation dissipated. He grabbed the back of my head and returned my kiss in earnest. His other hand skidded down my back and around my waist, pulling me down to my knees. *Yes!* This is what I wanted, what I needed. I'd take it all and wipe my slate clean. I felt his erection as he rubbed against me and I flooded with relief. We'd do this and he'd set me free.

His hands found the bottom edge of my tank top and he yanked it over my head. He unclasped my bra and threw it to the floor then captured my breast roughly with his hand. I watched him bend his head forward to suck my nipple into his mouth. The sensation of his tongue swirling around the tip made me kick my head back with a gasp.

He pulled me onto the cot and rolled me on my back, continuing his erotic assault, licking then nipping with his teeth. His warm palm glided over my ribs, down my stomach to my hips then over the fabric of my yoga pants. He pressed the heel of his hand into the junction of my legs, sending me arching to the roof, groaning as his fingers strummed the fabric beneath. His touch went through me like wildfire.

When I thought of Case, I thought of haunted eyes and bare feet in Keens. I didn't think of the body under the clothes, but I should have. He was muscled and smooth and I ran my hands down his sides, feeling the taut skin stretched over his ribs. When I found the waistband of his boxers, I pushed them down as far as I could, and then reached for his erection. I wrapped my fingers around the silk-smooth skin.

He inhaled with a hiss and looked down to watch my hands stroke his length from tip to base. I then dipped my left hand underneath to cup the weights that hung below. He pressed into my hands, biting his lower lip, retreating and surging again, urging me to take up the motion.

He filled my hands, but his boxers were twisted at his knees, thwarting his movement. He moved away to stand up and kick the boxers free. The cot was low to the ground and as he stood in front of me, he was at the perfect height. Boldly, I swung my legs around and licked the shiny tear off the tip of his erection. Case gasped. I licked the length of him and then all around the perfect rim before I took him in my mouth, tasting salt and musk. He braced his hands on the wall above the cot and shuddered as I applied every trick Jackson had ever taught me. He watched me, his lids heavy, his eyes unfocused.

This was so very much not the time to be thinking of Jackson, but there he was. Strangely enough, my heart didn't ache; instead, anger bubbled up in its place. Having Case in my mouth felt like a very satisfying "fuck you" to Jackson. Yes, this was exactly what I needed and as I worked Case into a frenzy, I wanted nothing more than for Jackson to have had a ringside seat.

Case kept his hands braced against the wall and I met his thrusts time and again. I felt his control slipping away and his breath becoming ragged. Sweat glistened on his stomach and he struggled between watching me and closing his eyes in ecstasy. He strained against his urge to pump his hips, but lost the battle and slipped a hand behind my head. And then every inch of him tensed and with one last thrust, he shuddered and his orgasm took over. He shouted out his release, tensing his stomach muscles and curling his hips one last pulsating time.

Silence pressed in on us. He dropped to his knees, wrapped his arms around me and held me tight. When his breathing settled, he pulled back and kissed me. There were tears on his cheeks.

"God, I'm sorry," he said in a whisper.

I brushed the tears away but didn't ask. We both had baggage and I could only assume he wanted to talk about his about as much as I wanted to discuss mine. He got up and I could see that his erection was past its prime. I shuffled back on the cot and leaned against the wall.

He unzipped the top of a cooler bag, removed two Coronas then popped the caps. He handed me one, sat beside me and tipped his head back, swallowing a long pull from the bottle. I took a small sip. The quiet wasn't uncomfortable, but I was sexually frustrated and hoping like hell to do something about it before too long.

"You've got to help me out here." Case fumbled with his words. "How did . . .? No, who sent . . .? Hell, I don't even know where to start. What are you?"

I understood his confusion, his questions, but they weren't questions I could answer. I looked away. Finally, guessing that his questions would go unanswered, he took another path. "You don't like Corona?" he asked, seeing my obvious disinterest in the bottle.

"Beer, actually, I don't like the taste of it."

"That's blasphemous you know?" And then he curled his mouth into a semi-smile. "How about water?"

"That would be better." He shuffled back to the cooler and pulled out a plastic bottle.

"Better? Than beer?" He shook his head as he cracked the seal on the water and handed it to me.

"Yeah, sorry about that. I'm more of a wine girl."

"Are you?" he said, as he settled back beside me and polished off his beer.

I handed him my barely touched Corona. He took a slug then set it aside. He lay down and rested the back of his head in my lap. His long legs hung over the edge of the cot.

As I looked down at him, he reached up to my face and ran his finger along my jaw and back behind my neck then pulled a length of hair around to the front. He smoothed the locks against my chest then lazily stroked the side of my breast, keeping me on the edge of frustration. I inhaled when he brushed his thumb over my nipple, hardening it instantly.

"How do you get up here?" he asked with quiet curiosity. I reached over and stroked his chest. His pecs felt firm under my touch. He reached for my hand and held it against his chest. "I guess it doesn't matter how you got up here—I'm glad you did."

He rolled toward me and pulled me down to the foot of the cot. It squeaked under the assault of our weight as we rearranged ourselves. He kissed me, softly at first, then aggressively pushing his tongue into my mouth. I gripped his butt pressing his groin against my pelvis.

He broke away, kissed the hollow at the base of my neck, and crawled slowly down my body, licking a trail to my bellybutton. He paused at my gunshot scar and kissed it gently before moving on. I sighed at the warm touch of his tongue drawing a line on the skin between my hips and begged for more.

He dropped to his knees off the end of the cot and removed my pants. I moaned in anticipation as he parted my legs and kissed the inside of my thighs. His clever fingers found me wet and eager, and I arched into his hand. God that felt so good. When I opened my eyes, he was watching me, stroking his thumb over that most sensitive part of me. The dual sensations of him touching me and watching me were erotic as hell. And then he leaned in and flicked his tongue over that knot of nerves that was, at this moment, the centre of my universe. Closing my eyes, I surrendered to him.

He teased and tested, explored and probed. He applied long, leisurely laps interspersed with short, hard flicks until I couldn't take any more. At long last, he latched on and suckled me into a cascading orgasm which he stretched out to impossible lengths.

When he lifted his face, I reached out to him, urging him up. "I want to feel you inside me."

"You don't know how sorry I am to say it can't be tonight—I don't have a condom."

"I do," I said, and his face lit up. "My hoodie." I pointed to the garment I'd tossed aside earlier. He got up to fetch it, his new erection leading the way. "The front pocket."

"I love a girl who comes prepared," he said, pulling out a strip of three. He used his teeth to open one of the little packages and rolled on the condom. His eyes were fixed on me like I was the last woman on Earth as he walked back to the cot, stroking himself. I spread my legs for him like a harlot and he eased down on the cot with his knees between my thighs.

The small cot creaked with our movement. He propped himself up on one elbow and looked into my eyes as he pushed the tip of himself into me. I shuddered. It was the moment I'd been waiting for. I reached my hips up to take him in and felt my body's resistance. I had a horrible moment's hesitation as I recalled my first time. Maybe it wouldn't work. He pulled back and gently pushed again. This time I felt my insides stretch to accommodate him. It hurt a little, but I didn't let on. I knew it would pass. He pulled back again and the next time he surged forward, I felt his pelvis push tight against mine.

He repositioned his arms on either side of me. "You feel incredible," he said, starting a slow pumping rhythm, thrusting hard at the end of each stroke. I felt my body react to him and it felt good, familiar. Images of Jackson flitted through my thoughts and I batted them away.

Beads of sweat formed on Case's chest and the muscles and tendons in his upper arms quivered under his effort. His face was a study in ecstasy. Oh, sweet ecstasy. I remembered that other Flier gift; the rush that Jackson used to send me over the cliff to orgasmic oblivion. I shivered at the memory. I didn't want Jackson here, but I seemed to have little control over his intrusion. I pushed the images away. It was like pushing my hand through smoke; it soon enveloped me again.

Case mumbled something incomprehensible as he drove his hips into me. I zeroed in on his face trying to ignore the intrusion of memories, but it was futile. I felt the familiar ache flare around my heart and tears spilled over the rims of my eyes. I squeezed them closed and forced myself to concentrate instead on the sweet friction that promised something unforgettable.

I wrapped my legs around Case's hips, changing our angle to give me a new focus. Now it was just me and Case and I felt the unmistakable pressure slowly building in my lower abdomen. It was close but took its sweet, sweet time radiating up and out. I curled my hips and met his strokes with new urgency as my orgasm closed in. When it hit, my insides gripped Case's erection and pulled him even deeper. He thrust hard and steady, riding through my waves until I settled, then he kissed me before he pulled out and told me to roll over.

I did as he asked and he tugged my hips up off the small cot and took me again, slamming home on the first thrust and stealing my breath away. This time was for him and he pushed deeper and harder, hitting that sweet spot in front, time and again. I loved the feel of him, the urgency of his desire. The cot squeaked in loud protest, but he kept up the onslaught at a frenzied pace, oblivious to the noise. I didn't think I had another one in me so I was taken by surprise when that sweet pressure blossomed once again, exploding into waves of pleasure that reached out to my fingertips and toes. My orgasm was the catalyst for Case and he shouted out as he reached his own completion, pulling me into his shortened thrusts and holding me close.

Just as his orgasm slowed, the cot collapsed under us. The momentum sent me sprawling flat on my face. Case landed heavily on my back.

"Oh, shit," he said, scrambling off me. "Are you all right?"

"I think so." I turned over and inspected my torso. "Yeah, I'm fine." I took the hand he offered. He pulled me up, and then pushed my hair back, searching my face for damage before pulling me into a strong embrace.

Then the giggles started. Quiet chuckles quickly escalated into raucous laughter.

When the moment passed and our laughter subsided into silly

smiles, we settled back down onto the sad flattened cot with our backs to the wall. There was no other place to sit. Case settled the blanket across our shoulders and pulled me into his chest. For the first time since I came inside, I heard the drone of the motor and the click of its gears. We sat there for a long time listening to the mechanical hum.

"I guess you get used to that," I said, referring to the noise overhead.

"I don't even hear it anymore."

The quiet crept over us again.

Eventually, I asked, "Have you worked here long?"

"Couple of years. How long have you been coming to the lighthouse?"

"I used to come here when I was a kid, but I've been away for years."

"Where have you been?" he asked, rubbing his thumb against the crook of my arm.

I could have told him, I suppose, but I balked. "Away," I said. I pulled free from his arm and looked around for my clothes.

"Where are you going?" he asked.

I felt the need to get away, to regroup. "Bathroom?"

"One floor down," he said, seemingly relieved. He held up my bra.

I took it from him. "Thanks," I said, and gathered the rest of my clothes then headed down the hatch. I tucked into the small bathroom and closed the door. I hadn't thought this situation through far enough. I wanted anonymous sex, but maybe Case wanted more. I dressed quickly, wondering how to end this encounter. I could slip down the stairs and be gone in a heartbeat, but I didn't. I wouldn't want him to do that to me.

When I returned to say goodbye, he was bent over the remnants of the cot, trying to resuscitate it. I didn't think there was much hope. "I think we killed it," I said, noticing he'd pulled on his boxers. "You might be sleeping on the floor tonight."

He stood and tugged me to him, stretching his chin over the top of my head and held me close. "When will I see you again?"

I pulled back and cupped his face. "No promises."

"Can I call you?"

"That's not a good idea." Tonight wasn't about a relationship, no matter how good the sex might have been. It was about moving on. And that's what I wanted to do.

"I hope you visit again," he said, as I pulled away. He brought the back of my hand to his lips and kissed it.

It was a sweet gesture. "Goodbye, Case," I said, then turned around and bolted down the hatch. I raced down the stairs and out the door in a flash, running out into the dark forest, never looking back.

I felt an incredible sense of freedom. Jackson was no longer my sole sexual experience. I found both relief and satisfaction in that knowledge. I briefly considered if Case really was that good or if I was just that hard-up. Maybe it was a bit of both, but at this point, I didn't care. It was fantastic sex any way I looked at it.

When I got to a suitable clearing, far from the lighthouse, I reached my mind's eye to the warm, smooth crystal and let it infuse its power into my still shaky limbs. It built to a crescendo and broke my body free from gravity. It was the first time since I'd gained control of my gift that I let the crystal take the reins. I floated up, rudderless over the tree canopy. It felt like being drunk, but it had nothing to do with alcohol. It was a post-coital haze combined with the surge of power in my limbs and it was intoxicating. I loved it: I wanted to stay there forever.

But my cellphone vibrated, ending my short-lived high. It was late for a phone call, which had me suspecting something else. I pulled out the phone and checked the display. Not again, I thought as I slowed to a drift above the trees. It was the alarm. What had set the thing off this time? Let me guess. I scrolled down to the particulars and sure enough—the attic motion sensor had been activated. Again. Damn, those squirrels were persistent. I quickly disarmed it while visions of flashing police lights danced in my head. The memory of Detective Jordan and company prompted me to pour some extra speed into my trip home.

I didn't hear the alarm as I got close, but it didn't mean the police weren't there. I didn't dare land on the deck or even the darkened lawn—just in case. Instead, I landed in the park and approached from the footpath.

Thankfully, there were no cruisers, no flashing lights. Inside, I dropped the keys and my cellphone in the bowl on the hall table and headed to the kitchen. The number for A-1 Pest Control was stuck to the side of the fridge. What was that guy's name? Andy or David, I thought as I plucked the magnet from the fridge. Andy—that was it. I set the magnet beside the coffee pot so I'd remember to call him first thing tomorrow.

I poured myself a glass of water and wandered to the patio door. The sky was a riot of twinkling diamonds, almost as if they were alive. That's exactly how I felt. I still couldn't quite believe I'd seduced Case. Further proof that I was a control freak? I closed my eyes and drew some of the hum of power from my limbs into my chest and held it there. It was an instant high—better than any chemical high. I inhaled a deep breath and gazed out again to the stars.

Movement to my left caught my eye. I swung my head toward it. The blue gingham chair in the corner of the room seemed to shimmer, like heat waves off asphalt. My eyes were playing tricks on me. I blinked and looked closer.

Then I screamed.

Chapter Fifteen

y water glass shattered on the floor as a dark figure materialized in the chair. He sat there calmly, looking like he owned the place, with his elbows on either armrest and his black-gloved fingers forming a teepee. His right ankle was propped casually on his left knee, but there was nothing casual about this man. His dark hair matched the rest of him: dark eyes, black shirt, black leather blazer.

More movement caught my eye, and I watched another figure emerge from the ether. This one lounged against the bookcase to the left of the flat screen. My heart squeezed up into my throat. He was also dressed in black, with leather from his neck to his boots. He too, wore gloves. I took a step toward the kitchen then made a dash for the front hall. I made it past the counter then slammed on the brakes and back-pedalled. Two more men took form down the hall. They also wore the black leather uniform. The one with brown hair wore a bomber jacket, the other one wore a car coat, but it was the gloves that were the most intimidating.

They slowly strode forward, stopping at the end of the hall, and then leaned leisurely against the walls on either side. Could I make it to my bedroom? I spun around and lurched in that direction only to catch myself short. A woman stood in my bedroom doorway, arms crossed. What the hell was going on? I had to get out. I turned back toward the front hall but the two men hadn't moved. Another woman materialized in the kitchen, watching me, her back resting against the counter. I took a step backwards, then another. My eyes darted to the dining-room table where another woman took shape, sitting comfortably.

They were all eerily calm, their eyes following my movements. Who were these freaks? What did they want? No one made a move toward me as I continued to step slowly backwards. The deck door off the living room was the only escape left. Two more steps and I'd turn and make a run for it. One more. I felt a hand on my shoulder. I screamed and jumped away from it, twisting around to see the man I'd backed into. He glared at me, his back to the patio door, cutting off my last escape route. He was tall and pale, his hair cut in a skull trim. Black, head to toe—they were all dressed in black: They were Fliers.

I had the presence of mind to throw up my protective block and then I found my voice. "Who are you?" My gaze darted around the room, wide-eyed with panic.

The man who'd been lounging in the corner chair spoke. "You have no idea?" His voice stabbed through my chest like a knife.

"No." I slid my gaze from his and scouted the room. No one had moved. I could hardly breathe. "How did you get in here?" What a stupid question: I knew exactly how they'd gotten in here. Outrage boiled up in me like molten rock. How dare they violate my home—my sanctuary?

"You made it so easy for us, Emelynn, the Prime Security signs out front, the security breach report there on the table. Thoughtful of you—practically an invitation. We would have phoned, but the attic sensor was so much more efficient don't you think?"

"What are you doing in my house?"

"We'll be the ones asking the questions." He stood up and took a step toward me. He narrowed his small dark eyes and took me in like an unpleasant thought. I recoiled. His thinning hair was brushed forward. He took another step. I backed away only to feel the man with the skull trim clamp his hand on my shoulder again. I gasped, looking down to the sausage-like fingers dwarfing my shoulder. I tried to think, to clear the panic long enough to remember something—anything, from the self-defence training. Escape—that was the goal.

"You're not going anywhere," said the man, tightening his vice-like grip on my shoulder.

The hell I wasn't. I'd never been more frightened in my life, but I wasn't about to just stand here and do nothing. I moved quickly, taking a step backwards into the man who clutched my shoulder. Using the momentum, I rammed my elbow into his stomach as hard as I could. He bent forward with a short grunt and I bashed the back of my head into his face, twisted to the right, and lunged for the glass door. I'd surprised him, but he was quicker than me and grabbed my right arm mid-lunge. He yanked me back so hard I lost my footing and his arm caught my waist on the rebound. He launched me across the plank floor like a bowling ball. I landed hard, flat on my back with the wind knocked out of me, and enough momentum left over for my shoulder to connect with the corner of my mother's blue sofa, dislodging it from its carpet divots.

"Enough!" shouted the man I assumed was their leader.

"Goddamnit!" skull trim man said, holding his nose. "I think she broke it."

I'd forgotten how much it hurt to have my wind knocked out. I fought the crushing weight on my chest and gaped like a fish to reinflate my lungs. When I got my breathing under control, I cradled my wrenched right arm.

"Rachael, Carrie!" the first man barked. Two women rushed in to stand on either side of me. They didn't look as threatening as the men, but they had the whole leather thing going on right down to the gloves.

"Stand up," the first man ordered. I glared at him. One of the women held her hand out to help me. Not bloody likely, I thought as I pushed with my feet, trying to scoot away from them, but there was nowhere to go. I couldn't fight my way out of this. My block might protect me from their jolts, but it wouldn't keep them from beating me to death.

I pushed myself up with my elbow. My shoulder protested the effort, but there was little choice. Rolling to my left, I made room to get my legs under me, and then pushed up to my knees. I winced and pulled my right arm close to my body. One leg at a time, I stood, and locked my knees to steady myself.

The leader approached, shaking his head. "Look around, Emelynn. Do you really think you're any match for us?"

I felt an energy swimming around me. It was similar to the hum of power that I felt in my limbs when I concentrated on the crystal, but this was outside of me, crawling across my skin and making the hair on the back of my neck stand on end. Black leather oozed from every corner. As my gaze passed over them, I counted. Nine Fliers and every one of them a Ghost. Nine. Oh my god. "The Tribunal Novem," I whispered. Somewhere in the frightened recesses of my mind, I remembered: nine founding coveys, one member from each.

"So you've heard of us?" the leader said with a triumphant smile. "I'm flattered."

I badly wanted to wipe that smile off his face. "Don't be," I said. "Your reputation isn't flattering."

He tilted his head and leaned in. "You should have more respect. We've made an exception for you." His words dripped with malice. "Your case is close to our hearts."

"My *case*?" I swallowed against the lump in my throat. What were the chances I could jolt him? "What could I possibly have done to get your attention?"

"Does the name Jolene Reynolds mean anything to you?"

Alarm spiked. "If you're here, then I assume you know the answer to that question."

"Don't test me—I'm not in the mood. Answer the question."

"The name rings a bell."

He backhanded me across the face. I fell backwards over the arm of the sofa then bounced to the floor, smashing my forehead into the coffee table on the way down. The metallic taste of blood leaked into my mouth. I felt the room close in around me as a horrible realization crawled up my spine: They were going to kill me.

The two women crowded in again.

"Get her up," the leader said, and the women reached for me. They didn't touch me, just held their hands out to me, and my body lifted from the floor like a puppet on a string. I felt their invisible pull vibrating through the hum in my limbs. Somehow they lifted me to a vertical position and then held me off the ground, bound so tightly I could barely move. I struggled in their hold, but it was firm. I felt like I was tied in a straitjacket with my head strapped to a board. Without being able to move my head, my view was restricted to the short sweep between the bedroom door and the blue gingham chair. Skull trim man remained by the patio door, clutching one of my towels to his nose.

"Now, let's try that again," the leader said, blocking my vision with his arrogant face. "Why does the name, Jolene Reynolds, *ring a bell* with you, Emelynn?"

I felt a warm trickle of blood trail down my temple and struggled to keep my block in place. I set my jaw and stared at him. He kept me in his gaze and sneered, then jerked his chin up. Despite my block, a searing pain shot down my spine, taking my breath away.

"I won't ask again," he said.

Scrambling for breath, I answered him, "Jolene gave me the gift."

"Who *helped* her give you the gift?"

"Helped?" I asked. What was he talking about?

"Don't make me hit you again, Emelynn. I don't like hitting women."

I think he liked hitting women just fine, but self-preservation made me keep that opinion to myself. "No one helped her. She came by herself. I was only twelve. I don't even remember how she did it."

"Tell me what you do remember."

"She asked me to keep it a secret. She pressed our fingertips together and mumbled some words I didn't understand. Then I woke up and she was gone. That's it. That's all I remember."

He looked at me as if he were weighing the truth of my words. "Where is Jolene now?" he asked, turning away from me.

"I don't know."

He quickly turned back to me and I flinched. "When was the last time you saw her?"

"The day she gave me the gift. I never saw her again."

The doorbell rang. "Get that," he said to someone I couldn't see.

Don't bother asking me, I thought, fuming. It's just my house, but hey, don't give it a second thought. The numbness began clearing from my forehead where I'd struck it on the coffee table and it started to throb.

I heard male voices approaching from behind. Their footsteps stopped abruptly where the hallway met the kitchen and then an uncomfortable silence hung in the air. They were only ten feet behind me.

A familiar voice that I couldn't place broke the silence. "This is a surprise." His voice had an undertone of disdain. I knew that voice. "What is it that merits the entire Novem's attention?"

It was James Moss! I couldn't see him, but I was sure that was his voice. Before tonight, I would have slotted James into the most-menacing-man-I-knew slot. What was Sandra's brother doing here? How was he involved with this group of hoodlums? Blood dripped from my jaw onto my collarbone.

"James Moss, I don't think you've met Mason." The leader spoke past my right shoulder to make his introductions. I heard more foot shuffling behind me.

A different, deeper voice identified himself. "Mason Reynolds."

The leader swivelled his gaze back to me. "Mason *Reynolds. Ring any bells*, dear?"

He turned from me again, speaking past me. "Thank you for coming," he said. He must have been talking to James. This was so frustrating. Except for skull trim man and the arrogant bastard in front of me, they were all behind my back. Were they sitting around the dining-room table watching the show?

Footsteps drew close on my right. "Sebastian, only you could make an order sound like a cordial invitation." It was James. He spoke in a quiet, controlled voice. Why was James taking orders from this man?

James came around on my right and finally into my line of sight. It really was him. I didn't know whether to be relieved or more frightened.

"Emelynn," James said, "what have you done?" It wasn't a question and there was genuine pity on his face. James hadn't changed. He still wore his dark hair long and tied back, which only emphasized his height and lanky build.

"You know her?" Sebastian asked in an accusatory tone that made it sound like a dangerous question.

"I met her last spring during a visit with my sister. She's affiliated with the local covey here."

Why was he lying? Who was he protecting? I'd taken a bullet rescuing his sister; was it enough for him to help me now? And what was his connection to these people?

"Well then. Maybe she'll be more cooperative with you than she's been with us."

"What do you need to know?"

"Mason Reynolds would like to know what's become of his sister, Jolene. This young lady claims Jolene gave her the gift. We'd like to know if she's telling the truth. Tell us what she remembers."

"James," I said through clenched teeth. "What's going on?"

"Sebastian would like me to read your memories."

What? I blinked at the inference. He'd said it like *Sebastian would like me to take your temperature*. Like it would be that easy. Thermometer in, hold, remove, read. Just like that.

"What the hell?"

"It won't hurt," James said in a calm voice, but it didn't erase my growing apprehension. "If I corroborate your version of events, then they'll know you're telling the truth."

"Get on with it, James. It's been a long night." Sebastian's impatience and arrogance suggested he was used to making demands. He moved out of my line of sight.

James stepped toward me. I held my breath and pushed back against my invisible straitjacket. He reached his hands out to me, one on either side of my head, and pushed his fingertips into my hairline. With the women holding my head immobile, I had no choice but to submit. His pale eyes were that combination of blue and green that was changeable. He closed them and I could feel the pressure of his fingertips . . . and something else. Something pushed against my block and I flinched.

And then I heard the strangest thing. His voice was in my head. My ears weren't hearing him, but an echo of his voice was there—somewhere in my head.

"I'm sorry, Emelynn. We have no choice here. We can't fight them so just give them what they want and let's hope it's enough to send them on their way."

He opened his eyes and pleaded with me inside my head. *"Please, Emelynn."*

"I can't."

"Don't speak out loud, say the words in your head and I'll hear you. Now try to relax and let me do my thing."

"Your thing *frightens me,"* I said without speaking.

"I know, but you've got to let me in. They'll hurt you, Emelynn, in ways you can't imagine and they won't hesitate. Do you really want to be another one of their accidents?"

I shook my head.

"You're blocking me."

"I'm scared." My block vibrated like a reflexive shiver against the cold.

"Don't be. Take your block down."

"Is there a problem, James?" Sebastian had returned and stood behind James.

James removed his hands from my head and addressed Sebastian. "It's going to take a minute, Sebastian. I'm working around her block."

"We can remove her block."

"That won't be necessary. Her block's not that strong."

"You've got two minutes," Sebastian said, then stalked off.

James turned back to me, placed his hands on my head and closed his eyes again. His voice washed through my head like warm water. *"I lied. There's not a hope in hell I'll get around your block. You're going to have to take it down, Emelynn, or they will and they are neither gentle nor patient."*

"I'm trying."

"Do you need help?"

"Help? How?" This was not the menacing James that I remembered. He sounded worried, and that, more than anything, frightened me.

"I can help you relax. You won't like it, but it's better than what they'll do."

Sebastian paced impatiently back into my line of sight.

"Do you want me to help?" He opened his eyes and looked at me.

My head was in his hands. I nodded as much as my bonds would allow but kept my eyes on Sebastian.

I heard James's voice in my head. *"Look at me, Emelynn."*

I did as he asked and the moment I saw the expression on his face I grasped his plan. He was going to use his rush to touch my libido with his gift. An icy dribble of dread trickled down my spine and I shuddered, breaking my gaze away.

"If you've got a better suggestion, I'm all ears, but we're running out of time," he whispered into my head.

I squeezed my eyes closed and concentrated on lowering my block, but fear overwhelmed my efforts and my block held firm, shaky, but solid. I felt James pushing against it. This had never happened before. It was as if my body was on autopilot, protecting itself.

It was useless. I opened my eyes in defeat and looked at him but only because I believed the man behind him would do worse. He held my head in his hands and trapped my gaze. I felt the warm brush of his caress inside my body, like warm breath on my neck. I filled my lungs and still couldn't catch my breath. No, this wasn't right. This was something lovers did—not us. It was too intimate: I barely knew him. "Get out!" I screamed, but it was too late.

The women on either side of me held me firm in their strange grasp and James had me locked in his gaze and neither were letting go. James stoked the embers of arousal with fluttering pulses beneath my skin. His hands didn't move, but I felt the pulses like heated fingertips down my neck and back and around my torso. He had me at his mercy as he built the sexual tension between us. I didn't want to respond, not like this, with James and strangers in the room, but I couldn't help myself. He continuously pushed at my block as he worked my body from the inside. I watched his eyelids half close and his lips part and knew then that I wasn't the only one responding. His pulse wound around the inside of my thighs and I closed my eyes. I couldn't watch his face as his pulse reached that most sensitive spot, like a delicate kiss. I inhaled sharply and in that instant, he breached my block. I gave myself over to him and the moment I did, he held me there, not fanning the fire, but not letting it die out either.

"I'm in, hold on just a little longer." I opened my eyes and sucked ragged breaths as I looked into his hooded eyes. I felt him touching my memories like fingers flitting through a file cabinet. But these fingers were cold. Each memory he touched lit up a photo in my mind. He looked at them all. Every moment of my life was laid bare for him to see. It was the ultimate invasion of privacy and there wasn't a thing I could do about it.

It was like watching a slide show of my life flashing by in reverse: Sebastian backhanding me; the other man throwing me across the floor; the diamond sky; checking my phone; kissing Case goodbye; Case naked and pumping his hips on top of me; taking Case in my mouth. Private moments never meant to be shared. It was beyond humiliating.

The pictures flipped by faster and faster. He touched a memory of Jackson and I saw Jackson's dark curls on the pillow beside me. The image caused the pain to flare up around my heart and I felt James flinch. He went back through my life touching off memories further and further back. I tried to ignore the images he saw and focus on the arousal he had created, using it like a shield, but the memories were more powerful.

Laughing with Eden at the Neon Turtle; splattering my opponent with paintballs; lying in a hospital bed; floating out of control in the storm; unpacking my father's photo; writing an exam. He kept digging. Floating near the ceiling of the condo in Toronto; greeting visitors at the SPCA; packing heavy cans into my knapsack; sitting across from the psychiatrist; being peeled off Nanny Fran at the Vancouver airport. I tensed, knowing what came next: a funeral in a chapel and a photo of Dad propped on top of an empty coffin. The memory touched off a grief too intense to bear and tears welled. James tensed, but kept going. The next image was of Dad as he boarded the plane that would kill him and then, finally, James made it to the memory of the beach with Jolene. It was almost over. He slowed down and cold fingers picked over every detail. He went back further to my twelfth birthday party. Molly smiled, her mouth smeared with birthday cake.

And then he was done.

"*I'm sorry*," he said, and released my gaze. He took a deep breath and relaxed his shoulders then finally dropped his hands. His face looked haunted.

Tears streamed down my cheeks and I couldn't even hang my head in shame. I lowered my eyes to the floor. I couldn't look him in the face: I was too humiliated, too embarrassed. I wanted to dig a hole and bury myself.

Sebastian called Mason over. I looked up through teary lashes as a tall man came to stand beside him. "Tell us," Sebastian ordered. James turned and the three men formed an ominous triangle in front of me. Mason loomed over James's right shoulder. He stood taller than James and wore an angry scowl. His blond hair was brushed smoothly back.

James spoke in a level voice. "Emelynn was twelve years old. The woman involved was attractive, slim. She had blonde, wavy hair, and blue eyes. She was small, maybe five foot three, about thirty-five. She was alone. It was just Emelynn and the woman. No one else participated. Emelynn has no memory of her beyond the day of the gifting." James held up his hands. "That's all there is. There were no witnesses, but the woman gave it freely—it was a gift."

Sebastian walked away, brooding. Mason brushed James aside and came to stand in front of me, unconvinced. "It doesn't make sense. Why you? You had no connection to her."

I glowered at him. They had just beaten the crap out of me and raped my mind and it wasn't enough? Something inside me snapped. If I could have freed my hands from this invisible hold, I would have clawed his eyes out. But all I could do was throw words. "What's wrong with you people?" I seethed, frustrated by my impotence. "Is the truth not enough? What more do you want? More pain! Is that what it takes to make the high and mighty Tribunal feel important?"

James whipped back around and raised his voice in alarm, "Emelynn, don't." He turned to Mason. "There's a letter in her nightstand."

"No! They can't have it. It's all I have." But Mason had already disappeared into my bedroom.

He came out, holding Jolene's letter. "How did you get this?" He stormed up to me and I closed my eyes against his rage. "Who are you?" His hot breath assaulted my face.

"Let me see that." Sebastian snatched the letter from Mason's hand.

"Where's Brian? What's your connection to him!"

I glared at Mason as fresh tears spilled down my face.

"Brian died in a plane crash soon after that woman gave Emelynn her gift," James said, his voice quiet. He glanced at me with a look of apology in his expression. "Brian was her father."

His words stopped Mason in his tracks. The wind went out of him and his shoulders slumped. "You're Brian Taylor's daughter?" His voice was quieter now. He pulled his eyebrows together and looked at me, as if for the first time. The examination continued as he stepped back and looked me up and down. He collapsed into the chair by the patio door and folded in on himself. Sebastian watched his every move.

"Release her," Mason said to no one in particular.

"You're satisfied?" Sebastian asked.

"Yes, release her. Jolene is truly gone." Mason looked broken and weak: The grief of accepted loss. I knew it well.

Rachael and Carrie each took hold of an arm and released their invisible hold on me then lowered me to the floor. I would have collapsed to my knees if they hadn't held on. My spine sagged.

"You don't know that," I said, seething. I refused to let pity for Mason cloud my anger.

"Until we found you, there was always some hope: but not now. Jolene loved Brian. If she was going to do this, then using you for her gift's vessel makes perfect sense. She trusted Brian to keep her gift safe."

"It might not have killed her," I said defiantly.

Mason looked at me, resigned. "She's dead." He said it as if it was a fact. It wasn't.

My anger caught fire. They'd violated my home, beaten me, raided my memories and now they wanted to crush my hope. That Jolene might still be alive was just a small wish, but they'd taken everything else and they couldn't have that.

"Get out of my house." My voice was quiet but steady.

"We have much to talk about—you and I," Mason said, looking up from the comfort of my mother's chair.

"We have nothing to talk about," I said, not quite so quiet, not quite so steady. "Get out—all of you!"

"See that she gets that cut tended to," Sebastian said, addressing James who took it as an invitation to move closer to me.

I put my hand up to him and stepped back. "Don't touch me."

James stood there, apology etched on his face, pleading wordlessly for an understanding I wasn't prepared to give.

The Ghosts blinked out of existence one by one. But I knew better. They weren't gone, not yet. They were Ghosts. Still here. Still watching.

"Let me take you to Avery," James said, trying again to step closer.

I motioned him off with my arm and strode to the patio door. Glass crunched under my foot. A key lay hidden on the top of the frame and I didn't care who in this corrupt crowd saw me reveal its hiding place. I slid the door open wide and stepped out onto the deck. For a moment, I considered the twinkling diamond sky. I'd never before wanted so much to be a part of it.

I ran for the stairs off the deck but didn't make it. When I reached the first step, instead of stepping down, anger fuelled my motion and I burst the bonds of gravity mid-stride, flying straight out across the Pacific to join the stars.

The break from gravity was violent and the resulting momentum felt like adding rocket fuel. I fanned the flames, accelerating to speeds I'd never flown before. It was a reckless, mind-numbing flight to outrun the memories, escape the hurt and grief. No one in that cottage could catch me. Some voice deep inside held that fact as truth and urged me on faster and faster until the cottage was miles behind.

I kept going, heedless of the dangers. It was just me and the stars in the sky and only dark water below. No one would find me here. No one could touch me. I kept going.

A dark land mass rose on the horizon, confusing me and shaking my single-minded focus. Where was I? Sanity finally returned to temper my anger-fuelled flight. I slowed to a more manageable speed and then coasted to a slow hover. My shoulder hurt and my forehead throbbed. I touched my eyebrow and my fingers came away bloody. I couldn't stay out here but I couldn't return to the cottage either. I would never forgive them for that invasion. My eyes watered, but I wouldn't give them tears. Revenge maybe, but not tears.

I checked my GPS. The land mass was Gabriola Island. I shook my wrist and reset the GPS because it couldn't be right. But once again, it pinpointed me just east of Gabriola. I'd flown almost all the way across the Strait of Georgia, a distance that took an hour and a half by ferry. I'd either been gone longer or flown faster than I realized.

I turned around and let the GPS guide me back to the mainland; back to that small sandy beach where I'd made my first big mistake. The soft sand cushioned my landing. I walked to where the sand met the base of the cliff and lay down between the cliff face and a beached log. It was cool and damp, but I was concealed and felt safe. Warm tears flowed without sobs. I shut my eyes and let the hum of power from my crystal lull me to sleep.

When dawn broke, I dragged my aching body out of my hiding place. The pain had grown worse in the cool, damp night and the cut over my eye felt stiff with dried blood. I picked my way north until the cottage came into view. It looked the same as it always did—safe, comforting. But that was just an illusion, wasn't it? Would I ever feel safe there again? Was safe even an option for me now?

Caution guided my steps as I approached, watchful for signs of life inside. I crept up the stairs and peered in through the patio door. Someone had closed it after I'd left but it wasn't locked. I stepped inside and looked around. The sofa was back in place and the carpet straightened. A check of the front door confirmed it was locked. Good. Someone had tidied up and cleared the broken water glass. I retreated to the bedroom, sat on the side of the bed and pulled open the bedside drawer. Lying on top was Jolene's letter to my father. It was back in its envelope. I ran my fingertips over my dad's name. At least they hadn't taken that away from me.

I felt weary to the bone, and lay on the bed, pulling the comforter over me. It hurt to roll onto either side so I stayed on my back. I would have changed into a nightshirt, but there was no privacy in here where those people could come and go so easily. Sleep slowly settled in around me like a leaden blanket.

It was midafternoon when I woke. I felt swaddled, unable to move in the twisted mess of my clothes and trapped in the comforter. I peeled an arm free and unwrapped myself. My body had seized up while I slept, amplifying my aches. I went to the bathroom in search of a painkiller. The face that stared back from the mirror didn't look like mine. It didn't look twenty-two. It looked older, meaner. Dried blood was smeared across my forehead from a ragged cut near my eyebrow. A bruise was blooming along my jaw and cheekbone where Sebastian had hit me. I ran my tongue over the cut my teeth had made on the inside of my lip. What story would I have to make up to cover the truth behind these injuries?

I poured a glass of juice and took it and the phone out to the deck. The day was bright but did nothing to lighten my mood. I settled into my usual chair and gingerly stretched my legs to the ottoman in front of me.

Avery needed to know what had happened.

The sharp edge of my anger had dulled but wasn't gone. I dearly wanted to turn the tables on each and every one of the bastards who'd invaded my home. I wanted to make each one of them feel as violated and victimized as I had. But I wasn't foolish enough to think I could do it. I was impotent in the face of their overwhelming power—a pebble to their Rock of Gibraltar. It ate at me.

"It's me," I said, when Avery answered his phone. "I need to see you if you've got some time."

Avery was his usual accommodating self. "I'll go unlock the door."

As I disconnected from Avery, I noticed that I'd missed a call. It had come in last night. Must have been when I'd been out over Georgia Strait. I punched in my password and Jackson's voice made my skin crawl.

"Emelynn, it's Jackson. Something big's going down, and it involves you. Call me when you get this."

Too late, Jackson. I deleted his message.

Chapter Sixteen

Thirty minutes later I parked the MGB in front of Avery's house. He stood just inside the small waiting room.

Something in me snapped the moment I saw him. He took in my battered face with a wince and held out his arms. I fell into them and all the tears I didn't know I'd been holding back, flooded out in heaving sobs. He held me and stroked the back of my head, whispering soothing words until I quieted. I finally felt safe.

"Don't you dare wipe your nose on my shirt," he said, pulling away from me and turning my sobs into blubbery laughter. "Come on. Let's get you a tissue."

We walked through the waiting room to the door that led to his kitchen. "We've got company," he said, gripping my shoulder. My tears would be embarrassing, but Victoria had seen me in worse shape.

But it wasn't Victoria, it was James, and I stopped dead in my tracks. He sat at the kitchen table. An array of emotions swept over me; anger, embarrassment, humiliation, guilt. I couldn't settle on just one. That's why Avery hadn't gone ballistic when he saw me—James had already filled him in. What the hell was James doing here anyway?

"Would you like tea or something stronger?" Avery asked, gauging my reaction.

"Nothing thanks, I just wanted to talk. I'll come back later," I said, turning around out of Avery's grip.

"Please don't go," James said, and I heard him get up to come after me. "I didn't have a choice, Emelynn."

I stopped my retreat but didn't turn around. "I've never been so humiliated in my life, James. I can't even look you in the face." I wanted to shout at him but my anger was drowned out by embarrassment. I didn't know which humiliation was worse: my reaction to James's rush or the fact that he'd seen such intimate moments of my life.

"I'm sorry, but you don't know the Tribunal like I do. They would have hurt you."

"They *did* hurt me," I said, clenching my jaw. "And *you* helped them." Avery came around in front of me holding a box of Kleenex.

"We need to talk about this," Avery said, and I felt fresh tears well up. "And I need to look at that cut in better light," he said, brushing the hair from my forehead.

I pulled out a tissue and blew my nose then let Avery turn me around and lead me back into the kitchen. "James, would you please get my kit from under the exam table in my office?"

James left the room without a word. He hadn't changed clothes from last night.

"Sit over there, by the window."

I did as he asked. Avery stepped away, set out three teacups and poured water from a kettle into a bowl.

"You should have come last night and let me tape that," Avery said. James returned and set Avery's kit on the table.

Avery motioned to him. "Would you pour us some tea while I clean this?" Standing beside me, Avery pulled packets of gauze and a bottle of liquid out of his kit. "Tilt your head and let me have a look." He sighed and then snapped on a pair of latex gloves. "I'm afraid this might leave a scar." He ripped a package of gauze open and soaked it in the warm water before placing it over the cut. "Just leave that there for a minute."

He pulled off the gloves and fetched our tea. James held a cup in his hands and leaned against the counter as far away from me as he could get while still remaining in the room.

"What are you doing here?" I asked James, not caring that I sounded rude.

"Here?" James asked, pointing his fingers to the floor and motioning a circle, "or here, as in Summerset?"

"Avery's."

"I knew you'd eventually show up here and we need to talk."

"Talk? You think talk will fix what happened last night? I came here for Avery, not to give you the opportunity to feel better about what you did." James looked like I'd slapped him and it felt good.

"At least hear him out." Avery set his cup down and snapped the latex gloves back on.

"Did he tell you what happened?"

Avery removed the gauze and started wiping at the cut. "I know the Tribunal paid you a visit. I can see they weren't exactly gentle. James tells me they summoned him to verify your version of Jolene's gifting."

"He left out a few details, and ouch—that hurts!"

"Do you want me to freeze it?"

"No, just stick a Band-Aid on it."

"I need to clean the edges and tape it. Can you tolerate a little more?"

I took a deep breath. "Go ahead."

"James said you tore out of there so quickly last night that he had no hope of finding you." Avery wiped at the cut until fresh blood stained the gauze. "Give the man some credit for sticking around to make sure you were all right." He sprayed something on the wound then taped it. "There. That's the best I can do."

"Thanks."

"Is there anything else I need to look at?"

"Nothing you can fix, unfortunately."

Avery reassembled his kit. "Let's go into the den." He headed toward the door on the far side of the kitchen and dropped the bloodied gauze and gloves into the trash bin on the way. James and I followed.

Avery's den looked like the men's clubs you see in glossy magazines. A heavy desk stood in front of French doors that opened to the back garden. The fireplace on the far wall was framed with a painted mantle, and bookcases lined the remaining wall space. The room was furnished with a small sofa and two leather chairs, which sat upon a rich Persian carpet. A second door of frosted glass led to a hallway on the other side of the room. Avery and I chose the leather chairs. James walked to the bookcase behind Avery.

"Tell me what happened," Avery said.

"God, there's so much. Where do I start?"

Avery didn't rush me. He sipped his tea and waited patiently.

"They're all Ghosts: every one of them."

"All who—the Tribunal?" Avery asked.

"That's who they said they were, but maybe James can confirm." I looked behind Avery to where James was trying to blend into the bookcase. "You're obviously on a first-name basis with them."

James ignored my accusatory tone. "I am. Not by choice, by the way, and yes, that was the Tribunal though I've never seen all of them together prior to last night."

"Before we go any further," Avery said, turning in his seat to address James, "I need to know, what's your connection to them?"

"My family is connected to them. Again, not by choice." He emphasized. "They demand our services and we deliver."

"Come on, I need more than that. Connected how? Deliver what?"

"Connected because the gift that runs through my family comes with an anomaly that the Tribunal finds useful. It was brought to their attention at the turn of the last century when one of my ancestors made an unfortunate error in judgment and our secret got out. Since then, the Tribunal have called on us regularly to assist them."

"Assist how?" Avery asked.

"With their investigations."

"James." Avery raised his voice, growing uncharacteristically impatient.

James exhaled heavily. "We can read memories."

Avery raised his eyebrows. "How does that work?"

"Through touch. I can pick up quick glimpses through handshakes, but I get more detail with closer contact and concentration." James looked over to me. "That's how I knew about you and Jackson. I saw him in your mind when I first met you and shook your hand."

"So, back to last night," Avery said, interrupting James. "The entire Tribunal showed up at Emelynn's house and you what? *Read her memories?* How did that help?"

"If I'm putting the clues together correctly, the woman who gifted Emelynn is, or was, the sister of Mason Reynolds," James said. "Mason is a member of the Tribunal Novem. The Reynolds family belongs to one of the nine founding coveys. None of them seemed to believe that the sister did this of her own free will. They thought Emelynn received the gift through coercion or on some other less-than-voluntary basis."

"And how did your input help?"

"I was able to confirm that no one else was involved in the gifting."

"By reading her memories?"

"Yes."

"Why would they believe you?"

"My family knows all too well what happens if we lie to them or give them cause to question the veracity of our information."

"But you did lie to them," I said, remembering his deception. "You told them you met me when you were visiting your sister in May. That's a bit more than stretching the truth."

"I didn't want to give them any reason to mistrust me where you were concerned. They got what they needed, and they didn't have to resort to unsavoury methods to get it."

That may have been true, but he'd covered his own butt in the process. "I can't help but notice that your lie also conveniently hid the fact that you and Jackson were only *visiting* because your sister had been kidnapped—something the Tribunal obviously knows nothing about."

"The less they know about my family, the better."

"I wish I had that luxury."

"In their minds, Emelynn, you messed with one of their own. That's why all nine of them were there last night. It was a show of force, and it was aimed directly at you. You don't want to know how they'd get to the truth if I hadn't been there."

"The truth or just what they wanted to hear?"

"Don't you dare suggest that I condone what they do or the methods they use. My family isn't given a choice. We do their bidding or they do to us what they do to all the others."

Avery snapped to attention. "What do they do to all the others?"

"They never, ever, kill a Flier before they confiscate their gift. It's how the Tribunal has gotten to be so strong over the years. You saw Carrie and Rachael, Emelynn. My great grandfather was witness to when those kinetic gifts were stolen."

"What's he talking about, Emelynn?"

"It was the freakiest thing," I said to Avery. "Two of the women were able to raise me from the floor and hold me there—mid-air— completely incapacitated. Neither of them was bigger than me, but I couldn't move, and they didn't even touch me—just held out their hands toward me, like this." I mimicked their stance.

"You don't know what they're capable of," James said. "They've been absorbing gifts and passing them on to their children for two hundred years."

"Thanks for scaring the rest of the crap out of me, James," I said.

"I just need you to understand that I had no choice. I didn't want to read your memories—believe me. That was as unpleasant for me as it was for you."

"I doubt that."

"Emelynn," Avery interjected, "tell me the whole story. Everything."

"That will require Scotch."

Avery smiled at me and laughed. "How about you, James? Do you need liquid courage for this recounting?"

"Why not? A splash of water in mine, if it's not too much trouble," he said, and Avery left the room to fix our drinks.

I turned to James. "I'm going to tell him everything, including the bit about my block, and how you got around it, so if you don't want to hear it, you'd better go."

"You don't need to share everything with him."

"Yes, I do, James. He's the only one, other than you, who knows that I'm a Ghost. He's been here for me through everything. We don't keep secrets from one another."

"Everyone keeps secrets, Emelynn. Believe me. I'm intimately acquainted with the secrets that people keep."

"I won't keep secrets from Avery. He's the one who taught me how to jolt, to flash. He might not be able to fix the new problem with my block, but he'll help me work through it. So no, I won't keep him out."

"Suit yourself." James turned to Avery, who was coming through the door juggling three cut-crystal tumblers. James took one, I took another. We didn't touch glasses—it wasn't a "cheers" type of occasion.

"Didn't you have your date with Dean last night?" Avery asked, as if he'd suddenly remembered.

"I did. It was a disaster."

"Disaster?" James said, interrupting. "I don't know a guy on the planet who would describe that date as a disaster."

"What are you talking about?" I said, and then the light slowly dawned. A hot blush bloomed up my neck and took over my face. James was right. We all had secrets. "That wasn't Dean," I said, looking away.

"Oh," he said. "Sorry." But his tone said "told you so."

"I was . . . out," I said, starting the story, "on my way home when the attic sensor was tripped. I thought the squirrels were back, so I disarmed it. But when I got home, I learned it was the Tribunal who had tripped the alarm. They were waiting for me and materialized one by one. They were hostile right from the start—assumed I was guilty of associating with whoever stole Jolene's gift. I tried to get away, but I didn't stand a chance against them."

I looked over to James. "I hadn't been home more than fifteen minutes before you knocked on the door."

"When did the Tribunal contact you?" Avery asked James.

"Yesterday, noon. They sent their private jet and told me to be on it. They gave me the address instructed me to stay close until they called. I didn't know it was your house, Emelynn."

"I'm sure it wouldn't have made a difference if you did. Anyway, by the time you arrived, I had already pissed them off, and they had me so scared that I couldn't shake my block."

"What do you mean?" Avery asked.

"I wasn't thinking straight. I was running on adrenalin and slammed my block into place as soon as I realized they were Fliers. When James showed up, I tried to release it, but couldn't. My block was stuck in self-preservation mode."

James continued the story. "They asked me to read her memories but I couldn't get past her block. Sometimes I can permeate a block—just leak right through it, but not hers."

"How did you get past it?"

"I did the only thing I could think of doing without hurting her. I used my rush to relax her enough to break through it."

Avery looked from James to me then back to James.

James traded his neutral expression for a defensive one. "Sebastian threatened to *remove* her block. I've seen him do that and it's not pleasant—like surgery without the benefit of anaesthetic. If he'd done that to her, she might never have been able to block again. The rush was a much better solution."

"So then you were able to read her memories and tell them what they wanted to know?"

"Yes."

"Not entirely," I said. "Mason still wasn't satisfied. He didn't believe his sister would give the gift to a stranger."

"She wouldn't," James said.

"You didn't have to tell him about the letter," I said, anger raising the volume of my voice.

"It was the only way to connect you to Jolene. Do you really think they would have left you in one piece if Mason wasn't convinced? I didn't expose the letter to hurt you. I did it to protect you."

"It was private." I squared my shoulders and glared at James.

"It saved your life."

I knew it, but I wasn't ready to concede the point. It felt good to be angry and even better to direct that anger at James—much better than feeling violated.

"Mason put the letter back," James said. "I don't think he wanted to, but I saw him do it."

"So they believed you and then what?" Avery directed his question to me. "They went home? Are they coming back?"

"They ghosted, but I knew they hadn't left, which is why I took off. I needed to get away from them. I have no idea when they left, where they went or if they're coming back."

"Do you know, James?" Avery asked.

"I'm not privy to their comings and goings, but I don't think Mason's done yet. He still has too many questions. The only other one who might have stayed behind is Ron. The rest are probably gone."

"Ron?" I asked.

"The guy whose nose you likely broke?"

A look of alarm clouded Avery's face. "Emelynn?"

"It was self-defence."

"He didn't think you'd fight back," James said. "Most people would have been intimidated by their presence, let alone the fact that Ron is a big man and scary as hell."

"What did they expect? They broke into my home and threatened me. It's not right. Besides, Ron got his revenge throwing me across the room. I think we're even."

Avery shook his head. "Do you think Ron will be a problem?"

"He wasn't happy about his nose, but I really can't see him coming after Emelynn. He might want to have a few words with her though."

"Do they know she's a Ghost?"

"It wasn't mentioned in my presence," James replied.

"Do you know of any other Ghosts who aren't connected with the Tribunal?" Avery asked.

"No, the only other one I knew of was Emelynn, and turns out she is connected."

"Like hell I am." My outburst hushed the room and the ensuing quiet claimed us for a few moments.

I turned to Avery. "Maybe I could stay here with you tonight?" It was an imposition, but I'd stayed before. "Just to give Ron some time to get out of town."

"The timing is lousy, Emelynn. Greg arrived this morning. He's already settled into my guest room."

"I forgot all about Greg's visit. Sorry, Avery. I'll figure out something else."

"I could stay with you at your place for a night or two," James said. "I was going to get a room anyway. You've got a spare room, right?"

I glared at him, bewildered. "You get that I'm angry with you, right?"

"Oh yeah, but I'm not the bad guy here."

James did look sincere, hurt even, but I couldn't let go of my mistrust. "I don't think so, James."

"Maybe you should consider it, Emelynn. Having James with you is better than being alone right now."

"I could bunk in with Eden and Alex for a few days."

"And make them a target of the Tribunal?" James asked.

"He's got a point," Avery said.

"Let me think about it."

James pushed off from the bookcase and set his empty glass on the desk. "Thanks for seeing me, Avery." He handed me a card. "My number. If I don't hear from you by eight tonight, I'll get a room in town. Thanks for the drink." He then turned and left.

"Do you think he'll hang around?" I asked.

"Why do you ask?"

"He seems to know so much about them. Maybe he knows if they're responsible for the hacking."

"They're not. Jackson called earlier. He gave me the name of the hacker. James didn't know the name."

"Who is it?"

"A guy named Rupert Dowling."

Just then a man I didn't know walked into the den. "Who is Rupert Dowling?" he asked.

"Ah, Greg. You're back. I'd like you to meet Emelynn Taylor. Emelynn, this is Greg Jeffries."

If I had to describe a computer nerd, Greg Jeffries was it, right down to the bowling shirt and loafers. He was mid-thirties, my height, with mousy over-gelled hair parted way off to the side. He had thick, oversized glasses and the only thing not nerdy was his broad build.

"Don't get up," he said, coming over to shake my hand. "My word—what happened to you?" He spoke with an accent.

"It was nothing. An accident," I said, then quickly changed the subject. "I'm trying to place your accent. British?"

"Australian. My family moved to the States when I was a teenager."

"How was your trip up from Portland?"

"Fine, thank you. I'm looking forward to a few days of sightseeing."

"Have you been here before?"

"Not to Summerset. It was good of Avery to offer me his guest room. Speaking of Avery." Greg turned around. "What's this about a Rupert Dowling?"

"He's the name behind the hacking. Jackson phoned after you left this morning. Does the name mean anything to you?"

"No. Do we have an address for him yet?"

"Not yet, but Jackson's people are on it."

"Yes, Jackson's crew seem to be very good at digging things up. He'll have an IP address in no time."

It was time for me to go. "Thanks for patching me up, Avery." I stood. "Nice to meet you, Greg. I'll see myself out," I said, walking toward the door.

"I'll walk you. Back in a moment," Avery called to Greg, closing in behind me.

When we were clear of the kitchen, Avery spoke. "I know you don't want to hear this, but I think you should call James."

"It just feels weird, Avery. I hardly know him."

"Do it for me? I don't think you should be alone, and James has come through for you more than once. I'd feel much better if he stayed with you for a few days. Just until everyone connected with the Tribunal leaves and things settle down with this hacker situation."

"You trust him?"

"You don't?"

"Trust and I aren't exactly seeing eye to eye these days."

"I trust him."

Avery looked so positive. I wished I felt the same way. "I'll think about it."

"Good. Call me if you need anything, and for god's sake, don't practice any more of your self-defence moves on Tribunal people."

That put a smile on my face. "See you later," I said, as I stepped out onto the sidewalk.

"Good night." Avery waved in the rear-view mirror when I pulled away from the curb.

Chapter Seventeen

Rumbles was closed by the time I drove by, not that I could visit Molly anyway. I'd need a cover story for my fresh injuries first. But it was too light outside to go flying, and I didn't really feel like going back to the cottage, so I pulled into the Safeway parking lot and dialled Eden.

"I was hoping you'd call," she said. "And please don't tell me you're only now getting home from your date?"

Was that just last night? "I'm afraid the date wasn't quite that successful." In the aftermath of the Tribunal's visit, my dinner with Dean had been relegated to distant memory. "I know it's Saturday night and all, but do you feel like getting together?"

"Sure. Alex won't be home for a few more hours. How about I come by?"

"No," I blurted out. "I'm not at home."

"O . . . kay," Eden said. "Is everything all right?"

"Yes, for now, but I could use your advice."

"Why don't you come over here then?"

"I'd rather meet somewhere else." I hadn't forgotten James's warning about making her and Alex a target of the Tribunal. "Have you eaten yet?"

"No. Do you want to meet at the Turtle?"

"That sounds perfect." The Neon Turtle was a Thai fusion restaurant tucked into a row of trendy shops not far from the other side of the park. Eden had introduced me to it.

The Turtle's neighbourhood was busy, which put parking at a

premium. The closest spot I could find was two blocks away on a dead-end residential street, abutting the park.

The heady aroma of Thai curry wafted out to greet me when I opened the door. The place was like those little SenSen liquorice breath fresheners—tiny but packing a lot of punch. A dozen tables crowded the restaurant's narrow floor space. Dim lighting added to the warmth of the textured yellow walls. I spotted Eden at a table halfway down. I used my hair like a curtain to hide the tape and the worst of the bruising and ducked my head as I seated myself.

"There's room outside on the patio—" She stopped abruptly when she got a look at my face. "What happened?" she gasped, reaching out to lift my hair away.

"Avery fixed me up. I'm okay." I re-established the curtain to camouflage my injuries from the other diners.

"This didn't happen on your date?"

"No. The date was a failure, but not because of Dean."

"I think you'd better tell me what happened."

I began with Dean. Eden was a quality listener, rarely interrupting and never second-guessing my actions, even the daft ones. "I'm sorry," was all she said when I told her how the date ended.

The satay and coconut chicken curry with cashews arrived with a big bowl of rice. We ate family style, sharing the fragrant dishes. My teeth ached where Sebastian had hit me. I skipped over my encounter with Case and picked up again with the alarm going off. She dropped her spoon and clutched my arm at the point where the Tribunal showed up in my house and squeezed tighter when she heard about Mason and then James.

She let go when I got to the part about Jolene's letter. Explaining all of that took us through to dessert. I finished at the part where I flew out of the cottage, but I skipped the whole Ghost business. Eden was safer not knowing that detail. She would understand me keeping it from her. She was, after all, the one who explained that Fliers lied to protect the people they cared about, and I cared about her.

Like Avery, she had a lot of questions about James and the particulars of his memory-reading abilities. She also offered a different perspective. "It must be hard for him, living with that quirk. Imagine never being able to shake someone's hand without learning stuff you don't want to know."

"What do you mean?"

"If he learned about Jackson from a simple shake of your hand, imagine what he gets when he meets someone who's just euthanized their pet or lost a loved one."

She made me wonder if I should have kept quiet about James's gift. The waiter came with our dessert: mango slices and coconut ice cream. I pushed at it with my spoon. The guilt of revealing James's quirk ate at me. "I shouldn't have said anything about James."

She reached over and patted my hand, offering a reassuring smile. "Don't worry. We Fliers are good at keeping secrets." She looked pointedly at the tape over my eyebrow. "How does Avery fit into your story?"

I ended my epic tale of woe by telling her about encountering James at Avery's.

"You sure pack a lot into forty-eight hours," she said.

"Not intentionally." I poked at my desert. "Would you trust James?"

"Avery thought it was a good idea, right?"

"He did. But I don't know James."

"He's pulled you out of the fire twice now. Maybe he deserves your trust. Besides, who else are you going to ask? I can't think of many Fliers who would willingly tangle with the Tribunal."

"If I don't call him by eight, he's going to find a room elsewhere."

"It's almost eight now. I think you should call him."

I fought a slippery slice of mango with my spoon.

"You can kick him out tomorrow if tonight goes badly."

Avery's trust and Eden's faith proved hard to discount. "You're right. Do you mind?" I asked, pulling out my phone. "I'll just step outside a minute."

I stood outside by a potted topiary cedar and dialled the number on James's card. Close by, two men in baseball caps spoke quietly to one another. My presence prompted them to move farther away. "I'll just be a minute," I said, apologizing for my interruption. James and I spoke briefly, agreeing to meet at the cottage at nine.

"Well, for better or worse, it's done," I said, when I rejoined Eden.

She opened the cellophane from the mint chocolate that the waiter had left with the bill. "Good. When Alex comes by to pick me up, I'll fill him in."

"Thanks. I met someone else at Avery's today," I said, as I pulled out my wallet. I was about to tell her about Greg Jeffries, when the man himself walked through Turtle's door.

"What is it?" Eden said, seeing the surprise on my face. She followed my gaze to the man at the door. "Do you know him?"

"Yes. That's Greg Jeffries, the man I met this afternoon at Avery's. He's the contact who found Jolene's identity. Avery invited him to visit."

The hostess took a menu and led Greg right by our table. He lit up when he saw me. "Emelynn, how nice to see you again."

"Greg, what a coincidence. What are you doing here?"

"I was hungry," he said, laughing. "Avery told me about this place. I thought I'd try it out."

"Where is he?"

"I gave him tickets to the dinner theatre on Granville Island. A little thank you for his hospitality."

"That's so thoughtful," I said. "Do you want to join us?"

"Oh, I don't know. It looks like you're finished."

"You can have our table when we leave then. Come on, join us."

He acquiesced, and the waiter pulled over a chair for him and left him with the menu. "Greg Jeffries, this is Eden Effrome."

Eden shook his hand and smiled. "Pleased to meet you, Greg. You're the one who runs the Infinity message board, right?"

"Yes, but you know, of course, that we're not using that one anymore. I'll shut it down altogether before too long."

"Emelynn tells me we have a name to put to the hacker now."

"Yes, though I don't recall it off the top of my head."

"Rupert Dowling," I said, remembering the name without hesitation.

"Yes, that sounds right. So what are you ladies doing for the rest of the evening?"

"I'm heading home to make up my spare room," I said.

"And I'm waiting for my husband, who will be by any minute to pick me up."

"Well then, I'll keep you company while you wait."

We didn't have to wait long. Alex arrived and Eden introduced him. "What the hell happened to you?" he said, when he saw my face.

"Eden will explain. I've got to get going or I'll be late." I stood and arranged the long strap of my purse across my chest. I kissed Alex on the cheek and reached down to give Eden a half hug. "Thanks for listening."

"Any time."

I turned to Greg. "Maybe I'll see you again before you leave?"

"I'm sure you will," he said with a smile, as Alex claimed my seat.

I headed to my car in the waning daylight. The sidewalk had quieted and only a few stragglers remained. I turned down the street where I'd parked. It was deserted and dead-ended at the park. If only I could fly to the cottage, I thought, checking the time. I'd be lucky to get home ahead of James.

My thoughts were on sheets and towels for the spare room when I first noticed the footsteps behind me. I crossed the street and considered whether being aware of my surroundings was a good thing or if it just added unnecessary anxiety. Regardless, I dug my keys out of my purse and laced them point out between my fingers like I'd learned to do in the self-defence class. The steady footsteps would probably turn any minute, but I felt better being prepared, even if it did make me feel paranoid.

But whoever was behind me didn't turn. Their footsteps followed, closing in much too quickly for comfort. My car was still half a block away. I stepped up my pace. My heart raced when the footsteps sped up in response and I glanced back. I recognized the two men with the base-ball caps from the restaurant. The moment they saw me turn, they started running, coming straight for me. I wasn't going to make it to the car. I didn't even have a panic button on my old key fob ... so I ran. Running I could do. I passed the MGB and headed to the end of the street, aiming for the park. If I could get into the thick of the trees, I could use their cover to escape. Even in daylight, I could hide above the tree canopy.

I jumped a low berm of scrub brush and landed too close to a sharp twig. It jabbed into my ankle. I ignored the sting and raced into the trees. Behind me, one of the men tripped on the berm. I heard the bushes snap under his fall. Adrenalin numbed my ankle and thrust me noisily through the ferns, over fallen trees and into the cool damp forest. When the undergrowth thinned, I picked up speed, but the two men's heavy footsteps were close behind.

Just ahead I saw a path and leapt over the low growth at the edge of it, landing sure-footed. Without breaking my stride, I turned right and kept going. My footfalls quieted on the earthen path. My pursuers followed close enough that I heard one of them shout, "Which way?"

The path had turned and they couldn't see me. They'd have to guess. I pumped my legs, thankful for Malcolm's insistence that I push myself. He'd be impressed, though not with my decision to head into a desolated park. What was I thinking? I couldn't take my eyes off the path long enough to find a clear shot into the sky. All I could do was keep running. The men had guessed the right direction and were gaining ground.

The path forked and I sprinted to the right. I'd run most of the paths in this park; this one should have been familiar. Where was I? I reached to flip on the GPS, forgetting that my keys were still woven between my fingers. I fumbled for the switch and paid for that brief distraction with a painful stumble over a root. I sailed forward, landing hard on my shoulder, the same one I'd ploughed into my mother's sofa with last night. Damn it! That hurt, but I didn't have time to coddle it. The heavy footsteps were closing in and before I regained my stride, I caught a glimpse of the men through the trees. They were too close.

Panic stole my breath, raising the fear I'd been trying to keep in check. I couldn't outrun them. With no other choice, I called on the crystal and recklessly broke free of gravity. The canopy was thick with no clear shot out, so I stayed low, flying off the path through the obstacle course of trees. It was a mistake. The trees were too tightly packed and unpredictably spaced. Their branches swiped at my limbs and eyes, making navigation impossible. A collision would be the end of me. I fought my way back to the path and heard one of the men shout, "There!" I didn't dare look back.

I flew above the path, hovering close to the ground, dodging the trees that altered the path's course. The baseball-capped men were finally losing ground. I could hear their footsteps falling back, but they weren't giving up. If I could avoid a collision and keep up this pace, I'd soon have enough leeway to find an opening in the tree canopy.

But my luck ran out. I heard children's laughter ahead and couldn't risk them seeing me like this. I had to land or get up and out of their sight. I chose up.

I sighted a cedar snag and shot straight for it then whipped around behind its rotting trunk. With difficulty, I quieted my heavy breathing. The decaying trunk's sparse branches didn't provide much cover, but at least it was up and people rarely looked up. Two boys on bikes passed beneath me riding toward my pursuers. The boys crossed paths with the men, oblivious to the chase underway. My hiding place felt dangerously inadequate as I watched the men run by below me. I lost sight of them and soon the quiet of the forest enveloped me.

I'd done it. The men hadn't seen my escape. How far would they continue along the path before they figured it out? Did I have enough time to return to my car? I stayed put, listening for their return. The GPS indicated the cottage lay to my left, probably ten minutes by air, but it was still too light out to risk flying.

The men soon made their way back along the path. "He's going to be pissed," one of them said, as they passed below.

"She probably doubled back," the other one added.

I watched until they were out of sight, then dropped down to the path, ignored the pain in my ankle and shoulder, and ran home.

CHAPTER EIGHTEEN

The cottage was just ahead. I slowed to a fast walk and gulped air in great heaves. My legs shook as I approached the house.

Out of nowhere, I heard a voice. "I thought maybe you'd changed your mind."

I screamed and turned around, ready to rake my keys across the face behind the voice.

"Hey! Back off." James leaned away from me with his hands in the air. "What happened?"

I closed my eyes. Relief flooded me as I let out a jagged breath and doubled over.

"Talk to me. What's going on?"

"Inside. We need to get inside." I straightened up and moved to the door. My keys had melded into my fingers and my hand shook as I unthreaded them. I isolated the door key then promptly dropped the whole mess. James bent down, picked them up and quickly unlocked the door. He ushered me inside, closed the door and turned the deadbolt. The alarm beeped quietly, waiting for the code.

"What's the disarm code?" he asked, poised to punch the keys.

I told him and he entered it. The beeping stopped. He stood there looking at me expectantly, his jaw tight, his eyes intense.

"I need water," I said, turning down the hall toward the kitchen.

James followed and headed straight for the patio door. "You want to tell me what's going on?" He'd found somewhere to change since I'd seen him last and wore a pale blue shirt tucked into jeans.

"I was followed from the restaurant," I said, after taking a big gulp, but the water didn't ease the burn in my lungs. "Two guys in baseball caps chased me into the park." I refilled the glass and took it to the dining room where I collapsed in the closest chair.

"Damn. How long ago?"

"Twenty minutes maybe. Why?"

"Do I need to clean up?"

"Clean up? What are you talking about?"

"How did you get away from these guys?"

"I ran, what did you think?"

"You're a Flier—I assumed you'd jolted them. In case you've forgotten, I've already cleaned up one of those messes for you."

The reminder hit hard. I *had* forgotten. James was the one who'd volunteered to deal with the armed guard I'd jolted unconscious at the shipyard during Sandra's rescue. I'd never even asked what happened to the man.

"He was okay, right?" I knew I'd knocked him out, but I'd never forgive myself if I'd done more damage than that.

"Okay? You jolted the man unconscious. He wasn't okay."

My face fell and James tilted his head and frowned. "Do you really not know its effect?" I shook my head, not trusting my voice. James softened his expression. "He was still breathing when I dialled 911. The paramedics would have found him quickly, but that's all I could do."

My hand flew to my mouth, covering my gasp. "I didn't mean to hurt him. We just wanted to get out of there alive." Eden was behind the wheel that night. We were trespassing in the shipyard when the guard came at us with his gun drawn.

"You might not have killed him, but you could have caused a brain bleed." James sat across the table from me. "You did the right thing with that guard. He was armed. Hesitation, when a gun's involved, will get you killed. Remember that. You're a Flier—you're not defenceless. Same goes for tonight. You were outnumbered and they were probably armed—you should have jolted them. But why didn't you just ghost?"

James didn't need to know how little I knew about being a Ghost. "I couldn't. There were other people around."

"If someone saw you vanish, they'd think their eyes were playing tricks on them and only a Flier would recognize a jolt. Witnesses would simply see the men drop. It would look like they'd fainted or at worst had a seizure."

"I feel like I've been pushed off the deep end."

James shook his head. "If you don't learn to swim, you'll drown." James stood and went back to staring out the patio door. "Were they Fliers?"

His question made me pause. "I don't think so."

"Did you recognize them?"

Condensation dripped from my glass. "I recognized them, but I don't know them. They were the same two guys who were standing outside the restaurant when I was on the phone with you. After I hung up, I went back inside. I didn't leave for another fifteen minutes or so because Greg showed up and after that Alex came in, but before . . ."

"Wait, wait, slow down. Start at the beginning."

I leaned back against the hard chair and recounted the details.

"So, when you left Avery's, Greg was still there, but you hadn't yet set up your dinner date with Eden?"

"That's right."

"And Eden was already at the restaurant when you arrived?"

"Yes, and Greg and Alex met us there."

"Then whoever chased you either followed you from Avery's office or followed Greg or Alex there."

"No, I saw the men outside before Greg or Alex showed up. Maybe they knew I was eating at the Turtle tonight."

"Could someone have overheard your conversation with Eden?"

"No. I was in my car. This doesn't make any sense to me. Does it to you?"

"Not offhand, but someone wants to get their hands on you. No doubt about that."

"Why?"

"You know why."

"Because I'm a Ghost?"

"Can you think of another reason?"

"But the only ones who know are you and Avery." I drained the glass.

"Someone else must have figured it out."

"Jackson?"

He shook his head. "I may not like the guy, but his first line of attack would be to try to charm it out of you. He wouldn't hurt you."

"Who, then?" I asked, ignoring the much too obvious retort about Jackson. "Someone with the Tribunal?"

"No, they wouldn't have to chase you."

"Cole, then. Maybe he's pissed about losing his meal ticket?" Cole was Jackson's half-brother and the one responsible for Sandra's kidnapping.

"I don't know. Maybe. I can check on his whereabouts."

I moved into the living room and dropped on the sofa. Would Jackson's half-brother really be so stupid as to try another round of kidnapping to get to Jackson's purse strings? "They said that someone would be pissed, so another person was definitely involved."

"Do you think they knew your car?"

"I couldn't tell."

"It's still at the restaurant?" he asked, and I nodded. "When it's dark, we'll go get it."

"Speaking of cars, where's yours?"

"Down the block. No one needs to know you've got company."

I called Eden to warn her. She and Alex were alarmed, as expected, but grateful for James's presence. My next call was to Avery. I filled him in on the evening's events. If I'd been followed from Avery's, then he needed to get Greg and Victoria up to speed fast, so they wouldn't fall prey to the same men.

"Thanks for the heads-up. I'll make sure they know," Avery said.

"I'm sorry, Avery, I haven't even asked you how your night at the dinner theatre turned out."

"It was great, thanks. Haven't been to a live performance in a long time." I promised to keep my phone close and let him know right away if anything else came up.

While we waited for dark, I found the sheets and James helped me make up the guest bed. While I cleaned the scrape on my ankle, he retrieved a small bag from his car and set it on the dresser.

When the blue hue of night replaced daylight, I changed into flying gear and we flew back to get my car. We emerged from the small neighbourhood park that Eden and I had used before to camouflage our landing. My hair was tied back, and I pulled the hoodie forward so it hung loose over my face. We retraced my steps from the restaurant to the car. I kept the keys woven through my fingers the whole time. James remained alert, watching for anything out of the ordinary.

"Get inside the car and lock the doors," James instructed when we were close to the MGB. "Don't start it until I'm back." He disappeared under the back bumper before I had the door open and reappeared at the passenger door a few moments later.

"It's clear," he said, buckling up.

"What were you looking for?"

"Tracking devices. There weren't any. Let's go."

When we returned home, I backed into the garage and didn't breathe easy until we were safely inside the cottage.

"I don't think they'll try again tonight now that they know you're on to them," James said, unzipping his jacket. He took it off and turned to toss it on his bed. That's when I saw the handle of a gun sticking up from the waistband of his black jeans.

"Do you always carry a gun?" The sight of a gun never failed to raise my anxiety level.

"Yes," he said without apology.

"They frighten me."

"That's because you don't know how to use one." He pulled the door to his room closed. "With the trouble that seems to follow you around, maybe you should learn."

I turned on my heel and strode to the living room.

"You keep your glasses in here?" James asked, opening a kitchen cupboard. Apparently, he would be making himself at home. "It's late," he continued, filling his glass from the tap. "We should get some sleep. Try not to worry. You're as safe as you can be."

"Let's hope so. Go ahead and use the bathroom." I crossed to my bedroom. "Good night." I closed the door and for the first time since I'd moved back to the cottage, I closed the bedroom curtains. It felt like admitting defeat, but this evening's events had scared me. I'd barely escaped and even having James in the house didn't make me feel safe. I changed into my nightshirt and waited until I heard him finish in the bathroom then took my turn.

When I turned out the lights, my thoughts raced around the trifecta of the Tribunal, my pursuers, and Jolene's letter. I re-fluffed my pillow half a dozen times and tossed from side to side, but sleep took its time finding me.

When I woke the next morning, I didn't feel rested. I dragged myself out of bed, put on my housecoat and headed to the kitchen. James was already dressed and staring out at the ocean. His chocolate brown T-shirt was tucked into last night's black jeans, and I could see the bulge from the gun he'd already tucked into the small of his back.

"Good morning."

"Morning," he replied. "Did you sleep okay?"

"I've had better nights. You?"

"Yeah, me too."

"You want coffee?" I asked.

"Sure."

I set the pot to brew and headed to the bathroom. James had left his Dopp kit on the back of the toilet. I popped a painkiller then retreated to the bedroom to dress. When I emerged, he'd already found the mugs and had left one out for me.

Steaming mug in hand, I reached above the patio door frame to remind him where I kept the spare key. A warm breeze rushed into the room when I opened the door. We went out to the deck and leaned against the rail. Being lanky, I was surprised to see such well-defined muscles in James's arms.

I'd thrown on a pair of jean shorts and a T-shirt which, though a little cool right now, would be perfect in an hour or so when the summer heat picked up. James had pulled his hair into a tight ponytail that sharpened the angles in his face. His pale blue eyes contrasted sharply with his dark hair, adding an icy touch to an already harsh facade.

"This is a beautiful spot. I saw it in your memories of course, but it's so much more seeing it in person. There's a peaceful quality to it."

Normally I loved it when people admired the cottage, but hearing James reference his ability to read memories in passing, like he'd seen this view on YouTube, was odd, to say the least.

"Are you sure your father wasn't a Flier?" he asked. "This is a Flier's paradise."

"I'm sure." My life would have been so much easier if he had been. According to Avery, if my dad was a Flier, I'd have been born with the gift.

"You can't tell from here," I said, "but the shoreline varies dramatically along this stretch. There's a sandy beach about a kilometre south of here. It's where I tried to learn how to control the gift before I knew what it was."

"I remember."

I glanced at him, surprised.

He looked down to the handrail. "I felt your panic when you were out of control that night. Before you fell."

"From my memories," I said, understanding.

"Reading memories is rarely a pleasant experience for me, Emelynn. It's not a talent I would choose if I'd had that choice."

"Can Sandra do it too?"

"No. That gene has been inherited only by the males in my family, and I have no intention of inflicting this on anyone else." He squinted out at the horizon and took a deep breath. "I'm the end of the line. The last one in my family who the Tribunal will ever be able to coerce."

"You look relieved at that."

"You have no idea," he said, smiling thinly.

Looking at him now, he didn't look very menacing. Maybe Eden was right about how difficult that little quirk had been for him and for his family.

"You hungry?" I asked. "I can make breakfast."

"No, but thanks. I'll get something when I'm out."

"Where are you going?" It was shocking how quickly I'd changed my tune. Yesterday I hadn't wanted him anywhere near me and today, he was my security blanket.

"I've got some investigating of my own to do and I still have contacts here. If they've heard rumblings about what's going on, I'll get more intel with a face-to-face visit."

"I'll go with you."

"Nothing personal, Emelynn, but you wouldn't be welcome. Stay in the cottage and keep away from the windows."

"*This* cottage?" I asked, questioning his powers of observation. "There's no avoiding windows in there unless you think I'm going to hole up in a closet? Besides, I feel like a coward hiding in my house. If I do that, then they've won."

"It's your choice, but if they get to you—they've won anyway."

He let me think on that while we finished our coffee in silence.

"I'll be out most of the day." He turned to go back inside. We'd barely crossed the threshold when the doorbell chimed. James caught my forearm. "Check the peephole first," he said, keeping pace with me.

"It's Molly," I said, relieved as I reached for the doorknob.

James stopped me. "Your face?" I'd forgotten. Molly would question the new cut and bruises.

I paused then nodded my head and opened the door. Molly looked like a blast of fresh air in a red polka dot skirt and white halter top. She wore white bauble earrings but had skipped the hair band today. I felt like a fashion pauper standing beside her.

"Molly, what are you doing here?" I laughed, hearing how that sounded and rephrased. "I mean, what a nice surprise."

Molly lifted her sunglasses to perch on her head and winced. "Not again."

It fit perfectly into the lie I'd been working on. "Afraid so," I said, making light of it. "Come in."

"You can tell me all about it over croissants," she said, leading her way into the house with a grease-stained paper bag. "They're still warm—."

She gave a little start. James wasn't exactly hiding behind the door, but Molly didn't see him until I closed it behind her.

"Sorry—this is James," I said, and suddenly I was in a bind. Fabricating two lies simultaneously had me reaching. Luckily James wasn't as stymied.

"James Moss. Lovely to meet you, Molly . . .?"

"Molly Connolly." She switched the bag to her left hand and offered James her right.

He shook her hand and flipped a switch, leaking charm all over the floor. It wasn't a side of James that I'd seen before, and it took me by surprise. "I'm a friend of the family." I couldn't figure out what exactly he'd done to soften his presentation. Maybe he'd rounded his shoulders or it could have been the beguiling smile. It was subtle, but it worked and Molly smiled back. Had he read her memories with that handshake?

"I was just heading out. Molly, nice meeting you." Molly had taken a few steps into the hall and James passed between us. "Emelynn, I'll see you later." He ducked his head, feigning a kiss on my cheek, but instead, he whispered in my ear, "Don't go out alone."

CHAPTER NINETEEN

After locking the door behind him, I turned to face Molly who was all raised eyebrows and curiosity. "We are definitely talking about this *friend of the family*, but first, what happened to you?" She pushed my hair aside to get a good look at my face.

"How about we talk over croissants?" I led her to the kitchen. She laid the croissants on the plates I set out while I made a fresh pot of coffee.

"So, talk," she said, tipping her head to indicate my face.

"I tried telling you the first time this happened. I'm a hopeless klutz."

"Did you need stitches?"

"No, just tape. It doesn't even hurt."

"You sure are hard on your face. Maybe you should practice falling on some other body part."

She had a good chuckle at that and then dove directly into the James topic. Having had some time to think about it, I turned him into the son of a friend of my mother's from Toronto. Hopefully, James could live with that.

"Between this," she waved at my face, "and James, you've completely distracted me from my real mission. How'd it go with Dean on Friday?" She had the hope of a ticket-clutching lotto player on her face.

"There's not much to tell. We had a wonderful dinner and then I scared him away with my glaring lack of trust in anyone of the male persuasion."

"Dean doesn't strike me as the type to frighten that easily."

"I'm not suitable date material, Molly. Not yet. I'll get Jackson out of my system eventually, but I think it's going to take more time."

"How did you leave it with him?"

"Badly, I think. He said . . . how'd he put it?" I searched my memory for his words. "He didn't want to be the 'focus of my fear.'"

"Ouch. That doesn't sound good."

"I didn't mean to jump every time he got near me, but I couldn't help it. It's not Dean's fault. It's me that's screwed up."

The Dean topic wore pretty thin after that, and I'd had enough bad-date talk.

"Do you want to help me pick out some curtains for the living room today?" I asked. Covering the windows seemed like a prudent compromise in the name of safety and with her background in design, Molly was the perfect person to help me find something that fit in.

"That'd be fun. We need to measure first though. Do you have a measuring tape?"

"I think there's a ruler in my dad's desk. Will that work?"

"As long as we're not going for precision, I think we can manage."

We measured and made a shopping list. Before we left, I scribbled James a quick note then maintained a firm grip on the alarm's panic button while I opened the garage. I know James thought I was safest staying inside the house, but I felt so much better once we got on the road.

While Molly shopped, I kept a vigilant watch on the people around us. Molly selected a ready-made curtain in a lightweight, cream coloured fabric with a vertical pale blue stripe. It had just enough blue to pick up the colour in my mother's furniture without seeming to add a new element to an already small room.

I stretched out our time away from the cottage, insisting on a long sit-down restaurant lunch—my treat for her help. Afterwards, we stopped at Home Depot to buy the hardware and tools needed to hang the new curtains.

When I ran out of delays, we returned home. Within an hour, she had the rod and curtains installed. We were standing back, admiring her handiwork when my phone rang.

It was Avery, checking in. "I'm fine," I said.

"Is James there?" he asked.

"No, he went out this morning, but Molly's here," I said brightly, knowing she couldn't help but overhear my conversation.

"That's good. When are you expecting James to return?"

"I have no idea. He said he had some contacts in the area he wanted to touch base with."

"Well, if Molly can't stay with you, come over here, okay?"

"Why, did you learn something?"

"No. I just agree with James. You shouldn't be alone." We hung up, but only after I agreed to call him later.

Molly didn't ask who was on the phone, but I knew her well enough to know the curiosity would be killing her.

"That was Dr. Coulter," I said, putting her out of her misery. "He was checking up on me."

"On a Sunday? Wow, he must be some doctor. Mine never checks up on me."

"I think he's taken a special interest because I told him my dad was a doctor. That, and he knows I don't have family here."

"I'm happy for you. Everyone should have someone to look out for them. Speaking of which, I'd better get going. Cheney and I are meeting the gang at Fast Eddies tonight." She smiled sheepishly. "I don't suppose you want to join us?"

"Thanks, but not just yet. I think Dean could use a break from my company. How about I drive you home?"

I dropped off Molly and phoned Avery. He invited me to join him and Victoria for dinner. He was making a seafood linguine with four-cheese garlic bread. I could hardly turn that down.

"I'll watch for you," he said before he hung up and sure enough, he was at the door when I pulled up in front. He ushered me inside.

"Did you get hold of Greg?"

"Yes, and I warned him to be extra cautious." We went through the waiting room toward the kitchen. "I'm glad I invited him. He's quite enjoying Vancouver; raves about Summerset. And he's such an easy guest—out all day and quiet when he's here. Self sufficient with his rental car and that iPad he never lets go of. I hardly ever see him."

When we got to the kitchen, Victoria was making a salad, and I could see a table set up in the back garden. It looked lovely, in fact, too lovely. Was I interrupting a romantic evening?

Avery had already filled Victoria in on what had happened with the Tribunal and the events of last night, but she still fussed about my face. Her attention felt awkward. It seemed like I was always the one in trouble and they were always the ones bailing me out.

"I should call James," I said. "Let him know where I am."

"Why don't you invite him for dinner?" Avery said. "We have plenty."

I called him and felt much less like a fifth wheel when he accepted Avery's invitation.

When James arrived, he joined us at the kitchen table. "Jackson's IT team got a fix on Rupert Dowling last night and were able to confirm a street address. It's just outside of Rockport. That's roughly halfway between Los Angeles and Portland. We got boots on the ground this morning, but our guy can't get near the place for police. Looks like someone killed Dowling a few days ago."

"Our hacker was murdered?" I said, alarmed.

"So it appears."

"By whom?" Avery asked.

"Don't know, and the police haven't charged anyone yet. But Dowling had an extensive record—identity theft, blackmail, forgery—all the typical stuff you'd expect from someone with a criminal mind and his skill set. Even more disturbing, he was a person of interest in an armed robbery that went bad and turned into a kidnap-for-ransom case. The victim turned up dead and mutilated. If Dowling was involved in that, we're well rid of him."

"Does it look like the work of the Tribunal?" Victoria asked.

"In the murder?" James asked. Victoria nodded and he shrugged. "Don't know, but it's not like the Tribunal to leave a body lying around for the police to find."

"Do you think it's connected to the men who were chasing me?" I asked.

"Could be. If someone hired Dowling to kidnap you and they thought Dowling screwed up, they might have been covering their tracks. But with Dowling's stellar record and the company he was keeping, who knows how many people were lined up to get rid of him?"

"What about Cole?" I asked. He'd already kidnapped once. He might be capable of murder.

"Jackson's brother?" Avery asked. "You think he's involved?"

"No," James interjected. "Cole's whereabouts are accounted for. It wasn't him."

"I'm sure Jackson will be relieved to hear that," Avery said.

"Jackson's the last person you need to worry about," James said, a little too snidely.

"Where do we go from here?" I asked.

"If there are no further attempts to get at you over the next few days, then I'd say it's likely Dowling hired the goons last night. They'll disappear as soon as they learn that their money-man won't be paying up."

"So, she just waits it out?" Avery asked.

James's defensive hackles came up. "Hey, I'm not running this show."

Avery looked at the floor and shook his head. "Sorry, James. I know you're doing all you can."

The discussion hit a wall and silence filled the room.

Victoria took the salad to the table outside, and Avery tipped a plate of seafood into the pot of cream sauce.

"Do you think there's anything to be gained by involving the police?" Avery asked, stirring the sauce. "We could identify my email account instead of Infinity as the target of the hacking."

"Maybe we could get Detective Jordan on it. Give him something better to do with his time," I said, not entirely kidding, but it brought a chuckle out of Avery and lightened the mood somewhat.

"Detective Jordan?" James queried.

"Oh, did I not tell you about him?"

"No," he said, and rolled his eyes. "Enlighten me."

While Avery finished assembling our dinner, I told James about Charles and his camera and the series of events that led to the detective's involvement. I was certain that James knew about it, but he reminded me he'd arrived late the night that Jackson told the rest of the covey about the camera. Avery plated his creamy creation and we moved to the table outside. Jazz music played softly from a small speaker.

"What's this detective look like?" James asked as he twisted the pasta expertly onto his fork.

"Six foot, broad face, brush cut—kind of looks like a boxer—maybe a wrestler, you know, big in the shoulders. The last couple of times I saw him he was driving a brown, unmarked police car."

"Did this Charles character work for anyone else on your street?"

"I'm not certain. Why?"

"A brown sedan was parked near the end of your block when I left your place this morning. I'd pegged it for an unmarked, which is why I noticed it, but there was no one in it."

"Oh great, he was probably spying on me again."

James chuckled. "I think they call it surveillance in his line of work." It was my turn to roll my eyes, but James wasn't done. "Don't knock it. He's doing you a favour. You couldn't ask for a better deterrent than a police presence."

"Good point," Avery said. "If the guys who were chasing you see the police, they won't risk getting spotted."

James addressed me. "I'll stick around a few more days in case something else turns up. That is, if you don't mind."

"Not at all." After last night, I felt safer knowing he was around.

"Good, that's settled then," Avery said.

As we finished the last of our wine, Avery pushed away from the table. "Dessert, anyone?"

It had grown dark, and my T-shirt and shorts were no longer warm enough for the cooling evening air. We moved inside to devour Avery's tiramisu. I helped clear the table and load the dishwasher before leaving.

"Thanks, Avery, Victoria. That was outstanding." I pulled my purse over my shoulder.

"Let me know if you learn anything more about Dowling," Avery said to James, offering his hand.

"You, too," James said.

I gave Avery and Victoria quick hugs then headed to my car.

"I'll be right behind you," James called, turning down the street.

I couldn't see his car. Maybe he always parked *down the block.*

"Drive safely," Avery said, waving as I buckled up.

I pulled away from the curb and kept an eye on my rear-view mirror for James, but he never came into view. It made me reassess just how far down the block he considered adequate.

The unmarked police car was nowhere to be seen along Cliffside. I pulled into the driveway and backed into the garage. James was probably parking a mile away, but given the bull's eye on me, I didn't think it was smart to sit outside and wait for him. With my keys out and the panic button under my thumb, I approached the front door. Once safely inside, my anxiety seemed silly, but this was probably going to be the norm for a few more days.

The living room looked strange to me with the new curtains drawn. The room seemed smaller somehow, closed off. It was the same effect with the curtains in the bedroom and I didn't like it. I ditched my purse beside the dresser and pulled the bedroom curtains open. Instantly, the room opened up.

　　　　　　　　　　　　　　　　　　　　　

I returned to the living room. Despite how claustrophobic it felt, Molly had chosen well. The curtains were as unobtrusive as they could be, but it would take some time to get used to them. I reached up and pulled aside the right half. A carpet of twinkling stars reflected off the calm surface of the ocean. It was a clear night, perfect for flying. I pulled open the other side and then my heart leapt into my throat, choking off my scream.

Chapter Twenty

Mason stared benignly through the glass at me. If the fact that his presence had been revealed bothered him, he gave no indication. Instead, he looked relaxed, lounging in the deck chair that I usually called mine. His calm demeanour in the face of my near heart failure pissed me off.

When the shock of seeing him dissipated, I opened the patio door. He'd frightened me more than I would ever let on. "What's wrong Mason—lose your lock-picking tools?" I said with contempt. "Oh, that's right, you don't need them." I turned, leaving the door open, and went back inside. I couldn't stop him from coming in anyway. He followed me in.

I marched toward the dining room, anger leaking out with every step. "At least last time you had the decency to set off the alarm so I'd have a heads-up."

"I thought I'd try for polite this time."

I turned on him. "Too late. Polite's a phone call, an invitation, and a little thing they call a doorbell."

Mason wore the standard Flier uniform, dark from head to toe, but he managed more leather than anyone I knew. I couldn't help comparing him to James. They both threw off a menacing glare, but Mason had removed his gloves and stroked the bunched-up leather, giving him the edge on intimidating.

"We need to talk."

"No. We don't." I rounded the counter into the kitchen, unsure what I was doing there, but trying hard to put floor space between us.

"You're the only connection I have left to Jolene."

"Maybe you should have thought about that before you invited your buddies in here to beat me up . . . while you watched . . . and did nothing. Did your friends send you a dead dove after your visit?"

He ignored my remark. "It didn't have to be like that. You didn't even try to cooperate."

"You didn't ask!" I turned to face him. "This is my house." I shook my head at his audacity. "You broke in and scared me half to death. What did you expect? I'd offer myself up for a beating? What kind of world do you live in where that's a reasonable expectation?"

"Reasonable? How's this for reasonable? I don't know you. Jolene didn't know you. No one had even heard of you until a few months ago. So you tell me—is it reasonable to expect me to trust you?"

"I don't care if you trust me. You shouldn't have been here."

"It's the reality of what we do, Emelynn. It's the world that Jolene brought you into and the same one you're now a part of, whether you like it or not."

I crossed my arms over my chest. "I didn't ask for any of this crap—none of it!" I turned my back to him. He wore a self-righteous look that I wanted to rip off his face.

"Yeah, but I'm betting you wouldn't give it up now even if you could."

I whirled around. "You arrogant ass." I let my temper get the best of me and hurled a furious jolt at him. It was one of my best and he wasn't expecting it. I rammed my block into place, expecting retaliation. He stumbled back a few steps, catching his balance. Chalk one up for me. I would have dearly loved to see him fall on his ass. That jolt would have knocked any other Flier halfway across the room, but not Mason. He just teetered then steadied himself.

"I guess I deserved that." He sat in the armchair closest to the patio door.

I shook my head at his arrogance. "By all means, make yourself at home." I reached for a water glass and turned away from him again. Just looking at him made me angry; made me wish I had a gun.

"Avery Coulter has been researching Ghosts."

My stomach dropped.

He waited until I turned back around. "Any idea why?" he asked. The threat was implied in the tone of his voice. Now I wished I knew how to use a gun.

"Why would you care?"

"You don't seem surprised, Emelynn. I thought you'd be more interested after the Tribunal's visit. Why is that?"

"I don't give a damn about your Tribunal or their tricks."

"I doubt that. I think you're very interested."

"Well, you're wrong."

"I don't think so. You fly like Jolene, you jolt like her and I'd bet my life you inherited her other little trick." He leaned forward, resting his elbows on his knees. "But my guess is . . . you can't control it."

I didn't say a word. He might have guessed that I was a Ghost, but I didn't need to confirm it for him.

"In our world, Emelynn, you will be treated like my niece."

"Whoop-de-do. So what? You want me to call you Uncle Mason now?" He thought that was funny. I didn't.

"It means you'll be treated like family. The Tribunal Novem is our covey and you're a part of that covey now."

"No, I'm not. My covey is right here," I stated, calm as can be. "This is where I belong." I made a circling motion to emphasize the point. "No one in my covey would have ever done to me what your twisted little group did."

"You're angry. I understand that, but you need to get over it." He pushed himself back up to his feet and raised his chin so he could look down his nose at me. "You're being petulant and short-sighted. I can help you. I'm probably the only one who can."

I left my untouched water glass in the kitchen and rounded the counter back toward the dining room, keeping the table between us. "I'm not interested in anything you have to offer, Mason. You can leave any time—the door's right behind you." I pointed the way, in case he'd forgotten.

"Do you know what the Tribunal Novem does?"

"You mean besides scaring the crap out of the rest of us?"

He chuckled. "Good to know, but yes, besides that?"

"Oh, do tell," I said, but even an imbecile wouldn't mistake the dead flat tone that meant, unequivocally, "Get out."

He ignored it. "We hold chaos at bay. We protect our secret from anyone and anything that threatens our free existence." Was he expecting a pat on the back? "Do you know how we accomplish that?"

"I think I have some idea," I said, tracing my hand over the bruise on my face.

"It's not always pleasant, but it's almost always a life-or-death scenario by the time we're involved."

"You're trying to tell me that *I* was a life-or-death scenario?"

"Jolene's gifting wasn't documented or witnessed, and she never once mentioned you or her plan to me or anyone else in our family or the covey. If Jolene had been forced against her will to transfer her gift to you, then you and anyone else connected with the gifting would have been responsible for her death. If James hadn't corroborated your story, you would have paid for her life with your own. So yes, it was a life-or-death scenario."

His words stopped me cold. I felt my way into the closest chair.

He looked smug and sat back down. "We're able to deal with these situations only because we're Ghosts. Ghosts have an edge that no other Fliers have. That's how we do it. If we didn't, people like Charles would sell us out to the highest bidder. You remember Charles, don't you? He wrote an impressive dissertation on us that would have made him famous; probably quite wealthy too. If he weren't so paranoid about someone stealing his research, he'd have already sent off a synopsis to the prestigious *Journal of Science*. That's who was considering publishing his work. Believe me, it was no easy task for us to have Charles discredit himself sufficiently to have the *JOS* dump his project."

I was speechless, first coming to grips with how close I'd come to the Tribunal's trash heap and now processing the Charles news bulletin. I didn't even hear James come in.

"Mason. I thought you were done here," he said, already through the hall at the kitchen.

"I don't think that's any of your business, James. What are you doing here?"

"Not that it's any of *your* business," I said, throwing Mason's words back at him, "but I invited him. He's staying with me."

"Well, isn't that cozy." Mason stood and rolled his shoulders. "Is there something going on between you two? Something the Tribunal missed perhaps, James?" He looked suspiciously from James to me then disappeared.

"Where the hell has he gone?" I asked, momentarily confused.

"My guess is he's checking our sleeping arrangements," James said.

"You're an intrusive prick, you know that?" I shouted, knowing Mason would hear me even if I couldn't see him.

He reappeared across the table from me moments later and I

jumped. "Sticks and stones, Emelynn," he said dismissively. "I find it's better to be certain whenever possible. It saves on unnecessary coercion." The last remark was aimed squarely at James.

"You and I aren't done," he said, pointing a determined finger at me. "Take as much time as you need, but don't fool yourself. You may not have asked for this, but it's yours now, warts and all, and if you're not inclined to forfeit it, then you'd best accept what you are—and that's one of us and it's not an easy ride."

Mason reached into his pocket, pulled out a business card and tossed it on the table. "If you don't get yourself killed before you get off your high horse, call me. Very few of us can teach you how to use my sister's gift. I'd suggest you don't waste the opportunity." He turned around and crossed to the patio door. "And get rid of those earrings." Instinctively I reached up to touch the amber earrings my mother gave me. "Amber traps Fliers like you and me as easily as it trapped insects when it was tree sap." He didn't wait for me to show him out, he just vanished—literally.

"Do you think he's gone?" I asked James, still fingering the earring. First the psychic and now Mason. What the hell was it with these earrings?

"I can't tell. But you might be able to." My confusion prompted him to continue. "I've seen the others do it—they seem to be able to sense if another Ghost is around."

I had, in fact, felt something in the air when I stood in the Tribunal's presence before. It had made my skin crawl. Closing my eyes, I tuned in to the hum of power running through my limbs and tested it, pulled on it, but didn't feel anything more than my own familiar measure.

"I can't feel anyone else, but who knows if I even could."

This time it was James's turn to look confused. "No, I don't suppose you've had much experience around other Ghosts."

"I can't control it, James—the ghosting," I confessed. "At least not yet, but Avery and I are working on it."

James frowned, digesting the news. "Mason knows you're a Ghost."

"He's just guessing."

"He offered to teach you to use his sister's gift. That's a little too close to the mark if you ask me."

I couldn't argue. Mason probably did know. How that might impact me, I had no idea. Right now, I didn't want to think about

Mason, period. "Let's go flying," I suggested. "I need to get Mason out of my head."

"Fly where?"

"Anywhere. It doesn't matter. I just want to forget about Mason and Ghosts and those men who chased me—just for a little while."

James frowned. Did he not understand the appeal of flying for fun? "It's an unnecessary risk. You can go play another time when the threat is behind you." He'd said *play* like it was a dirty word.

"Well then, make yourself at home." I retreated to my bedroom, changed into flying clothes, and pulled my hair back into a ponytail. He was elsewhere when I came back out, thankfully. I didn't want to argue with him about my flying. It was something I did for me, for my sanity, and I didn't need to justify it or ask for anyone's permission.

I set my phone on vibrate and tucked it into my pocket then stepped onto the deck. The stars sparkled brilliantly as I slipped down the beach stairs and headed south. If the people pursuing me were still out there, they couldn't touch me once I was airborne—no one could. I was safer there than anywhere else and it was a perfect night for flying. I lifted off the moment I was clear.

A steady offshore breeze accompanied me high up the cliff face and out over the trees into the park. I settled into a horizontal position and flew slowly, dangling my fingers to skim the treetops. Reaching out, I plucked a shiny arbutus leaf from a lurching trunk. The rust-coloured bark had split and peeled, revealing a brilliant green undercoat. Like floating in a wave pool, I dipped down and surged up, flowing over the contours of the tree canopy. Occasionally, I stopped to watch the birds that nested high in the massive cedars. Mine were the only hands that had ever touched these boughs and flights like this on such a perfect night made my heart sing. I was glad now that James had opted-out of tonight's flight. He would have spoiled the magic for me.

Last night's whirlwind chase through the park prompted me to embrace a new flying trick. At the first break in the tree canopy, I dove through the small opening and hovered horizontally a few feet above a path I knew well. I started slowly, threading my way just above the packed earth and clear of the trees that crowded in on either side. There was a rhythm to the flight, similar to the motion above the tree canopy, but more restricted, like navigating a twisty tunnel. I kept my arms tight to my sides and frequently ducked my head out of reach of branches that tested me every few feet. Sometimes the branches won, and I'd get swatted, but only once did my Ryders go flying without me. I landed to retrieve them, pleased with my progress, and decided to add low-level flying to the growing list of skills I practiced regularly.

Rising once again above the trees, I turned south, bearing toward the distant lighthouse. Would Case be there? Just thinking about him made me crave the physical possibilities. Sex was like chocolate—sweet temptation that was hard to resist once you'd had a taste. Had he thought about me—about our encounter? He must have. The real question was, did he regret it? How would he react when he saw me again—if he saw me again? I held my course thinking I'd decide when I got there.

As I approached the clearing to the lighthouse, I caught a glimpse of Case's Jeep parked near the trees at the edge of the clearing. I landed close by and touched the hood. Cold. He'd been here a while. Looking toward the white tower, I made my decision. My craving for the feel of his touch outweighed my concern about my new role as seductress. The speed with which I'd surrendered my virginity and perpetuated the headlong fall into moral debauchery was setting speed records, and it didn't even bother me.

I strode into the clearing and across the moonlit lawn. I may have been fine with the debauchery, but I wouldn't risk Case getting a first-hand glimpse of me in flight. As I approached the lighthouse, I wondered if there was a doorbell or did visitors knock? The base of the tall structure was at least fifty feet below the living quarters—would he even hear a knock? Before I got close enough to find out, the door swung open. Case stood in silhouette on the threshold and my heart skipped a beat. Had he been waiting? He wore nothing but jeans and boat shoes. I reached for his outstretched hand, and he pulled me through the door, banging it closed behind him with his foot as he pushed me up against the wall. This was not the passive Case I'd seduced two days ago.

His eyes lit up when he brushed the hair from my face. I pressed my fingers to his lips to silence him as he touched the tape above my eyebrow then traced his fingers gently along the bruise on my cheek. His hands cradled my face and his lusty expression faded, replaced with concern under a furrowed brow.

No, no, no—sympathy was not what I wanted. I turned my head sharply and bit into the flesh at the base of his thumb. Surprise replaced concern. He dropped his hands and took a step back, studying me.

Pity was the last thing I wanted from Case. I licked my lips, laid my hands flat against the wall behind me and waited. He held my gaze and tested my intention, moving in until our bodies were a breath apart. I didn't waver. His resolve was almost audible as it snapped back into place and lust once again crossed his face. He brought his lips to mine in a rough, urgent kiss that tasted nothing like regret. So much for me being the seductress, the one in charge. Case had upped his game and I liked it.

He reached down, pressing his hands against mine, pushing me into the wall and holding me there with his body. He thrust his tongue into my mouth, breathing like a freight train as he ground his erection into my stomach. He was hungry—just how long had he been waiting? The pained, cold Case was nowhere to be seen tonight. In his place was a blond firestorm of need and pent-up frustration. I happily bent to his will.

He released me long enough to pull my fleece over my head and kick off his Topsiders. I popped the top button on his jeans, and he quickly pulled my tank top up and off. He grabbed both my wrists in one hand and held them against the wall above my head as his lips found mine again and his urgency drove my desire through the roof. I jammed my toe against the heel of my shoe and kicked off one, and then the other. It felt like we were both making up for lost time. I pulled my hands free and broke from his lips long enough to unzip his jeans and push them off his hips. I pressed back against the wall and hooked my foot into his waistband shoving his jeans to the floor. He smiled his approval and I realized he'd gone commando. It was my lucky day. He stood before me naked and erect. He looked delicious—like the hard caramel after the milk chocolate is all licked off.

I let my eyes take in the sight before me, running my hands down the smooth skin of his torso and then wrapped my fingers around his erection. He inhaled on a hiss and threw his head back, pushing into my hand as I stroked him. His reaction was just what I craved. I loved that I could make a man feel like this and savoured every nuance on his face, every twitch of his body. After a half-dozen thrusts, he put his hands over mine and held them still, shaking his head and pulling my hands away from him.

He reached behind me and unfastened my bra, leaning in to reclaim my lips as he did so. For just the briefest of moments, I thought the move wasn't as smooth as Jackson's one-handed release then I pushed the thought aside. Jackson wasn't welcome here. Case removed my bra and took a moment to weigh my breasts in his hands before he slipped his hands under the waistband of my yoga pants and shoved them down, going down to one knee. I steadied my hands on his shoulders and stepped out of my pants. His beard stubble was rough against my skin as he pressed kisses between my breasts then licked a trail down to my belly button. The muscles between my hips contracted with a mind of their own.

A smile crossed my lips as I looked down at the top of his head and combed my fingers through his hair. Who this man was should have meant something to me. It didn't. How did I come to be that woman? He wound his arm around my waist and brushed his fingertips over the shiny pink skin of my bullet scar then kissed it gently. He oscillated between rough and gentle. I watched him slide his fingers under the top edge of my panties and sit back on his heels to pull them free of my feet. On his way back up, he trailed his fingers along the back of my legs. His left hand wound around to my backside, but his right hand detoured between my legs and found out just how wet he'd made me. He met my gaze to watch my face as he pushed first one, then two fingers inside. When he leaned forward to lick between my legs, a moan escaped my throat. I closed my eyes and laid my head back against the wall, afraid my knees would give out.

His clever manipulation brought me to the edge of orgasm, but he stopped short of letting me step off. I gasped at his abrupt inter-ruption, searching his face, desperate for him to continue. He smiled knowingly. I bit my lower lip to keep the agony at bay and watched him lean in for one final lollipop lick before turning aside to stand. He moved desperate hands to my breasts, rough and needy then followed suit with his mouth. I could hardly bear the anticipation. The condom appeared out of nowhere and he rolled it on then put his hands on my shoulders and pushed me back against the cold wall. He kissed me hard and deep and I tasted myself on his tongue.

Case reached down for my leg and lifted it, arranging it around his hip. He guided his erection to my core and thrust up. With a single push, he buried his entire length inside and held it there while my insides quivered and stretched. Don't stop, I begged with my eyes, needing his movement inside me more than air. He pulled out slowly and when just the tip of him remained, he thrust again, hard and deep and I dug my fingers into his shoulders. The intense foreplay didn't lend itself to a slow, building climax: it hit like a lightning strike and I shouted out with the force of it. Case rode it out and then took up a punishing rhythm in double time. It was pure lust to the hundredth power. The rough wall bit into my spine, but I was enraptured, beyond feeling pain.

Case's rhythm faltered and his face contorted. Watching the ecstasy roll across his features and knowing how close he was, took me over the edge again, and I curled my hips into his spasms as they overtook us both, driving him even deeper. He threw his head back and shouted a few choice words through a clenched jaw as I raked my teeth across the thin skin of his collarbone. We held each other up, the twitchy after-shocks making us both gasp and murmur contentedly while we recovered our breath.

I lowered my leg when calm returned, and he looked down at me then kissed me gently. "Hi," he said, breaking our silence.

"Hi," I replied as we unwrapped ourselves from each other.

"What happened?" he asked running his fingers over the tape on my forehead again.

"I'm clumsy," I said, tracing my fingers over the mark my teeth had left on his collarbone. He didn't push, he just smiled an incredibly warm smile that I suspected no one had seen in a long time.

We gathered our clothes and headed up the stairs to the bathroom where he insisted we share the tiny shower stall and wash each other off; that's all there was room for. We lathered our hands and gently caressed each other as if to make up for the rough coupling. The soap stung the wall-rash on my spine.

After we dressed, we headed up to the catwalk level. Music played quietly from an old iPod stereo. A bottle of red wine stood already open on the low table beside the cot. He'd remembered. I watched his lips curl into a smile as he poured a glass. He ransomed the glass for a kiss before retrieving a bottle of beer for himself. He'd been thinking of me and he'd remembered. I felt hot tears burn at the back of my eyes and ducked my head, turning away to fight the inexplicable waterworks. I took a gulp of wine.

He unlocked the balcony door. We stepped out and leaned against the rail. "It's so beautiful up here," I said, admiring the panoramic view.

"Yeah, it is. I looked for you out here when I arrived."

I didn't respond. We enjoyed our drinks, standing side-by-side, breathing the salt air and the silence. The lantern above made its trek back and forth, clicking out its progress.

"Beth was my wife," he said, startling me. I looked over to him, but he didn't move his gaze away from the horizon. "She was killed in a sailing accident off the New England coast two years ago."

"I'm sorry." I reached to touch his shoulder.

"I thought it would be easier for me here, you know—different coast, different ocean," he said, motioning toward the water. "But it isn't, really."

"Grief doesn't respect physical boundaries," I offered, knowing that fact well, having carried my own grief for my father all the way from BC to Toronto and back again. He let out a sad sigh, shaking his head.

"I've got to go," I said, handing him my empty glass.

"Will I see you again?"

I leaned over and kissed him. "No promises." He looked sad and tired. "It's better this way."

"For whom?" he asked, quietly. Jackson's ache flared in my chest and I had to look away.

"Goodbye, Case," I said, turning to walk away before I did something regretful, like promising something I didn't have to give.

I raced down the stairs and across the clearing knowing he would be watching me. As soon as the forest claimed me from moonlight's grip, I dove headlong into the path and flew fiercely, riding the tunnel like a roller coaster. A few tears escaped and I brushed them angrily away. I felt like I was drowning again and this time I was pulling Case down with me.

CHAPTER TWENTY-ONE

A branch whipped across my shoulder and the sting reminded me that one misstep in this tunnel would have painful repercussions. I was too distracted to fly at these speeds. It was dangerous. I immediately slowed down.

The next few days would be trying. My independence was on hold and I couldn't take my guard down. I searched for a break in the cover then rose above the tree canopy and headed home.

The lights were off and James had closed the new curtains. I couldn't see through them into the cottage, so they at least achieved their purpose. James was probably asleep. I removed my shoes to make as little noise as possible. When I got to the patio door, the vibration of my cellphone startled me. It was the house alarm. I scrolled down: the beach stair trip-alarm. Damn, James must have set the alarm. I punched in the disarm code and took a calming breath.

As quietly as I could, I unlocked the patio door and slid it open then reached inside to pull the curtain aside. The next series of events happened in such quick succession that I couldn't do anything but ride the violent storm to the floor.

Someone gripped my forearm, jerked me inside then twisted me around and kicked my feet out from under me. I fell forward and my cheek bounced off the hardwood. A firm hand pushed my face down and held it to the floor. My left arm was trapped under my body and my right hand was shoved sharply up between my shoulder blades. My attacker's knee pressed heavily into my back, making it impossible to breathe. The slightest movement caused excruciating pain. I was helpless—completely immobilized and in such distress that I didn't immediately notice the gun barrel poked into my temple.

"Emelynn?" It was James's voice. "What the hell?" The gun disappeared and I heard a metallic click. "Stay still," he instructed as he released his hold on me piecemeal, starting with his knee off my back. I was finally able to inhale again. He held my shoulder in place while he dislodged my right hand from the impossible angle up my back. My arm felt cold and my shoulder was on fire. Crap that hurt.

James jumped up. I rolled onto my back and looked up at him. "Jesus, James. What are you doing?"

"Where have you been?"

"Flying. Like I told you." I rolled my shoulder and winced. "God, that hurts."

"You're lucky I recognized you—I nearly popped your shoulder." He shook his head and turned away, hands on hips as he paced in a small circle. "Who is that guy?"

"What guy?" I asked absently, looking at James for the first time. He wore underwear. Just underwear. I tried not to stare, but they were tight, black boxer briefs and he rocked them. There wasn't an ounce of fat on him anywhere and that left a lot of lean muscle to distract me from my shoulder. I looked away then sat up and rolled my head. Nothing new hurt.

"The blond," he said, waiting for my answer.

"Damn it," I said, finally figuring out what James was on about. "Just because you can do that thing, doesn't mean you should."

He tilted his head like I'd suggested something ridiculous. "Who is he?"

I pressed my lips closed and looked away. I did not have to explain myself to James or anyone else.

"What's his name?" James said, raising his voice.

"Case. Are you happy?"

"Case who?"

"I don't know—just Case."

"You're fucking a guy and you don't even know his name?"

"You don't get to judge me," I said, fuming. "You may have seen into my life, but you don't know me."

"I think that's the exact same thing you said to me just before I told you Jackson was married."

"Thank you for bringing that up. Now my evening's complete."

When I stood up, I saw the bed sheet on the sofa. "Were you sleeping out here?"

"I can hear better out here." He stopped pacing and rubbed his hands through his hair. "I thought we'd agreed that flying was a stupid risk."

"No, *you* thought that, and I didn't feel the need to justify myself. Did you sleep here last night, too?"

"How the hell am I supposed to protect you, if you won't do what I tell you?"

"Who said you're supposed to protect me?"

"Why else would I be here?"

"I thought you needed somewhere to stay. You're not my bodyguard, James. I don't need a bodyguard."

"You sure as hell do. How do you know this Case guy isn't connected with those men who tried to snatch you?"

I shook my head. This was ridiculous. "If Case was part of this thing, I'd be in the thick of it by now. He's had lots of opportunity to get to me. Besides, he doesn't know a thing about me. Emelynn. He knows my first name is Emelynn, that's it."

"That's fucked up. Why are you sleeping with guys you don't know? Is that how Jackson got to you?"

The pain around my heart flared to life at the mention of his name and my rage burst free. "Jackson is why I'm fucking guys I don't know! And if it takes fifty of them to get that bastard out of my system then that's how many I'm going to do." The anger brought my tears, and I curled my shoulders in around the aching hole in my chest.

James stepped close. "Don't touch me," I said. He looked stricken. I crumpled into the corner of the sofa where he'd been sleeping and let the tears fall, unchecked.

"That was harsh. I'm sorry. I shouldn't have said it." He disappeared and moments later shoved a Kleenex box in my direction then sat beside me.

I dried my tears and blew my nose until the sobs stopped and the anger subsided.

"It's none of my business," he said. "I don't have to understand it."

"I feel a 'but' coming on," I said, my voice nasal.

"No. No *but*."

He pulled the sheet around his hips to cover his boxer briefs. James was out of line, but he wasn't wrong. It was fucked up.

"I didn't know Jackson was married," I said.

"I know. I'm the one who told you, remember? You don't have to explain yourself to me."

"Jackson was my first, that's all. I think that's why it hurts so much."

My little confession took James by surprise, but he tried hard to cover it. "Did Jackson know that?"

"Yeah—I told him, but a lot happened that night. He'd just fished me out of the Pacific and saved my life. I knew what I was doing."

"He should have known better."

"I should have, too. I didn't expect him to use me like he did, but it's not like I didn't play a role in it." James fidgeted with the edge of the sheet, not looking at me. "Jackson took something from me I didn't know I could lose. Now I can't seem to get it back. With Case it's different. I protected myself this time. He can't hurt me because he doesn't know me, and I don't know him. And that's the way it's going to stay. I won't let him get close. So, it may be fucked up, but it's working for me."

"All men aren't like Jackson. You can't paint half the world's population with the same shitty brush."

"I just need to protect myself right now." I was tired and it was late. "Thanks for being here," I said. "I appreciate your efforts, but I don't want a bodyguard and I sure as hell don't want you getting hurt on my account. Good night." I turned to leave, but James grabbed my arm. I wrenched free from his grasp.

He let his arm fall. "First thing tomorrow, how about we work out some basic safety boundaries we can both live with for the next few days?"

I studied his face. All I saw was concern. "All right."

"You can trust me."

"I guess I'll have to. After all, you're sleeping on my sofa. In your underwear."

"Yeah, but we know each other's last name, so I'm safe. You can cross me off your to-do list." James the comedian—that was unexpected. He softened his scowl, and I wondered if he wore it like a shield.

"Good night." James may have earned my trust, but he was never on my to-do list.

I finished in the bathroom and closed my bedroom door. It was one thirty in the morning and I was tired. Avery had been right; I did feel safer with James staying here. I crawled into bed and pulled the sheet up under my chin. It didn't even seem awkward talking to him about the Jackson fallout. He wasn't obvious friend material, but other than the odd callous comment, he'd done right by me. I rolled over and wondered why I had to keep convincing myself that I trusted him.

By seven thirty in the morning, I was awake and surprisingly well-rested despite the short night. But I needed to get moving because Malcolm would be here soon. I grabbed my housecoat and opened the bedroom door, tying the belt as I crossed to the kitchen.

"Good morning," James said, looking up from a newspaper. He'd already been out for a paper? And who read the real thing anymore? He sat in the chair at the far side of the room with his feet on the ottoman. The curtains were wide open behind him letting in the morning sun. His bedding was gone and I smelled coffee. Man, Avery thought Greg was a good guest. It looked like James could give Greg some competition in that department.

"Good morning," I said, then headed to the bathroom. I cleaned up and dressed for my run before I poured a coffee.

James looked over my clothes. "You going somewhere?" He folded the newspaper and laid it on the ottoman.

"Malcolm and I run for an hour first thing each Monday, Wednesday and Friday. On Tuesdays and Thursdays, I meet him at the Y for weight training." I sat down on the sofa facing him.

"Since when, and Malcolm who?" James put his feet on the floor and leaned forward with his elbows on his knees.

"Since early July and his name is Malcolm Perreault."

"Where do you go for your run?"

"The park, usually. Why?"

"Basic safety, remember? We were going to talk about it this morning."

"Right. Okay, shoot."

"You should change your route every day and avoid the park for the next few days or at least until we settle the safety issue. Run in populated areas, like Deacon Street."

"Okay, that should be easy enough. What else?"

"Don't go outside alone—not even to walk to your car. When you're inside, keep the curtains closed and the doors and windows locked. Your panic button should be with you at all times and don't answer the door or the phone unless you know who it is."

"That sounds reasonable. I'll try not to disappoint you."

"You won't disappoint me, Emelynn. These measures are for your safety, not mine. In case you hadn't noticed, *I* can take care of myself. These precautions might seem ridiculous, but it's your life. You should take it seriously."

"I'll be careful."

"Good. One more thing, put Case on hold for the time being. Unless, of course, you want me to accompany you out there?" James stood with his coffee cup in hand and crossed toward the kitchen.

I rolled my eyes. "He's not involved." It was disconcerting how much information he could pick up with just a short touch. I'd have to remember that.

He poured more coffee. "You're vulnerable when you're alone."

There was no point arguing, but I didn't like the restrictions. I watched him walk back to the chair, curious now. "Don't take this the wrong way, James, but why are you here?"

He looked over at me, raised his eyebrows and smirked. "I was in the neighbourhood. Remember?"

I returned his smirk but pressed on. "Funny. But I'm serious. We're even now, you and I. You know my secret, I know yours. You could have gone home days ago and avoided all this hassle."

"It just so happens I'm between jobs right now so you can blame my presence on good timing."

He picked up the paper and tried to look absorbed by it, but he didn't fool me. "What job would that be?"

He looked up from the paper and sipped his coffee, as if he was trying to decide what to tell me. "I'm an investigator."

"Did you just make that up?"

He jerked his head back. "No."

"What do you investigate?" I asked, eyeing him suspiciously.

"I have a wide range of interests. If someone hires me, I investigate."

"Who hires you?"

"Now *that* I'm not at liberty to discuss."

"Okay, then, where do you live?"

"What's with the thirty questions?"

"You're being secretive. Secrets usually mean you've got something to hide."

"It goes with the territory in my business."

I would have quizzed him some more, but the doorbell rang.

"That's probably Malcolm," I said to James, standing. "Did I tell you yet that you're the son of one of my mom's friends in Toronto?" He looked suitably confused. "It's your cover story."

"Oh, good to know," he said, accompanying me to the door.

"It's him," I said, and opened the door. I made the introductions then explained away my face with the usual excuse of being clumsy before turning back to get my fanny pack and fill my water bottle.

Malcolm and James were laughing when I returned and I thought it odd that he could so easily slip into this happy-go-lucky persona. It was so not James—or at least not the James he usually showed me.

Malcolm didn't hesitate when I suggested Deacon Street for our run. He was very accommodating that way. If I'd had bad knees, the concrete and asphalt route would have been jarring. As it was, I was grateful for the cushioning of my shoes and would be glad to get back to the softer path of the park, once the danger passed.

"We made it past eight kilometres," I said, proudly tapping the face of the wrist-mounted Garmin. We were almost back to the cottage, and I was still breathing hard and walking my cool-down, but it felt good to be pushed physically. We finished our stretches in a shady patch on the front lawn and confirmed tomorrow's time at the Y before Malcolm pedalled off.

I wanted to shout "Honey, I'm home," when I strolled into the house, but I wasn't sure James shared my sense of humour. It was a moot point anyway because James wasn't there. I called his name, but the curtains were closed. He must have gone out. He hadn't left a note.

After my shower, I poured a bowl of Cheerios. Would James consider sitting out on the deck "risky" behaviour? I opted for the dining-room table instead and flicked the power button on my computer. The emails crawled in as I absently munched on the crunchy O's. I set my bowl down to type. It was a prudent move because seconds later, I jumped when James knocked on the patio door.

"Emelynn, it's James," he said, his voice muffled behind the glass. A key turned in the lock and the door slid open. James pulled the curtain aside. "How was your run?"

"Good, thanks. We broke eight kilometres today."

"That's what, five miles?"

"Almost, I think. Where were you?"

"Checking out the beach."

He didn't elaborate and I didn't feel like pulling teeth. If he found something important, hopefully, he'd tell me. He settled into his corner chair, his newspaper still draped across the ottoman.

My send/receive was finished. I dumped the usual junk mail and clicked on the email from my mother "What else are you *checking out* today?"

He shot a glance my way and paused. "I'm waiting for word from our guy in Rockport. He's working his connections."

"Looking for?"

"A positive ID to start with. Rupert Dowling's in the system, so they'll do a DNA match, but that could take a while. Until then, the best we can do is work the angle of his known associates and any recent contacts he's had that we can trace back here."

"You really are an investigator." It wasn't until that moment that I realized I hadn't completely believed him this morning.

"You doubted me?" He looked surprised.

I laughed and shook my head. "Trust issues," I said, returning to my computer.

The doorbell rang. I looked up, quizzically at James. "Are you expecting someone?"

"No, you?"

"No."

We headed to the door in tandem, and it struck me as funny, like when all the girls go to the restroom together. He stood to my left as I checked the peephole. "Detective Jordan," I said, unable to hide my annoyance.

James shrugged. "Might as well get it over with. I'll be in my room." He darted to the left and closed the door quietly behind him.

I took a deep breath, steeled myself then opened the door. "Detective Jordan." I didn't invite him in. "What can I do for you?" His brown sedan was parked in the driveway.

"Ms. Taylor. May I come in?" His voice was deep and gravelly, the kind of voice you would hear in a crowd. He had on the same worn jacket that hugged his shoulders and gave away the bulge of the gun under his left arm.

I hesitated and then opened the door for him. He searched the hallway, noting James's closed door as he walked ahead of me. "May I?" he asked, nodding toward a dining-room chair at the end of the table.

"Of course." Gabe's comment came to mind. The detective would be watching my reactions. I had to be careful. "What brings you by?"

He motioned for me to sit in the chair kitty corner to him. Though it grated me, I dutifully took the seat.

"What happened?" he asked, indicating my face.

"I fell. How can I help you?"

"Looks like it hurt." I shrugged. "We found the Wright's car."

I mustered the enthusiasm of an innocent person. "That's good news, right?" The detective gave nothing away. "Did you find any new clues to their whereabouts?"

"Don't you want to know where we found it?"

He had a way of putting me on the spot. I arched an eyebrow. "I guess." Why had he focused on that? Was he trying to throw me off to get a reaction from me?

"State troopers in Renton raided a chop shop. Found the Prius in pieces. Hybrids in that price range aren't the usual fodder for chop shops so it got special notice." He pulled a pen out of his wrinkled jacket and clicked the end of it absently with his thumb. "Do you know where Renton is?"

"Washington, I believe?"

"Just south of Seattle." He pulled a notepad out of his inside pocket and flipped through it as he spoke. "You were in Seattle recently, weren't you?" He found the page he was looking for, read it, and looked up at me again.

I was tired of playing this game.

"Delaney Developments chartered a plane to Lake Union in June," he said, watching me.

This was a no-win situation. Even giving him my blank face gave him something.

He checked his notes. "Here it is, yes, June 14th. You were on that plane."

Of course he'd know that. "We went sightseeing. It's a pretty area."

"You weren't on the charter when it came back the next day. How did you get home?"

"For crying out loud!" I raised my voice as my temper gave way. "We had a fight, okay. I hitched a ride back. That's all there is to it."

"Hi," James said, interrupting. I caught my breath, unsure of James's intention.

"You must be Mr. Moss," the detective said, standing.

"James," he said, offering his hand. He didn't even question how the detective knew his name.

"Detective Samuel Jordan," the detective replied, shaking his hand.

I twisted in my chair and James caught my eye. He asked, "What's going on?"

"The detective here would like to know why I didn't return on Jackson's charter from Seattle."

"You can tell him." James looked sane, but he'd obviously lost his mind. He walked behind me and put his hands on my bare shoulders, making it look like we were a couple. He spoke over my head to the detective. "He's going to find out anyway." That's when I heard him. In my head, just like the night when he'd read my memories. "*Just go along with me.*" It was eerie and instinct made me want to turn around and look at him, but he gripped me tight, holding me forward.

The detective watched us, intrigued.

James put on an act, leaning down as if he were trying to see the expression on my face then straightening back up. "It's okay, I'll tell him."

"*Oh good,*" I thought, hoping he could hear me, "*because I haven't a clue where you're going with this.*"

"Jackson neglected to tell her he was married. When I set her straight, she ditched him."

"Is that right?" the detective said cautiously, looking from me to him. "Looks like that turned out all right for you." Now he was just being a pig.

"Oh, no," James said, whipping his hands away from me like he'd just heard I had leprosy. "We're not together." I shook my head. Trust him, he'd said. Yeah, right. "I'm just passing through. Emelynn offered me her spare room in exchange for some help with her computer."

"Why weren't you on that return charter, Mr. Moss?"

James laughed like he didn't have a care in the world. "Jackson didn't appreciate my honesty. But I wasn't planning on coming back here. I carried on home to New Orleans."

"And what brings you back now?"

"I'm between jobs. Vacationing."

"So long as you're not working a case, here. The local PD wouldn't appreciate your interference as much as PDs south of the border seem to."

"You've done some homework, Detective," James said, nodding ruefully. "But I'm not hiding anything." If James was worried, he sure disguised it well.

"Is that all, Detective?" I said, anxious to put an end to his visit.

"For now," he said, clicking the end of his pen. He reluctantly tucked his notepad back into place.

"Good to meet you, Detective." James offered the man his hand. "I'm glad to see you're keeping an eye on her. I keep telling her she has to be more careful, living alone out here, especially with that couple still missing."

When the detective was clear of the driveway, I turned on James. "What the hell was that all about?"

"He's digging, trying to make connections. We didn't give him anything he didn't already know." James had his phone out and was dialling. "Call Eden. Be discreet—the detective may be listening—but give her the heads-up." He turned his back to me. "Danny, hey man, how are you?"

I grabbed my phone off the hall table and called Eden. It was the strangest conversation I'd ever had with her, but Eden was sharp. She knew something was up and didn't question me lamenting about Detective Jordan. She listened as I told her all about him rehashing the business of our sightseeing trip to Seattle and the fact that he knew who was on the outbound flight and that I wasn't on the return flight. She uh-huhhed through the whole story of his visit, which I couched in words and tone that wouldn't give me away if the detective had my phone bugged.

"I understand, Em, and don't you worry about it. This will all blow over, eventually."

I can only hope, I thought, hanging up. James came down the hall with my GPS in his hands. "This is slick," he said, playing with the Garmin.

"Thanks. It comes in handy. Eden was cool, but she'll have questions next time she sees me."

"I'm sure, but at least the immediate danger is taken care of."

"What should we do about Detective Jordan?"

"There's nothing we can do. He's going to keep digging—it's his job and he has a lot of resources at his fingertips."

"What do you mean?"

"Detective Jordan is part of a cross-border task force. They're investigating several missing persons cases stretching from California to British Columbia. The cases must have something in common, but I haven't been able to access their files. Just don't let him rattle you.

You had nothing to do with the Wrights' disappearance. The only connection he has to you is that they worked here. Well, that and your reactions."

"He's insinuating that I'm involved." My voice was louder than I'd intended.

"See," he said. "Defensive." I took a deep breath and puffed out my cheeks then slowly exhaled. "He's just poking around to see if anything shakes loose. You've got to give him credit though—he's good. I didn't even see him follow me to the car, and that's got to be how he traced me. At least the pressure will be off you while he checks me out."

"Yeah, but he'll be back."

"Maybe, but the focus will shift down to Renton now. I bet those chop shop guys wish they'd never seen that Prius." James stood up. "Come on, I'll take you to lunch. Get your mind off this for a while."

"Okay," I said. "Where to?"

CHAPTER TWENTY-TWO

I hadn't expected Harvey's, but that's where he took me. We drove all the way out to the airport and paid for parking, just so we could eat fast-food.

"Most places fry the meat or nuke it then slap it on a griddle. It should be outlawed," he said. "Open flame's the only way to go."

James had a quirky side to him that I would never have guessed. It certainly didn't fit with the persona he wore around me. I was coming to realize that I really didn't know James at all.

He idled the car in the driveway when we got home. "You're not going to park down the block?" I asked.

"I'm dropping you off so I can check my trapline."

"You're what?"

"My contacts."

"Oh," I said, surprised he hadn't said anything sooner.

"Don't forget our agreement. Curtains closed and no solo outings."

I had my hand on the door handle ready to get out when a thought occurred to me. "There are some boxes in the closet in your room. Do you mind if I go in to get them?"

"No. Do you need a hand?"

"I can manage, but thanks. I'll see you later."

He waited until I was inside before he drove off.

James kept his room tidy. It didn't even look like he was staying there. His black leather satchel was packed, ready to pick up and go. I didn't snoop inside it, though I was sorely tempted. Brownie point for me.

The two boxes were heavier than I remembered, and I ended up dragging them down the hall one at a time rather than lifting them. I pushed them between the sofa and the coffee table.

The closed curtains blocked out the light, emphasizing my state of house arrest. It won't be forever, I reminded myself, but I missed the freedom of just walking out the patio door and down the stairs to the beach. Funny how the things we take for granted loom large when they're out of reach.

I made a cup of tea, put the radio on for background noise and opened the first box. More journals. There were issues of the *Journal of the American Medical Association* and more from the *New England Journal of Medicine*. None of them held anything published by my dad. At most, they contained tick marks or underlines.

There were two from the *American Journal of Ophthalmology* and each of these was littered with underlines. My father had even scribbled names in the margins in several places. To anyone else, the notes would be insignificant, but to me they were precious. This was exactly the type of thing my mother had asked me to look for—evidence of his research. I set the two journals on the bookcase then repacked the box and dragged it to the front door ready for recycling.

As I settled in to tackle the last box, my phone rang. It was Avery wanting to know how things were working out with James.

"We had a minor misunderstanding last night, but we've come to an agreement."

"Minor misunderstanding?"

"We disagreed on the precautions I should consider."

"Please tell me you took his advice, Em. This is his area of expertise."

"So he says, and yes, I did. I now have curtains shutting out my view and can't go out alone. I feel like I'm under house arrest."

"It won't be for long. Did James hear anything further about Rupert's murder or the men who were chasing you?"

"Not that I know of, but he's been out most of the afternoon. It's so frustrating that this pair of goons has the power to turn my life upside down. Speaking of goons, Mason paid me another visit."

"Why?"

"I'm not sure, but it wasn't to apologize. I think he might suspect I'm a Ghost. He knew you'd been researching them."

"Do we need to be concerned?"

"I don't think so. He said Jolene's gift makes me his niece. I made it clear I wouldn't be calling him uncle." My phone chirped. "Can you hold on? another call's coming in."

The minute I accepted the incoming call, my screen lit up to tell me the house alarm had been set off. In a mild panic, I scrolled down to find that the trip alarm on the beach stairs was to blame. I looked up to the curtains and froze. Was someone out there? I stood up and backed away from the windows, toward the protection of the hall. What should I do? Disarm it or let it go to the police? I had forty seconds to decide when someone knocked on the glass of the patio door.

"Emelynn, are you there? Em, it's Jackson."

His voice hit my stomach like a fist. Twenty seconds to decide . . . fifteen . . . ten. I entered the disarm code and dropped the phone on the hall table.

He knocked again and called louder. "Emelynn, it's me, Jackson."

I stood there with my stomach in a knot, unable to move my feet forward to answer his knock. Why should I? He knew I didn't want to talk to him and I sure as hell didn't want to see him. Why was he here?

His next knock was so loud I thought he'd break the glass door.

Damn it! If I stayed here cowering in the hall, then Jackson was still pulling my strings. I couldn't let him do that. I strode to the curtain and yanked it open. He took a step back from the door and lowered his arm, staring at me.

I watched his expression soften from anxious to relieved. His dark, windblown curls were shorter than before, but he was as handsome as I remembered. The straight, square lines of his face were *GQ* perfect and highlighted against the black flying clothes he wore. I opened the door and stood there, fighting my resolve, but one look in his pale hazel eyes and I was undone. I meant to be angry with him, to push him off the deck. Instead, I found myself wrapped in his arms, tears rolling down my face.

He held me tight, and it felt good. It shouldn't have, but it did. I waved the hurtful truth away and let him hold me, remembering how good it felt. At least until I stopped sobbing. Then I came to my senses and pushed away from him.

"I was right to be worried," he said, reaching for my bandaged fore-head. "What happened?"

I leaned back, out of his reach. "The Tribunal happened."

He stepped closer and grabbed my arms. "I tried to warn you. Why didn't you return my call?"

I threw up my block and pulled out of his grip. "I didn't want to talk to you. That should have been obvious."

"Let's go inside," he said, stepping toward the open door.

"No." He looked up, surprised. "How could you do that to me, Jackson?"

"I'm sorry," he said, bowing his head. "I never meant to hurt you."

"Yes, you did," I said, and the pain flared around my heart as he met my glare. He lowered his brows, puzzled. "You knew exactly what you were doing."

"Let's talk about this inside," he said, once again stepping toward the door.

I barred his way. "No."

He stepped back. "I was blinded. It was a foolish, selfish thing I did, and I'm sorry." He reached out and this time I was strong enough to step back from his proffered embrace.

"You didn't even come to see me when you knew I'd been shot."

"I couldn't. You were in good hands, and Sandra needed me."

"You mean your *wife* needed you."

"I'm sorry, Emelynn. I wish I could take it all back."

"I would have helped you. The whole covey would have helped you. You didn't need to lie to everyone."

"I know that now."

"You knew it then, Jackson. Tell me—how did you justify it to yourself?"

"Emelynn," he said, pleading.

I stepped toward him. "No, I want to know. Give me one good reason why."

He stepped back, unsure. "I was out of my mind with worry. You dropped into my life and I liked you. I liked the distraction of you. I liked teaching you how to fly. And I fell for you. Is that so hard to understand? Didn't you feel it too? Didn't you enjoy what we shared?"

"Didn't I enjoy that you turned me into your mistress?" I laughed and finally found my anger. "Didn't I enjoy that you made a fool of me?" I stepped forward until Jackson had to back up. "Didn't I enjoy that you manipulated me?" He continued to retreat from my advance. "I should thank you, I suppose."

"Emelynn, please."

But I couldn't hear any more. I should have just slapped him, but

I'd lost my temper and threw a jolt at him instead. He needed to hurt as much as I did.

Regretfully, his block was up. "Stop it!" he shouted, unaffected. "It kills me to see you hurt. I care about you."

"No, you don't."

"I do. I've been worried about you. That detective, Samuel what's-his-name—he was poking around and then the Tribunal were asking questions. When I heard about those thugs that chased you, I got worried. You may think I'm a bastard, but I'm not heartless, Em. I do care what happens to you."

"Go home, Jackson."

"I just want to talk, Emelynn."

"Is there something more you want from me, because I'm not clear on why you're here?"

"Jackson," James's voice called from inside the patio door.

Jackson stepped back and paused. "What are you doing here?"

"I think the more appropriate question is—why are *you* here?" James said, matching Jackson's anger.

"None of your fucking business! Did you follow me?"

"No. Unlike you, I was invited."

Jackson paused and looked to me. "You *invited* him?"

I stepped back and blinked, dumbfounded. "What, exactly, are you accusing me of?"

"Are you sleeping with him?" Jackson asked.

His accusation brought a bitter smile to my lips. "You arrogant bastard! Do you really think you get a say in who I sleep with?"

He turned to James. "So this is what it's all about? You stab me in the back and then twist the knife by fucking her?"

This time there was absolutely no forethought. I bowled a jolt into Jackson that would have toppled any Flier I knew, except maybe Mason.

James shouted, "No, Emelynn!" and pulled me back.

Jackson took the hit, bowing backwards but quickly recovered. He glowered at us but didn't back down.

"Go home, Jackson. I'm not interested in your apologies, and I won't ever forgive you."

"That's enough!" James yanked me back farther, and then I heard his voice in my head. *"You can't risk triggering your ghost—he can't know."*

That's when I noticed we weren't alone. Ten feet off to my left, behind Jackson, Danny hovered, watching. I looked to my right and saw

Alex. He too hovered, witnessing. Behind Jackson, I saw Gabe. My face crumbled. Someone had called the covey. Jackson's own words echoed in my ears; *Covey protects one another. That's what we do.*

"You're not welcome here," I said, then turned away from him and walked back through the patio door.

Angry words followed in my wake, but I didn't stop. I ended up in James's room, as far from the raised voices as I could get. I sat on the end of his bed and waited for the commotion to subside. The patio door closed. I heard the curtains being drawn, and footsteps approached, pausing at each door until they finally stopped.

"How are you doing?" James asked, leaning against the door frame.

"Thanks for that."

He shrugged.

"Where'd everyone else go?"

"Home."

"I didn't think I could be more humiliated than I was by Jackson's betrayal, but I was wrong. Again."

"Not really. Alex already knew. He wanted to throttle him. Probably would have if calmer heads hadn't prevailed."

"I'm sorry. This is so embarrassing."

"You've got a good covey, Emelynn. They did nothing different from what you'd do if you were called on."

"I owe them all an apology."

"Maybe, but I think they appreciated the opportunity to have a conversation with Jackson." He chuckled to himself.

"That's a wicked laugh."

"Jackson made this mess—he can clean it up."

"Did you call the covey?" I asked, curious.

"No. Avery did. I was already on my way and the others dropped everything to get here. Avery didn't know it was Jackson, he just knew you'd cut away to take another call and when you didn't get back to him, he redialled. It kept going to voice mail."

"I'd better call him."

"I already did. Avery's fine."

"Thank you."

"The covey's training is paying off. They were calm and coordinated tonight, but tactically, they left themselves vulnerable. I could help them with that."

I studied his face. James wasn't a fool. He must realize that the covey saw him and Jackson in the same light. "The covey doesn't trust you, James. You misled them about Sandra and Jackson. I don't know how to fix that."

"You can't. That one's my mess and I'll take care of it. Eventually. But not tonight. Come on, let me buy you a drink," James said, offering me his hand.

We returned to the living room and he poured two glasses of wine. He handed me one and sat opposite.

"What was Jackson referring to when he said you'd stabbed him in the back?" I asked.

"As soon as Sandra was well enough, I told her about Jackson's infidelity."

"You what?" I said, raising my voice.

"Not about you. Just Jackson. Sandra's my sister, Emelynn. I can't just pretend I don't know. I love her, but she's blind where Jackson's concerned. She needed her eyes opened—she needed to see what he's capable of. But I'd never expose you. It really wouldn't have mattered who the other woman was. Sandra understood that."

"She asked?"

"Oh, yeah. She wanted to know, but I didn't tell her."

"How did she take it?"

"She moved off the *Symphony*."

"That explains why Jackson's pissed."

"Sandra may still forgive him. She hasn't closed that door yet."

"You sound disappointed."

"I'll support her no matter what she decides. I'll even make nice with Jackson if that's what she chooses, but it doesn't mean I'll like it."

We talked easily. Another hour passed before I'd settled enough to feel drowsy. We said good night and I lay in bed thinking about Jackson. This time my heart didn't flare. I was sorry and numb, but I couldn't muster any of the anger that I'd felt earlier. The fire had been quenched.

When I awoke, James was gone. He'd left a note by the coffee maker. *Gone to check the trapline.* I helped myself to a mug and got ready to meet Malcolm at the Y. With my panic button firmly in hand, I made an unapproved solo trek from the house to my car.

James hadn't returned when I got back to the cottage just past noon. I felt like I'd gotten away with something and laughed at the absurdity of my imprisonment. After a hot shower, I dressed then made myself a sandwich. I looked down at the last box of my father's books and decided to tackle it—one final chance to find an undiscovered piece of my father. I pulled the flaps open and exposed the tightly packed spines of dozens of journals. This box was much the same as the last one. The now familiar journals were equally disappointing in terms of notes from my dad. I paged through every last one from the box. Not one journal with research worth saving, and no treasures.

I gathered the loose journals, straightening the piles to ready them for repacking, and pulled the empty box closer. But when I picked up the corner of the box, there was weight to it. Strange, it looked empty. Reaching inside, I picked at the seam in the bottom of the box and the cardboard loosened. I removed it. Underneath was what looked like a piece of brocade. It was a bag of sorts, a big cloth envelope. Its shape gave away its contents: a book. The brocade was hand-stitched and the flap closed with a loop around a knotted leather button. It smelled of mothballs.

"What did you hide in here, Dad?" My anticipation mounted as I carefully carried the bag to the dining room table. The brocade was lined with coarsely woven fabric. It protected a large book with a smooth leather cover. The only marking on the front of the faded cover was a crest. It looked like what you see sewn on the breast pocket of a private school jacket.

I ran my fingers over the embossed crest. Was it a drawbridge or some sort of gate? Whatever it was, flowering vines grew up either side of the structure, and a small fox or dog guarded the top. The book could be a journal or perhaps a diary. The pages were heavy-weight vellum the colour of well-milked tea and had ragged edges. However, they were in better condition than the worn cover had suggested. Intricate calligraphy adorned the pages, but it wasn't all drawn by the same hand. The style was inconsistent with a mix of both black and dark brown ink. I'm sure it was written in English, but the complexity of the decorative text made it difficult to decipher. Maybe Dad had bought it as an investment and stored it in the attic for safekeeping.

A richly coloured drawing preceded each section of the book and larger, stylized letters in old-style English, appeared throughout, some-times at the head of paragraphs. One section looked to be either an eighteenth-century ledger or a farm's inventory, if I'd deciphered "swine" and "equine" correctly.

I was so engrossed in trying to decipher the complex script on the front page that I didn't hear James until he called my name from the front door. "I'm in the dining room," I answered, my back to the hall. "Any news from the trapline?" I asked, not taking my attention from the page.

"What have you got there?"

"I don't know. It reminds me of the books I'd seen photographs of in my art history classes. It could be from medieval times or possibly the Renaissance, but some of it's more recent. I think it's a journal."

I sat back in my chair so he could see. "I found it hidden in the bottom of one of the boxes my dad had stored in the attic." I let him reach across my shoulder to flip back the cover. "Be gentle," I said. "I don't want to damage it."

"This is a family anthology."

"You've seen it before?"

"Not this one." He'd studied the cover, and then flipped it back to examine the same page I'd been trying to decipher.

"I think my dad might have bought it as an investment. Do you know if it's valuable?"

"Yes, it is," he said, looking bewildered. "But books like this one aren't for sale."

"What do you mean?"

"This book looks very much like the Flier bloodline anthologies that the Tribunal has been rounding up for decades. If they knew you had it, they'd confiscate it."

"Really? Whose bloodline is it?"

"See this here?" James pointed to the first line of what I'd have called the title page. "That's an *R*. I think the rest of it spells Reynolds." The writing was complicated, but if the drawing to the left of the cursive was an *R*, then the rest of the lettering could be *eynolds*.

"And this is a *G*, which makes that word *Genus*, which is Latin for family."

"Are you suggesting that this book is a history of the *Reynolds* family bloodline?" I couldn't hide my excitement. I'd hit the Jolene motherlode.

"I'd bet my life on it."

"What would my dad be doing with it?"

"If Jolene didn't give it to him, then he got it from someone else in her family." James carefully turned the page. "The Tribunal considers these books dangerous."

"Dangerous? They're just books," but even as those words left my mouth, I remembered something Avery had told me, something confidential about how he and a childhood friend had gotten their hands on an old book. It attracted their teenage curiosity. A curiosity that led to Avery losing his ability to fly and his young friend losing his life. Could this be one of those books?

"Here," James said, pointing excitedly to an entry near the bottom of a page. *Jolene Elizabeth*. And right beside her name, connected with a broken line, was my father's name, *Brian Edison Taylor*. "This is the family's genealogy," he said, flipping back a page, and then another. We studied the entries. The older entries on the first two pages were more complex and more elaborately decorated.

"Please," I said, stopping him. I flipped the pages forward, returning to Jolene's name. I followed the line that connected Jolene to my father and then down where one name stood alone.

Andrew Reynolds Taylor
b. March 2, 1986 d. April 13, 1986

I ran my fingers across the name. My brother's name was Andrew. I sank back into my chair. He'd lived just six weeks. Andrew. I would have called him Andy, or maybe just Dee, like people called me Em. Who'd had the sad task of recording his name here, I wondered? Was it my father? Jolene?

Mason's name was there too, Mason McKenzie b.1969. Jolene was born in 1961. So she was Mason's big sister. There were no lines extending from his name, but then again, this book had been in the attic for at least fifteen years, probably longer. He could be married with five kids for all I knew.

"Do you have a safe here?"

I jumped at the sound of James's voice. It took a second for his question to sink in. "For the book?" James nodded. "No, but I think Avery does. You think this should be locked up?"

"Yes. I'll call Avery right now."

While he talked to Avery, I thumbed through the pages of Reynolds descendants. The name at the very top, the name that had started it all, looked like Edward. I couldn't make out his other names. He was born in either 1760 or 1769, though the six could be a zero. No wonder the literacy rate was so low back then—who could read this writing?

James put his hand on my shoulder. "Avery's home. He's expecting us." I shrugged away from his touch and he moved his hand. "Sorry."

I slid the book carefully back into its brocade cover and followed James down the hall.

"Your car is closest," he said, which made me the designated driver. He stared at the brocade bundle in my arms. "Do you have something to hide that in?"

I returned to the kitchen and opened the cupboard door under the sink. Lurking under there somewhere was a stash of bags. The one from Rumbles was the perfect size. I slipped the brocade bundle inside and tucked it under my arm.

CHAPTER TWENTY-THREE

Avery locked the waiting-room door behind us and ushered us into the bright kitchen. "Is that it?" His eyes flitting excitedly to the package under my arm.

I laid the book flat on the round table and slid the brocade bundle free of the bag. I'd never seen Avery so on-edge. He stood over me like I'd brought him the Holy Grail.

James was more detached. "Will that fit in your safe?" he asked.

"Yes," Avery said, as I pulled the old book free of its soft fabric covering. He turned to me, reaching out to swing the book closer to him. "May I?" I nodded. He opened it delicately, treating it as if the pages would disintegrate. "I didn't think I'd ever see another one of these."

"You agree with James, then? This is the *Reynoldses' Anthology*?"

"I'm sure of it."

"Can you make out the words?" I asked.

"Not easily. The script is beautiful though, isn't it?" He carefully laid back page after page until he neared the end of the book, then paused, taking more time to identify the words. "This section right here," he said, pointing to a heading that started with *R*.

"It's not Reynolds," I said.

"No, it's *Remedia*. Latin for remedies." He continued, carefully laying back pages until his fingers came to rest on a short passage.

"Why Latin?"

"It's not all Latin. The section headings and some of the older entries are, but see here." He pointed to a paragraph in the *Remedia* section. "That's an *A*. The word is *absent*, and here, *full of the moon.* The sentence reads *Absent the full of the moon.*" He traced each word with his finger. "This here is *inside a circle*. Some of these entries were likely translated from Latin or maybe even Gaelic long ago."

The *Remedia* section had Avery's full attention. I watched his eyes rake over the script, searching. He bent his head down and squinted, concentrating. Were those the words that had stripped Avery of his gift of flight all those years ago? He'd asked me to keep that to myself, so I didn't raise the subject in front of James, but I was curious.

At the sound of someone coming into the house, we all froze.

"That will be Greg," Avery whispered with urgency. "He can't see this."

Avery turned and took a step away from the table. I closed the book and carefully slipped it back into its protective brocade envelope.

"Greg, you're back. What'd you get up to today?" Avery asked, surreptitiously positioning himself between Greg and the book.

Before Greg could answer, James stepped forward and further obstructed Greg's view. I quickly slid the brocade bundle into the Rumbles bag.

"Greg, Avery sings your praises, man." James offered Greg his hand. "I'm James Moss." He had intentionally directed Greg's attention away from me as I set the bag on the floor.

"Hey, Greg," I said, straightening. Greg's glasses overpowered his face.

"Emelynn," he said, smiling at me before he turned to James. "James Moss," Greg repeated slowly. "Why is that name familiar?"

"Perhaps through Jackson Delaney. I'm his brother-in-law."

"Of course. Good to meet you, James. What brings you to the Vancouver area?"

"Oh, just touching base with some old friends."

"How long are you in town?"

"A few more days. How about you?"

"I'm leaving tomorrow. I've already overstayed my welcome," he said, laughing and looked over to Avery.

"Oh, come on. I've already told you to stay as long as you want. You're the easiest guest I've ever had."

"That's very kind of you Avery, but I promised my sister I'd visit before I went back to Portland."

Maybe his sister would help him out with a better "look." The glasses and side-part weren't doing him any favours, and he needed to lighten up on the hair gel.

"If you'll all excuse me," Greg said, turning back the way he'd come. "I've got to find room in the suitcase. Canucks T-shirts for the nephews," he said, referring to the shopping bag he held up. "Will I see you later?" He'd addressed the question to James.

"No, we were just heading out. Maybe another time?"

"Sure. Good to meet you, James. Goodbye, Emelynn."

As soon as Greg was out of sight, Avery turned and reached for the Rumbles bag. "I'd better put this away." He disappeared into his study and returned moments later, empty-handed. "It'll be safe now."

After thanking Avery, we made our departure. "Does your family have one of those books?" I asked on the way home.

"No. It was confiscated by the Tribunal when they learned about us. I don't think many anthologies remain out there."

The mess I'd left in the cottage awaited my return. I tidied the jumble of journals scattered over the living room floor and repacked the box.

Later in the evening, I ordered a pizza for our dinner. James's cellphone beeped. "Do you recognize any of these men?" he asked.

The photo was a head shot of a tattooed man. "Is this a mug shot?"

James inhaled, impatient all of a sudden. "Do you recognize him?"

"No."

"What about the others?"

"Others?" He looked at me like I was a dolt then reached over and swiped the screen to reveal another mug shot. More tattoos. "No. Who are these men?"

"They're Rupert Dowling's known associates."

"He hangs around with some scary people."

"Hung, past tense," he reminded me. "He was in a scary business."

I swiped again, this time a businessman, but not a mug shot. More like a surveillance photo. The next was like that too. "Where did you get these photos?"

"Never mind, just keep looking."

I swiped through three more mug shots before I stopped and stared.

"You recognize that one?"

"He and his partner chased me through the park." I squinted. The photo was dated today, but more curious was that it looked like it had been taken from a security camera at an airport. "You have access to airport security?"

"You're sure?"

"I can't be positive, but it looks like him."

"He landed in Portland this morning. Go through the rest of them."

I swiped through them before handing James back his phone. "The second guy's not here."

"He could be new." James texted something then tucked the phone into his pocket. "What?" he said, looking at the question on my face. "This is good news. I think we'll be able to wrap this up soon."

"How did you get those photos? I can't imagine the police or immigration handing them over."

"Lucky for us, I know the right people."

He was being secretive again, but I didn't let it bother me. "You think the danger is past?"

"I won't be happy until Dowling's body is positively IDd, but there are too many coincidences for him not to have been behind this."

The doorbell rang. "That'll be our pizza," I said.

James accompanied me to the front door but let me pay without an argument. When we returned to the living room, I put the box on the coffee table, and we dug in.

"I think Dowling found out about you and sent muscle to get to you," James said. "What I don't know is how he found out or who else he might have told."

"He's the hacker. That's how he learned about me."

"But how did he know to use Jolene's name as the trigger?"

I thought that over. "He must have known Jolene was a Ghost. Or maybe he just speculated, like Jackson."

"Maybe."

We finished the pizza in silence and I cleared up. "I'm going to call Avery then turn in. Are you planning to sleep on the sofa again?"

He chuckled. "I think I can surrender the sofa. Good night."

I closed the bedroom door behind me and waited until James was in the bathroom before dialling Avery.

"Sorry to call so late. I hope I didn't wake you."

"No, I haven't gone to bed yet. What's up?"

"One of the men who chased me returned to Portland this morning. He's one of Rupert Dowling's friends. I identified him from photos James had."

"What does James make of that?"

"He's cautiously optimistic, but still concerned about how Rupert learned Jolene's secret and who he might have told."

"But he thinks the immediate danger is past?"

"Yeah."

"That's a relief."

"I wanted you to know."

"Thanks for calling, and Em, thanks for bringing the book. You're one of the few people who know my history with a book like that. I appreciate your discretion."

"Quid pro quo, Avery. I owe you. Are you going to look for the offending incantation in the book?"

"I am, but not until tomorrow, after Greg leaves. Will you come over?"

"Sure, as soon as I'm finished with Malcolm, okay?"

"Great. I'll see you tomorrow."

Things were looking up. Avery would find his answers, and the threats that hung over my head like a black cloud seemed to be dissipating.

The next morning, James was up and about before me. Again. "How'd you sleep?" I asked when I emerged from my bedroom.

"Better, thanks." He was distracted with his phone. "Just reading the headlines," he said, when he noticed me watching.

I joined him for coffee after I'd dressed for my run. "Any more news?"

"No. But I'd say you're in the clear: at least as clear as you're going to be until we get that 'Jolene is a Ghost' rumour quashed."

"I'm glad to hear you say 'we.'"

"I'm not the one with the IT resources. I thought we could get Greg involved after he gets back home. Of course, we'd have to do that without revealing your secret, but I'm sure we can think of something."

"I'm just glad you didn't suggest Jackson's IT team."

"No, that wouldn't work. Jackson and Rupert will be Greg's first leads."

"Targets, don't you mean?" I said, and James smirked. I opened the curtains and unlocked the patio door. "Coffee on the deck?" I asked, pulling the door open. The morning air was crisp and fresh. James followed me to the deck chairs.

"Have you made plans to leave?"

"I booked a flight out tomorrow morning."

The small talk was pleasant enough, but it was the stuff of fare-wells: last-minute safety tips and teasing. He'd tucked his menacing persona away this morning and acted almost relaxed—probably happy to get away from the stress of the past few days. He wasn't alone, I thought, soaking up the small freedom of sitting out on the deck.

"I've got my run with Malcolm this morning. Will I see you later?"

"Yeah, sure thing."

"Great. How about I cook you dinner—a thank-you dinner?"

"Don't go to any trouble."

"Okay. Kraft Dinner it is." I left him smiling, and he returned to his headlines while I headed out front to wait for Malcolm.

I phoned Molly while I waited, curious about what Dean might have said on Sunday night at Fast Eddies.

"He didn't show up," she told me. "Cheney called him later, but he didn't say anything terrible about your date. He said you guys had a nice time."

"Really? He thought that was a nice time? I'll assume he was being a gentleman because otherwise, he needs better dates."

"I don't know. When Cheney asked if you two were going to go out again, he said maybe."

"Maybe? Really?" That was a surprise.

"I've got to go. We've got an early delivery coming in."

We hung up. I finished my warm-up then greeted Malcolm as he pulled up on his bike. We took another busy street route at my suggestion, and I was worn out an hour later when we returned.

James was gone, but his Dopp kit was still in the bathroom. After my shower, I phoned Eden to give her the update I'd given Avery last night.

"Eden's working," Alex said.

"Thanks for last night, Alex."

"We've got each other's backs, Em," he said, and we left it at that. It was less embarrassing to just move forward. I updated him on the news about the mug shots and James's thoughts on the reduced threat. "That's great. I'll call Eden on her break. She'll be relieved. We were just saying last night how we'd maxed out our drama quota for the year."

"I'll try to keep it down on my end from now on," I said, laughing. Next was an update to my mother, minus the scary parts. It felt good, like putting away the Christmas decorations after the big event. Tidy up, clean and dust, then settle back down to the rhythm of everyday life.

I phoned Avery. "Has Greg left?"

"Yes, earlier this morning. Are you coming over?"

"On my way." I grabbed the car keys, set the alarm and locked up. It felt good to have my independence back.

When I arrived at Avery's, he had the book out on his desk in the den. "How's it going?" I asked. I noticed he hadn't shaved. Nor did it look like he'd slept.

"The book is very similar to what I remember of Jimmy's family anthology. This one's older with more entries, but it's all here. The genealogy goes back to the mid-eighteenth century listing births, deaths and marriages. See here," he said, pointing. "There was a baron in the clan in 1874. The section on land ownership seems to end when the family left Scotland, but the section on coveys has been updated in the past fifty years. It's a work of art, Emelynn. If it weren't about Fliers, I'd say it rightfully belongs in a museum. Just look at the craftsmanship here in the colours and symmetry." He turned to a section title page that I couldn't read.

"Can I make you a cup of tea?" I asked, concerned about his appearance. I'd never seen him so unkempt. He didn't look up from the book.

"Ah, yeah. That'd be good."

"Have you eaten yet?"

He looked at me curiously. "Are you mothering me?"

"Sorry, but you look like you could use some mothering."

He rubbed the stubble on his jaw, as if he'd suddenly become aware of it. "Oh, god."

"What's going on?"

Avery sat down heavily behind the desk and ran his hands through his hair. "I never thought I'd find out what happened. I've been haunted by Jimmy's death since that day in his basement. Now I might finally learn what went wrong. I need to know if Jimmy's death was my fault."

"Avery, you were fifteen—a kid. You couldn't possibly be responsible."

His eyes took on the saddest look. I wouldn't be able to stand it if he cried. "Go have a shower. I'll make us something to eat and we'll look at it again after you've freshened up."

He looked like he was about to protest so I cut him off. "Go." I turned and headed for the kitchen.

I smiled to myself when I heard his footsteps headed toward the stairs. Now all I had to do was raid his fridge for something to cook.

It wasn't a difficult chore. Avery's fridge was stocked. I settled on a mushroom and cheese omelette with toast and fresh tomatoes. I sliced potatoes into a second pan and let them brown in butter with a sprinkle of salt and pepper.

"That's better," I said, when Avery reappeared, freshly shaved and wearing something that didn't look like he'd slept in it.

"What smells so good?"

"Mushroom omelette," I said.

We loaded our plates and took them to the table in the garden.

After he'd finished, he leaned back, sipping the last of his tea. "Thank you. That was just what the doctor ordered," he said, and winked.

It felt gratifying to look after him for a change.

"How are you holding up after Jackson's visit? Okay?"

"I am." It felt good to say it out loud and know it was true.

"I'm glad. You ready?" he asked after we'd cleaned up.

"I'm all yours, but at some point, I've got to head to the grocery store. I've promised James a thank-you dinner. Did I tell you he's leaving tomorrow?"

"No. I guess that means he's convinced you're out of danger."

"Yes, thankfully." I dried my hands and we returned to his office.

He dragged a chair around so I could sit beside him. With a pad of paper between us, he turned to the *Remedia* section of the *Reynolds Anthology* and we started examining the script. I wrote down the words that he deciphered. Some of it made sense, but it was tough going. The script was dense and many letters looked alike. Half a dozen times we'd get partway through an entry before Avery would shake his head and acknowledge that it wasn't the one he was looking for.

"It's got to be here," he said, doggedly continuing on.

"Okay, write this down," he said, starting with a new entry. "Absent a full moon."

I wasn't hopeful. They all seemed to start in the presence of, or absence of, a full moon.

"Under a clean—no, clear sky." I wrote that down and he continued.

"Inside a . . . protected? Yes, protected, circle of wool ash. No, that doesn't make sense. Wood ash."

I was losing patience with the process, but I could see that Avery was keen to keep going, so I kept pace.

"The four corners of the compass ablaze." That was new. I perked up.

"Pure up, no . . . pure of intention, free of encumbrance, unadorned fingers joined by touch." Avery looked across to me, his face expectant. "I think this is the one."

"Are you sure?"

"So far," he said, hopeful. "Keep writing."

I poised the pen and wrote. When he'd finished, the text read:

> *With the power of my birthright in the palm of my hand, we call on the grace of the ancient ones to grant the covenant of transference once and only once. This is our bargain. I gift thee flight that thou may take to the heavens. I gift thee vision to light the night. I gift thee in peace and health of mine own free will. So be it decreed and sealed.*

"This is it." Avery sat back with the notepad in his hand. "Such a small handful of words. They look perfectly harmless, insignificant." His eyes raked the page again, from top to bottom. "These very words altered the course of my life and ended Jimmy's."

I squeezed Avery's forearm. "It was a long time ago. You couldn't have known."

"Yes, logically, I know that, but emotionally, I'm still back there with Jimmy."

"Seeing it now, can you figure out what went wrong?"

"I think the better question is, what went right." He returned to the top of the page and pointed at each line. "We didn't check the lunar cycle, so who knows if we were absent a full moon. We definitely weren't under a clear sky; we were in his basement. I don't remember saying half these words, though I must have, or at least up until the part about gifting him my night vision because I walked away with that intact. How could we have been so careless?"

"Avery—at the risk of repeating myself—you were a kid. Kids do stupid things. It's built into their DNA."

He looked at me and smiled. Soon after, a genuine laugh broke through. I laughed, too, relieved.

"Have you shared any of this with Victoria?"

"She knows about Jimmy. There's no hiding the fact I can't fly, and that leads to some obvious questions."

"You and Victoria are good together."

"She's been great, but—" He left it there, shaking his head.

"But what?"

"I haven't been able to fly since I was fifteen. I can barely remember the sensation at all. But since Victoria, I'm acutely aware of what I'm missing. Each time she leaves, I feel like I've let her down. I want to be with her—to fly with her. I've never thought of it as a handicap before, but I do now. I worry that I'm holding her back."

"I can't know her heart, Avery, but I've seen the way she looks at you and I don't think that's what she's thinking."

His demeanor remained unchanged, and it broke my heart.

"How about we put this away for today?" he said.

When the anthology had been returned to the safe, he sat me down to remove the tape over my eye. "I'm sorry about the scar," he said. "It'll fade."

"It's not your fault. I'll just add it to my growing collection," I said, shrugging. "Hey, I was planning on taking James for an after-dinner drink over at Fast Eddies tonight. Why don't you join us?"

"Thanks, but I don't think I'm in the right frame of mind for socializing."

"Well, if you change your mind, call me." I thanked Avery, said goodbye, and gave him a big hug. "Victoria didn't know you when you could fly. That's not what she's attracted to."

He paused then smiled again. Maybe I was finally getting through to him.

"See you tomorrow?" he asked, referring to our usual Thursday session.

"I'll bring more milk jugs," I added with a nod.

Chapter Twenty-Four

Thoughts of Avery and Victoria consumed me until I turned off the ignition in the Safeway parking lot. I was making dinner for James and had to get my head in the cooking game. I locked the car and headed for the automatic doors that swooshed open ahead of me.

I settled on salmon with asparagus and rice then backtracked to the wine store where I picked up a bottle of Cupcake Chardonnay.

It wasn't even five when I pulled into the garage. I unlocked the door and called to James as I pushed it open.

"Hey," he said, coming down the hall from the living room.

"I hope you like salmon."

"I love salmon, but I can't stay. I'm sorry, Emelynn, but I've been called away."

"I've got wine," I said, hoping to entice him. "Can't you postpone it for a few hours?"

"Sorry, Emelynn. It's the Tribunal. They've sent a car. It'll be here any minute." He looked out the door behind me. "I was just writing you a note."

I saw his satchel packed and ready to go by the front door. "But I haven't thanked you."

"Yes, you have."

There was nothing to be done about it. He had to go. "I'll make it up to you next time you're in town, okay?"

"It's a deal."

I walked to the hall table and set the groceries down. The crunch of gravel under wheels announced the approaching car. It was a black airport limo with darkened rear windows.

"Thanks, James."

He nodded his head once. "How's that block of yours working?"

I looked at him, confused.

He took a step closer. "I think you should put it up now."

By the time his arms were around me, I'd figured it out and rammed my block into place.

"There you go. See? Safe as can be. Take care, Emelynn."

Had he just kissed the top of my head? I couldn't tell for sure and then he was gone, walking to the limo with his leather bag in his hand.

The limo was out the driveway in an instant and quite suddenly, I felt all alone. I put the groceries in the fridge, having no interest in cooking for one. Instead, I poured a glass of wine and drank it on the deck. He hadn't been here that long, but the house seemed empty without him. Maybe I should think about getting a roommate.

After the wine, I took a long walk on the beach. I poured myself a bowl of cereal when I got back. Feeling sorry for myself was ridiculous. I pulled my phone out and dialled Molly. "You want to go for a drink?" I asked when she picked up.

"Ah, okay. Sure. Where?"

"How about I meet you at Fast Eddies?" I could at least follow through on that part of my evening plan.

"Okay, I'm off in twenty minutes. Meet me there in half an hour."

A sure cure for melancholy was looking fabulous. I started with a sexy bra and matching panties then pulled on a tight spaghetti strapped camisole and a short chiffon skirt that bounced to a flare with little effort. The butterscotch-coloured top was perfect. A strappy pair of sandals finished the outfit perfectly.

I leaned into the mirror and inspected my new scar. It wasn't that bad—a jagged cut about an inch long just above my eyebrow. It was still red but would fade to white soon enough. Maybe I should cut bangs to hide it. The bruise had faded to an almost unnoticeable yellow. By the time I put on some makeup and loaded my purse with wallet, phone and GPS, my glum mood was almost gone. I wore the amber earrings just to thumb my nose at Mason then grabbed my jean jacket and left.

The cab dropped me off in front of Fast Eddies and I felt like a million bucks walking through the front door. The hostess didn't recognize me as one of Cheney's crew.

"I'm meeting someone," I said, and she nodded as I headed to the bar. Molly wasn't there yet. I ordered two dirty martinis and smiled, remembering that it was Molly who'd introduced me to the drink.

Molly arrived just as the drinks were dropped on their napkins. "Wow, look at you." She admired my outfit and my spirits soared. And then she eyed the drinks. "Are those dirty martinis?"

"I didn't even have to show cleavage to get served."

"What do you call that?" She laughed, looking at my cleavage. I suppose the top was a bit revealing, but it looked great. Maybe even as good as Molly for a change. She wore a pale blue sleeveless shift with a small white belt and white slingback shoes with kitten-style heels.

We carried our drinks to a high table close to the window. Across the room, a pool game was underway, accompanied by the sporadic clack of balls.

A pale blue hair band held back Molly's dark curls. She wore a pearl necklace with matching pearl studs. She always looked perfectly put together. We toasted our friendship and settled into comfortable conversation, stopping once in a while to follow the outbursts from across the room at the pool table.

"How's the job search going?" she asked.

"I haven't put much effort into it, I'm afraid."

"If you're interested, I can put in a good word with Ruth and Anne. You know—the sisters who own Rumbles."

"I wouldn't have thought they had enough work for you, let alone me."

"Not at Rumbles. They just bought a second bookstore, and they tell me its records are a mess. They're looking for someone to sift through the paperwork and input the details into their computer system. You can probably do it from home."

Me and paperwork and computers: sounded like a recipe for frustration, but I needed to start somewhere. "That sounds . . . promising?"

Molly laughed. "Great. I'll mention it to them. How are things going with your roommate?"

"James?"

"Unless someone else is living with you," she said, raising her eyebrows.

"He was not *living with me*; he was visiting. Besides, he's gone now—left this afternoon."

"That's too bad." She curled her lips seductively.

"You keep that up and I'm going to tell Cheney," I teased, and she sighed heavily, feigning defeat.

"Hey, guess who popped up at my place, day before yesterday?"

"Who?"

"Detective Jordan. Has he told you that the Wrights' car was found in a chop shop in Renton?"

She shook her head. "No, but it's only a matter of time before he tries to hang that on Cheney and his dad. They're mechanics, after all," she said with a derisive laugh.

"He quizzed me on that sightseeing trip I took because Seattle's close to Renton. I swear the guy thinks I'm the one responsible for the Wrights' disappearance. He'd even followed James and traced his name through his rental car. The man never quits."

"Next thing you know he'll be putting a case together against James." Molly's phone rang. She looked at the phone's display and her face lit up. "It's Cheney. Do you mind?"

"Go ahead," I said, and pulled the final giant olive off the bamboo skewer with my teeth. Molly was too engrossed in her conversation with Cheney to notice me watching her. She flushed and absently twirled a curl in her fingers; a woman in love, no doubt about it. I envied her that.

"Just a minute." She covered the phone with her hand. "Do you mind if Cheney drops by?"

"No, of course not."

Molly smiled, chirping happily into the phone before ending the call. "Do you want another?" she asked, signalling the waitress.

"Another martini would be the end of me. How about a glass of wine?"

Molly had joined the ranks of the hometown regulars and was on a first-name basis with the staff. She introduced me to Meg, our waitress, before ordering our wine. While we waited for it to be delivered, she updated me on the latest antics of her twin brothers. "They hitchhiked all to the way to the Calgary Stampede," she said proudly. "Unfortunately, they got stranded there," she said with a laugh. Molly had done something similar with a music festival on Vancouver Island when she was their age so she was sympathetic. "Mom and Dad bailed them out with bus fare home, but now they're complaining about the chores they have to do to work off their debt."

I faced the bar's entrance, so I saw Cheney before Molly did, and motioned him over. Molly turned in her seat and a slow smile spread across her face. Cheney leaned over and kissed her. Did they know they were in love? Had they told each other yet? I hoped so. He sat down with his back to the room.

"We should have invited Eden," Molly said.

"She's working afternoons."

The waitress brought Cheney a beer. "Thanks, Meg." He hadn't ordered it, but that was one of the perks of being a regular.

I nursed my wine while Cheney and Molly updated each other on their days. My eye was drawn to a man nervously twitching in the entranceway. Something about him looked familiar. I watched him looking over the crowd. It was Greg. What was he doing here? Avery said he'd left this morning. His eyes met mine. He put his finger to his lips to gain my silence and beckoned me over. I excused myself and headed toward the ladies room.

"Avery's been hurt," Greg blurted out.

"He's what! How?"

"Someone broke into his house. He's in the hospital. We need to go. Right now."

My heart dropped to the floor and Greg grabbed my shoulders. "Make your excuses to your friends and meet me in the parking lot. I'll drive."

"I thought you'd left," I said, absently, grasping for details that made sense.

"My flight was cancelled. Hurry up." Greg gave my arms a squeeze. He let me go and turned for the door.

I stood there with my mouth agape. Avery was hurt. How bad was it? Had someone gone looking for the anthology? Could the Tribunal be involved? My whole body trembled as I made my way back to Molly. I couldn't risk telling her—she'd want to come with me. If the Tribunal were involved, I didn't want her or Cheney anywhere near me.

"I'm going to catch a cab," I said in a whisper that I hoped wouldn't give my panic away.

"You're white as a sheet, Em. What's wrong?"

"I think I had too much to drink," I said. "There's a cab outside. I asked it to wait for me."

"I don't think so," Cheney said. "I'll drive you."

"No." I cut him off. My two worlds were colliding. "The cab's right there. You and Molly go have a nice dinner."

"I'll walk you out," Molly insisted.

"Please don't. Enjoy your wine. It's embarrassing enough that I've had too much to drink. I'll talk to you tomorrow."

Molly and Cheney sat back and eyed me suspiciously but let me go. I grabbed my jean jacket, threw my purse over my shoulder and bolted for the front door.

Greg was in the driver's seat of a nondescript sedan and had pulled up in front. I opened the passenger door and jumped in. "Which hospital?"

"Richmond General." He stepped on the gas and squealed away from Fast Eddies. I folded back into the seat and reached around to pull the seat belt across. I felt a sharp jab in my neck and an arm reached around the head-rest to cover my mouth. I screamed against the hand but could already feel the tug of darkness as my strength waned.

"That's it." The voice came from far away. "That's what I like to see."

Greg's eyes went wide as he struggled with the wheel. Would we crash I wondered without alarm as the blackness came to call and someone said, "Sleep tight."

Chapter Twenty-Five

What was that smell? Musty, damp and foul. I opened my eyes and rolled my head from side to side, blinking to clear my vision. I was on a bed in a small room. A ratty pink towel covered a small window set high in the wall. Brown stains marred the ceiling. My neck hurt like a son of a bitch. I raised my hand to rub the hurt away and discovered that my hands were bound together. What the hell? I blinked my eyes to focus on the thick black cable tie that held my wrists tight then slowly pieced together my journey from Fast Eddies to here, wherever "here" was. They'd jammed a needle in my neck. Who were these people? I pulled at my wrists but the bindings had no give to them.

The pink towel wasn't dense enough to cover the fact that it was night. I heard the muffled laugh track of a sitcom drift through the half-open door. The sporadic flicker of the TV's light played off the wall in the hallway. What did these people want?

Where was Greg? Had we crashed the car? And then a horrifying thought struck me. Had he been a part of this? No, he couldn't have. I'd seen his face. When I was attacked, he'd been shocked, barely controlling the car. I remembered hearing squealing tires. He must have swerved the car to dislodge my attacker. Was Greg all right? What about Avery? God, what had happened to Avery?

The small bed I lay in was stained and pushed up against a wall mottled black with mould. I looked down to my feet. My shoes were gone and my ankles bound with rope. I brought the thick black plastic that bound my wrists, to my mouth. It was impossible to chew through.

Other than the TV, the house or cabin or whatever disgusting hold we were in was quiet. I ignored the lingering ache in my neck and stretched my legs out to examine the knot at my ankles. I glimpsed the rope's loose ends. If I pulled my knees to my chest, I might be able to undo the knot.

I shifted my knees and the bed let out a loud squeak. I froze. When no one stirred, I tried again, slower this time. Feeling around for the loose end, I wriggled it blindly backwards through the big knot, stopping each time the bed squeaked.

The stained mattress smelled like mildew. I frantically picked away at the rope. How long had I been here? Was this the same night or the next? Ken Gillespie's voice from the self-defence class echoed in my head, "The primary objective is to get away." Each time I lost track of the rope's loose end, I had to straighten my legs and look down at the knot then reposition myself to work at loosening it further, without setting off that damn squeak.

When I finally pulled the rope free from my ankles, I stilled and listened. If they hadn't heard me yet, then they weren't expecting me to be awake. I would have to keep quiet if I wanted to slip away. I waited until the feeling had fully returned to my limbs before I swung my feet to the floor and sat upright. Once again, I tried to chew the cable tie from my wrist, but there was no hope of getting rid of the restraint without a knife.

I stood and tiptoed to the door. The laugh track roared. Stepping through, I turned toward the TV's flashing light. The hallway opened to an archway. On the left was a kitchen and beyond that, to the right, was the living room. A man slouched down in front of the glowing TV; his hand dropped away from the rifle that sat across his lap. He snored softly. I spotted a door on the far side of the living room, but I'd never make it there without waking him.

There had to be another exit. I turned back and stepped into the kitchen. Sure enough, there was another door. I crossed the kitchen floor, quiet in my bare feet and approached the door, examining the lock. It was flimsy and I easily turned the latch, releasing the bolt without a sound.

Almost there. I turned back to search for something to sever the cable tie on my wrists. A tug on the closest drawer released a low creak. I held still, waiting for a reaction from the sleeping man, but none came. Damn! I might be forced to escape with bound hands, but not without

Greg. He had to be here somewhere. I had to find him. We'd make it out together and laugh about it later—I hoped.

I crept down the hall past the room I'd been in and found a bathroom. Beyond the bathroom were two more doors. I pushed gently against the first door. A man's hand dragged on the floor beside the bed. His shoulders were naked, but his bald patch told me it wasn't Greg and the gun on the bedside table confirmed it. I pulled the door closed.

The last door was on the right. It opened quietly with a small push and my eyes caught sight of Greg's hideous bowling shirt. He was curled on his side. His thick glasses lay on the bedside table beside a handful of thick cable ties. I smiled with relief. They hadn't tied his wrists yet.

I approached him soundlessly and clasped my bound hands over his mouth. "Wake up," I whispered in his ear. "Shh . . . Don't say a word." Greg came to and blinked open his eyes, focusing on my face. "It's me, Emelynn. Be quiet," I cautioned. He looked suitably confused and I immediately worried that he was still drugged. "There's a back door off the kitchen. The watchman's asleep. I think we can get out of here if we're absolutely quiet." He looked at me and nodded while I made my way back to his doorway and glanced out. I motioned him to follow me.

We tiptoed down the hall, passing the other guard's door then the bathroom and turned left into the kitchen. I stopped to listen for activity ahead, toward the TV's glow, but it remained quiet. I glanced around to find Greg. He had fallen behind and looked confused and weary. We were almost there. I moved to the unlocked door and motioned for him to follow me. Silently, I turned the kitchen door handle and opened it.

The moment I stepped out the door, I heard a thunderous crash and looked back to see Greg frozen to the spot where he'd knocked something to the floor.

I slammed my block into place and felt it close like a vault. The man from the living room came to life. "Hurry!" I held my bound hands out to Greg. He dozily tripped toward me, obviously still suffering some effects of the drug. Damn! He wasn't wearing his glasses either. I could jump-start and carry him if I had to, but hopefully, he'd be able to fly on his own.

I heard someone stomping toward us and stepped back into the kitchen. I grasped Greg's hand firmly and dragged him bodily out through the kitchen door. As I pulled him across the lawn, it became clear to me that he wouldn't be able to make it on his own.

With bound hands, I had to improvise. I took three quick steps toward Greg and ducked, ramming his midsection with my shoulder. He folded over me, and I used the last of my momentum to push off with my feet. Gravity snapped free, and I steadied myself as I rose up and away.

Greg squirmed. "Stay still!" I was only ten yards from the house—not far enough away yet. I heard a few pops from the kitchen door, and felt a sting in my hip and another in my thigh. Had I been hit? My thoughts scattered and Greg's weight fell off my shoulders. For a horrifying moment, I thought I'd dropped him to his death and then . . . I didn't have any other thoughts.

When I woke, the depressing reality sunk in quickly. With no doubt at all, I knew I was lying on that filthy mattress again. The mouldy smell was inescapable. Something was tied tightly around my eyes, blocking my vision, and that awful smell of decay permeated the air.

My shoulders ached from the strain of my arms being tied above my head. I heard metal clang when I reached around and fingered something hard around my wrists. It wasn't a plastic cable tie this time: handcuffs, I thought. They were threaded through the top of the bed's metal frame. My ankles were also bound, not tightly together, but not with rope either. The harsh ring of metal sang out when I pulled my knees up. It sounded like a chain, but at least I could move my legs.

Damn! I'd blown my best chance for escape. Had I dropped Greg? Was he hurt? And what the hell was itching at my waist? I rubbed my torso against the mattress and felt a lumpy belt around my middle. With a shock, something else registered. Something more frightening than the restraints: I couldn't feel my skirt or top. My bra and panties were there, but nothing else. A choke of panic took my breath away. I pulled uselessly against the restraints.

"You can stop struggling," came a man's gravelly voice right beside me and I screamed. I swung my head around straining to see through my blind. "You won't be getting away so easily this time." I rammed my block up and felt it quivering like a freshly embedded blade.

"Who are you? What do you want?"

A second, deeper voice spoke from the direction of the doorway. "We were told not to talk to her."

"Where am I?" I asked. "Where's Greg?"

The first man with the gravelly voice responded, "You should be worrying about yourself, not Greg."

"Come on out of there," the deeper voice said.

I heard the man beside me stir. "I'll check on you later, darlin'," he drawled, whispering in my ear. His words raised the hair on my neck.

The door clicked shut, muffling their voices. My head felt thick, as if the drugs still coursed through my veins. What the hell had they done to me? With the blindfold on I couldn't tell the time of day. I pulled at my arms and found no give at all to the bindings. Ken Gillespie's words echoed in my head, "Your first priority is to get away." What's your second priority, Ken? I thought, gloomily, pinned to the bed in this prison.

They'd stepped down the hall, but I could hear their muffled voices through the thin walls. The gravelly voiced one spoke loudly, his voice harsh. "You can't expect me to sit on my can for two more days in the middle of godforsaken nowhere with one beer."

"You're the one who can't go a day without. You go to the fucking store."

"You know I can't do that. If someone recognizes me, then it's game over for both of us."

"You'd rat me out?"

"In a split fuckin' second."

"You and I have a deal. We back each other up and stay put until he relieves us."

"Yeah, well if you want me to back your ass up then you'd better get down the road and restock."

"You think you can keep your dick in your pants that long?"

"Fuck you."

"If you damage the goods, we won't collect and that will make me very unhappy. You don't want to make me unhappy."

"Since when has a little fuck damaged the goods?"

"She's dangerous—we were warned. Don't fucking touch her. You hear me?"

"Then I'd suggest you hurry back."

"Goddamnit! You're going to blow this for us. Leave her alone." A door opened and closed. It had the distinctive heavy thud of an exterior door. A car roared to life. Wheels crunched on gravel then faded away.

Had he left me alone with the rapist? I had to get out of here. I rubbed my head frantically against the mattress, trying to loosen the blindfold. It was tied so tightly my eyes hurt, but no amount of pushing against the back of my head loosened it.

We were in a trailer. I knew that, after my brief escape. I heard footsteps, but couldn't tell if they were in the kitchen or living room. The only time I could tell for sure was when they stopped outside my room. The door swung open. I couldn't tell if my block was stuck, but I didn't dare lower it.

"Who's there?" I asked. No one replied, but someone was there. I could hear him breathing.

"My partner's gone on a beer run." It was the rapist's gravelly voice. "He could be a while 'cause we're in the middle of no-fuckin'-where, but don't you worry." I heard him step into the room. "I'm going to take very good care of you."

"He told you to leave me alone."

"Yeah, well, he's not here and he's not the boss." His voice was right beside my head and I pulled away. His breath smelled foul. "You don't look dangerous to me—just a waif of a thing, really. Pretty to look at. And ... so ... very ... helpless." A chill raced down my spine. Goosebumps made my skin tingle. He was close enough that I could smell his stale body odour.

He was going to do it—he was going to rape me.

I pulled uselessly at the bindings. He brushed his hand alongside my outstretched arm, from my elbow, down the fabric on the side of my bra and ended in a lazy circle drawn on my stomach. I squirmed, but there was no getting away from him.

"We figured you'd be less inclined to run without your clothes."

My only option was to jolt him. I had to lower my block to do that, and what if he was a Flier? I needed to think.

I tried to refocus his attention, but my voice came out with a quiver. "What do you want with me?"

"Not me, darlin'. All I want's a little poke. But the boss will be here soon, and he tells us you have something of his." His fingers traced the skin above my bra, from the top of one breast across to the other.

I twisted under his touch. "Please, take the blindfold off," I begged, my voice quaking. "It's hurting my eyes."

"No can do, darlin', but I can take this bra off," he said. "It's hurting *my* eyes." I heard his clothes rustle as he fumbled with something. I heard a click. Panic raised its familiar head. My lungs lost their elasticity. I couldn't breathe. I fought against the binds, knowing it was useless. The sharp edges of the cuffs cut painfully into my wrists.

"Settle down, darlin'. I'm not going to hurt you."

I tried to push the panic away. "Please," I begged. "Don't do this." Then I felt a sharp cold pressure between my breasts and gasped when the halves of my bra gave way.

"That's better," he said, and I felt rough fingers peel the fabric away. I screamed with every ounce of breath I had.

"You go ahead and scream, darlin', if it makes you feel better. We didn't pick this place for its cozy charm, you know. There's nobody around us for miles. No one to hear you scream." I could hear the smile in his voice. Control escaped me then and panic took the reins. I heard myself scream over and over again.

When the screaming stopped, I felt exhausted and separate from what was happening, as if someone else had been doing the screaming. Had he left? I strained to hear his breath. My wrists and ankles burned where the skin laid raw against the metal.

I needed to think, not panic. I heard Jackson's voice in my head, *Panic is not your friend, Emelynn.* It was a lesson I'd learned the hard way. Now it threatened me again. With my breathing still shaky, I forced big inhales. In through my nose, out through my mouth: calming breaths.

I wasn't helpless. I was a Flier. I reminded myself of James's caution. I wasn't defenceless, he'd said, and I knew it: My jolts were powerful. The rapist was going to return and when he did, I had to lower my block and jolt him. I didn't have a choice.

But what if I knocked him out and his partner didn't come back? How long until someone found me? Would I be left here to die? What if his partner came back and wanted to join in the fun? If only I knew how to trigger my ghost. As the *what if's* piled up in my mind, the rapist came back to my door.

"Are you done with the screaming now?"

"Not if it will keep you away from me." I heard the *kitschh* of a pressurized can opening. He'd have to be closer for me to jolt him or I'd risk missing him. My eyes ached behind the tight blindfold, but I'd jolted with closed eyes before. Even if my achy eyes worked, what if my block was jammed?

"I don't mind a little screaming. I can gag you if it gets annoying."

The man was all heart. "Just what is it that your boss thinks I have?" He was drinking beer; I could smell it now. I breathed steadily and tested my block.

"Said it was a crystal. But he also said you'd have it on you, and you don't. You can ask him yourself when he relieves us." The beer can crackled as he took another drink.

This was good; as long as he was talking he was keeping his distance and eventually his partner would return. My block wasn't stuck. Thankfully something was finally going my way. "I don't know anything about a crystal."

"NMP. Know what that means? Not My Problem. It's a little something I picked up from TV."

And they say TV dumbs you down. "I've got a hundred grand sitting in my bank account. Let me go and it's yours. You don't even have to share it with your partner."

"I don't think my partner would appreciate the way you're thinking." Without being able to see his face, I couldn't tell if he was considering the offer or not. He belched. "Let's have a little fun here first and then you can give me all your money."

Damn, we were back to the rape. "You don't want to do that."

"Oh, darlin', yes I most certainly do."

"Let me go. I don't know what you look like. You can still walk away."

"And waste a fine little piece of tail like you? I'm hard just looking at you." He took another loud swallow, and then I heard the can hit the wall and bounce to the floor.

"Can I have a drink?"

"That was the last one. I'd have shared if you'd of said something sooner."

He stepped closer, his footsteps barely audible. Panic was trying to get hold of me again and I fought to keep it at bay, taking big breaths, in and out, in and out. Focus, Emelynn. As creepy as it was, he needed to be closer. I couldn't risk botching this jolt.

"You can struggle if you want, I kinda like that."

"Please don't do this," I begged again, but I heard him unzip his pants and they fell to the floor with a quiet clunk, as if a belt buckle had hit first. He wasn't going to stop. "I don't want to hurt you." He laughed, grabbed my ankles, and yanked, forcing my legs apart as far as the chain would allow.

"This isn't going to hurt me, darlin'," he said, and the bed shifted under his weight.

Time's up. I couldn't put it off a moment longer. This is exactly what Avery and I had been practicing and if he was close enough, I wouldn't miss. I lowered my block and wrapped my hand around my crystal. But something was wrong. It didn't feel as warm as it should. The power was there but diminished. I pulled everything I could forward and visualized a white-hot ball of energy, then let loose, blasting it toward his head.

But his head wasn't where I'd expected it to be. He'd bent lower and I'd missed. Damn! I felt the dull edge of a knife at my hip, cutting through the fabric of my panties. The bed squeaked. It wasn't too late. I could still do this.

"You disappoint me. No screams, no struggle. Almost takes the fun out of it," he said, yanking my panties to the side. His fingers dug between my legs and I bucked, momentarily losing myself in a screaming panic.

"Ah, that's better," he said, and his voice was the slap in the face I needed to bring me back. I was going to kill him. I gathered the waning strength of the crystal again while he crawled between my legs. The jolt would make his brain bleed and I'd be happy about it. The thought chilled me. My gathering jolt wasn't even at half strength when I felt his greedy hands squeeze my breasts. When his foul mouth covered my nipple, I knew exactly where his head was. I hurled the half-formed ball of energy straight down at him, not more than eight inches away.

This time I didn't miss. His elbows gave out, and he collapsed on top of me without a sound. I wanted him dead. Hopefully, I'd made up in proximity what I lost in power. My crystal was suffering and I didn't know why. What had they done to me?

The man's weight was crushing. I wiggled and shifted under him until his body was jammed between me and the wall. Then I finally broke down and screamed, "Get off me!" I repeated my plea at the top of my lungs like an inmate in an asylum. The man pissed himself and the hot urine ran down my thigh. He made strangled wet drooling noises and then started convulsing.

I turned my head away from him and pulled as far as the restraints would allow, repeating my mantra: *I am not defenceless; I am a Flier; panic is not my friend.* Eventually calm returned. I thought of the cottage, the pungent smell of the ocean and the heat of the rocks after they'd absorbed the afternoon sun. I tried to feel the warmth of a coffee mug in my hand as I wandered to the water's edge and dipped my feet in the cool, summer water.

Did anyone miss me yet? I'd told Molly I'd call her tomorrow. Was it tomorrow yet? Would she wonder why I hadn't called? Maybe

Malcolm noticed my absence and was worried enough to call someone. Avery was expecting me Thursday afternoon. Oh my god, Avery. Was he all right? Had he truly been hurt during a break-in? If Detective Jordan was any good, surely he'd notice I was gone. How long did I have to be missing before someone started looking for me?

The rapist stopped convulsing, but he was still breathing. His urine was cold now. It smelled foul. My thoughts wandered through the cottage then back to the mantra. This must be what losing your mind was like. I counted the man's breaths, hoping he'd stop breathing, but he didn't, and time droned on. I lost track of my counting around eight hundred and started over. Each time he inhaled, I willed it to be his last. The next time I lost track of the count, it was over a thousand.

Car tires on gravel broke me out of my clinging-to-sanity exercise. A heavy door opened then closed, and I heard the man with the deep voice call for his partner. "Here's your fucking beer." Something heavy dropped on the kitchen counter. The jingle of keys preceded him down the hall until he stood in my doorway.

The jingling stopped. Was he enjoying the view? The thought brought fresh anger boiling to the surface.

"Oh for Christ's sake, get the fuck away from her." He hadn't figured it out yet, but he soon would.

Silence preceded cautious footsteps into the room. "I have a gun, Emelynn. It's aimed at your head so don't do anything stupid." I heard him step closer. "Jesus . . . what the fuck have you done?"

"Me?" I shouted, seething. I'd jolt him if he got close enough. I was already gathering the crystal's waning power.

"Emelynn, listen to me. We call the boss every six hours. If he doesn't hear from one of us, he won't show. He'll leave you here to starve. You hear me? You need me."

I chortled like a madwoman and started forming a jolt. My crystal was weak, but if he got close enough . . .

"We're thirty minutes from the nearest neighbour and fifty from the nearest town. No one will hear you and you're not getting out of those cuffs. If you do to me whatever you did to him, you will not get out of here alive. You hear me?"

He needed to be just a little closer. "If you say so," I said, too angry to be cautious.

The blast of his gun forced a scream from my lungs. My ears rang, the shot nearly deafening me.

"You think I'm fucking around? The next one's going in your head!"

I couldn't stop my body's reaction to the shock of the gunshot and tremors shook through me. I clamped down on my teeth, but they chattered anyway. The weak jolt I'd been forming evaporated.

The rapist's body slid off me and onto the floor. Then I heard it being dragged out of the room. The door slammed and the smell of urine and mould nauseated me. I vomited, and the hot bile dribbled down my underarm, settling under my shoulder blade. I wretched until I thought the pressure would rupture my eyeballs then laid back and tried to breathe through my mouth.

"Oh, Christ," the man said, when he finally came back. I was still trembling and felt numb and weak. "My gun's in my hand, Emelynn. Don't make me use it." I heard him approach. He snapped something cold around my neck and my head jerked when he tugged it. "It smells like a urinal in here," he mumbled, releasing my ankles. Then he released my wrists and quickly locked them behind my back. My shoulders screamed out from the sharp change of position.

"Sit up," he said, shoving me roughly. I moved my legs to the side and straightened. My nakedness barely registered over the fear that paralyzed my mind. "Up!" He tugged at the collar until I was standing. I felt shaky and weak, and he had to push me to get me to move forward. My torn panties fell to my ankles and then off as I stepped into the hallway. I could feel whatever they'd put around my waist. The skin under it itched and had become painful, as if a string of blisters had formed.

I could tell we were in the bathroom from the echo. He prodded me forward until my knees hit the toilet then he turned me around. "Sit." He pushed down on my shoulders. "I'll be back in a minute. Don't forget—I've got a gun." His footsteps faded down the hall.

He returned a moment later and pushed me up against the side of the tub. "Step in." He wrapped his hand around my arm to steady me. I lifted one leg and then balanced to get the other leg over. He pulled my neck forward by its tether and I heard the harsh clank of metal on metal before he stepped away. Instinctively, I pulled against the band around my neck and felt its solid hold. The bastard had chained me to the wall. He muttered angrily and removed my ruined bra.

I heard the spray of water before I felt it. The cold liquid hit with a shock. He hosed me down and wiped a rough cloth over the vomit. I cringed from his touch but couldn't get away from his harsh cleansing.

My shaking was out of control by the time he hit me with another sharp
blast of cold water. It stung my wrists and ankles—even my waist where
the skin was broken.

He released my neck and the cold chain dropped between my
breasts. Using the hard point of his gun, he prodded me ahead of him. I
sensed the end of the hall. He guided me into a different room, pushing
me until my legs hit the side of what must be a bed. "Get up there.
Kneel." I did as he said and felt him lift the chain off my stomach and
pull it tight, forcing me farther forward. He pushed me down, face first,
and then secured the tether with a clang.

"Please, take off the blind," I pleaded. "It hurts."

"No." He dropped a blanket on me. The door closed. I pulled
against the tether. It was short and didn't budge and I was cold and
exhausted. The blanket felt like heaven and even the mouldy bedding
didn't smell bad to me now. I don't know if I fell asleep before or after I
stopped shaking.

Chapter Twenty-Six

I woke, stiff and sore. The cuffs on my wrists were tight but there was enough leeway to allow me to rub my forearms against the knobby belt at my waist that itched so badly. My eyes pulsated under the blindfold. I listened for signs of life, but it was quiet in the trailer. Songbirds sang outside the window without a care in the world. It occurred to me that songbirds sing in daylight. It was daytime. That little bit of knowledge made me weep. What day was this and was anyone looking for me yet?

My ears perked up at the ring of a phone, but I couldn't make out the conversation. Moments later I heard footsteps in the hall then the toilet flushed. It was a long time before the man came into my room. "I'm going to take you to the can," he said, and I heard his footsteps close to the bed. He pulled the blanket off my shoulders and pressed the hard, cold barrel of his gun into my back; the shock of it made me gasp. "That's my gun, in case you've forgotten." After unchaining me, he wrapped the blanket around me and escorted me to the bathroom. He stuffed toilet paper into my hands then left. He'd obviously never tried to wipe himself with his hands cuffed behind him. Back in the bedroom, he fed me a banana with a drink of orange juice, then chained me face down again and left the room, closing the door behind him.

I am not defenceless; I am a Flier; panic is not my friend. Without a clock, the passing of time lost its meaning; had an hour passed or ten minutes? I learned how each one of my movements made the bed creak. The house noises became familiar too, the thunk of the fridge door, the knock of kitchen cupboards, the squeak in the floor down the hall. Each door had its own distinct hinge noise as did the scrunch of the vinyl sofa when someone sat on it.

When the man came again, the birds had stopped singing. "What's your name?" I asked. Silence. "What day is it?"

"One day closer to me getting out of this shit hole." He offered me no such assurance. We went through the bathroom routine again and he fed me another banana and more juice, then left.

I drifted in and out of sleep, completely void of any sense of time. Voices in the hallway outside my room eventually woke me.

"You'll get your money." A new man. "Just as soon as I confirm her good condition." The new voice was quiet, unrushed.

Their footsteps came into the room. "Emelynn, how are you, dear?"

Dear? Was he kidding me? I turned my face away from him.

"Have your hosts been taking good care of you?"

I ignored him and his sick sense of humour.

"I wish you'd talk to me." His voice sounded cultured. I didn't detect an accent.

The blanket lifted from my shoulders and cool air chilled my back. I smelled cologne.

"Her wrists are a mess, but her fingers look good. Have you had her blind off?"

The rapist's buddy let out a mean laugh. "Ask Dan how much that blind helped. She complains it hurts."

So the rapist's name was Dan.

"Is that right? Does the blind hurt, Emelynn? Do you want me to remove it?"

"Yes," I blurted out. "Please," I said, pathetically.

"Ah, so you do speak. You can hear too. That's good." The blanket settled down on my back again.

"Let's go," the boss said. Their footsteps left the room and trailed off down the hall.

The rapist's buddy made two trips to the room across the hall. I heard a heavy zipper and imagined a duffle bag. My captor was leaving.

"Keep your phone on," the boss said.

"This job's done."

"Yes, and thank you, but I may have further need of your services."

The front door opened and closed. Moments later I heard car wheels on gravel, fading into the distance. Two voices remained. The boss and a second one I hadn't heard before. The second voice was deeper than the cultured voice, but there was nothing distinctive about it. The trailer grew quiet again.

I stirred at the boss's voice. Perhaps I'd fallen asleep. I slammed my block into place.

"Good. You're awake. How about you and I have a little chat?"

I didn't bother turning to face him.

"Do you know why I invited you here, Emelynn?"

Invited—now he was a comedian.

"You have something that belongs to me, and I intend to get it back." I kept him on ignore and noticed his voice travelling but no footsteps. Was he a Flier? "Do you know what it is?"

I turned my head toward his voice. "Your buddies told me you think I have your crystal. I'm sure they also told you I don't have it. I don't know who took it, but it wasn't me."

"You think we've made a mistake?" His voice dripped with sarcasm.

"Colossal."

He laughed a full-throated roar. "Ah, Emelynn. I've been biding my time for more than ten years: watching, waiting, setting my trap. I've been a very patient man—it's a virtue, you know—patience."

"Yes, you're a paragon of virtue." I didn't mean to be snide, it just slipped out.

"Perhaps you don't appreciate the time and effort I've expended to find you. It was a gamble. I put my money on the chance that whoever had Jolene's gift would eventually return. Now my gamble's paid off."

He knew about Jolene. How? His voice had moved again with no accompanying footsteps. He had to be a Flier. I shifted to face his voice. "I was terribly upset when Jolene disappeared. Her brother, Mason, was beside himself. He helped me search for her; questioned anyone who'd seen her. Her last known whereabouts was Summerset, but then, you already knew that."

His voice was on the move again. "It was me, you see, who set up the birders. Me, who baited them to keep them vigilant all these long years since Jolene's disappearance. It was quite clever really; we had such a large area to monitor." He was bragging, like he'd waited years to tell this story. "There were several birders watching, but it was Charles who found you; unwittingly, yes, but effective all the same. It was easy, really. All I had to do was tempt them with a few doctored photos; rare sightings close enough to keep them looking. They did the rest. The best watch dogs I could possibly want. Thankfully Charles had already done the heavy lifting by the time the Tribunal picked him off."

My body stilled. I had to remember to breathe. This man was far more dangerous than I could have imagined.

"Am I sounding more like I know what I'm talking about now? Still think I made a *colossal* mistake?"

His roving voice made me think he was hovering. He was definitely a Flier; I was certain of it now. "Who's Jolene?" I asked, feigning ignorance. If he knew about Jolene, did he know she was a Ghost?

"Don't play dumb. It'll make me think you're a liar."

"I'm not lying. I didn't know Jolene. I met her a few times when I was a kid, but I don't know her."

"Well, she certainly knew you. Why else would she give you her gift?"

I swallowed hard.

"You don't even know what she gave you, do you?" His voice was near my ear this time. "What a fucking waste. How old were you? Thirteen? Couldn't have been more than that."

"Twelve, actually." My voice sounded small.

"Like I said, what a waste; a massive, fucking waste. It's about time we fixed that, don't you think?"

"There's no fixing this," I said, but it was futile. He'd been on this path far too long to let mere words sway him.

"You underestimate yourself, Emelynn. We *are* going to fix this, you and I, because you're going to give me Jolene's gift, and you're going to give it the way it needs to be given—freely and unencumbered."

My ears pricked up at those words. They were the words from the anthology. Did he have access to one of the books?

"Ah, I see you recognize those words. Do you remember them?"

"No."

"Well, never mind. I know them by heart. I'll write them out for you when the time comes."

I lay very still. Gifting would likely kill me. Did he know that? Of course he knew that. Did he know I was a Ghost? My mantra ran through my head, cooling and calming: *I am a Flier; I am not defenceless; panic is not my friend.* I'd have to be quick to jolt him. With my crystal fading, would I be able to re-block fast enough to protect myself?

"Who are you?"

"I suppose there's no harm in telling you now. My name's Carson Manse."

"How do you know Jolene?"

"She was my lover many years ago."

So Carson Manse was probably in his fifties. "You already have the gift. What could I possibly give you that you don't already have?"

"Now you're playing the fool again."

"Not intentionally, I'm just trying to figure out what any of this has to do with your missing crystal? Did Jolene take it?" He didn't answer me. Was he still in the room? "Carson?"

"We searched your house. It's not there, not in your car and you're not wearing it."

"That's because I. Don't. Have. It." When did he search my house? "Jolene never gave it to me. I can't help you. I'd give you the damn crystal if I could. Hell, I'd buy one for you if I could." How did he even know about my crystal? It wasn't a physical thing, and I hadn't told a living soul about my talisman—not even Avery.

"That we can't find it, isn't a deal breaker. It's a disappointment, yes, but I always knew the crystal would be the weak link; I procured a substitute a long time ago. You don't plan for something as long as I've been planning for this, and not be prepared for every possible scenario. You can act like you don't know the significance of the crystal, but I don't believe you. You see, I know your good friend, Avery, has been researching Ghosts, and that belt you're wearing, well you can't hide how badly it's irritating your skin. Are you going to try to tell me you aren't a Ghost?"

Carson knew. I wilted into the filthy mattress. But what did being a Ghost have to do with the crystal? And what was the significance of the belt that had rubbed my skin raw? I shouldn't have pushed Mason away. He'd been right. I needed him and now my ignorance was going to get me killed. I didn't understand half of Carson's innuendo, and I needed to. "What have you tied around my waist?"

"You don't know?" My silence answered his question. "I suppose I can believe that one. It does explain your bold earring choice."

"Amber?" I asked. Mason had known about amber. He told me it trapped Fliers like us. He was referring to Ghosts. Even Cassandra hinted at it. Why hadn't I listened?

"Not just any amber, Emelynn, quality amber. It's from the Baltic Sea. I'm surprised Avery hadn't at least discovered that much by now."

This is what Avery had warned me about; why it was so critical that no one learned I was a Ghost. Neither money nor pleas would alter

Carson's course. He was willing to kill me to get what he wanted, and nothing was going to stop him. "You killed Jolene."

"No, she killed herself, unless you want to take the blame."

"Jolene was running *from you*. She gave me her gift to protect it— *from you*." Now it all made sense. I remembered Jolene's visits to me on the beach that summer. She'd tucked her hair under a big floppy hat and used it to shield her face. It wasn't sun protection—she was hiding. It was Carson she was afraid of; Carson she looked for over her shoulder; Carson she ran from.

"That was a mistake. If she'd given it to me in the first place, we wouldn't be in this predicament. My mistake was letting her get away. I won't be repeating that mistake with you."

I turned my head away from his voice. That's why he'd been hovering; knowing what I knew now, he knew I'd kill him if I got the chance. It was him or me.

"Carson," I said. "You'd better have a good block."

"You can't break my block, Emelynn. Jolene already tried that."

The only advantage I had was that he wanted my gift, and he'd have to remove my chains to get it. *I am a Flier; I am not defenceless; panic is not my friend.* I smiled. Carson was a dead man. My heart froze over, cold as ice.

"You'll have to entertain yourself for a while. I've got some preparations to make. If you need something, just shout. Rupert will tend to you, but don't make the mistake of underestimating him. He's highly motivated to protect your eyes and hands, but not much else."

Rupert? Could he mean the recently murdered Rupert Dowling? A few moments later, I heard voices in the hall, close to the kitchen. Then the kitchen door opened and closed.

Footsteps approached, stopping at the door. "Hello, Emelynn." It was the voice of the man who'd arrived with Carson. His voice had a lower tenor than Carson's.

"Rupert . . . Dowling?"

"You've heard of me?"

"I heard you were dead."

"Yes, I heard the same. If being dead weren't so bloody convenient, I'd be upset about the rumour. But no worries: Carson's taken care of the DNA so I can stay dead."

"How very thoughtful of him." Carson may have been able to avoid a jolt with his hovering, but Rupert had walked down the hall so maybe he wasn't a Flier. Maybe I could get Rupert close enough to put him out of action. "I'm thirsty. May I have a drink of water?"

He hesitated for just a moment. "Sure," he said cheerfully. He left me and went down the hall and into the kitchen. The cupboard door banged closed, the faucet ran and then his footsteps returned.

This might be my only chance to eliminate Carson's backup. I had to be patient and wait for the perfect opportunity. One jolt and he'd be down like Dan the rapist. Then it would be just me and Carson, the dead man.

The bed shifted under his weight. I froze. Not again, I thought, but Rupert didn't remove the blanket, he straddled my back, grabbed my hair and yanked my head back. "Here, drink." He pushed the rim of the glass against my mouth. "You're thirsty, remember?" He tipped the glass. I opened my mouth and swallowed what I could and choked on the rest, coughing and spitting out what didn't run down my chin to soak into the mattress.

He released his grip on my hair with more force than he needed, leaving me to my coughing fit. "I've played this game before, Emelynn." He crawled off the bed. "Carson warned me about you, and I saw what you did to Dan. I won't be making that mistake."

I caught my breath. "It's not too late for you to get out of here," I choked out between coughs. He'd retreated to the doorway.

"I'm not going to ditch Carson. He's already given me a taste of what you people can do and now I want it, all of it. After I've done my part here, playing second for him, he's going to find a donor for me and return the favour."

"A donor?"

"Yeah, someone like you."

"You have a brand-new identity, Rupert, and I haven't seen your face. You could start fresh—a whole new life. Just walk away."

"I've already started my new life, Emelynn. And you've already seen my face. More than once."

Had I? His voice wasn't familiar.

"I've been watching you for a long time. When Charles first reported something suspicious, I came up to have a look. Toured the whole beach from Sunset Park to the public access. Checked out you and your neighbours, looking for clues."

Was this the man who had loitered in the sand at the foot of my stairs to the beach all those weeks ago?

"But that was before we knew your name. Since then, well . . . I played with your new house alarm and watched you and your running buddy scurry around looking for burglars."

I swallowed hard.

"I drank a Bud while you mingled with your friends at Fast Eddies. I even played a little game with you that night. Do you remember?"

What was he talking about? I couldn't place his voice and suddenly the creepy spider-crawling-across-my-shoulders sensation flared up. I squirmed under the blanket, cursing. Not now. This was not the time for my nerves to act up.

"I ate a basket of chips while you yukked it up with your chums at Clam Diggers, remember?" The spider sensation morphed into warm fingers across my shoulders.

Finally, the light dawned. "You're doing that?"

"Yeah, cool isn't it? Carson gave me that." He was like a kid showing off his new toy. "I can feel it, too, you know." The sensation intensified until I felt hands on my shoulders. "Feels nice; soft, warm, but don't worry, I'm not as ugly as Dan. I don't need to force myself on women." His voice was still in the doorway, so the sensation couldn't be real. Could it?

"Don't get me wrong, I'm a dead shot with a gun." The hands moved to my neck and tightened their grip. Despite the stiff collar around my neck, he started to choke me. "But I don't need my gun to control you. So don't fuck with me."

The sensation of his hands disappeared, his footsteps faded, and then I heard the TV come on.

Shit! Shit! Shit! I hadn't even tried to block him. What was wrong with me? And what the hell good was a mantra when it was just words. I was a sorry excuse for a Flier: I couldn't block or jolt when I needed to, and panic had frequent flier points in my life. It was impossible. I was going to die in this filthy trailer chained up like an animal.

I lay there wallowing in self-pity for a long time. I thought about my mother. Even though we weren't as close as some mothers and daughters, I knew she'd be devastated when I was gone. She'd probably blame herself for making it so easy for me to move back here. She'd blame the cottage, the same way she blamed the ocean for taking Dad away. She'd sell the cottage for sure when I was dead.

Would Molly miss me? We'd barely reconnected. Would Cheney remember that he kissed me once? Had I had an impact on anyone's life? Avery would miss me. He'd been so careful with my secret. If Avery learned that Carson knew he'd been researching Ghosts, he'd blame himself. Hell, he was still blaming himself for a tragedy that happened when he was fifteen and that was no more his fault than this. And what about the rest of the covey? Eden and Alex, Danny, Gabe and the others? They'd take it hard. Covey protected one another. It's what we do. I'd heard that repeatedly.

I couldn't let that happen. If there was anything I could do to stop Carson and get out of here alive, I had to figure it out. I owed all of them that much. I repeated the mantra and tried once again to draw strength from it: *I am a Flier; I am not defenceless; panic is not my friend.* Nor is pity, I added. Incapacitated and humiliated, yes; scared, definitely; but I wasn't dead yet.

Soon I heard voices mingling with the TV and then Rupert returned to my room. He released my neck tether and draped the blanket around me before pushing me ahead of him to the bathroom. Next stop was the living room.

"Emelynn." Carson said my name with excited anticipation, like we'd met at a dinner party.

"Carson." I turned my face to his voice. Jolt then re-block, that's all I had to do.

"I've assembled everything we need, so it's time. It's your choice how we proceed from here." He was hovering again, like a bad smell. "If you cooperate and do everything you're told, the process will be painless, and Rupert will make sure you have the best recovery possible." As soon as I thought I had a fix on him, his voice would come at me from a different spot. "If you choose not to cooperate, Rupert will make the process as painful as possible. Should be a simple decision."

"Yeah, you'd think, but it's all pointless, isn't it? There's no *best recovery possible*, is there? There's a better than fifty percent chance that the gifting process will kill me on the spot, and if it doesn't, my body will be left so weak that a good case of the sniffles could do me in."

"Fifty percent is a damn sight better than zero, Emelynn. Besides, it's not like you have a choice. Why not make it easy on yourself and take the less painful route?" He was close to my left shoulder. This was my chance. I dropped my block and reached for the crystal. It was so cold it frightened me, its power barely humming beneath my skin. I kept talking as I called to the crystal, gathering its dim strength. I needed more time.

"Oh, I don't know. Could be that I don't trust you or your friend, Rupert. Or maybe I don't think Jolene would appreciate that I so easily gave away the very thing she gave up her life to protect." I pulled all I could from my crystal. It was barely a fraction of the power I needed.

"You have NO connection to that woman!" He moved closer when his temper flared. "You have no reason to—"

And then I let him have it. It was all I could muster and I might never get a better shot. His fall confirmed that he'd been hovering, but his voice said it wasn't enough.

"Son of a bitch!" he shouted. "Rupert! Get her the fuck away from me, and when you bring her back, make sure she's ready to cooperate."

Chapter Twenty-Seven

Rupert shoved me roughly from behind. At least I thought he was behind me. He hadn't spoken so I couldn't place him. For all I knew he could have been in another room, but I felt his hands push me anyway.

"Stupid bitch," he said, after he'd pushed me into the bedroom. He chained my neck tether so tightly that my chin pressed against the metal rails of the headboard. "This could have been so fucking easy."

He disappeared and raised voices echoed from the living room.

I recognized Rupert's footsteps when he finally returned, but he remained silent.

"He's going to kill me, Rupert." I kicked at him but couldn't stop him chaining my ankles.

"Maybe not. Some of you live."

Oh my god, he'd been through this before. A chill ran through my body. "He told me his name, Rupert, he's not going to let me live." How many other Fliers had they done this to?

"You should have taken the easy route." His voice sounded removed, like he was daydreaming. Rupert had checked out. Why?

"Rupert!" I shouted as the blanket lifted off.

"Shut up." He unlocked my wrists, re-fastened them to the wall above my head and then stepped away.

"What are you doing?" A second later I heard the sound of a whip slice through the air.

It struck my back, taking my breath away as effectively as the cold Pacific, but this hit left a sting like a hundred yellow jackets in its wake.

Before I could catch my breath, Rupert's whip cut through the air again, laying down a second stinging line as painful as the first. I tried to twist away, pulled at my raw wrists, but the neck tether held me tight.

"No!" I screamed, but he didn't stop. He rent the air again and burned a third line beside the others. "Please, stop!" I begged after the fourth. My back was on fire. He showed no mercy and struck again. When the next stroke struck skin already raw from the amber around my waist, the pain proved unbearable. I screamed until my lungs gave out. Then I must have fainted.

I came to in the same position—neck tight to the headboard with my arms strung over my head. My back blazed. It stung like the freshly exposed skin under a giant, peeled blister. An open wound. My bottom lip quivered and my whole body took up the rhythm. How many times had Rupert rained his whip down on me?

The next hours, or maybe it was days, drifted in a haze. My body was in control and its exhaustion dictated sleep, tremors and fever. The pain woke me regularly, and I sobbed. Then the cycle repeated.

"Dry the tears, Emelynn." Carson's voice made me still. Was I dreaming? "This is your doing. We gave you the easy option and you chose the painful one. Rupert's done a lovely job; I do hope it met your expectations."

It wasn't a dream. "Screw you," I whispered.

"Do you really think this is as bad as it can get?"

"You're going to kill me anyway. I'm not giving you Jolene's gift. It'll die with me and then you can get your jollies watching your big plan die along with me."

"What about your friends? Are you willing to sacrifice them too?"

I tried to focus on his voice. What was he talking about?

"Show her, Rupert."

I felt a hard edge against the back of my scalp and then the pressure from the blindfold let go. My vision went from black to bright white in a painful flash as the free flow of blood returned to my eyes. I tried to open them, but they were glued shut.

"Give her a minute," Carson said.

He gave me two. I worked my eyes, squeezing and straining until finally the left and then the right opened a crack. All I saw was grey. They had blinded me. I blinked and then blinked again and opened my eyes wide. Shadows. This time I saw shadows.

Carson grabbed my chin. "Look at me."

His face was a blur. I squinted to focus but couldn't see more than shadows. "Shit," he mumbled under his breath. "Cuff her arms behind her. Get her up and give her something to eat."

His footsteps trailed away. Rupert approached the bed and leaned over to unlock my wrists. I screamed when he moved my arms. However, the pain in my shoulders paled in comparison to the fire that erupted on my back with every twitch of muscle under the raw skin. He sat me up and the fact that I was naked wasn't even a factor against the pain and nausea at being yanked upright. My eyes welled up. Warm tears ran down my face as he clicked the cuffs shut behind my back. I whimpered when he draped the rough blanket over my shoulders. He left me sitting on the edge of the bed shaking and I heard him go down the hall toward the kitchen. Voices spoke and I strained to hear their words.

"We need her eyes, damn it," Carson said.

His concern about my eyes was well founded. I couldn't see more than shadows. I worked my eyes, rolling them, blinking hard and forcing them to focus. If I could recover more of my vision, I might be able to fool him and then I'd have an advantage. Rupert's footsteps approached, and I frantically blinked, trying to gain vision. The tears had helped.

He arrived with something wrapped in cellophane. I heard the wrapping crinkle as he removed it, followed by the unmistakable stench of sulphur and onion. Why did egg salad have to smell so bad? He reminded me of his gun before he fed me the sandwich.

It was light outside; I could tell that much. Rupert's face was a blur, but I saw that he had short, dark hair. He was built, not fat, but definitely not thin. He wore a light-coloured T-shirt and dark jeans. I recognized the room as the one I'd found Greg in the night we tried to escape.

"Where's Greg?" I asked, ashamed that I hadn't thought of him before now.

"Just eat," Rupert said, as he pressed the sandwich against my mouth again.

He helped me wash the dry bread down my throat with a drink of water then left for the kitchen. The throbbing in my head had gone and my vision was clearing. I could now make out the stains on the mattress and the brown-ringed water marks on the ceiling. It would take an Academy award-winning performance to pull off vision impairment now, but I had to. I needed Carson to get close enough to hit him with another jolt. Despite bragging about his block, my last jolt nearly did him in. He was either lying or he didn't have his block up when I'd jolted him.

But the amber worried me. It was killing my crystal. I reached inside to hold it and found it cold, its power barely there. Would I be able to gather enough juice from it to do the damage I needed? Would the crystal recover if I could somehow get the amber off? Squinting at my stomach through the gap in the blanket, I could make out the outline of the amber belt. Each piece was the size of a hazelnut, strung together like a pearl necklace. I could see the burnt yellow colour of the amber now and knew my vision was almost back.

I bent my elbows, inhaling through my teeth to swallow the pain, and ran my bound hands awkwardly along the lumpy rope behind my back. It was tightly fastened but there had to be a clasp of some sort. The surrounding skin was blistered and moist. I felt a small gap between two stones on the right side. There was a knot of twisted metal, like florist wire. I wiggled the knot with my fingers, jabbing myself on a stiff end. I pulled it loose and soon found the other end. The ends were twisted and the first twist came apart easily, but the knot of wire was far from undone. I worked at it until I'd untwisted a second loop. If I'd had more time, I might have been able to loosen it completely, but footsteps approached.

The performance began. I lowered my head and stared at the floor. It was Rupert—I recognized his footsteps. I could see well enough to tell he wore runners. I concentrated to keep my eyes steady and not let them follow his feet as he crossed the floor. He got behind me and helped me stand, arranging the blanket to cover me. It provided minor modesty but wasn't worth the flare of pain it caused as it shifted against the torn skin of my back. Rupert poked the barrel of his gun into the back of my head and prodded me down the hall into the living room. He retreated a safe distance, leaving me standing in front of the window. I squinted against the blinding daylight, listening for Carson. Was he hanging around the ceiling like a bat? I didn't want to give away my vision, so I kept my eyes still and my head level, biding my time until he spoke.

"Are you feeling better now?"

"Peachy." I turned to his voice but intentionally directed my eyes to a spot left of him. It was incredibly tempting to look him full on and finally know the face of my tormentor, but I didn't dare. The only sense

I got from my peripheral vision was that he was bigger than me and bald. He moved when I did, hovering sideways a few feet, watching my movement like a hawk. I wrapped my fingers around the cold crystal and willed it to give me its strength.

"Are you ready to cooperate?"

I moved my head so I looked just left of his new position, as if I'd followed his voice and not his hovering form. The power I'd gathered wasn't nearly enough.

"Cooperate? Don't you mean sacrifice?"

"Emelynn, you make this so much harder than it needs to be."

He'd moved again and I let my eyes follow. "Harder than dying?"

"Yes," he said, and I could hear the promise in his voice even without seeing it in his face. "Rupert," he called, and I heard Rupert's footsteps down the hall. I narrowed my eyes to see him open the door to the room where Dan tried to rape me. I still didn't have enough power to damage Carson. If only I could get rid of the amber.

"Do you want to know how?"

I swung back to his voice by the window. The blanket around my shoulders shifted, making me gasp. I heard Rupert's steps coming back into the room behind me, then the quiet thump and scrunch of the vinyl sofa.

I turned toward the sofa and saw a blanket-wrapped bundle. As I stepped closer Rupert swung his gun in my direction and I heard an ominous click. "Step back," Carson warned, and when I did, he added, "Show her."

Rupert turned back to the sofa and tugged the corner of the blanket off revealing a shock of spiky red hair.

"Eden?" I took an involuntary step forward. "Eden!" Rupert stopped my forward momentum by firing his gun over my head. I leapt back and covered my ears, too late to prevent the noise from deafening me. My eyes darted to Rupert.

"Yes, Eden," Rupert said, as my head spun and my ears rang. "Nice girl, Eden. Do you think she'd mind my whip?"

I would have cursed, but the sight of Rupert struck me dumb. I just stood there, staring at a familiar face that I now saw clearly.

"What? Don't recognize him without his Australian accent?" This from Carson, who'd moved to a new perch behind me. "Rupert has proven indispensable. He's the one who planted the Trojan Horse—the honey that caught the fly so to speak. Clever, don't you think?"

"You bastard!" I spit the words at Greg. But it wasn't Greg; it was Rupert. He no longer wore the glasses, and the dorky hair was gone, but it was more than that. It was subtle, his eyebrows or maybe his nose?

"Yes, well, a clever bastard nonetheless," Carson said. "He's also rather adept at B&E. Dr. Coulter never did suspect a break-in when Rupert relieved him of your file two weeks ago. Dr. Coulter should really be more careful about his paperwork, but his description of your abdominal scar was quite accurate—very helpful."

"Where's Greg? The real Greg?"

"I'm afraid Greg's had an accident," Rupert said.

I'd never met Greg, but he'd been a friend and because of me, he was dead. And now Eden's life was also in my hands.

"What's wrong with Eden?"

"She's just sleeping. She doesn't even know she's here yet. But she will if you don't cooperate."

I turned my gaze to Carson with all pretense of impaired vision gone. His eyes, like his heart, were black as coal. He stood, not hovered, six feet away. He wasn't tall but had a powerful build. He'd shaved his head to hide a receding hairline. He didn't look surprised that I'd pinpointed him. And I couldn't do anything about it: There wasn't enough power in my crystal to make a night light glow let alone deal him a fatal jolt. Eden had to be my focus now.

"If I do this thing, how will you guarantee Eden gets out of here unharmed?"

"The moment the transfer is made, Rupert and I will leave." Carson's thin lips curled into a benevolent smile, belying his complete control over me. "I'll leave a phone close by so you can call for help before we're out of the driveway."

"How do you know I'll be able to dial for help? I might not live through the gifting."

"That's not usually how it works. Even if you don't survive, you'll linger for a few hours. Your night vision will be gone because the gifting shatters your second lens. Remnants of the lens will eventually blind you, but you'll have enough sight and strength to walk away, to get help." Carson tugged at the cuffs of his jacket then brushed at his shoulders, primping, as if my life was an inconsequential bit of fluff on the nap of his suit.

"But I'll be no match for you or Rupert after the gifting. How can I trust that you won't harm Eden afterwards?"

"I'll be incapacitated immediately after I receive your gift, and Rupert will be too occupied getting me safely away from here to interfere with your phone call." Being incapacitated rang true. I remember waking up on the beach after Jolene gifted me. Even Avery remembered being rendered unconscious after his ordeal.

"Even if you don't survive it, the drugs wear off in three to four hours. Eden will wake eventually, and she'll find the phone."

If I had a choice, I'd let the gift die with me, but Eden didn't deserve this fate. They'd already killed Greg and what they'd done to me was proof enough that they'd hurt Eden. I had no illusions that if it came to that, they'd kill her too. My crystal was failing and without its strength, I couldn't fight them. This was the best I could do for her. They'd eliminated my options. They'd won.

"I'll do it," I whispered, closing my eyes in defeat.

"Good. We'll make the transfer as soon as it's fully dark," Carson said. "Now, you need to rest." He motioned to Rupert.

Rupert was on me in a flash, but instead of escorting me down the hall, he plunged a needle into my shoulder. "We can't have you plotting another escape," he said, as my knees gave out. I couldn't even manage a scream when his arm caught the welts on my back.

I fought the drugs, but it was no use. The darkness claimed me.

Chapter Twenty-Eight

Waking from drugged sleep is disorienting. It feels like you closed your eyes only moments before, yet, in waking, you know that time has passed. I lay on my side and my back burned. The amber belt was still in place, but my hands were cuffed in front of me this time and my ankles weren't restrained. Someone had dressed me in Greg's ugly bowling shirt. No, Rupert's ugly bowling shirt, I reminded myself. I sat up carefully and fought off a wave of nausea. The shirt had stuck to my back and tugged painfully.

When my head cleared, I realized it was dark outside. I had to get that amber off and fast. I removed my amber earrings and dropped them to the floor. Dried blood painted my forearms. I contorted my hands, searching for the wire that held the amber to my waist. The knot that I'd loosened earlier was unreachable with my hands bound in front. I sucked in my breath and pulled the beaded belt to my left. I felt the sharp sting of fresh scabs tearing. I inhaled through my teeth then gave another tug until the knot was in front.

When my breathing settled, I found the gap between the two stones and fingered the twisted wire knot. The loose ends had folded back in. I pried the sharp ends free, but there were no more twists. The wire had been knotted underneath. I pierced my thumb as I pushed against the sharp ends until they gave way and could be bent back through the knot. Grasping the bend I'd created, I pulled until the loose end came free. I repeated the process. It was working. I was close, but whoever had knotted this wire hadn't intended it to come off.

Rupert's footsteps down the hall stopped my progress. I held in a gasp as I quickly lay back down on my side and feigned sleep. He needed to think I was unconscious for just a few more minutes. That's all it would take to free me of the amber.

"It's time, Emelynn. Get up." The click of his gun chilled me. "I heard you. I know you're awake."

I opened my eyes and looked at him. "I need to use the bathroom."

He escorted me down the hall with the barrel of his gun pointed at the back of my head. Once inside the small bathroom, my eyes confirmed the filth I'd smelled in previous visits.

"Go on," he said, and I stepped to the toilet.

"You want to give me a minute, please?"

"Not tonight," he said, his gun poised.

"I need some toilet paper."

Without taking his eyes off me, Rupert wadded the tissue and jabbed it into my cuffed hands. "Here."

If I ever got out of this alive, I would make Rupert feel the humiliation of this moment, and then I'd make his back bleed like mine. I paused at that thought. I may have been going through the motions to my doom, but if I could think about retribution, then I hadn't given up all hope.

A cold smile flickered at the corners of my mouth.

Rupert pushed me down the hall. When we were abreast of the room I thought Eden was in. I stopped. "Where's Eden?"

"Sleeping."

"I want to see her."

He hesitated, probably thinking of saying no, but something made him give in. Maybe it was easier to show me than to argue. He opened the door and Eden's small form lay on the bed. All I could see of her was her flaming red hair. He pulled the door closed. "Now go," he said, urging me toward the kitchen. We went through the door I'd heard open and close many times and stepped outside. How long had I been here? It felt like weeks.

The night was clear and warm. Frogs croaked loudly close by. I inhaled deeply of the fresh air and looked up to the stars. It wasn't a full moon, so Carson had got that part right. Tall fir trees encroached on the trailer's yard. A blue sedan was parked in the driveway, pointed toward the road.

Carson sat cross-legged inside a crudely rendered circle about three metres across. He'd created the circle outdoors; that made two things he'd gotten right. He'd ditched his jacket and looked relaxed in slacks and loafers, as if he'd dropped in unexpectedly on a yoga class.

"Go on," Rupert said, and Carson held his hands out, inviting me to join him.

I walked to the edge of the circle and studied his handiwork. Four candles blazed at an equal distance from one another around the circle's edge. The circle would be made of wood ash if I remembered the words Avery had deciphered from the Reynolds Anthology. Carson knew what he was doing. Rupert had his gun trained on me.

Maybe this was really it. Maybe I'd just been fooling myself with thoughts of retribution. "Where's the phone?" I asked.

Carson pulled a phone out of his shirt pocket. "Right here."

"Show me that it's working."

He pushed the keys and the display lit up. Then he tossed it outside the circle to his right, midway between us. "Your turn," he said, beckoning me forward.

I stepped across the ash and felt a wind lift the back of my hideous shirt. It was probably just my imagination, but it sounded quieter inside the circle, as if a barrier had closed around us.

"Sit," Carson said, and I lowered myself to the ground in front of him. His beady black rat's eyes followed my every move. A small velvet bag lay between us. "Rupert knows what to expect. He's seen this before, so if he suspects that things aren't going according to plan, he'll put a bullet through your head."

"You say the nicest things." I had no assurance that he wouldn't put a bullet through my head no matter what happened, but I was long past the point of worrying about such trivialities. I'd done all I could, save getting free of the amber. Even if I could get free of it before Rupert got a shot off, I had no idea if my crystal would recover. It was too big a risk to take with Eden's life on the line. I held my wrists out to Carson. "Take the cuffs off."

Carson stared into my eyes, cautious, but unafraid and didn't look away as he pulled the key from his shirt pocket. He was flaunting the fact that he wasn't worried about me jolting him. He was well versed in amber's effect. I could no longer feel that thrum beneath my skin. The power that once took only a thought to stir, was still. The crystal was quiet. Not dead but sleeping. Looking at my bloodied wrists, he inserted the key. The cuffs sprang loose. He threw them and the key beyond the circle. I flexed my wrists, relishing the freedom.

Carson pulled a cue card out of his pocket and held it out. "After we're in position, these are the words that you'll recite—precisely as they're written. When you're done, Rupert will come into the circle and take care of me, and you can go to the phone. Eden's inside, first door to the right of the kitchen."

I took the card and looked down at the very words I'd written for Avery just days ago.

"After you've read it, give it to Rupert. He'll prompt you."

I reread the words. Then I let my glance drift from Carson to his ash circle and his candles. Had Jolene made an ash circle? Surely I would have remembered that? There weren't any candles that I recalled either. In fact, Jolene had gifted me in broad daylight. I held the card out, and it was pulled from my grasp.

"Do you believe in Karma?" I asked. Up close, I could see his age in the tone and texture of his skin.

"No. I believe you make your own luck in this world and only the strongest thrive and survive."

"I believe you reap what you sow, and you have a duty to your fellow man."

"I hope that gives you peace, Emelynn."

I smiled at that because I realized it did. Carson would get his just reward, I had to believe that. "The Tribunal will hunt you down for this. You won't have a moment's peace when this is done."

"The Tribunal's days of sitting on high, dictating the rules and meting out their justice are numbered."

"Oh?"

"The Tribunal has made a lot of enemies over the years. I'm only one of a growing contingent of Fliers who have decided to do something about it and every one of us is growing stronger." He untied the ribbon that cinched the small velvet bag. "You see, we've learned a thing or two from our exalted Tribunal. They may have a hundred-year jump on us, absorbing gifts from the Fliers they condemn, but we're catching up. And now, at long last, one of us has a Ghost within our grasp." He tilted his head in deference, as if thanking me. I wanted to claw the contented look off his face. "After we're done here, it'll be so much easier for me to help the others find their own Ghosts. Soon we'll be strong enough to take out the Tribunal."

"And then what? What's your end game?"

"Justice," he said, as he tipped the bag's contents into his hand. It was a crystal: white, not clear like mine, and smaller than the one that slept inside of me.

"But none of that changes what's going to happen tonight. We've wasted enough time. Now, raise your hands," he said, demonstrating with his own.

Maybe I didn't want to live in a Flier world controlled by the likes of Carson, or maybe I'd just resigned myself to doing this for Eden's sake, but in either case, I felt completely calm. When I raised my hands, he placed the crystal against my right palm, and then pressed his own against it to hold it in place. I watched his face as he arranged his fingertips so they touched each one of mine. He was excited about this, happy even. I didn't see a hint of doubt in his eyes or a drop of remorse.

"Jolene didn't want you to have this."

"It's not up to Jolene anymore." He tried to lock onto my eyes, but I broke away to look again to the bright night-sky. How could such a horrible thing happen on such a beautiful night?

"Enough, it's time."

I let him lock onto my eyes and Rupert spoke the first line.

"With the power of my birthright in the palm of my hand," I repeated and felt a breeze pick up.

"We call on the grace of the ancient ones," I said, precisely as Rupert dictated. The breeze swirled lazily around us.

"To grant the covenant of transference once and only once." The breeze picked up momentum.

"This is our bargain." I squinted against the debris that now danced with the strengthening wind.

"I gift thee flight that thou may take to the heavens." Rupert spoke louder now, competing with the breeze.

The wind blew my hair around my face. "I gift thee vision to light the night," I said, loud and clear above the din.

The churning air rushed under my shirt, tugging at the fabric that was glued to my back. I spoke the next line. "I gift thee in peace and health of mine own free will." At that point, the shirt pulled loose, and I gasped. The copper scent of fresh blood stole my concentration.

"Go on," Rupert urged, prompting the last line a second time.

"So be it decreed and sealed." I spoke the final words and Carson fell back from my fingers, landing heavily on the gravel. The wind died. The crystal fell to the ground between us.

A heavenly quiet settled around me and I felt like I was floating in it. The ancient words really did have power. I'd felt it and it was a wondrous thing. Rupert reached down to snatch the crystal. I watched him in a daze as he placed it carefully into the velvet bag and drew the bag closed with the ribbon. He stole glances at me as he raced around Carson. Strangely, my night vision was intact. Wasn't it supposed to be gone? I felt numb, like I was in a dream, but I wasn't night-blind and I wasn't dead.

I needed to get to that phone. I turned my head and saw it lying in the gravel about fifteen feet away. I crawled toward it, feeling the gravel bite into my knees and hands. Finally close enough, I reached my arm to take it and a shot rang out. The phone shattered into pieces. I stared at the spot where the phone had been just moments before. It took me a second to look back to Rupert. He kept his eyes on me as he stuffed the gun down the front of his pants.

Bastard! He bent down to get his arms under Carson's shoulders. I reached for the amber belt and with benefit of sight and free hands, I worked the twisted knot. I heard the shifting gravel as Rupert dragged Carson to the car. When I looked up, he'd already opened the rear passenger door. The belt's knot sprung free.

Rupert propped Carson into a sitting position on the ground by the rear door and ran around to the far side of the car. While he was reaching through from the driver's side, hauling Carson across the back seat, I peeled the amber beads away from my ravaged skin, wincing as each bead pulled free. When the last one fell away, instantly I felt a warm flush flow over me. The heat flared. It filled me and bubbled out, warming the air and ground around me. The crystal was free. I could see it. It pulsed white, not clear as it had always been before and I reached for it instinctively, wrapping my hand around it. I'd never felt it so intensely before. The crystal was hot; its power overwhelming.

The slam of the car door brought me around. The fog cleared from my head and my strength returned. I stood and walked toward them. An eerie calm settled around me. This is what karma in motion looked like. They would both feel its wrath tonight. I only had one objective now: one deadly objective. Kill them.

Rupert had Carson tucked safely in the back seat and glared at me over the roof of the car as I approached. He was still thirty yards away. I saw his shoulders move, but not toward the driver's door to make his escape. He was pulling his gun out. I watched him as if he was moving in slow motion. The gun came up in his right hand. He lifted his arm into position, steadying it on the top of the car, but he wasn't near fast enough. My jolt hit the gun before he could pull the trigger and it flew out of his grasp, clattering across the gravel, well out of his reach. I smiled at his startled reaction and hurled a jolt at his head. But my pause for self-satisfaction cost me. He'd ducked behind the car and the jolt hit something behind him.

He jumped into the driver's seat as a loud crack reverberated from the woods beside the car. After a pause, the treetops fluttered. The car started and Rupert hit the gas. An ominous splintering sound grew louder, and the wind stirred with a rush. I glimpsed a dark hulk teetering toward me and I turned and ran. The tree landed with a thunderous boom behind me. I spun around. The huge fir lay across the driveway right where the car had been seconds earlier.

"No!" I cried as I realized Rupert was getting away. The downed tree lay between me and his car. I could hear his spinning tires spitting gravel. I screamed at the branches fluttering madly above the massive trunk. I squeezed my crystal tightly and felt it melt into me, as if I'd popped its casing and the essence of it was absorbed into my skin. I looked to the ground and saw the crystal's white glow all around me. I lifted off in a blur of light. It wasn't a conscious decision and gravity didn't snap away. I just thought it—and I was in the air. Rupert and Carson were not getting away. I would shoot a jolt through both of them, if it was the last thing I did.

The heat of the crystal poured through my veins as I cleared the felled tree. My body glowed, casting a shadow of light on the ground beneath me. The radiance was all around me. I felt the power in it, and I felt something else. I felt warmth nearby, in harmony with my own, like a second wave of heat. I turned toward it and found the source. Mason was in the air and closing in fast. I spun away from him but he managed to get in front of me. He held his gloved hands out to stop me.

His action was incomprehensible to me. "They're getting away!" I yelled and deked his move. He countered, blocking me and I jolted him. Light flared around me and I paused, feeling the power crackle in the air.

Mason seemed unaffected and blocked my movement again. "You're going to break your crystal, Emelynn. Let me help you."

"There's no time!" I pointed toward the direction Rupert's car had gone. "They're getting away!"

"Over here," Mason called to someone over his shoulder.

"No!" I shouted at him and drove another jolt at him. The light flared bright again and the air vibrated. Once again, I tried to out-maneuver him. But he was quick and blocked my escape.

"You have to stop this, Emelynn. You're going to hurt yourself." He spread his arms, holding his hands out to either side. I felt the other Flier approach before I turned to see her. I recognized her as one of the women from the Tribunal. Her presence brought another wave of heat. She grabbed Mason's hand and I spun around to see Ron, whose nose I'd broken, join their hands, forming a tight circle around me. Their clenched jaws and rigid postures presented a formidable front. As before, they were dressed in black leather from their gloved hands to their dark shoes.

"Get away from me," I snapped and pushed up, but I couldn't break away. My glow lit us all up like a flare, and their heat pulsed around me. They had me trapped inside their circle, and then they too started to glow. I tried to drop down but couldn't do that either. "What are you doing?" I shrieked.

"We're quenching your crystal. If we don't, you're going to shatter it."

"But they're getting away," I said, feeling the first effects of the drain they were putting on me. My energy waned.

"They'll be taken care of."

The glow diminished. They were taking me back to the gravel on the far side of the tree. The haze returned, thickening my head and weighing down my limbs. "Let me go," I said in a slur, blinking slowly.

"We're not alone. The police will be here any minute and when they arrive, you need to be inside, away from all this," Mason said. We landed just outside the ash circle, and they dropped their arms, releasing me.

I took a step away and stumbled. Mason caught me with an arm around my waist and I shrieked from his touch on my back and dropped to my knees. Tears of frustration and pain spilled out of me. "Don't let them get away with this." I whimpered, sitting back on my heels, losing steam with every breath.

"We won't, but we have to get inside. Now!" I heard the faint thump of an approaching helicopter. "Can you stand?" he asked, offering me his hand.

I reached up and winced when he pulled me to my feet. "Come on," he said, dragging me to the kitchen door.

"Here," Ron said, scooping the abandoned handcuffs off the ground. "You'll need these." He handed them to Mason.

No fucking way. Not again. I pulled free of Mason's grip and ran blindly. The woman was close and reached out, snagging the sleeve of my shirt. I heard it rip then half of the shirt fell away from my shoulder. My legs betrayed me and I tripped, sprawling forward on the gravel.

I heard her gasp and saw Mason's feet land in front of me. "Oh, Jesus!" he said. They were silent while I sobbed in defeat. "We're not going to hurt you. Emelynn, listen to me. We need to stage this so the police don't suspect anything more than a kidnapping. Do you understand?"

The thump of the helicopter grew louder. "We need to hurry," Mason said. "Come on, sit up. I'll help you."

I let them help me up and after I was on my feet, Ron and the woman ghosted, but I could feel their presence. They hadn't left.

Mason helped me in through the kitchen then asked, "Which way?"

"Right," I said. "Wait. Eden!" I found the energy to round the corner and pushed open the door to her room. "Eden?" I called, falling to my knees beside her. "Eden!" I pulled the blanket away, shaking her shoulder. "No," I moaned looking down at a lifelike dummy with spiky red hair.

"Eden's safe. She's with Alex." The helicopter's rotors were close. "Which room were they keeping you in?" he asked, helping me up again.

"End of the hall."

He hastened us to the room and closed the door. "How?" he asked.

"Don't leave me here," I pleaded.

"I'll stay with you until the paramedics arrive."

I searched his face for trickery but found only sympathy.

The hardest thing I'd ever done was lay back down on that filthy bed and let Mason re-fasten the neck tether and then the leg chains. I watched him reach down and pick up one of my amber earrings. He quickly destroyed it, pulling the amber free from its silver wire. "Swallow this," he said, pressing the amber to my lips. "It'll keep you from disappearing when the paramedics treat your back." The lights from the chopper flashed behind the dirty window covering and I swallowed the amber.

He snapped the cuffs closed. "I'll be right here," he said close to my ear, and I felt his gloved hand on the back of my head. "I won't leave you."

The percussive thump of the helicopter frightened me and the commotion that followed ramped up the terror. Doors burst open and shouting followed. The door to my room was the last to be opened, and I cowered back from the bang as the door hit the wall. Bright light beamed through a cloud of dust into the room and heavy footsteps approached with caution.

A man knelt down beside me putting his face in my line of vision. He lifted his visor and smiled. "We've been looking for you. You're safe now. We'll get you out of here."

He turned and barked, "Ann, get video and quickly. George, bolt cutters, and clear the paramedics." I closed my eyes and tried to sense Mason. I felt his warmth—he was still here, just like he'd promised.

CHAPTER TWENTY-NINE

I woke in a comfortable haze, surrounded by bright lights and a steady beep. Hospital, I remembered, looking around. I lay on my stomach with a pillow under my hips. They were kind enough to knock me out when they cleaned the wounds on my back. It felt tight now, wrapped in bandages. It was no longer on fire. That was a nice improvement, and the hospital smelled great. I inhaled deeply. I used to think hospitals smelled like sickness and disinfectant, but not today.

"Sweetheart? Are you awake?" The soft voice was familiar, hopeful.

"Mother?"

"Yes," she said, approaching from the foot of the bed. God, I'd missed her. I hadn't realized how much until she took my hand. The wall between us crumbled with the warmth of her touch. She lowered herself to the chair beside me. "I'm right here." She smiled thinly. Her green eyes were bloodshot. She looked tired. "I've been so worried. I thought I'd lost you." Tears welled up in her eyes and spilled silently down her face. The only other time I'd seen her cry was when Dad died.

"Don't cry. I'm okay."

"Yes, yes you are. And you're going to be fine." She sniffed, drawing strength, and her smile brightened. She shook her head, and her short hair came loose from where she'd tucked it behind her ears. I hadn't noticed as much silver in her hair before.

"How'd they find me?"

"Your friend, James. He found the registration for your GPS and used that to trace you. Eden assured me you never went anywhere without it. We just prayed she was right."

I smiled at that. She'd already met James and Eden. Who else had she met? "What day is it?"

"Monday—afternoon."

"How long have I been here?"

"They found you early this morning. You've been missing for four days—since last Wednesday night."

It felt like four years. "When did they figure out I was missing?"

"Detective Jordan phoned me on Friday. He'd already had calls from Dr. Coulter and your trainer, Malcolm. I talked to Molly when I couldn't reach you and when she told me how you'd left things at the restaurant, I told her to call that detective then caught the next flight out. They started looking for you right away."

"I'm so sorry, Mother. You must have been terribly worried."

"We all were, especially with Charles and Gabby still missing. I'm so glad you're okay," she said, brushing my hair back. "Dr. Coulter asked me to call him the minute you woke. Is that all right?"

"Yes, of course," I said. She pushed away from the bed but didn't need to make that call because he'd come into the room.

"She's awake," my mother said.

"I can see that." He came to the side of the bed and crouched down to meet my eyes.

The moment I saw his face, I started to cry. He reached over and wiped the tears from my cheek.

"What are we going to do with you, Emelynn," he said, smiling my favourite crooked smile.

"I'll give you some privacy," Mom said. "I need to make a few calls." The door clicked closed behind her.

"Did they find Rupert and Carson?"

"Yes," he said slowly, looking confused. "They're both in the hospital, under arrest."

"This hospital?" I blurted out, tensing.

"No, not here," he said, and I relaxed again.

"I thought they'd be dead." I sniffled. Avery found a Kleenex to press into my hand.

"The police got to them first. One of the helicopters ran them off the road and their car rolled. Carson's still unconscious. Greg broke his back."

"Greg? No. Rupert," I said.

"What are you talking about?"

"Rupert Dowling was the man we knew as Greg Jeffries."

"That can't be. Rupert Dowling's DNA matched the dead man found in his townhouse in Rockport. Rupert Dowling is dead."

"He's not. He's been posing as Greg. Rupert told me that Carson switched the DNA. Rupert wanted it to look like he was dead. I'm sorry, Avery, but I think something bad has happened to Greg." I saw the distress on his face. He stood up and turned his back to me.

"Then the body they found in Rockport is probably Greg's. Damn." Avery turned. "I've been so angry, thinking Greg had betrayed us and all along, he's been in the Rockport morgue."

"When I get my hands on them, I'll kill them," I said. It wasn't a figure of speech.

Avery winced at my words.

"They were going to kill me, Avery. It was just like you warned. Carson figured out my connection to Jolene, and he wanted to steal my gift. I had no choice. They'd already told me that Greg had had an *accident*, and they made me think they had Eden. I thought they would hurt her. The amber drained my gift so badly that I couldn't jolt anymore. So I did it. I gave him my gift. But I don't think it worked. Or maybe it did, I don't know. I still have my night vision and I can still fly." I was babbling.

"What did you say about amber?" he asked, drawing his eyebrows together.

"They fastened a string of amber beads around my waist. Mason had warned me about amber, but I was so angry with him at the time, I didn't listen. Now I know better."

"That explains why the wounds around your waist look different from the lashes. Your waist injury looks more like a burn."

"At first, it just itched, like an allergic reaction, but the longer the amber stayed against my skin, the worse it got. After a while, I figured out that my gift faded more each day I wore the damn belt."

"And you think it was the amber?" He sat back down close to me.

"I'm sure it was. And you know those amber earrings I wore all the time—the ones my mother gave me? They were probably the reason why you and I had such inconsistent results testing my ghost. The instant that amber belt was off me, I was able to function again."

"I'm so relieved, Em. And I'm very glad you're back." He brushed his hand across my cheek. I covered his hand with my own and held tight.

"Me too." That smile of his made me feel like everything was going to be okay. "How's my mother doing? She looks like she hasn't slept in days."

"I don't think she has. She went to your cottage straight from the airport to help James and Eden and then she camped out at the police station with Detective Jordan." Avery sat back in the chair. "When word came down that you'd been found, the detective drove her here and she hasn't left since."

"She needs to go to the cottage and get some rest."

"Maybe she will, now that she's seen you and heard your voice."

"I'll talk to her."

"That reminds me, Detective Jordan's been hounding me. He'll be back to talk to you soon, I'm sure."

"What do I tell him?"

Avery stood up. "As little as you can. James tells me they have Carson's fingerprints on the handcuffs and Greg's—sorry, Rupert's on the whip and the other restraints. You don't need to add much to seal their fate."

"Can you hold the detective off a little longer?"

"Sure." Avery checked the readout on my beeping IV. "Get some rest. I'll check on you in a few hours." He turned, heading for the door.

"Avery," I called, and his footsteps stopped. "Thanks for being here."

"Always," he said, and then left.

I shut my eyes and let fatigue drain my consciousness.

When I woke, I knew Mason was in the room before I opened my eyes. I could feel the warm glow of his presence.

"Mason?"

He revealed himself, appearing in the chair beside my bed. "Hi," he said, looking relaxed and leaning back in the chair. "I would have phoned for an invite and then knocked, but you were out of it."

I smiled at his attempt at humour. "You stayed."

"I told you I would." His wavy blond hair stood out sharply against the black leather he wore, but he'd removed his gloves. He must have been overheated in that gear.

"Thanks."

"You're welcome."

"Do you know Carson?"

"I thought I did."

"So he really was Jolene's lover?"

"He was the first man she allowed herself to get close to after your father. He betrayed her. He'll pay for that."

"What about Rupert?"

"I don't know him, but he'll pay, too."

"Good."

"It won't be easy. The police complicate things for us."

"How so?"

He straightened up. "We need to question them. Questions the police won't be asking."

"Carson said there were others—other Fliers who were unhappy with the Tribunal. He said they're absorbing gifts and gaining strength."

"They call themselves Redeemers." Mason sneered. "Carson's the first one we've caught. We need to know who his associates are."

"You knew about them?"

"We know they exist and they're getting stronger. These so-called Redeemers vow to eradicate the Tribunal as it stands and they're responsible for a number of Flier deaths."

"Is Carson a Ghost now? Did he get Jolene's gift?"

Mason smiled. "No. If it were anyone but you, he would have, but no."

"Why not . . . and why me?"

"The gift isn't yours to give. Remember the words 'once and only once'?" I nodded. "Jolene gave you her gift—it can be given only once."

"But he collapsed."

"Even a failed transfer steals consciousness."

"I don't remember Jolene using candles or an ash circle."

"She must have."

"I would have remembered."

"She was a Ghost, Emelynn, and you were a child. You probably just didn't see her do it."

"But it was daylight."

"It wouldn't have mattered, as long as it was a clear sky."

He leaned back in the chair again and silence fell over us until I spoke. "How long before you can question them?"

"Carson's in a coma. If he comes out of it, we'll extract what we can. Rupert's out of surgery, but still in ICU. The moment he's conscious, we'll isolate him—find out what we need to know."

"I thought I heard voices in here," my mother said, sweeping into the room. "I didn't see you come in." I could tell from her tone that she wasn't pleased about that.

"Mother, hi. Yes, Mason stopped in for a visit. Laura Aberfoyle, this is Mason Reynolds."

Mason stood.

"Mason," my mother said, reaching out her hand.

"Laura, lovely to meet you," he said, taking her hand in both of his. "Emelynn, I'm glad you're okay. I've got to go."

He left with my mother watching his wake. "I don't remember you mentioning Mason before. How do you know him?"

"He's a friend of James's." I wished Mason didn't have to leave. I had so many more questions and I hadn't thanked him properly.

A nurse pushed the door open. "Good, you're awake. I'll help you take this painkiller and then we'll set up to change your dressings."

"Already?"

"It's been ten hours. Dr. Coulter's on his way in."

"Mother, why don't you go home and get some sleep? The painkiller will probably knock me out after this anyway."

"I don't want to leave you."

"She's in safe hands," Avery said, coming into the room. "And she's right, you should get some rest." He put his hand reassuringly on her shoulder. "You'll be able to take her home soon."

"Is that right?" I asked.

"We're watching for infection, but it looks good. We're treating your wounds with a new hydrogel product that's shown great results. It'll speed the healing and help minimize the scarring."

"See Mother, I'll be out of here in no time. Go get some sleep."

She looked drawn and anxious but leaned in and patted my head. "All right. I'll get some rest and come back as soon as I can."

"Thanks for being here."

"Oh, sweetheart—where else would I be?"

The nurse followed my mother out the door and I told Avery about Mason's visit. "I need to give James a heads-up. I told my mother that Mason was a friend of his."

"James was just here. I told him you'd be out of it for a while after they change your dressings."

And I was. The painkiller zonked me out. The dressing change was painful, but nothing compared to the burning of before.

Avery couldn't hold Detective Jordan off any longer and the next morning, when the sedatives released me from their fog, the nurses helped me sit up and the detective came in.

He wore the same old sports jacket—the one that gave away the bulge under his left arm. He might as well ditch the jacket for all the camouflage it provided for his gun. Constable Wong accompanied him, standing guard by the door.

"Ms. Taylor," the detective started. "I'm sorry for your ordeal. You remember Constable Wong?"

"Yes, how are you, Constable?" I asked.

"Fine, thanks. Constable Mendel sends her regards." Chris Mendel had been Constable Wong's partner when they'd brought me home from the hospital after my fall in the park. That was before I'd learned I was a Flier—a lifetime ago.

"Ms. Taylor, we need to record your recollections of the events that culminated in your arrival here at the hospital. Do you mind if we record this conversation?"

He'd already set his slim recorder on the table, recording. Being "sorry for my ordeal" hadn't softened the man. "Go ahead." I told him how I'd accepted a lift from a man I thought was Greg Jeffries and how someone else in that car had drugged me.

"Unfortunately," I told him, "I was blindfolded and restrained so I can't provide a lot more information." When he asked, I told him it was a crystal they were after. "I had no idea what they were talking about. It was crazy talk, like they were members of some kind of cult."

"Can you identify the kidnappers?" he said, dealing photos like playing cards on the rolling table in front of me.

"This is the man I knew as Greg Jeffries," I said, pointing to a mug shot of Rupert Dowling. "He's the man who hurt me."

"Whipped you?"

"Yes." I couldn't bring myself to say the word.

The photo of Carson was not good. It had obviously been taken in the hospital and the lighting made his skin tone waxy. His eyes were closed, his jaw slack and a ragged line was stitched in black across his forehead. "This man is Carson Manse. He was the man in charge. He's the one who ordered Rupert to hurt me."

"You don't recognize anyone else?"

"No. There were two other men there, but I only heard their voices, I never saw them."

The detective pointed a thick finger to a photo of a balding man with small, narrow-set eyes and a skiff of thin hair. "This man was found on the premises."

I shrugged. "I'm sorry. I don't recognize him."

"He died of a massive brain hemorrhage. The coroner puts his time of death around noon on Friday. Do you remember anything significant occurring around that time?"

Only that I'd jolted a would-be rapist named Dan. "No, sorry."

"Okay, thank you, Ms. Taylor. This has been helpful."

"But only three of the men are accounted for. What about the fourth man?"

"We have no leads on him yet."

"Where are these two now?" I said, pointing to Rupert and Carson's photos. I wanted them as far away from me as possible.

"In a hospital on Vancouver Island."

"That's good. Thank you for moving them."

"We didn't move *them*, Ms. Taylor, we moved *you*."

"What do you mean?"

"You were found in a remote area on the north end of Vancouver Island. They were in critical condition and were sent to the closest trauma unit. You were in better shape, so you were transported here. You didn't know?"

"I hadn't thought to ask."

"We have video from the Duke Point ferry terminal that shows Rupert Dowling paying for passage on the last ferry to Nanaimo, Wednesday night. You appeared to be asleep in the passenger seat. He must have driven north from there."

"I didn't know where I was."

"That's understandable. But don't worry about them. They won't be going anywhere soon. Rupert will be charged with aggravated assault and kidnapping and a string of other crimes. He's also wanted in the States. Carson is still in a coma, but we have fingerprints that tie him to both you and the trailer where you were found."

"Thanks."

Detective Jordan turned off his recording device and gathered the photos and other papers that he'd strewn about. "Emelynn, do you have any reason to believe that these men had anything to do with the disappearance of Charles and Gabby Wright?"

With regret, I said, "I don't know." I wondered if they would ever make the connection.

After they left, I phoned Malcolm. It took a few moments to reassure him I was all right. His calm voice felt like a soothing balm. I thanked him for his role in my rescue, and in typical Malcolm fashion, he tried to shake it off. But I didn't let him. I would think of something special to do for him. He'd once told me he made a choice each day—a choice to be happy. It worked for him. Maybe it would work for me too.

Avery arranged for my discharge that afternoon. Mother showed up in Dad's MGB with the top down, to drive me home. Watching her behind the wheel gave me a glimpse of the first genuine smile I'd seen on her face since she'd arrived at my hospital bed.

"Your father and I had a lot of fun times in this car," she said. "I'm glad you had it restored."

She made me a cup of tea when we got back to the cottage, and we took our mugs out to the deck to enjoy the warm afternoon sun. I sat back gingerly in my favourite deck chair, revelling in the beautiful day. Painkillers dulled the pain and the hydrogel they'd applied soothed my raw skin. The police estimated Rupert had lashed me twelve times. They needed a precise record for the case they were building against him. It was a fact I would have preferred not to know. I also would have preferred not to know that the whip he'd chosen had been made to inflict pain, embedded as it was, with small, roughened steel balls.

It felt strange to be back in the cottage with my mother. She acted stiff and remote, like she was confronting ghosts of her own in every room. She'd taken the guest bedroom though I'd offered her mine. "It's easier this way," she'd said, and I knew it was true. Dad's memories were stronger for her in their old room than in my childhood digs.

"Cheney seems like a nice young man," she said.

"He is, and Molly's crazy about him."

"I could see that." They had stopped by the hospital shortly before I'd been released. The bouquet of sunflowers they'd brought me brightened up the dining room table. "I remember as a child she looked like such a ragamuffin, but you'd never know that now. She told me you may be interested in working with the sisters that own Rumbles."

"Yes, it's a possibility."

"After all that's happened, I thought you might want to come back to Toronto with me."

The thought hadn't crossed my mind. I searched her face wondering how committed she was to the suggestion but found no clues. "I'm not ready to leave here. This house, this beach—it feels like home."

"You were always happy here. I wish I could stay, but I have to get back to my work."

"I'm glad you came. And I understand about your work. Besides, I have Molly and Eden, and Dr. Coulter is very good to me. You heard him—I'm going to be fine."

"Yes, you've always been so independent." The doorbell rang and Mother looked at me with a question in her eyes. "Is that a new doorbell?"

"I had to have the old one replaced," I said, apologetically.

"You probably wore it out years ago," she chided then went to answer it.

She returned with Eden. "Would you like something to drink? The tea's still hot." Eden asked for it black and Mom disappeared into the cottage.

"Have you learned anything new about Rupert or Carson?" I asked.

"No." She sighed. "The Tribunal isn't saying a thing and the hospital won't release any details. At this point, you're in the best position to get information. The police might tell you more than they're telling the rest of us."

"Here you go, Eden," my mother said, handing Eden her tea. "What were you girls talking about?"

"I was just telling her how lucky it was that James knew how to trace my GPS. Who called him anyway?" He'd left on Tribunal business the afternoon I was abducted.

"I did," Eden said.

"Who called you?"

"Molly." I realized then how fortunate I'd been that they knew one another. Eden had been so very right to insist that I meld my two worlds. It may have saved my life. "Thank you," I said, and reached out to squeeze Eden's hand.

We talked a while longer, Eden telling my mother about her work at the hospital and Mom telling Eden about her research. Eden left after arranging to come by in the morning to change my dressing. After that, Mom went to lie down. I pulled a baggy long-sleeved dress shirt over the bandage that covered my back from neck to hip, slipped on a pair of flip-flops and headed to the beach. The tide was just starting its long trek back out and I walked to the water's edge to dip my toes into the cool water.

My mother needed the rest. She looked better than when I'd first seen her in the hospital, but she remained pale and drawn. This was the first time she'd been back to the cottage since Dad died. I'd been watching her and sometimes she would just stop and stare. She'd done it earlier when she'd run her fingers along the top edge of the bookcase with a distant look in her eyes. I imagined her remembering him; remembering our family as it used to be, like the games of "nicky nicky nine doors" that she'd alluded to earlier. Being here was hard for her—as hard as dealing with what had happened to me. I would be all right, but I wasn't so sure about my mother. Maybe next time she visited it would be easier for her. Right now, she needed to get away, back to the comfort of her lab.

I'd been warming myself on a slab of sandstone for a while when James came down the stairs. I returned my mother's wave, and she disappeared back into the cottage.

"You're looking better," he said, sitting down beside me.

"Thanks. My mother told me you're the one who figured out how to find me."

"When we couldn't locate you with your phone, Eden reminded me about your GPS."

"If it weren't for you, they'd have killed me."

"Mason wouldn't have let that happen."

"You called him?"

"No. Avery did. He saw that the police were complicating things for us. The whole covey was on alert, but we couldn't do a thing with Detective Jordan and the police hounding our every move. Mason and the others slipped right past them."

"The covey must wonder what's going on with me. I never meant to cause so much trouble. It just seems to follow me around."

"You don't need to worry about the covey—they're loyal to a fault. And you don't need to worry about Rupert Dowling any longer either. I understand he suffered a brain bleed and died late this morning."

I was taken aback for an embarrassingly short moment. "Good. I hope the Tribunal learned something useful before he died." That sounded harsh, but not as harsh as my inner thought that I hoped it was a painful death. Just a few days ago, I'd been horrified that I might have hurt a gun-wielding guard with one of my jolts and now I was happy someone was dead. I hardly recognized myself underneath those callous thoughts.

"There's something else." He reached into his pocket and handed me a folded piece of paper. "I found it taped to the balcony door at the lighthouse."

"You went to see Case?"

"It's the first place I looked."

The note was written in small, neat handwriting.

Thank you, Emelynn, whoever you are. You gave me back my life and now I need to go and live it. I'm returning to New England to say a proper goodbye to Beth. Take care of yourself and if you're ever able to share your life, look me up.

Casey Stockton, NH

I refolded the note and tucked it into my shirt pocket. Case had left and another small piece of me fell away. Not the devastation that I'd suffered when I learned the truth about Jackson, but Case leaving, left me hollow somehow, as if there was no weight to me and a strong wind might blow me away, a castoff plastic grocery bag.

"Why is it, James, that when you show up, the men in my life run away?" I meant it as a quip, but Case leaving hurt more than it should. So much for anonymous, no-strings-attached sex. I guess once a man's hands roam over your body, there's no keeping them out of your heart.

"I like to think I'm doing you a favour."

I couldn't help but laugh at his retort.

"Emelynn, the damage Jackson's done isn't going to be undone by Case or anyone else. You need to forgive him and move on."

"Forgive him?"

"This thing you're doing with other guys is only going to hurt you."

I hadn't thought I'd been blaming Jackson, but maybe I was. Maybe all my talk about it being just as much my fault as his was just that: talk. We sat quietly watching the waves ebb with the tide.

"One of the kidnappers is still out there. Do you think he knows who I am?"

"I don't know."

"I'm worried about my mother. She's not a part of our world but she's still in danger. Just knowing us puts her at risk. I don't know how to protect her."

"You can't remove all the risk. Even if she knew about us, she wouldn't agree to sever her ties to you. She goes by a different name; that helps. But there are other things we can do to make her harder to find."

"Like what?"

"Well, you can change how you contact one another and remove any reference to her in your phone or address books. Make sure she's not listed as your *In Case of Emergency* contact with anyone like the security company or on your passport. We can alter your birth certificate and scramble any other electronic record that might point in her direction."

"You can do that?"

James smiled arrogantly. "I'm good at what I do, Emelynn."

That smile made me believe him. "Will you help me?"

"Will you stop sleeping with men you don't know?"

I laughed. "How about I promise to know the full name of the next guy I sleep with?"

"It would be an improvement."

We sat in comfortable silence looking out over the water. The surface was smooth as glass, unusual for this time of day. "Detective Jordan asked me if I thought Rupert or Carson were involved with the Wrights' disappearance."

"What did you tell them?"

"That I didn't know. If he's as good as you think he is, he'll figure out that they're connected."

"I got a look at the names on the task force's list of missing persons."

"Oh?" How had he managed that?

"There are four Fliers on that list."

"I'm sorry to hear that, but it might not be a bad thing. Maybe the detective will put some more Redeemers out of business."

"Maybe," James said. "It would keep him busy, get him out of your hair."

I could always hope.

My mother made mac and cheese for dinner. She'd baked it with bacon and onions and browned breadcrumbs on top. I hadn't had it prepared that way since I was a kid. It was wonderful.

She flew back to Toronto the next day. Eden took her to the airport after she'd changed my dressing. The hydrogel was working miracles, or so Eden said when she saw how well the wounds were healing.

When they'd left, I was finally alone and had time to think again. My back felt good. Not healed—that would take weeks—but it no longer hurt. Better still, my crystal thrummed with energy again. I could see it when I closed my eyes, clear again and ready. Soon I'd call on it to break away from gravity's hold and soar once more into the treetops. Flying and breathing were synonymous to me now. The revelation that flying made me whole somehow—like flight had always been missing— made me feel like the sky was where I belonged. Not quite a sanctuary, like the cottage, but it held a rightness, like the smell of the ocean and clean fresh air.

It used to be that my gift was the biggest out-of-control area of my life; funny how time had changed that. Now my gift was the only thing in my life that felt in control. But then again, control was just an illusion, wasn't it? A concept. Something to make us feel more secure, but which didn't really exist except in our minds.

I'd revisited my kidnapping a dozen times. Could I have done any- thing differently to prevent it from happening? No amount of physical fitness or self-defence training would have dented that scenario. Even if I'd stayed in Toronto, they might have eventually found me. My mother would have been far more vulnerable there, and in Toronto, I wouldn't have had a covey to help me.

Carson remained untouchable, protected by his coma, but others like him were still out there. And so was the kidnapper who had gotten away. They might not know about me, but they had their sights set on other Fliers. Everyone in my covey was vulnerable. We were all going to have to be more vigilant going forward. Avery had already met with the others to discuss precautions. Identities would no longer be assumed, and Fliers were putting check-in procedures in place for their families. As frightening as it seemed, the threat hadn't really changed; we just knew its name now—Redeemer. The knowledge would help keep us safe.

But what about me? What would keep me safe? The cottage was alarmed; my physical fitness was the best it had ever been; I'd learned basic self-defence; and my flying skills were as good as any born Flier. Yet none of that had kept me out of Carson's clutches. In fact, I wouldn't really be safe anywhere. That I was a Ghost only heightened the threat for me and the covey, and because I'd been gifted, I couldn't even give it away. It was a part of me. A part I had to learn to live with. A part I knew virtually nothing about.

I walked into my bedroom and opened the bedside table. Mason's card lay on top of Jolene's letter. I picked it up and fingered its edges. Mason could teach me how to control my ghost, but at what price? The price of not learning might be higher still. I dialled the number.

"Emelynn?" he answered.

"I think I'm ready now."

THANK YOU

Thank you for reading *Hidden Enemy*. If you enjoyed it, please tell a friend or consider posting a short review where you purchased it. Reviews help other readers discover the books and are much appreciated.

—JP McLean

EXCERPT FROM BOOK 3

BURNING LIES

Emelynn survived her painful initiation into the world of Fliers, but are her secrets safe? Were the whispers true? Are powerful people searching for proof of their existence and do they know about Emelynn? Can she guard her secrets and her life now that she knows how easily either could be lost?

Read on for an excerpt . . .

The black granite hadn't lost its lustre. I should have known it would be black, but still, it threw me. I'd expected soft white marble and cherubic angels, maybe harps for an infant's grave, but cold, stark granite?

A gentle breeze stirred the dry air.

"Emelynn, are you all right?"

Mason could have passed for a bodyguard or a hit man. He kept a cautious watch over me as I kneeled at my brother's headstone and traced the engraving with my fingers. A tear escaped.

Andrew Reynolds Taylor
Beloved
March 2, 1986 ~ April 13, 1986

"Yeah," I lied. My half-brother had lived just forty-two days, and I'd only recently learned of him. I didn't have siblings. Maybe that's why I didn't like referring to him as a "half." Somehow, it diminished him. But the tears weren't for the boy I never knew; they were for my father. The agony he must have suffered burying his son made my chest ache. I knew that ache well. Was it he or the child's mother, Jolene, who had the sad task of writing the epitaph? I wiped the tear away.

"Were you here? For the funeral?" Though in his early forties now, Mason would have been a teenager when his nephew died.

"Yes." Whether he spoke softly in reverence for the setting or in sadness, I couldn't tell.

Andrew would have turned twenty-five this year—just three years older than me. What would he have been like? Would we have been close?

I glanced up at Mason and he forced a thin smile. "Are you ready to go?" he asked, offering me his hand. He'd forgone his usual black leather gloves; they would have drawn attention in California's late-September heat. The rest of his attire made no concession to the temperature: black slacks, black shirt and black shoes. Mason was always prepared; all of the Tribunal Novem were, especially now.

I nodded then reached for his hand. "They picked a beautiful spot," I said. Turner Acres was a small cemetery nestled in the hills northeast of Oakland. Mason helped me to my feet, a small courtesy I was both grateful for and resentful of. I brushed the grass from my capris and straightened my hideous blouse. It was a loose-fitting, multi-hued fashion misstatement, but a necessity that helped conceal the fact I wore no bra. I wasn't yet able to tolerate anything tight against the tender skin on my back.

"Yes, they did," he agreed, and we strolled through the sombre grounds of the cemetery back to his Audi. The air smelled like freshly mown hay.

Mason and I had gotten to know each other better in the month since my ordeal. I now knew he'd never married nor did he have children. I'd also learned that he lived with his parents, a fact which stunned me and didn't fit with the imposing image of the leather-clad man who'd stormed into my cottage mere weeks ago. Since then, he'd been making an effort to be kind and keep his menacing tendencies in check. It was working. I was actually starting to believe what he'd said about considering me his niece since his only sibling, Jolene, had gifted me.

He looked down at the car keys in his hand. "If we ever find Jolene, we'll lay her to rest with Andrew."

Although I didn't like to think about it, Jolene had likely died as a result of giving me her *gift*. If the process itself hadn't killed her, it would have weakened her to such an extent that a bad cold could have ended her life. Sadly, half the documented cases of gifting ended in death and no one had heard from Jolene in a decade: there was little room for hope. Mason and I talked about Jolene a lot. She'd captivated my father years before he met my mother.

"Thanks for bringing me here," I said. Mason had made all the arrangements. The Tribunal's private jet had flown me directly from Vancouver to San Francisco, where he'd picked me up. We'd driven straight from the airport to the cemetery.

"You're welcome." He opened the passenger door and waited until I'd tucked in my legs. "I'm happy you wanted to come." The door closed with a soft thunk. His gaze shifted left and right as he walked around to the driver's side. He'd been vigilant since we left the airport. It reminded me that we were never really safe—even here in the peaceful countryside.

He crammed his six-foot frame into the driver's seat, pushed in the clutch and jiggled the stick shift in neutral. "My father is anxious to meet you," he said, shifting into first. He slowly released the clutch and the car inched forward. Gravel crunched under its wheels.

We turned onto sun-faded asphalt outside the front gates of Turner Acres. I pulled my new Garmin GPS from my purse and input the cemetery's location. The GPS was a wrist-mounted model just like my last one. Unfortunately, that one was tagged as evidence in the Major Crimes Division lock-up in Vancouver. My kidnappers had known to destroy my GPS-enabled cellphone when they'd drugged me and taken me to their filthy trailer in the woods, but they hadn't a clue that the wristwatch they'd thrown into a bag with my clothes was, in fact, a GPS. It was the only time I'd been thankful for my dismal sense of direction that ensured I wore it everywhere.

"I booked you a room in Bodega Bay, although I wish you'd reconsider and stay with us."

"I appreciate all you've done for me, Mason. I'd just feel more comfortable in a hotel." I didn't mean to be difficult, but I didn't think of him as my uncle—not by a long shot. Besides, he probably lived in a dank basement apartment and I didn't want to impose on his parents.

But more than that, his family had ancient ties to the Tribunal

Novem—the judge, jury and executioner for our kind. I didn't want to be any closer to them than necessary. Mason was a card-carrying member of this so-called judicial body. I learned that the night I met him . . . the night I'd been the unlucky focus of the Tribunal's attention.

The Tribunal had paid me a visit when they learned that I possessed Jolene's gift. They had a well-earned reputation for brutality; a fact I learned first-hand. Mason was there the night the Tribunal bloodied me and forced James Moss to read my memories. It was only after Mason and the others were satisfied that I hadn't *stolen* Jolene's gift, that they released me. I couldn't just ignore that.

After that violent encounter, I shut Mason out of my life. It wasn't until after he helped rescue me from my kidnappers that I finally understood how much I needed him. Mason was one of only a handful of people who could teach me about a facet of Jolene's gift that continued to elude me. A facet that would get me killed, if I didn't learn how to control it. So I'd swallowed my pride and forced a change of heart where Mason was concerned. It's why I was here. Well, that and also to learn everything I could about Jolene and the time she spent with my father.

The Audi's engine purred as we headed toward the San Rafael Bridge. During the long drive, Mason recounted stories about Jolene from when they were children. Jolene was eight years older than Mason. They'd grown up just north of Bodega Bay on an estate he called Cairabrae. These were happy memories for Mason, and he spoke about his childhood home with pride. "The name's Scottish," he explained. "It's been shortened, and the spelling's been bastardized, but it means dear friend on the hill." I tucked away the fact that he thought of his family home the same way I felt about my cottage.

"Jolene went abroad to study art when I was ten, first to Paris for a few years, then to Rome. She came back for breaks or we'd visit her, but we didn't have a lot of time together until she returned to Cairabrae. I was fourteen then. She would set up her easel in the solarium or out in the pasture somewhere and paint all day. Sometimes, she'd head out to the beach or down to San Francisco and fill a sketchbook. We'd ride the horses on the weekends and my friends all thought she was hot." Amusement crinkled the corners of his eyes.

I didn't doubt him. I could still picture her from our brief encounters on the beach outside my cottage that fateful summer when I was twelve. I'd only met her a few times before naively accepting her gift: a gift that altered my life's path. Mason had the same wavy hair as Jolene, but his was now flecked with grey and he kept it short, brushed back from his forehead.

"She brought her share of boys home but none of them compared to your father. When she brought Brian home, we all knew he was special and not because he was a doctor. She looked at him like he was her whole world. I think she fell for him the moment she laid eyes on him. If they hadn't lost Andrew, I'm sure they'd be together still."

And if they'd never parted, I thought, I would never have been born. But they *had* lost Andrew and Jolene lost herself. For three long years, the man who would become my father reached out to her, but she didn't reciprocate. Grief paralyzed her. Eventually, my dad met my mother, Laura. They married when she became pregnant with me, and Brian made a new life for himself. I'd only recently learned about Jolene and their son from a letter I found in a box of my father's things I'd discovered in the attic of my cottage. It had left me reeling. Neither he nor my mother had ever shared that part of his life with me. Maybe it wasn't the kind of thing you shared.

We travelled north on Highway 101. Mason kept a keen eye on the rear-view mirror, his left wrist bent over the steering wheel, his right hand loose on the gear shift. The cityscape increasingly gave way to larger green spaces, or what would have been green space if it weren't for the drought. Now the scenery was largely tan and yellow except for the deep green of trees that punctuated the gently rolling slopes.

"Why do you think Jolene felt she had to forfeit her gift?" I asked.

"I wish I knew. A part of her died with Andrew. She ran away— settled in Greece for a time. When she finally came home, we thought she'd come to terms with his death. I didn't realize she'd reached out to Brian until I read that letter you found. She must have realized that she'd lost him, too."

"I can't imagine giving this wondrous gift away. She must have been desperate."

"Jolene struggled with depression after Andrew's death. She never painted again. Mom went to great lengths to get her to stay at Cairabrae. She even cut off her trust fund. But Jolene would never stay for more than a month or two. I was away at school then and wrapped up in my own life. I think Carson Manse was the final blow. God, how I wish I could go back and reach out to her. We could have protected her."

Jolene had been running from Carson Manse at the time she gifted me. He'd been her lover and was the same man who, years later, arranged to have me kidnapped. Mason and I speculated that Carson had tried to steal Jolene's gift in much the same way he'd tried to steal mine: inside a circle of wood ash and under mortal threat to her or someone she loved. He would have tried to force her to recite an incantation that would transfer the gift to him, but somehow, she'd escaped him all those years ago. I wasn't so lucky when he found me.

"But she coped for fifteen years after Andrew's death," I said. "Surely she found some peace and happiness in that time."

"She was never the same."

"I can't decide if Jolene was terribly brave gifting me, or a coward."

"She was exhausted," Mason snapped. Immediately, I regretted my insensitive choice of words. He shook his head and softened his tone. "Her depression was never treated."

I turned to study his face. "Suicide?" I asked, shocked at the realization. That possibility had never occurred to me, but it made perfect sense. It also explained why she hadn't ensured there was someone in place to help me transition into the world she'd inexorably made me a part of. Mason shrugged, and we drove on in silence.

We exited Highway 101 at Petaluma and headed west toward the coast. Half an hour later, we hit the postcard-perfect Shoreline Highway at Bodega Bay and turned north. The narrow highway wound precariously around bluffs and beaches for another fifteen miles before he signalled a turn to the right. The steep, winding road was marked "private." The nearly bald ocean cliffs gave way to pasture and sagebrush, as we climbed higher into the hills. Rocky outcrops and eucalyptus stands marked the slopes. We wound our way uphill for another five minutes before we came to a stop at the gates of Cairabrae. I recognized the Reynolds family crest on the wrought-iron gates. It also adorned the cover of the Reynolds family anthology, a leather-bound heirloom that Mason didn't know I carried in my luggage. Mason clicked what looked like a garage door opener and the big gates swung open.

We drove over a rise and Cairabrae came into view. Clearly, I'd underestimated Mason's definition of estate. Cairabrae was a sprawling two-storey stone mansion with wings on either side of a large columned entryway. Formal manicured gardens surrounded a circular drive that passed under a wide porte cochère. Outside the porte cochère, opposite the front doors, stood a larger-than-life marble fountain. It consisted of three Greek-inspired female figures standing shoulder to shoulder, facing out. Their stone dresses were wet from water that spilled from the heavy vases on their shoulders. Each of the figures held a dove in an outstretched palm.

"This is beautiful," I said, my voice filled with awe. He pulled in under the porte cochère and parked. Mason definitely did not live in a musty basement.

"Dad's had a late lunch prepared for us. I'll take you to your hotel after we eat."

"Thank you." I reached to open the car door. Mason came around and held it for me then offered his hand. I took it, once again apologizing for my frailty. Mason winced in sympathy.

I hated feeling weak. "It doesn't hurt that much." I smiled brightly as I straightened my clothes. "Avery says two more weeks and I'll be as good as new." Avery was my doctor and the closest thing to a father I had in my life. The new skin on my back hadn't hurt this much since he'd removed the bandages a week ago. But I'd been on the road since seven this morning, most of that time strapped in with my back against a seat—almost five hours in the plane and another hour and a half in Mason's car. The pressure irritated, but the skin would soon toughen up. I'm not sure the same could be said for my psyche. The horror of my ordeal still woke me some nights.

The right side of the big double-entry doors opened before Mason reached them. A man, who could only be described as a pro-wrestler, held it ajar. He was dressed in black and had biceps larger than my thighs. His neck was even thicker. All he needed was the ornate gold belt and spandex tights.

"Mason," the man said, dipping his head. His clean-shaven face was kindly but a smile wouldn't have gone amiss.

"Ryan. Where's Dad?"

"Out back. Do you have luggage?"

"No. Emelynn's not staying. Emelynn, Ryan," he said.

"Ryan." I offered my hand. He darted a glance to Mason. Was a handshake inappropriate, I wondered?

He forced a brief smile. "Nice to meet you, Emelynn." Ryan was too intense to be the doorman. He must be security.

"This way," Mason said, steering us forward.

I considered myself lucky to come from a family that was well-off, but this was well-off to the hundredth power. It was easily the most beautiful house I'd ever been in, though "house" was a misnomer: it was a palace. We stepped over the threshold into an expansive vestibule. Pale marble floors gleamed all around and a six-foot-wide staircase curved up on the left to a second-storey atrium. A round claw-foot table sat in the entrance and it was bigger than two of my dining-room tables put together. In fact, my dining-room table would have collapsed under the weight of the enormous bouquet of flowers that graced this one. A thick oriental carpet was centred under the table and a chandelier the size of an armchair lit the lofty two-storey entryway. It put me in mind of a hotel lobby.

We crossed the floor and descended three steps to a formal sitting area. The scale of the room was huge. To the right was a fireplace I could almost stand upright in, and I'm five foot seven. In the corner to the left sat a beautiful, red-lacquered grand piano. Floor-to-ceiling folding glass doors stretched across the back wall.

We strode through the room and stepped outside onto a vast covered patio, beyond which lay an expanse of pavers drenched in sunlight. Potted palms were artfully scattered about and blue water sparkled invitingly in a pool off to the left. The back lawn, cut short and faded to a crispy pale brown, stretched on for an impossible distance. Horses swished their tails in a paddock beyond the lawn.

I spotted Mason's father sitting just inside the shadow of the covered patio. He set his glasses on the table and rose to greet us. Pure white hair framed his tanned face. He smiled at me like an indulgent grandfather as Mason made the introductions.

"Dad, I'd like you to meet Emelynn Taylor. Emelynn, Stuart Reynolds."

I offered him my hand. "Mr. Reynolds." He was shorter than Mason and handsome despite the deep lines on his face.

"Stuart, please," he said, crinkling the edges of his dark eyes as he grasped my hand firmly between both of his. His hands were rough; a working man's hands.

"It's so nice to finally meet you, Emelynn. Please have a seat." He gestured to a chair on his right. I perched on the edge of it while Mason took a seat on Stuart's left.

Stuart turned to Mason. "Any trouble along the way?"

"None," Mason said.

Stuart nodded and turned back to me. "How was your trip?"

"The jet was a nice touch," I said, embarrassed at the extravagance.

He shrugged like it was nothing. "It wasn't being used today. Please, make yourself comfortable."

Mason interjected. "She's still healing, Dad."

The reminder stung, but not as badly as the whip that my kidnappers had used to persuade me to cooperate with them.

"Forgive me. Can I offer you a refreshment?"

"A glass of water?" I suggested.

"Still or sparkling?"

"Ah, still please." Tap water would have been fine. I felt like such a poseur in this palace.

"Iced tea," Mason said.

Stuart raised his hand and movement in the shadows close to the house caught my eye. A woman I hadn't noticed before moved silently behind a bar and moments later delivered our drinks. She was dressed in a black shirt and slacks, just like Ryan. Maybe she was also security. She certainly didn't look like a barmaid. Her brown hair was pulled back and twisted tightly in a chignon and she looked as fit as an aerobics instructor. She blended discreetly back into the shadows as quickly as she'd appeared.

"I'm very sorry about your run-in with Carson Manse," Stuart said. "Rest assured he'll be dealt with appropriately if he ever regains consciousness."

I could only nod. Their version of *appropriate* meant he'd be dead. You would think that would upset me. It didn't.

"What's his status?" Stuart asked Mason.

"He's still in a coma. James is keeping tabs on his condition."

"Good." Stuart turned his attention back to me. "I've taken the liberty of ordering our lunch. I do hope you enjoy salad niçoise. Maria makes the best one in California."

"Then I'm sure I'll love it."

Stuart wasn't wearing the basic black uniform. He dressed casually in a blue checked shirt, and cowboy boots peeked out beneath the legs of weathered jeans.

"Maria's your wife?" I asked.

"Maria's our cook," Stuart said. "Regretfully, my wife's in poor health and isn't able to join us."

"I'm sorry. I didn't know."

Stuart breezed over the subject. "I understand you'll be with us for a few days?"

I shot a glance at Mason. Had he told him I was staying here? "I'm returning home on Friday," I said with no mention of my accommodations.

"Good. That gives us some time to get to know one another. Next time, you'll stay longer."

I raised my eyebrows. Now I knew where Mason learned to be so presumptuous.

"You must take after your mother," Stuart said, studying me. "I don't see much of Brian in you."

My heart lurched at the mention of my father's name. "Did you know him well?"

"Yes. He and my Jolene were very close. They planned to marry right here at Cairabrae after Andrew was born."

"I didn't know that."

"Yes, well, it didn't come to pass. Terrible thing, losing a child." A shadow of his own loss crossed his face.

"How did they meet?" My curiosity burned to know every detail of my father and Jolene's time together.

"He walked into the gallery one day when she was working."

Mason interrupted his father's narrative. "The gallery was in San Francisco."

That fit. My father had worked in a clinic in San Francisco in the early eighties.

Stuart frowned at the interruption then continued. "The gallery was a cooperative where the artists took turns running the shop. After Jolene met your father, she came home lit up like the fourth of July. Jeannette knew right away." He shook his head, smiling at the memory. When he saw my confusion, he quickly clarified. "Jeannette's my wife— Jolene and Mason's mother."

"She knew Jolene was quite taken with the young man who'd admired her work. Jolene kept Brian coming back with promises of more pieces from the same artist. She strung him along for weeks before telling him that she was that artist. But by then, I don't think it was the art that drew him to the gallery. She was talented with a paintbrush, but no one likes seascapes that much." He chuckled and winked at me.

I couldn't help but smile back and told him of the painting of Jolene's that still hung in my father's study. "I remember him looking at that painting absolutely mesmerized," I said. "He never tired of it."

Stuart seemed pleased with that.

"So, Emelynn," he said, "tell me about yourself."

I knew they'd be as curious about me as I was about them, but talking about myself made me uneasy. I felt uncomfortable being in the spotlight, so I'd prepared a Coles Notes version of my life. "There's not a lot to tell. I lived with my parents in Summerset until I was twelve. Summerset's on the west coast of British Columbia," I said, describing the location of a hometown I'd learned few people had heard of.

"Just south of Vancouver. Yes, I know it," Stuart said, nodding.

Surprise registered on my face. "Well, the summer I turned twelve, I met Jolene and that October my father was killed. After the funeral, my mother moved us to Toronto."

"I'm sorry. I liked Brian very much. How did he die?"

"His float plane disappeared on its way to a fishing lodge in the Queen Charlottes. They never found him."

"That must have been difficult."

Some days it still was. My recap was finished, but they both looked at me expectantly. I wanted to tell them—I'm only twenty-two—there isn't more.

Stuart spoke, breaking the awkward lull. "If you wouldn't mind, tell me about Jolene."

"Jolene," I said, wondering where to start. "I met her on the beach in front of the cottage in the summer. She visited a few times, just briefly. She was soft-spoken. Wore a big floppy hat and sunglasses, as if she was hiding from someone. Carson Manse, I suppose."

Stuart and Mason listened without touching their drinks. "I liked her. She asked about my family and brought me feathers and pretty beach glass for the sandcastles I liked to build. The day she gifted me, she told me she had to leave soon. She said she wanted me to have something special but insisted I keep it a secret. The next thing I remember was waking up on the sand and wondering where she'd gone." I look furtively over my shoulder. The woman with the chignon stood quietly behind the bar.

"You can talk freely," Stuart said, correctly guessing the reason for my hesitation.

"All right." Did all of the staff here know about us?

I continued. "I discovered my night vision a few days later and knew then that she'd given me something special." I paused, remembering the first night that darkness didn't fall. Even though I was just a child, there was no mistaking when the night took on a blue hue and my vision remained clear as day. The miracle of it has never faded. "I didn't understand what it was, but I kept my promise; I didn't tell anyone."

"She never contacted you after that?" Stuart asked.

"No. Maybe she tried, but we'd moved to Toronto. I looked for her when the floats started, but I only knew her first name."

"The *floats*?" Mason and Stuart said simultaneously.

I stifled a laugh and not just because of the matching quizzical look on their faces; most people would think I was a lunatic in search of an asylum for telling this story. But not these two men. I had their undivided attention.

"That's how I thought of it before I knew what the gift was. It started with sleep-walking, or at least my mother thought I was sleepwalking. It was years before I figured out that I was losing gravity in my sleep and drifting around the condo. Thankfully, my mother never got a live-action view of it and, luckily, the condo was small so I couldn't float too far away."

"You could have been seriously hurt," Mason said. He leaned back to let the woman with the chignon refill his glass.

"That came later. The summer before I started university, I began experiencing the floats when I was awake. There was no predicting when it would occur, so I started packing weights around to keep me grounded. I thought I'd lose my mind. Jolene wasn't my favourite person during those years. When the floats took me unawares, I'd usually end up hurting myself." I took a breath, allowing myself a brief wallow in the torment of my awkward childhood. I now knew that the vast majority of Fliers were born with the gift. The few like me who were gifted would normally be mentored, but I'd been left on my own to figure it out.

"That's what finally brought me back to the cottage in Summerset. When I finished university, I figured there'd never be a better time to learn how to control this thing. I knew if I wanted any kind of a normal life, that's what I needed to do. The cottage was the ideal place; it's isolated and private, and my mother had no interest in returning with me. In fact, she gave me six months' living expenses for my graduation gift."

"I'm so sorry, Emelynn." Stuart reached forward and took my hand. "Please believe me when I say that my Jolene would never intentionally hurt you or anyone else. She was a gentle soul—too much so for our world I'm afraid. I have to believe she wasn't in her right mind at the time."

He released my hand and sat back in his chair. "How did you learn about the gift?"

"Foolishly, I thought I could teach myself how to control it, but I was wrong. I ended up in the hospital after a spectacularly bad fall and, fortunately for me, Dr. Coulter was on duty in the ER that night. He spotted the second lens in my eyes and recognized me for what I was. What I am," I corrected, feeling the weight of the words.

"He arranged for Jackson Delaney to take me under his wing. I thought Jackson was delusional, but who wouldn't? His impossible notions flew in the face of everything I knew about physics, but the proof was undeniable. Jackson introduced me to the local covey and, with their help, I learned about your world."

"I imagine it came as a shock," Stuart said. He had no idea.

"Mason tells me your covey is admirably loyal to you."

"Not just to me." With only eleven of us in the covey, we all knew one another. It felt like family. We were tied together by our gift and depended on one another to protect the secret and each other. We'd worked hard to develop our defensive skills and we'd proven that we could protect our own. I was enormously proud of that.

Maria arrived with our lunch, and the woman with the chignon set out wine glasses.

"The Gerty today, I think, Debbie," Stuart said, and the woman, who now had a name, quickly produced a chilled bottle of Gewürztraminer for his inspection.

"Yes, that's the one. You'll join me, I hope," Stuart said, turning to me.

At this point, I was famished and would have eaten with my fingers and stuck a straw in the bottle. But then again, I drank tap water. I nodded and Debbie poured us each a generous glass of wine. Over lunch, they asked me endless questions about my *floaty* episodes. Maria's salad niçoise really was the best I'd ever tasted. The tuna was grilled rare and the tarragon was fresh. It was after three o'clock by the time coffee was served.

"If you don't mind, Emelynn, I'll take my leave," Stuart said. "I like to visit with Jeannette after lunch and I'm sure you're tired after your trip." He stood. "Finish your coffee and Mason will show you to your room. Feel free to use the pool or wander around and get to know the place."

"That's very kind of you, Stuart, but I think there's been a misunderstanding. I'm staying in Bodega Bay."

"Oh?" He tipped his head. "You know you're welcome to stay here. Lord knows we have enough room."

I swallowed, feeling awkward. Mason sat there like he knew nothing of my plans. Was this his way of pressuring me to stay?

Stuart must have sensed my unease. "Well, whatever you're most comfortable with," he said. "Dinner's at eight."

"Thank you for lunch," I said, pondering his dinner statement. Or was that an invitation?

"My pleasure." Stuart nodded at Mason before turning and strolling back into the house.

"Thanks for your support there, Mason."

His lips curled in a wry smile. "He's right, you know. Look at this place and just three of us live here."

Though tempted, I hadn't changed my mind. Mason didn't understand how much it had taken to get me this far. I'd come despite the loud and insistent protests from James Moss. James had become a good friend despite not one, but two fiery introductions. He'd proven himself highly skilled in the security arena. I paid attention. "Something's not right," he'd warned. "He's trying too hard to get you to visit."

Mason's persistence that I stay at Cairabrae reminded me of James's warning. Right now, however, I needed Mason. I was only staying three days and I'd assured James that I would leave at the first sign of duplicity. That didn't do much to appease James, but I was living *my* life, not his.

"Would you like to see Jolene's room before I take you to your hotel?"

My face lit up. "Yes, I would."

"Come on then. I'll show you." He stood and led the way into the house.

ACKNOWLEDGEMENTS

Hidden Enemy was originally published as *The Gift: Revelation*. The title change is a result of overwhelming feedback from the books' readership. My gratitude goes to Elinor Florence, who was instrumental and supportive throughout the rebranding process.

After the first draft of a manuscript is completed, the real work begins. The book you hold in your hands took the time, enthusiasm and dedication of many generous and knowledgeable people. I'd like to take this opportunity to thank my editor, Nina Munteanu, who is also a writing coach and author (https://ninamunteanu.me). Nina once again applied her superb story-editing skills to wring every last drop of intrigue from the story.

My heartfelt thanks also go out to the very best group of cold readers an author could ask for. You all deserve a medal for bravery. Thank you Colleen, Sue, Denis, Kathy, John, Gee, Jean, Cathy, Eleanor, Anna and Sally. The editing process wouldn't be nearly as entertaining without your input. And I mustn't forget Bill, whose two cents is much appreciated, or Elizabeth, who helped proof the proof. To Jasna, thank you for your input with the new summary and the cheerleading.

Thanks to the design team at JD&J Designs for *Hidden Enemy's* enticing book cover design.

As always, my love and thanks go to my supportive husband and family. And a special thanks to Mom—no one can spot that extra *to, at, that, up, out* or *down* like you can (I know . . . omit the *can*).

Copy edit provided by Nancy Wills, ILEX *indexing and editing* (https://ilexindexingandediting.com).

All errors in the research and writing of this novel are entirely my own.

Glossary of Terms

Covey: A group of Fliers who are geographically connected. Older coveys were and still are connected by family rather than location. All Fliers belong to a home covey and are expected to check in with coveys in areas they are visiting. Coveys are a source of information and are trained to protect their Fliers.

Crystal: All Ghosts need a crystal to achieve ghosted form. The two exceptions to this are Emelynn Taylor and the woman who gifted her, Jolene Reynolds.

Flash: Fliers can use the second lens in their eye to produce a flicker of light within the eye that other Fliers recognize.

Flier: A human either born or gifted with a mutated gene that allows him or her to shed gravity and take flight. The gene can also manifest with additional facets, such as memory reading and telekinesis. The mutation produces a second lens in the eye.

Founding families: The nine founding coveys are comprised of the oldest and strongest families within the Flier community. Centuries ago, these family coveys founded the Tribunal Novem to police the Flier ranks.

Ghost: A Flier with the ability to dissipate into molecules too small for the human eye to see. Ghosts are rare. The process of turning into this form is called ghosting. All members of the Tribunal Novem are Ghosts.

The Gift: The mutated gene that allows a Flier to shed gravity. The mutation produces a second lens in the eye. The gene can also manifest with additional facets, such as memory reading and telekinesis.

Gifting: The process of transferring the gift, in whole or in part, from one Flier to someone else. The receiver can be any human. The process strips the donor of the element gifted. When the entire gift is given, the process weakens the gift-giver and is fatal half the time. Giftings are strictly controlled by the Tribunal Novem. A Flier who has been gifted is considered a second-class Flier.

Jolt: Fliers can use the second lens in their eye to produce a wave of energy along a spectrum from sparks, which are like static shocks, to jolts, which are painful and can even be fatal. The degree of energy produced depends upon the Flier's particular gift and varies from weak to strong. A fatal jolt causes a brain bleed (hemorrhage or aneurysm), which is medically classified as a stroke.

The Redeemers: A group of Fliers who feel they have been wronged, or are not represented, by the Tribunal Novem. Their goal is to replace the Tribunal Novem. They are led by Carson Manse.

Rush: Fliers can use the second lens in their eye to produce a stimulative energy that falls within the low-end of the spectrum of energy they are able to produce. It's sexual in nature and used to heighten sexual arousal. Referred to as the/his/her rush.

Spark: Fliers can use the second lens in their eye to produce a wave of energy along a spectrum from sparks, which are like static shocks, to jolts, which are painful and can even be fatal. The degree of energy produced depends upon the Flier's particular gift and varies from weak to strong.

The Tribunal Novem: Judge, jury and executioner in the Flier world. They are comprised of one representative from each of the nine founding coveys. They are always Ghosts. Their identities are not known within the Flier community. The Tribunal's leadership rotates every five years. At any given time, five Tribunal members provide day-to-day investigation and enforcement.

Discussion Questions

Spoiler alert: These questions contain spoilers that will ruin the story for those who haven't yet read the book.

1. In Hidden Enemy, Emelynn finds an ancient book hidden among her father's journals. Have you ever discovered a hidden treasure? What was it and where did you find it?

2. Detective Samuel Coulter is introduced in Hidden Enemy. Is he a friend or foe of Emelynn Taylor's? Why?

3. If you were casting Detective Samuel Coulter's role in a movie, who would you choose to play him?

4. In a culture where one-night stands and walks of shame are, if not commonplace, certainly a part of our lexicon, how does Emelynn's relationship with Casey Stockton compare? If you were her best friend, how would you advise her?

5. The Tribunal Novem's calling card is a dead dove. How is this choice symbolic? Effective?

6. The Tribunal Novem practices vigilante justice. Is there a place for vigilante justice in society?

7. What makes it possible for the Tribunal Novem to act with impunity? Can you think of other organizations that act with impunity?

8. In Hidden Enemy, James reveals that he can read memories. Is this a skill you wish you had? Why? What would be the upside and downside of having this skill?

9. When Emelynn is at the mercy of Carson Manse and capitulates to his demands, do you think she made the right choice? Were you disappointed? What other options did she have?

10. The author had a real-life villain in mind when she chose the name Carson Manse. The real-life killer and Carson Manse share the same initials, and their names are similar. Can you guess who that mass murderer was? Who would you cast in the role of Carson Manse for a film adaptation of Hidden Enemy?

11. If you could ask the author one question, what would it be? Would your organization or group like to arrange an author appearance in person or online? If so, please contact the author at jpmclean @jpmcleanauthor.com.

A printable version of these discussion
questions is available at jpmcleanauthor.com/extras.

About the Author

JP (Jo-Anne) McLean writes addictive supernatural fiction. She is an Eric Hoffer award winner, a two-time silver medalist in the Wishing Shelf Book Awards, a finalist in the Chanticleer International Book Awards and the Independent Author Network Awards. She is a B.R.A.G. medallion honoree and four-time Literary Titan Gold Award winner. Reviewers call her books *addictive*, *smart*, and *fun*.

JP holds a Bachelor of Commerce degree from the University of British Columbia's Sauder School of Business, is a certified scuba diver, an exploratory chef, and an avid gardener.

Raised in Toronto, Ontario, JP now lives with her husband on Denman Island, which is nestled between the coast of British Columbia and Vancouver Island. When she's not writing, you'll find her cooking dishes that look nothing like the recipe photos or arguing with weeds in the garden. She enjoys hearing from readers. Contact her via her website, jpmcleanauthor.com, or through social media.

 Sign up for her newsletter ~ jpmcleanauthor.com

 Find her on Goodreads ~ goodreads.com/jpmclean

 Like her on Facebook ~ facebook.com/JPMcLeanBooks

 Follow her on Twitter ~ @jpmcleanauthor